Critics

CHOCOLATE DAYS,
POPSICLE WEEKS

Have You Read These Current Bestsellers from SIGNET?

☐ **THE FRENCH LIEUTENANT'S WOMAN by John Fowles.** By the author of The Collector and The Magus, a haunting love story of the Victorian era. Over one year on the N.Y. Times Bestseller List and an international bestseller. "Filled with enchanting mysteries, charged with erotic possibilities . . ."—Christopher Lehmann-Haupt, N.Y. Times   (#W4479—$1.50)

☐ **LOVE STORY by Erich Segal.** The story of love fought for, love won, and love lost. It is America's Romeo and Juliet. And it is one of the most touching, poignant stories ever written. A major motion picture starring Ali MacGraw and Ryan O'Neal.   (#Q4414—95¢)

☐ **JENNIE, The Life of Lady Randolph Churchill by Ralph G. Martin.** In JENNIE, Ralph G. Martin creates a vivid picture of an exciting woman, Lady Randolph Churchill who was the mother of perhaps the greatest statesman of this century, Winston Churchill, and in her own right, one of the most colorful and fascinating women of the Victorian era.   (#W4213—$1.50)

☐ **THE AFFAIR by Morton Hunt.** Explores one of the most engrossing and profoundly troubling of contemporary concerns. Morton Hunt allows the reader to enter this secret underground world through the actual words and experiences of eight unfaithful men and women.   (#Y4548—$1.25)

Chocolate Days, Popsicle Weeks

Edward Hannibal

A SIGNET BOOK from
NEW AMERICAN LIBRARY
TIMES MIRROR

SIGNET TRADEMARK REG. U.S. PAT. OFF. AND FOREIGN COUNTRIES
REGISTERED TRADEMARK—MARCA REGISTRADA
HECHO EN CHICAGO, U.S.A.

SIGNET, SIGNET CLASSICS, SIGNETTE, MENTOR AND PLUME BOOKS
are published by The New American Library, Inc.,
1301 Avenue of the Americas, New York, New York 10019

FIRST PRINTING, JUNE, 1971

PRINTED IN THE UNITED STATES OF AMERICA

For Maggie, Margaret and Peg

One

———◆———

IF IT HADN'T BEEN for R.O.T.C., Fitzie might have become something nice and Catholic, like a C.I.A. agent or insurance man; or something nice and Jewish, like a lawyer or broker; or something nice and Protestant, like a marketing executive or editor. He might even have stayed in the Army. He joined R.O.T.C. his first year at B.C., brown bagging it out from Craig Street, on the outside edge of Boston, every morning with four others in Rich Picardi's '38 Plymouth. Fitzie was the only one of his car pool day student guys who joined and he did, not because he had any desire for going Army—Korea was long past by then—but because he knew then that he'd be marrying Janice at the end of his four years and the Army would be something they could go off with fast. An immediate living, maybe even a ticket far away. Also he figured the monthly check he'd get for his junior and senior years would let him get her a diamond. It worked out exactly that way, too, except that in the summer between his third year and last year he had to go for six weeks to R.O.T.C. summer camp at Fort Devens. This messed up his summer job at the J. L. Powell and Sons ice cream plant, where he had worked every summer since right after high school. Not that he wouldn't have loved to be one of them who whipped off to Cape Cod every June to waiter and tan and make out at the resorts and hotels, but Fitzie had to make a grand and no less each summer if he was to get through school. Only the factories could let you make that. Beaches have bad years and lots of ways to spend dough in good years. Factories don't.

In fact, by the summer after his sophomore year, his mandatory Greek and Latin behind him, Fitzie got promoted from demolder to supervisor of the Tank and was up to around twelve hundred clear, working through the week after Labor Day. Seventeen girls and three guys under him: the Tank made chocolate covereds and Popsicles, although they had a different trade name; fed by gravity through pipes from the huge, cold mix vats on the

7

floor above, the liquid ice cream or the orange, grape, raspberry, lemon-and-lime or sometimes pink lemonade Popsicle mix would be squirted by the feeder into the twenty-four-slotted copper molds. Fast. A hiss of compressed air, two dozen purple or yellow or whatever color shafts in the air, suspended, then full. The girl would shove the mold forward onto the center chain belt with one hand, pulling in a new mold from the return tunnel. If more than eight inches came between the molds moving along the belt the Tank was working slow and Fitzie would have to see if the feeder was asleep or fooling around, or check his lines up to the vats or call a mechanic to the feeder box. Standing in cockpits above the mold belt, two on each side, the four stick girls would air-shoot the sticks into the heavy metal trays, lock them fast by pushing down the wide hard clamp, then drop them into the molds as they passed by toward the pit. Company-union rules said only males could work in the pit or as demolders, and these were sometimes full-timers but usually college guys. Fitzie had started in the pit, where the job was to stand waist-high to the mold-carrying belt, between it and the end of the pool-sized tank of brine, kept around thirty-two below zero. Because of the brine, the men wore rubber gloves to the elbows, but even so got spot-burned on the face—like flying bacon grease—and had Captains Courageous hands by September.

The pitman would slide ten filled-and-sticked molds from the belt, line them up perpendicular along the Tank's counter, then push them forward into the cradle. A punch of the overhead microswitch, more air-shooting, and the cradle in one operation would plunk straight down, move one mold-length forward, come back empty and submerged, then whoosh and slam back up out of the brine for the next load, surfing up a nice spray-wave of cold burn and tough luck to the pitman who didn't step back out of range. The new row of molds would force the front row, at the further end of the Tank pool, up onto the counter there for the demolders to grab, five apiece, and dunk quickly into their boiling-water tubs. The molds, empty, would fall away down the slide through the rubber curtain of the return tunnel for the trip back to the filler. The demolder would hold on to the trays, now with their load of frozen color hanging heavy, lift them above his chest, then insert them into the upper tunnel to be moved by steel fingers along parallel runners. Fitzie had also done a summer as a demolder. Forward, the fingers would

8

brace themselves stiff, to slide the trays squeaking ahead; back, the fingers would pivot up helplessly and weak, clacking across the tray handles, then forward, strong again, pushing the trays steadily through the dark tunnel. An old full-timer in the locker room once told Fitzie, "A week demolding, a man can spend a million dollars and go sex crazy." To talk to each other, the demolders had to yell over all the air hissing and finger clacking and mold slamming and brine sloshing; they also had to be good, had to have done it enough so their bodies had got the rhythm of the pulling, dunking, up, in; and would keep going, not to miss a space, when their minds shut off to talk or daydream.

If the Tank was making chocolate covereds, the little up-and-down basin in the center of each upper tunnel would be kept filled with warm chocolate all day, also fed up an upstairs vat, and each tray of dangling rock-hard, naked vanilla stalagmites would get up-dunked brown as it passed along the runners. If Popsicles, the basin simply carried cold water and washed the white frost from the brown root beers or the orange oranges. As supervisor, Fitzie liked Popsicles, because the chocolate was just one more thing that could stop the Tank-calliope's relentless song. As pitman and demolder, he had prayed for chocolate days: one break after another. A chocolate week was a vacation. Mostly, though, it was chocolate days in Popsicle weeks. At the end of the tunnel, stationary steel fingers would lift the tray handles upright, dropping the ice cream down onto a rubber belt. The trays would ride ball bearing rollers back to the stick girls; the clumps of red or lime-yellow would spread and chug along to the baggers, five to a side, who would grab them by the sticks as they went by, one in each hand, slip them down into the paper bags held open-mouthed by shoots of air, then into cardboard two-dozen boxes. The same girls, when each box got full, would fold in the cover, tape it and push it onto the final conveyor, which would send the boxes tumbling through the floor-hole to the mackinawed men waiting in the freeze-room below to stock them onto pallets. Fitzie had tried twice to get made a freeze-room man because the pay was higher; for the same reason he never got it. He did get made supervisor though and that he loved. Not just the money. The days. The Tank. The first thing he did was introduce the rotation system: every half-hour, he'd whistle and people would swap jobs, the pitman moving to demold, a demolder climbing into the pit, a bagger becoming the filler, the filler taking a stick machine. Fitzie had seen the sense of that his first summer on the Tank, but had known enough to keep it to himself until the right time. And, three summers later, he received fifty dollars from the Incentive Awards Committee, plus the respect of the girls and the boys. The respect he blew, his first week as supervisor.

Free of the oppressing Father Dunpheys and Epistemologys and Ciceros and Transubstantiations and Henry-the-V's and passing, feeling a man, Fitzie pushed the Tank. He moved over it like Cary Grant across rooftops and windowsills. Straightening fingers before they clogged. Helping trays and molds along their routes by hand. Teaching the pitmen how to feed the cradle two molds at a time. Switching to Vat #2 *before* the first ran out, eliminating the customary downtime for changeover. Resetting the timer on the upper tunnel to move the fingers, hence the demolders, hence the pitmen, hence everybody, faster. Friday night, he learned he had broken the Tank's output record by four hundred boxes and felt glad. Saturday morning, at home, not working, without overtime pay, he learned he had been stupid, and felt black.

Monday morning, he learned he had lost his people. Six girls came late, all worked sullenly, spatting, tearing bags, jamming trays, breaking product, getting headaches and cramps, tipping over filled molds. The boys, less offended, more afraid of him than the girls, were okay, but somewhat down. At midmorning coffee break, Fitzie climbed atop the pit's platform.

"Hey, wait a minute," he called over them, stopping them in their move away from the Tank.

"Save ya goddamn speeches till we get back!" It was Rosie, full-time and unofficial forelady of "Pig Alley," as the Tank's girl-end was called. She had a dead-end face like Huntz Hall's and Fitzie, from his first summer, loved her. Very tough, very straight. Very sad, Fitzie thought, and bought her beers sometimes after work.

"Shut up and listen," he said. "Listen, I just noticed somebody pushed up the timer on us."

"I told ya, Gloria, didn't I, didn't I tell ya?"

"Them bastards."

"No wonder!"

"Ssh, quiet now. It was probably just a mistake. It'll take me a while to fix it, so why don't you stay out another ten minutes, okay? Okay, go ahead, and I'll see you in a half-hour." It worked. They came back chirping. The Tank ran Saturdays at time-and-a-half that week and every week that summer.

And when the Tank ran well it was beautiful. Fitzie would roam around it, picking up sticks, hosing down the floor, relieving a demolder or pitman for a quick smoke in the hall, giving back rubs to the girls. "You hurt your back?"

"Whatdya mean?"

"Well, you got it all strapped up."

"You're a riot."

He'd get them singing, too. His favorite was to get one side of the Tank to sing "ooom, poop-poop, ooom, poop-poop," and then when they were going strong and together, he'd bring in the other side with the old carnival midway flying horses tune: "da da, da *da*, da da *da* . . . da da da, da da *da*, da da da!" It made the Tank even more of a calliope, almost a real one, only with people-parts; sometimes it made Fitzie break out laughing. He stayed away pretty much from the one or two college girls working there for the summer from Salem Teachers or Framingham—they were too much like Janice, eligible— but as the summer days of chocolate and Popsicles tumbled along, he and the full-timers got all kinds of games going. A swift hand around beneath her uplifted, bagging arm during a back rub for a quick feel; an anonymous backhanded squeeze of his sex when he'd be standing behind the bagging line preoccupied with a sound from the filler or passing in sticks to a stick-girl. Laughs, bells and overtime, week after week.

Once, in August, Fitzie himself came close to getting oiled out of the overtime. Somebody with a tie over at the milk plant had a son he wanted to give part-time work to, so Fitzie's foreman brought the kid to Fitzie one Friday afternoon. Sheepishly, he told Fitzie that *Dickie* would be coming in to run the Tank on Saturdays for the rest of the summer, so would Fitzie check him out on it? Dickie was a tall, blond crew-cut Swede from Prides Crossing or Marblehead who went away to school, to Stanford, and Fitzie, pissed, said, "Sure." Nobody could tell, afterwards, whether Fitzie explained wrong or too fast, or whether the management son got it wrong. All anybody knew for sure was the vivid, costly fact that that Saturday morning, five thousand gallons of cold, purple, grape Popsicle mix somehow went gushing from its vat through valves and pipes not down to the Tank but out onto the vacant railroad loading platform in the rear of the ice cream factory. Dickie and the girls had waited at the Tank, but nothing came. Dickie ran upstairs and checked his valve settings at once, of course, but they all seemed right as he

11

understood them. And the girls did say it took quite a while sometimes for the mix to start down. And there really didn't seem to be anyone around to ask until it was too late. And it *was* terrible about the old watchman taking the morning sun on the platform under the pipe, but Dickie certainly couldn't have known that. In the end, somebody got Dickie a job at the Myopia Hunt Club and Fitzie rode his Tank into September and cleared his twelve hundred dollars for the summer.

It wasn't until he was back at school for junior year that Fitzie finally put together two sure things in his life and discovered that they fought each other. He obviously couldn't go back to running the Tank next summer *and* go to Fort Devens for six weeks with the goddamn R.O.T.C. Yet, he still had Janice and together they still had their getaway plan that depended on his being commissioned at graduation. So goodbye Tank, that's all there was to it. But he bit his thumb knuckle over it. Not counting the truth that he, personally, hated the thought of never running his Tank again, how could he make the money next summer for his last year? The Army would pay him something, but it was practically zilch. And Janice would be working, graduating from nurse's training in June, a year ahead of him, but that would have to go in the bank. Aware that the ice cream plant wouldn't know anything themselves until the time came, Fitzie had to carry his worry around with him like a cyst on his soul through the whole dreary, preachy drag of his third year. He tried working Saturdays but his marks fell off. He delivered mail at Christmas, but that went for presents. In May, he cut some classes one morning and took the trackless trolley to the plant. There he was given a cup of niceness that surprised him very much, solved his problem, and eventually led to his meeting Gene the Shirt Platt.

The company informed Ftizie that since they had decided to be offering him a spot in their management training program after he graduated—nice jolt number one—they should certainly be able to come up with a plan that would accommodate his summer conflicts—nice jolt number two, relief, and quick knowledge: he'd never take their real job. He didn't need the college-thing for that. Whatever he was going through that four-year Gothic block of loveless dust for, it wasn't to be anybody's management trainee. Their ass. Still, they did do the trick for him. In the weeks before his military obligation he could resume, with a raise, his job as Tank supervisor. When he

12

returned, well, actually the only availability would be on the night cleanup crew. A little grisly, but there was the night differential and it wouldn't be for long ... "Terrific," Fitzie grinned. So, came June and his Tank sweet, too brief; and then the brown, hot days in steel pot and M-1 in the stubbly fields and sticky clay roads and night pine groves that weren't pine groves to these people, but areas to be secured by setting out a perimeter defense. Puerto Rican sergeants teaching broken mortar nomenclature. Tear gas. Maggie's drawers. Broom straws under bunks are logs. With dirt on them. Five gigs, no pass. So, for Christ's sake, you pick up the straws. That's all. She-it. Easy. Especially with Sister Mary Musntoucher, the indestructible Tinker Bell nun perpetually, since first grade at Saint Paul's, living there in Fitzie's ear, calling all the signals of right and duty and conscientiousness. A D.M.G. —distinguished military graduate—went to him at the end, meaning he could get a Regular Army commission upon graduation if he so opted, and Fitzie went back to the ice cream plant.

Lester Belheumer took him through the job on the first night, which began at 9:00 P.M., broke for lunch at midnight, and ended at 5:30 in the morning. Lester was retiring after thirty years with the company, the last eight on vat cleanup. Fitzie, of course, didn't need to be told anything about the giants #1 and 2, his old 5000-gallon Popsicle vats, but he listened as attentively, nodding, to the old man's grave lessons on those as on the twenty-one other vats to be cleaned for use in the morning. Ammonia shutoffs, pipe valve settings, tricky areas such as under the rubber sealers around the glass porthole doors. They wore rubber boots over the company white denim trousers, and tee shirts. Seen through the roof, the vat floor would look like an oil refinery inside a building. Old Lester's system was to knock off 1 and 2, the big babies, first; then 22 and 23—both big but not quite as large as the Popsicles—which loomed adjacent there in the rear of the building and held, during the day, the thick mixes for the pints, quarts, half gallons and cookie sandwiches. These four were like house-size Hawaiian Punch cans set on their sides. The Popsicles were cold and fruit-smelling, clean after a quick brushing, hot hosing and cold rinse. The ice creams were nightmare evaporated milk cans inside, smelling rancidly of sour milk and caked with slippery yellow-white scum that had to be scraped and squeegied out through the drain hole before any real

13

scrubbing could be started. Fitzie threw up in 23 and old Lester phlegm-chuckled.

Vats 3 to 11 and the pipe work Lester would finish before midnight. After lunch, 12 to 21 and really hustling so as to be able to change and wash up on company time, before punching out at 5:30. Fitzie went home and slept for twelve hours after that first break-in night, a Friday-Saturday. He left Janice early Saturday night and slept until noon Sunday. Monday night was out of Poe; he washed up on his own time. Tuesday he went in early, and walked among the vats in his street clothes. His leather heels on the red tile floor echoed in the stainless steel whale abdomen. At nine, in boots and pants, shirtless, Fitzie was hosing out all scum vats, large and small, from outside, squatting on the tile, valves open full, temperature up to near steam, the boiling stream shooting like a flame thrower through the portholes. Then slamming the portholes shut, the drains unopened, he'd leave one stench vat to blast the next likewise. The Popsicles and no-scums he entered and cleaned only after the last scum vat had been blasted and locked tight. Finished, he returned to the first scum vat, opened the drains and, the scum out and on its way to Boston Harbor, he crawled in to soap-scrub and hose the vat clean, as easily and quickly as any Popsicle or wet cream vat. By lunchtime, in three hours, he had all the vats cleaned except for the pipes and valves. Like a stage propman, he picked a vat, set a hose through its porthole, leaned a longhandle brush against the front, threw a sponge and chamois inside in the light, and lifted in his bucket of soap solution onto the curved steel vat floor.

After lunch, Fitzie gave his set a once-over, then walked to the dark side of the building, to the storage area. By the dim night bulbs and by memory and feel, he arranged a bed of empty paper freeze-bags on full fifty-pound sugar sacks, stretched out on his back, hands cupped for a pillow, and slept from one to four-thirty, waking himself by mental Baby Ben as mastered at Fort Devens. He struck his set, washed and reconnected his valves and pipes, washed and dressed himself and punched the clock at 5:30 sharp. This system stood for two solid weeks. He changed it one night not because it stopped working but because he found he couldn't sleep and got bored lying there on the sugar sacks in the dark. Gene the Shirt worked in an area between the vat room and Fitzie's sleeping quarters, cleaning out the hundreds of five-gallon milk cans used throughout the plant in a day. Gene the

14

Shirt did it cheerfully and mindlessly, as if he weren't heaving leaden cans up and over the geyserlike water spout all night, to the all-night blare of WHDH. Gene's name came from the Hawaiian shirts he wore coming to work, at work, going home.

"Hi, Shirt," Fitzie said, his mouth dry.

"Hi, kid. Want a cigar?"

"No thanks," Fitzie said and took out his Pall Malls, lighting one from Shirt's cigar.

"Boogieman get you?" Shirt grinned.

"Huh?"

"Drink some warm milk why don't you? I do anytime I can't sleep. The old lady, too."

"Smart old bastard, aren't you."

"Aw, what's the dif?"

"Steve know too?" Steve was the night foreman.

"You ain't scared of Stevie-boy, are ya?"

"Shit. What's *he* gonna do to *me*? Want me to spell you on those awhile?"

"No thanks. The arms is all that's workin'. You know all about little Stevie, do ya?"

"Hell, I got her in the box room once myself. Rita the Heater." It was nearly true; it would have been completely true if Fitzie, struck by a thunderbolt of guilt and fear about zero minus one second, hadn't pulled out and lurched to his feet, preventing ejaculation even then until he fainted and fell straight, flat one his face onto the piles of cardboard flats. His nose bled but didn't break: the blood and the sperm pouring forth while he was still out—involuntarily.

"And except you ain't trying to be no company man neither."

"Right. Poor Steve, he's a good guy, too. His *grand*father worked for them, you know that?"

"Know?" Shirt laughed. "Hell, I know his old man! Still driving a milk truck to this day. Every single morning, Charlestown. Ninety a week right through the depression. Can't beat that."

"Guess not," Fitzie said, and wondered if he should ask Shirt how he got the Continental he parked in the lot every night.

"Ah, Stevie'll be okay, though. They're just teachin' him a lesson. Can't have the supers in the floor broads' pants."

Everybody, Fitzie decided, had some reason for working the night crew. Night people. Himself. Steve. Angel, named for The Angel for the same reasons: he was a horror, a quiet, soft-moving giant freak; an ex-wrestler

15

from Lynn, his pinhead totally hairless, his ears cauliflowered and a nose a glop of window putty nearly hiding his eyes. *Don't look, Kathleen! It's not nice.* Who needs that? Ralph, the Ph.D. from Mattapan, father of seven and teacher of high school math, did it for the summers for the money, but also for the labor. Fitzie one night talked to Ralph of the strange power of the Tank. It turned out it was Ralph's as much as Fitzie's: Ralph cleaned it, as unhappy over chocolate days and chocolate weeks as Fitzie had been, for the molds and trays and tunnels crusted and added to the work. Still, like Fitzie, the immensity of the great machine—as eerily awesome when dead and silent as when alive and throbbing—its touchable, hard bigness challenged Ralph and filled some void in him. Fitzie understood. The German half-wit Der Dummy was somebody there at night in the ice cream plant, sweeping his red tile floors and shining his fire extinguishers with Noxon. Shirt spoke to Fitzie of the night Angel and Der Dummy fought in the vat room and the tremble Fitzie caught in Shirt's omniscient, I've-done-and-seen-everything voice gave him a vague taste of what King Kong terror that conflict must have ignited, and it was enough; he didn't regret not seeing it.

Even old Lester: his wife, long-drained and warped by disease, had gone out one night with her head in the open gas oven of the black stove in their Revere flat, and Lester could never stand being in their place at night after that. Shirt gave Lester no more than six months after his forced retirement. Listening, Fitzie felt a distant nausea of guilt for having scorned the old man's sacred system, but it passed. One night just before lunch, Shirt poked his head through a vat porthole and asked Fitzie, sopping wet and scrubbing away inside, if he'd mind running up to the all-night deli in Sullivan Square for him.

"Sure, glad to," Fitzie said, welcoming any change in routine that came his way.

"Two pastrami on hard roll. Mustard, no pickle." All the night men drank the free, icy, creamy company milk from the lunchroom cooler. "And Fitzie—ask for kosher, okay?"

"What are you, a Jew?" Fitzie laughed.

"Yeah," Shirt said, straight.

"Son of a bitch," Fitzie said and sloshed over to his friend's face in the vat wall. "You're my first Jew, you know that?"

The man smiled, softly, unlike him. "Well, you ain't my first mick."

16

Nicko looked up from his slicer when Fitzie ordered and said, "This for Shirt at the ice cream?"

"Yeah," Fitzie said, "I'm working with him."

The man winked, reached to the shelf holding rows of tiny corn flakes boxes, took down a small, white plastic statuette of the Virgin and made a pass with it over the tubes of meats in his steamy glass cabinet. Fitzie snarled, "Hey, cut that out. The man wants it a certain way, he ought to get it."

"Listen," Nicko said, "Me and Shirt know each other from Curley days, for Chrissake, so who you talkin' to? Listen, you think I can order kosher meat for one guy? I been doin' this this way for years. I don't do *nothin'* to the meat, do I? If Shirt thinks he's eatin' kosher meat, ain't he eatin' kosher meat? *You* gonna tell him, buddy-boy?"

When Fitzie tried to give Shirt his change from a five, Shirt said, "Keep it." Fitzie wouldn't. He went to Nicko's every midnight after that, and every night Shirt would try to tip him but Fitzie kept refusing. "Come on. I like to get out in the air. And Nicko gives me hard-boiled eggs and sometimes a beer."

"Look. Never do nothing for nothing." Shirt said. One night, toward the end, Shirt threw Fitzie a shiny object from his pocket as he was flushing his jugs and Fitzie was loafing there with him, smoking. It was a silver cigarette lighter, heavy, made in Britain. On the side was engraved THE MICK. "Hey, what's this for?"

"Ah, a guy I know down Nantasket give it to me. I got two hundred if I got one. When I saw the words on it, I thought you'd think it was funny."

"Well, thanks a lot. It must be worth about twenty-five bucks, though."

"Oh, I dunno, you can't tell."

Fitzie wasn't conned. He knew and kept the lighter, glad to have it and touched. Shirt waited until Fitzie's last week before school to tell him. Shirt had a deal. He was in with some people. When Shirt drove from the ice cream plant mornings on his way home to Everett, he would stop at the dog track and sign a piece of paper. He'd drop down around four in the afternoon and sign the paper again. In winter, it would be at the Garden. Fridays he would go home with two paychecks. That was why Shirt was one of the night people.

"Christ, Shirt," was all he could manage, "that's a crime, isn't it?" He now felt a little frightened for the man—as well as by him.

"Well, depends on what you think *ain't* a crime, huh?"

Fitzie lit a Pall Mall and held the lighter in his hands, looking at it hard. It seemed to burn slightly.

"I do some work," Shirt was saying. "I get paid for it."

"Tell that to the judge," Fitzie laughed, "and you'll get twenty years."

"Depends on what judge," Shirt said seriously. "Fitzie," he stopped with his jugs, straightened up and lit a fresh cigar from the stub of the one in his mouth. "What do they get for an ice cream cone in the drugstore, now?"

"I dunno. A dime, I suppose, fifteen?"

"Sometimes a nickel extra for jimmies, too, huh?"

They both laughed. Shirt went back to his jugs.

"How much you think it costs them to make it?"

"Uh, uh, that's no good, Shirt. That's just simple profit, that's what makes any kind of business work. You think Ford ought to give you that Continental for what it costs them to make it?"

"But who says *how much* they oughta mark things up?"

"Well, there's a lot of middlemen in everything, too, you know. That jacks up the cost. Ice cream or anything. Anyhow, the government runs prices, keeps everything fair."

"They teach you that at B.C.?"

"Yeah."

"You believe it, Fitzie? You believe everything the jebbies teach you out there?" Fitzie couldn't answer. It had suddenly occurred to him that he had never considered not believing anything in school. Outside, yes. But never in school. He felt off balance. "That isn't it," he said. "The thing is," and his voice seemed to drop to a whisper on its own, "that the whole is no better than its parts. In other words, what *you* do might be okay, but if it's part of something that includes white slavery and pushing dope and murder and the Mafia and protection and all that, then it's wrong. It's got to be."

"White slavery," Shirt muttered. "You are a cutie."

"No, but you know what I mean," Fitzie said, feeling like Donald O'Connor.

"You're goin' in the Army next summer, huh, Fitzie?"

"Yeah, June."

"Gonna be an officer and a gentleman by an Act of Congress."

"You bet your ass."

"I was in the Pacific, you know, in the war. You shoulda seen what I saw some U.S. Marines do, Fitzie, to kids, too. And women."

"Yeah, yeah, yeah, I've heard all that."

18

"Ain't that a part of your whole, Fitzie? Don't that make your government a little shitty?"

"Yeah, but the government didn't *tell* those Marines to commit atrocities. The government, in fact, has laws *against* them."

"Oh! I see."

"I mean, it's not the same as the rackets, where they *want* all the bad ..."

"What rackets?"

"Well, I mean ..."

"Who said rackets? Me? Did I say rackets?"

"No, Shirt. But I just assumed."

"Yeah, I know. Look. Doesn't it all boil down to the guy? Each man? You. Me. I mean, who has to go around worried about the big picture. Can't ya just do what you do and try to get along as best ya can?"

"Yeah. I guess so."

"How long you gotta do with Uncle?"

"Depends. Two years, unless I go Regular. I got a thing that'll let me go Regular if I want to."

"Just like a West Pointer, that's my boy. You gonna?"

"No. At least I don't think so. I don't know."

"Well, what are you gonna do after you get out?" This depressed Fitzie. He didn't want to talk anymore now, but Shirt was, after all, the only one who'd ever asked him. So he told him. "Shirt, I haven't thought that far ahead," he said so low that Shirt stopped manhandling his jugs.

"Ain't you studyin' for somethin'? Accounting or somethin'?"

"No."

"Then what the Christ you doin' out there?"

"Well, the first two years you don't get much choice. Now, I'm taking just what I like. I mean I'm taking a lot of stuff like theology and philosophy and Spanish, too, but I do just enough to keep my eighty with them. I just like the lit, so that's really all it get into."

"Stories and books and that?"

"Yeah, sort of."

"You gonna teach, then?"

"Jeses, I hope not. I just don't know. Listen, I got enough to get through now. In June I'm getting that degree and that commission, I'm getting married and I'm going as far away as I can. That's all I know."

Shirt had come closer. Fitzie was sitting up on some stacked barrels of mix-powder near the freight elevator. Shirt leaned against them, his face near Fitzie's knee. "Gimme one of your cancer sticks, will ya? I'm outa cigars." Lighting up, he said, "Everyplace's the same, but I guess you oughta go see somethin' for yourself."

"I'm going to try to."

"Thing is, Fitz, I got somethin' for ya. Been talkin' you up to some people what are lookin' for some young guy like you. You know, with an education, but what knows up from down. Except I thought you was goin' to be a lawyer or somethin', which'd be better. Don't matter, though, you got the stuff."

"You mean a job with them?" Fitzie knew enough to say it very flat, no surprise, no comment in his voice.

"Yeah. Nice. Dress up, drive your own car. Nice, clean work. A lotta talkin' to people. I said how you was good on your feet."

"Well, jeez, you know I signed up. I mean I gotta go into the service right away."

"No hurry, Fitzie. Just thought I'd let you know, huh? It's good. You go way with Uncle, that's the best thing for ya right now, come to think about it. Always be a job for ya, don't forget that, huh?"

Relieved, Fitz slid off the barrel edge and dropped to the floor. "I've got to wrap up my pipes, Shirt. See you tomorrow night, huh?"

"Good-night, Fitzie."

"Shirt?"

"Yeah?" The noise was rising once more, his jugs and water were moving. The cigarette looked puny where the cigar should have been.

"Thanks, Shirt."

Two

IT WAS 1958, the year when new officers assigned to Intelligence didn't have to undergo the Fort Benning Infantry Training, so Fitzie went straight to Fort Holabird in Balitmore, the College on the Colgate. He and Janice found a small place, for less than his housing allowance, nearby in Dundalk. It was school again, for nine months, and it was just fine. Within the yeast smell from the beer factories, with their new friends from Texas, Kentucky, all over—especially with a small group from St. John's of Minnesota who knew everything from Nabokov to pot even then—Fitzie and Janice ate oysters at the Friday night buffet at the officers' club; learned the Block, where Lady Zorro stripped downstairs at the Oasis and where the Miami Club, next to the police station, let the girls show hair; found the Bookstore's backroom Sunday afternoons for coffee and folk music, eating out at Miller Brothers and amid the paintings and statuary of mobbed Hausner's. $222.30 a month, plus another $100.00 for being in school: meager, but buying Fitzie more than he had ever had. Even Baltimore seemed *away* to him. For a while, Janice nursed at the Baltimore City Hospital. She had her R.N., a rarity there then, and soon became head nurse on the maternity ward. She and Fitzie had to get up at 5:30 for him to drive her up to the bleak castle on the hill to work, but her money was good, made them flush as well as able to sock some away. It ended after six months, the night Janice told him about the French tickler.

"I didn't know what the hell it was! But I let on I did."

Fitzie went crazy. "Who had it? Who showed you?"

"An intern brought it around in a jar. They took it out of a whore. The guy brought her in himself."

"And your *doctor* friend thought that was pretty funny, huh?"

"Well, it was, sort of. I mean it was *yech*, but don't be such a prude for God's sake."

This angered him even more because he was just becoming aware that it was true. It bothered him too that

21

Janice seemed to know so much more about life than he; why hadn't he realized this before? How had she grown older than he when he had never had his eyes off her for four years? He made her quit, actually drove to the hospital and resigned for her when she refused. It was their first real clash and they were through it and on the other side in little more than a week, but it still clung on in the private corner of Fitzie's self. He refused to let himself regret what he did, yet knew he had been a fool. Was a fool in so many ways, so raw, so dumb, so unprepared by anybody. Goddamn them! It particularly irritated him that his friends from St. John's, locked up in the snow for years, off in a monastery where nuns made *bread!*—knew so much, about liquor, about drugs, about studying, about even just talking. They were Catholic too, but were so much looser than he was, so on top of things and unafraid. He envied them and hated himself and felt a new awe of Janice. Waking before her in the morning, lying there looking at the Chesapeake dawn coming through the wear-holes in the green window shades, he would try to ease himself out of himself in order to look at it. It was a boy, he decided sadly, not a man; worse, it was his B.C. take-a-course boy, not his Tank-vats boy. He would have to change it, it wasn't good, it was just another smug nobody in the schoolyard, stopping stickball when the bell rang and getting obediently into line.

Scoring high in the language aptitude examination and being Liberal Arts, Fitzie wanted the agents' course— C.I.C.—so was handed a slide rule and assigned instead to Photo Interpretation. The mathematics, the measuring, the scale-finding never did become easy, but the rest made him eventually excited and satisfied with P.I.—the poring through the stereoscope over the overlapping aerial photographs, the world jumping up in three dimension, like spending the day looking down from a low-flying airplane. As his group progressed they worked with World War II photographs, then later, Korea. It was a time machine for him. He would pretend that it was 1943 or 1944 and that he was really somebody back then, the guy who had to draw truth from the elusive earth down there. *By God, it's Hamburg! The bastards have the harbor filled with barges, with houses built on them, and sheets or something in between for streets. Get me Churchill, Patton, Eisenhower. Our boys won't miss this time.* Their final exam was the Inchon landing, rife with challenge and urgency, full of details and trivia (the harbor master for the entire show was an Army engineer!), and the scary reality

22

of having history grade their work: if *your* answers had been used for planning, would they have made it? Would more men have been killed, or less? Fitzie filled with it.

His best day, to a point, happened at the Ordnance Center at Aberdeen, where they went to observe a fire-power demonstration of new, experimental weapons. On a tour of the grounds later, they were shown the tank graveyard, a vast field lined with the hulks of some two hundred tanks of all shapes, dating back to the first war, coming from Japan, France, Britain, Russia, all over. The young second lieutenants were given an hour to prowl around the ranks of rusting, weird monsters-of-war, and climbing onto decks and down through open turrets moved Fitzie into another life-plane. He was Bogart, burnt, dry, desperate, hard, sure in *Sahara*.

Within the dampness, inside the soul-abandoned iron corpse, he heard march music, faint and stirring; he peered out to see the long line of enemy he had to face alone, with only Sergeant Foster left with him, manning the .50 caliber above. So be it. One by one, wasting no shots, outmaneuvering the mass of fire-spouting devils from Hell, Fitzie pounded destruction through hull after hull, detracking when he couldn't puncture, leaving the flushed-out creatures for Sergeant Foster's merciless hand, which gunned them down as they scampered away. The instructor in charge at last blew his whistle to signal them back for the march to the bus. The sun had dropped away, leaving a pearly mist of light in the air in the graveyard. Climbing to where his Sergeant Foster's gun had been, Fitzie paused for a last look at the tanks and something crazy happened. He saw six white deer at the far edge of the great field, dancing off, back into the black woods. But the sounds of tracks and shells and ack-ack and march music blared on in his head. He couldn't shut them off. He saw some white deer and heard his killing sounds at the same time, and it struck him down immediately and abruptly into a black, painful depression that stayed with him for hours and wasn't gone until he awoke the next morning in his bed with Janice. He never told her about it and gradually forgot it himself, but never completely. Never explained, it stayed a new part of him and would return as a feeling, brief but complete, whenever it chose to. Fitzie would try to grab it, to hold it still and figure it out, but he never made it. All he came to finally was the surety that it was somehow not a bad, but a good thing to have in him. He couldn't tell why.

Janice, with the small hands and great water-blue

23

Limerick eyes, shook him again, became still more a strange, new woman-creature to him, the night he came home with the news about Germany. A captain from Personnel had interrupted class that afternoon to give those officers without orders twenty-four hours to decide whether they would like to volunteer for assignment to Seventh Army, in West Germany. Fitzie's impulse said no. Janice said, yes, at once. "You're the one who always talked about getting away," she said to him.

"Yeah, but, I don't know. If I take you on concurrent travel, it's a minimum of thirty-six months," he said.

"So what?"

"Christ, that's three years," he said. "I'll have to extend to Voluntary Indefinite. I'll be twenty-five before I can get out."

" 'Voluntary Indefinite'—the story of our life," Janice said. They were in a Laundromat, on a bench, smoking and waiting for their wash. "Where have we got to go anyhow? When else will we ever get to Europe? Come on, baby, let's live it up." He hated her for saying the words he knew should have been his. He loved her, this new, unknown girl, for getting them said. Still, he had always imagined being *sent* somewhere—this volunteer basis put him in the position of wanting somebody's permission to do it. "And how do you know," she said, "maybe you'll want to stay in?"

"Mm. Looks like the alternative is Texas. That's what the word is, anyway."

"Two years in Texas. Terrific."

"I don't know. We could get to Mexico, maybe."

"Yeah. That's better than Paris or Madrid, any day."

"You think we ought to go, huh?"

"We'll do whatever you decide to do, lover. That's what I signed up for, didn't I."

"But you do want to go, don't you?"

"Goddamn you!" she said and went to open the machine.

Without taking leave, they flew a chartered TWA flight from Idlewild, stopping at Gander, to Frankfurt am Main. Coming in, the woods outside the city looked to Fitzie just like New Hampshire. He didn't know enough to stay overnight at the airport hotel; he processed his travel orders through, received train tickets, and the two of them went straight on the eight-hour ride south through Stuttgart to their post, a *Kaserne* in Swabia, in the southwest corner of West Germany. They arrived stupid with fatigue, frightened and lonely, only to be told that Fitzie's unit had been in the field, at Rommel's old panzer-training grounds at Grafenwöhr, near the Czech border, for two weeks and wouldn't be back for another six. They were to take their time getting settled. There was no hurry at all. Fitzie felt like a fool. He felt betrayed by his own conscientiousness, which he suddenly suspected of being only plain, dumb fear, in disguise. He took it as a lesson and learned it.

Once Fitzie got to Grafenwöhr, met Major "Duke" Pacheck, the C.O., and Captain Paul McGregor, O.I.C. of the Security Section (C.I.C.), the Army was fine.

Duke did one good thing for Fitzie, McGregor did another. Duke was old to be only a major. He was fifty-two, and this was both his last tour before retirement and his first command of a uniformed, tactical outfit. He had been under cover since the war. Huge, Duke had a great, beefy, square face with tiny blue eyes in it, smoked enormous cigars all day long, lumbered around like a rhino yet went "hee, hee" when he laughed, didn't know how to salute or to wear his brass, and turned his outfit over to the young Fitzie. Overloaded with young P.I. and Order of Battle lieutenants, he made Fitzie unofficial Executive Officer. None of them had been there long. The unit was a mess, ready to be wiped out or absorbed by the first passer-by who noticed it. But it was easy. Duke simply gave Fitzie, McGregor and two other young lieutenants full run of the place. McGregor had been around as long as Duke, was also an ex-agent, but had always pined for troop duty and was flying high as the children. The key was Sergeant Beisch. Top. He knew the regulations. They spent a little more than a year putting the Tank—Fitzie named the unit that, the others liked it— into proper, by-the-book working order. Finished, they had Duke request the first Inspector General inspection the detachment had had since it had arrived overseas with the Gyroscope, passed with Letters of Commendation flapping in from all amazed corners—then cooled it for their remaining two years. In the end, Fitzie wrote his own, as well as others', Recommendation for the Army Commendation Medal. They all got it.

In giving him the place, Duke was giving Fitzie his real education: "Nobody knows anything and the rest don't have any balls. Do it the way you want it and it'll be right." In peacetime, the unit's Translation and Interrogation Prisoner of War sections were detached, and spread out in team offices along the East German and Czech borders—the Curtain—under operational control of the bigger spook organizations. When and if the balloon went up they would revert to Duke's command. In the meantime, they were on Fitzie's Morning Report for administration and supply—meaning once every six months Duke, Fitzie and Sfc. Gargano, the supply sergeant, would make a week's run in Fitzie's new Opel to those towns east of Nuremberg where the teams passed their time remembering the golden, busy years when the Curtain had holes and men would cross both ways: running West; being pushed, for pay, East. It was on one of their trips to the border that Duke told Fitzie the people trick: the secret of travel, the seeking out of at least one person, a child, a cop, an old man, a fat drunk—anyone, wherever you go, and talking to him. "And not about the goddamned Eiffel Tower or London Bridge, either. About his feet. Ask him about his feet, or about his food, or what he thinks about pigeons. Do that and you'll get a piece of them to carry around. The rest you can see in the movies or on a post card. When the hell you going someplace, anyway?"

"August," Fitzie said.

"Not till then? Don't you have the leave?"

"Yeah, but Janice has to have the baby first. And I have to save the money."

"Jesus, I forgot that. When's she due?"

"The day we get back."

"God, you can't screw up on the first one. We'd better cut it short and get back. We can go tomorrow morning."

"You mean it, sir? I was starting to sweat it a little."

"Shit, yes. We're just loping the mule out here anyhow. Where you going in August?"

"London. And Ireland. A week each."

"And how much loot will you have?"

"Eight hundred. A hundred a month, three to go."

"On what you get? What do you second-johns make now, anyhow?"

"Two-two-two."

"You little bastard, you ain't savin a hundred out of that."

"I am, too."

"How, for Chrissake? Your daddy helping you?"

"Ha-ha. Owe you one. We just decided, and we're doing it. I'm smoking C ration cigarettes out of the NEO kit, for one thing."

"And staying away from the club."

"And staying away from the club."

"Ha! Good for you. You son of a bitch, there might be hope for you yet."

"Thanks a lot."

"But I doubt it. Hee-hee."

Janice had their baby and nine stitches at the Army hospital in Bad Cannstatt, Stuttgart, and they did go to England and Ireland and did talk to people. One, a farm wife outside of Cork, some relative of Janice's, turned them away from her great, whitewashed kitchen and into her musty parlor where they sat touching knees in the airless August heat. "And how would a nice glass of ale go for ye?" she asked Fitzie.

"Fantastic," he said.

It came, tall and pale amber, and Fitzie poured it in— warm and ginger.

"Ginger goddamn ale" he cursed at Janice later, driving away in their rented Consul. "They're *all* Pioneers, for Chrissake."

But they weren't, not all, and Fitzie and Janice met the others. In London, Fitzie talked to a man in a park who asked them if they needed help or directions. Fitzie asked about his feet and he walked them around the city all afternoon, an encyclopedia of history. At the end, he hit them for five pounds and Fitzie paid it and was back in their hotel room before he multiplied it out and realized he had been conned. "Well, we would've had to pay for a guided tour and Jimmy was much better than that," Janice said.

"Not fifteen bucks' worth, he wasn't, that limey bastard!"

Together, they saw Alec Guinness in *Ross*, and *My Fair Lady, Flower Drum Song* and *West Side Story;* they ate and drank wine and watched the jugglers and strippers at the Churchill Club. It was strange; they didn't feel married. They felt as if they had only met. For the rest of their leave they made believe they had picked each other up and were staying with each other, sleeping together, for the good time of it. On their last night in London Fitzie dropped a fortune for tickets to the Sadler's Wells Ballet, including the long cab ride there from their hotel. Running up in the evening rain, they just barely made it in. Janice had wanted to see real ballet since the second grade. Tonight it wasn't ballet, they hadn't read the tickets. It was opera. In English. Sadler's Wells was on tour for the summer. In its place was an all-female school company. The hero was a skinny girl with red hair being dragged around by her sword and making love to a maiden of two hundred pounds. After the first act they left the audience smoking on the sidewalk and walked away. Janice was on the verge of tears.

"I'm sorry I dragged you out, Liz, old girl," Fitzie said, "but after seeing it with Tallchief, I just couldn't bear these amateurs."

"Oh! Did you? Moscow?"

"Ed Sullivan. There's a cab."

They kissed to Trafalgar Square. "Listen," Fitzie whispered, "I have to move out tomorrow. Come with me. To Germany, where I must rejoin my regiment. I'll give you a baby."

"Okay, ducks."

It wasn't the Army for them, really. Their apartment was spacious and bright. They saved and drove to Copenhagen, fourteen hours straight, and bought furniture one weekend on a pass. Isolated, Duke demanded no reveille, very little chicken; the standing rule to the thirty-odd men was blow it and you're out. Everyone played the game and enjoyed the life. Beefeater gin was about eighty-five cents at the Quartermaster liquor store in the basement of the B.O.Q. In Fitzie's unit alone there were five couples their own age, all in the same buildings or close by. Fitzie's days were spent with Top and Captain McGregor, mostly, reassembling the Tank.

McGregor, like Duke, never talked of the past except to curse his latter years doing dumb background investigations in Newark; McGregor was a gung-ho, hyperactive hummer and finger thumper; running around as if he were on his first tour instead of his next to last. Weekends, he belonged to the local German glider club, a throwback to his World War II bombardier years. Once he embarrassed Fitzie by taking a week's leave to work behind the counter of a *Metzgerei* downtown, slapping meat around in a huge white cloak, not for money: for lessons in wurst-making and beef-drying from the owner. McGregor had plans to go farming somewhere in the Carolinas when he retired, and thought such knowledge would come in handy. Fitzie couldn't decide which had become his father, Duke or McGregor. Both, he guessed. What McGregor gave to Fitzie was praise.

"You're the last of the barbarians, you know that?"

"What do you mean?"

"You're a killer. You and Kennedy."

"Balls."

"No, you're really after yours and that's good. Putting

28

yourself through school. Working. You don't owe anybody a thing. I envy you."

"*Everybody* did. It's what you did, that's all. I didn't know what I was doing. No points. Cut it out."

They'd talk, walking through the town in the morning, McGregor making his liaison calls on the police and so on, taking beer break at ten like natives. McGregor had spent some twelve years of his career in Germany; he thought it hilarious to be stationed in Swabia. "In Berlin, they used to go to balls dressed as Swabians. Like we'd go as a hillbilly." Like Duke, McGregor wanted Fitzie to stay in, to go Regular. "All us old farts from forty-two, forty-three will be gone in a couple years. You'll have it made. The only time you might have to be at this level again is as the C.O.—but you'll only be around thirty. We'll all get out and break the hump for you."

"I thought you liked it with a combat unit."

"Ah! I'm playing soldier. This isn't the real thing. Telling some poor old ugly platoon sergeant that if he marries his little *Schatzie* he can't get her into the States because she's a pro, or has some screwball East Zone connection. A lot of crap. No, you'll get sent to school, Fitz. They've got all kinds of programs now. Do a tour in the Pentagon."

Fitzie made first lieutenant and Duke had orders cut making him exec officially.

"See?" McGregor said. "You're filling a captain slot, already. A barbarian."

"Uh, uh. If anything, I'm slipping. It meant more when I was a second-john, right? Now I'm a first, so it isn't that great."

"Man, I'd hate to be a WASP with you around. Come the revolution, huh?"

"I'm telling you, I'm not after anybody. All I want is a good job, and make some good money."

"Right. Right! In the immortal words of Max Shulman, 'Screw 'em all and sleep till noon.' "

Between Duke and McGregor, Fitzie for the first time in his life became very conscious of himself, and very confused. He had no plan anymore and this worried him. But this concern was a vague thing that ran only beneath the crust, in a vein under the daily strata of doing his work and living with Janice, their baby and their friends. They saved and they traveled. Frau Bitzer came up from the town to stay with the baby in their apartment for five dollars a day and food. Two fifteen-day trips each year and many long weekends on passes. On a pass, they could

29

get to Paris, Zurich, Cologne, Nuremberg, Munich, Garmisch. And they did. In 1960, they left Baker Barracks one summer morning at 2:00 A.M. and drove to Oberammergau for the Passion play, then returned that night. And they found Mutters, high in the thin air above Innsbruck, and the pension there that leaned over a bottomless ravine, with the honeycomb underneath its porch for fresh honey on the buttered croissants in the mornings—four U.S. dollars a day, total. Sleeping and loving under the quilted eiderdown bed throws, then riding the lift in the day to the inn atop the mountain, sitting outside at the ledge tables; one afternoon watching the runaway, grunting hog plow through the door to the dining room inside, rousting the flock of British ladies on tour running and screaming across the slope. Three years of it they had, and it tanned them. On a Sunday, they would walk in the swept forest above their *Kaserne*, pushing the stroller over the smooth-stoned paths, climbing to come out of the woods at the Gasthaus with the terrace that looked fifty miles down the valleys, to learn the taste of May wine with the sun in it, and of Löwenbräu in pewter steins. Or they would drive to Baden-Baden and walk among the flowered streets around the Casino. Ten hours, stopping only at the Air Force snack bar on the way, put them in Paris and into the third-floor room of an old hotel on the Avenue Carnot. They made this trip four times: on the first, Fitzie faced the truth that only Fitzgerald, Hemingway and Joyce had with any reality reached him—out of all those days and books and papers called college. Only them! Snapping open to this, not having realized it before, happened in Paris and Fitzie went half mad he felt so free and new. He had got something, after all, not nothing.

They bought cheese and wine and carried it as they were supposed to, in a webbed shopping bag and ate it, with fruit, in parks and on the quays along the Seine. He read poetry aloud to Janice from a book he bought in a stall near Notre Dame, and after a while they weren't even embarrassed about it. Fitzie took Janice's hand suddenly and led her into the doorway in the middle of a tumble-down block facing Notre Dame from the Left Bank. Inside was quiet and darkness, and the smell of rain. A narrow staircase of footworn wood, very old, leaned like a ladder against the left wall. They climbed it, not speaking, trying not to look sneaky. A landing, then another steep set of stairs. They looked sanded. The banister felt like stone. On the third story the stairs ended in soft, lemony light from a skylight in the roof. Two narrow doors faced them. Fitzie opened one and startled a small old man washing lettuce inside at a tin sink. The room was no larger than the toilet in an airplane. He looked like Eduardo Cianelli and also like the face in the famous photograph of the man weeping in the crowds on V-E Day. He jabbered at Fitzie and Janice, an open faucet of French. The only word they could recognize was "Yank." He shook their clasped hands in both of his, then opened the other door. The wrinkled woman who rushed up from the inside and slammed the door shut behind him could have been the man's twin sister, yet they looked just different enough to have merely lived together for decades. Through the slammed door, Fitzie and Janice, like waiting beggars or salesmen, heard two faucets now: her words chirping parakeets twittering and swooping in frantic, upward loopdeloops; his answers stouter crows perched and reassuring. Then the door was opened by the old man, and the woman, smiling and blushing, came forward and asked them in with her hands. For a long minute they all stood smiling at each other. They were poor people. Their home was the one room, not counting the lettuce closet, with the bed against the wall in an alcove, so that one of them must have had to climb to the inside; it was a crowded room. Tables, an opened ironing board, a one-ring gas range, a hassock. The single rectangular window was opened: in it was the rear end of Notre Dame with its awkward stone props, and a little sky. Fitzie remembered the camera he was fingering. In Tarzan English he got them all off the hook.

"Me," he said, pointing to every noun, "picture, cathedral. Church. Notre Dame. Picture?"

"Fenestra!" Janice yelled.

"Ah! Ah! Oui, oui," the old people beamed, the woman even clapping her dark-freckled, veiny hands. Fitzie leaned out the window and snapped his picture of the ass end of Notre Dame. The woman produced a half loaf of bread from a large flowered cookie tin and spooned Nescafé into cups. The man cleared space on the main round table and they sat and ate the bread with guava jelly and drank the coffee; smiling at each other, blurting occasional brave words like "Bon. C'est bon," and "Merci." When they finished, Fitzie took out his Pall Malls and offered them. Both the old man and the woman accepted one and lit up with much faucet-splashing. Fitzie placed the pack beside the man's cup, but he pushed it back, shaking his head, "Non, non!" When they finished smoking, Janice got up brightly and said, "You're wonderful. Merci beaucoup."

31

"Should I slip some dough someplace?" Fitzie whispered.

"Oh, my God, no!" Janice hissed back.

At the door they shook hands all around. On the landing, Fitzie held out the cigarettes again and said, "S'il vous plaît?" The man nodded, smiled and took them, "Merci, au revoir." Outside, without speaking directly about it, they rode in a taxi back to their room. It was just noontime, and it was there and then that their loving passed into a new sanctuary, a beginning beyond the simple act that had been all for them before. His mouth, her petals; her mouth, his stem; then together in old-new turnings, giving and receiving at once. They slept and woke and slept, apart and entwined. "My lover," Janice whispered once.

"No booze, either," Fitzie said seriously, awed.

"Oh God, it's delicious."

"Fucking seems like a very nice word, all of a sudden."

"Fucking is a beautiful word," Janice said. They went out to eat dinner after eight in the evening. By then, Fitzie had begun to feel proud of himself and he resented the feeling as an intruder, a spoiler. They went to the Algerian restaurant just down from the hotel, although they had avoided it before because of the Algerian crisis. As they ate, the last of the purity of their afternoon was driven from Fitzie's heart: he suddenly thought of Father Carrol in senior ethics teaching: *any act is natural so long as the sperm arrives in the womb.* They hadn't been alone after all! Fitzie felt as if he had just been unfaithful to Janice, chattering merrily across from him, as if he had just sold pictures of her to a stranger. The nun is his ear. Nun, sin, nun. They hadn't sinned. Oh, terrific. Driving the green Opel back on the black, wet ribbon through the gray French fields to Germany, they hummed and chatted within the ember of their new secret; but inside, he couldn't get rid of the Jesuit's unsolicited, nun-sent, resented sanction. He wrestled, punching, afraid that unless he could knock it out, the priest's voice, his words, his goddamned okay would become forever a part of his and Janice's time capsule of that afternoon; and spoil it. He couldn't pretend he hadn't had the thought; he had. But wait. Only after, long after, when they had washed and dressed and left the room and the hotel, had the Church's comment sounded. During their fuck afternoon, his mind had been pure, had contained only her and themselves. They were all right, then. After didn't count, was too late to do any harm. The nun must have looked away or dozed

32

off. Thank Christ. Washed, free, Fitzie pushed the Opel's red speedometer ribbon up to 100 kilometers and turned his whole mind now to this strange creature with him, this mysterious new woman he had known so long yet hadn't. He felt quite new and strange to himself, and it felt good.

Their longer leave-trips took them to Spain, to the Riviera, to Berlin and Salzburg and Rome. They went alone, in their Opel, asking people about feet. The Tank finally got running smoothly, and Fitzie, at the beginning of the third year, was coming closer to deciding to stay in, to apply for a Regular Army commission—now that Intelligence had been made a career branch and there would be no off-assignments into the Infantry or Artillery. It looked good. They were making captain at twenty-five now. Fitzie could look forward to more schooling in Baltimore, most likely a tour at the Pentagon, then to Monterey for a language with good chances for a master's at Columbia or some other civilian college. Oh, there were some negatives. At least one "undesirable" tour in three was part of it, probably Korea, and that would mean a separation. But the bad with the good, and what the hell, how far ahead can you think? There was also this Vietnam thing which seemed to be becoming something, but again that was one of those things. Duke and McGregor weren't pushing him, but he knew they both were tickled at the route he seemed to be taking.

He had had a truck driver grandfather who, the day before he finally died at fifty-six of the cancer that had rotted him to bones and took his testicles, being shaved by Fitzie in their back yard on the Boston & Maine tracks had whined, "Take the Civil Service, Johnny. Get into the P.O., it's the only way you'll ever get anything." The Army had been Fitzie's P.O. Nor had he ever thought beyond it, except in a vague way, except to figure that if he could ever somehow be making ten thousand a year he would be fine. But they were into the nineteen sixties now, and he wasn't really in the Army anymore; he had passed the line and was on his way out of it, moving toward the blurry tomorrow that kept coming closer without getting any clearer. All Fitzie knew was what he was not going to do. He was not going back to Boston. He was not going to teach or sell insurance for John Hancock or Prudential, or go to law school. Simply because these things were what everybody from Boston College did, unless their fathers owned liquor stores or car dealerships. Everybody that Fitzie knew anyway. Sometimes he thought he would

33

like to go back and just make Popsicles—not train to be any kind of shirt-and-tie type, just run the Tank. But he knew he could never make his ten grand doing that. And for some months, all this drove him crazy. To Janice, talking at night in their living room, aware that they did not sit in the kitchen anymore, Fitzie would sometimes even begin cursing himself for going to college at all, would curse whatever and whoever he could remember had played any kind of hand in pushing him to go—which boiled down really into only Janice herself and one nun in high school, the one who had unfairly made him editor of the newspaper despite the fact he had never lifted a finger on it for three years. But it was too late now and he knew it. The damage had been done. He had a degree and was an officer and therefore had responsibility to live up to. More scary, he was now actually a twenty-five-year-old man, a husband and a father—not just once but again, pretty soon now. Jesus Christ Almighty!

One day the anguish wasn't there anymore. No thanks to Fitzie: he had neither come to any plan, nor said screw it. It just went away on its own. What was there now, somehow, was this new cool; this light feeling of *self*. Work wasn't life anymore to him. Janice was. Walking in the woods was. Getting loaded on beer Sunday afternoons was. They all became *it*, rather than simply what you did in between, when you didn't have to work. And what seemed to have just come along with this switch was the suddenly easy possibility of staying in the Army. What the hell difference did it make what he did for work? He still, of course, did his jobs right, and felt guilty whenever he'd take an afternoon off to drive Janice to Stuttgart or something, but generally life, became much more of a simple proposition.

Although Janice was due soon, was in her last six weeks, they still made awkward love, sweet and gentle. Then they took another chance and took leave. Their last trip. They drove south, through Switzerland, to Bolzano in northern, Germanic Italy where they walked the paths above the crisp, bright city at night, then went on to the Adriatic, to Cattolica on the coast below Venice. Fitzie and Janice, sitting on the beach, watching the boys and girls play volleyball; walking out on the wooden quay there to see the men drop their square, sheer nets into the calm waters and bring them up alive with the dancing, small silver fish; eating the scampi off bamboo sticks. And Fitzie, running into the water, shooting headfirst into it, deep, staying under, swimming until his chest ached, then

34

kicking up to take air and swim fast and hard, trying to hurt the cool, salt-heavy water with his arms and hands and legs, then rolling over, way out. Janice a round, small, yellow-dressed knickknack among the others back on the sandy mantel. Floating, frog-kicking slowly, taking the heat on his face and chest, the dark chill on his back and buttocks. Ah, to be able to stay here forever, for life. But no, damn it, there was a pull to go back, some kind of call, like the hated nun in his ear, to return and do whatever he was supposed to do. Not that he knew what that was. He only knew now what else he wouldn't do, couldn't do. He couldn't stay in the service. He was missing a screw somewhere inside him, he decided; some joint, some wheel, some pin either had been left out or pulled out or stuck somewhere along the line of his twenty-five years. *He didn't get it*, that's all. He couldn't understand how to run a Tank that didn't pop out full boxes of something good at the other end. He had to find some kind of machine that did that.

The white deer ran.

They went back, driving at night. Four days later Janice gave Fitzie a son, gave their little girl a brother. Fitzie spent the last days writing: he wrote his request for separation from the service; he wrote 180 letters for jobs, to companies, to magazines, to the networks, to advertising agencies—all in New York. They had gone to Germany, now they were going to New York. Not because they knew what it was; because they knew what it wasn't. It wasn't home. It wasn't the Army. It was away, and maybe it would be their place.

Three

━━━━━◆━━━━━

IN THE END, the Army itself squelched whatever doubts
Fitzie had about leaving it. It flew them to Newark
instead of to Idlewild. It was the third of July and Fitzie
hadn't been paid for June— he was to get it all in a lump
sum when he separated at Fort Hamilton in Brooklyn.
They had to take a Trailways bus into the Port Authority
building, the baby boy blackening the front of Fitzie's
tropical worsted shirt with sweat. The builders' houses
alongside the New Jersey Turnpike looked like nothing
they had seen in Europe for the three years, looked as if
they would vanish as soon as the bus passed them, and fed
more their fatigue and dread than their excitement. Without the money for a cab, they had to wait two hours for
the Army bus to come and get them. People stopped to
hold the children, to ask if they were all right and to
speak of people they themselves had in the service. One
old man gave Fitzie a bag of pears. The post was closed
when they got there, and of course would stay closed all
the next day, Independence Day. In the transient billets,
Fitzie borrowed ten dollars from a black sergeant taking
his six children to Kansas, where his sick wife had been
evacuated to the week before. They ate in the snack bar
and went to bed. All were wet with heat but so tired they
quickly escaped into sleep. They spent the next boiling day
sitting on the grass outside the officers' club, looking out at
the waters of the Atlantic on the edge of New York
Harbor, staring up at the bones of the Verrazano Bridge
being built. The kids were hot and dazed by the time
change and cried; Fitzie and Janice were abrupt and mean
to each other. They ate the pears, which were no longer
cold and hard. On the fifth, they got the Opel from the
Brooklyn Navy Yard and cleared Fort Hamilton physically and spiritually, driving over the Whitestone Bridge and
up the Merritt Parkway toward Boston, fast.

So they went home, but didn't, either: they weren't
going to be staying any longer than they had to. Both
families had been primed by letters in advance, so there

36

were no shocking announcements to be made. The children ran perfect interference for them. It was all merry and glad, first at Janice's house, then again in the Craig Street flat with Fitzie's parents and younger sister. And it all was like visiting someone in a hospital: from the moment of arrival, there was only the waiting for visiting hours to be over; there was no really being there. From everybody, eventually, the "So, how was it?" and always the "Terrific, we loved it," in reply. As if it had been a Bermuda cruise.

Janice's family never did ask the other question directly; Fitzie's father, Spider, did: "Well, what are you going to do?" But Fitzie knew he expected no solid answer, had asked it only because he felt he should. So Fitzie's flat "I'm going to New York" was answer enough—as if it meant something, as if Fitzie himself knew what it meant. After the welcome-home celebrations came the lull, but there was no father-son retiring to the study to discuss the future because there was no study, and since there never had been any serious discussion of anything ever before, how could there be now? Who could tell him anything? Not his father, not Janice's father or brothers. After going away on their own so far and for so long, he and Janice were like the genius child or the problem child: they could be neither helped nor hindered, only watched to see what they'd do next. Nobody ever asked, "Why? What the hell you want to go down there for?" And this made Fitzie sense something else alive in the people around him: fear. They were afraid, at some sublevel of feelings, that he might answer them, might finally say out loud how deeply he hated it all there, and nobody wanted to hear that. Not that he would have said it to them; not that he even knew it then. If his father, or anybody, had asked why, Fitzie probably would have crumbled. He couldn't say, "To get the hell out of here!"—that might have hurt them; also, you don't go *from*, you go *to*. And to what was he going? He had no idea.

He got a little of the old P.O. talk, but not much. Spider, himself working in a scab shipyard since the war, had heard the Navy jingle enough times to believe it: ". . . you're sure to go higher and when you retire you'll only be thirty-eight!" And he mumbled something about he hoped Fitzie was sure . . . but he let it go; hell, the kid was out already, it was too late now. His mother said even less to him, she said nothing. They had never been close, but there seemed to be new distance between them now that he had returned—ah, yes, he was the boy no longer; now

37

he was somebody's husband, the Army officer who had been in Europe. Fitzie's senses could read it: now he was a college-educated worldly man to her and he knew that if she would ever venture out of her *mea culpa* Irish meekness far enough to dare a mother's word to him—which she wouldn't—it would be only, "Watch out, now, just don't think you're a big shot, that's all." But the only stated comment he got from anybody came from Janice's father, old man Mose, Joe Kennedy, Abraham. It filtered through Janice's mother to Janice to him and it was simply, "Ah, that one'll do all right for himself." Janice took it as confidence and encouragement and Fitzie pretended to: "You bet your sweet ass." But inside, he resented it—thanks for nothing. Because inside he secretly half wished somebody would bang a nail into his bravado, talk him out of it, tell him what the Christ to do.

Not even the professionals did that, although they did, unknowingly, make it all simpler for him. Hoping to flesh out the skimpy list his mountain of job letters had borne, Fitzie went out to the guidance and placement people at B.C. They obligingly called alumni in New York for him—men in several different fields, since his basic description boiled down to bright putty. That done, they smiled and said the words that convinced Fitzie that he would, for sure now, get a job in New York. They said, "There now, that's a pretty good start for you. Call us when you get back and we'll go to work and see what's around Boston for you."

Fitzie said, "What do you mean, when I get back?"

"Well, let's face it, Jack, New York's a pretty tough nut to crack unless you really have an inside track someplace. Most of our boys who've gone down come back soon enough, but you go ahead, it'll be good for you."

Fitzie knew then that it would be only a matter of time. If that was the deal, he would have to make it; he could never come back. That was a Friday. He left Janice and the children with her family and was in New York Monday morning. He had enough money for about four or five, maybe even six weeks of job hunting in Manhattan, staying at the Y and busing home weekends.

Fitzie made Grand Central his headquarters. He broke a dollar into dimes and began his list. Six dollars later he had made one appointment, for Wednesday. He ate in Grand Central, either hot dogs and orange in the Rexall up the stairs from the waiting room, or cheeseburgers and french fries and milk shakes for thirty cents down Forty-second Street in the Ranch Burger. He went to the bathroom in Grand Central, down the white stairs from his telephone booth. He virtually lived there, his four weeks of all-chocolate days, no Popsicle ones at all. He listened to the lady spieler in the Kodak display room seven complete times. He circled the want ads there in the papers he bought there, and made copies of his résumé and sample ads, when he got them, in the machine there, four for a quarter. Some days he never left Grand Central from eight-thirty to five-thirty or six. Later than that there'd be no answer. He was interviewed by public relations people up Fifth at Rockefeller Center, by editors of girlie and combat magazines off Times Square. He was offered ninety a week on a magazine for shoe stores. A tanned, crew-cut old man high over Sixth Avenue gave him three travel books. "Read them and write me a critique of each."

Fitzie said all right, explaining timidly that his timetable would make it pretty hard, and spent one whole weekend in Boston locked in a room in Janice's house. He turned them in Monday and when he called Tuesday was told, "Listen, they're lousy. Sorry." Interelectric, Inc. burned up another complete day. They had sent Fitzie air fare to their upstate New York headquarters. There, five men received him into their offices. Each one had a pot belly, wore a white shirt, smoked a pipe and was nice. At the end of the day he went back to the first man, the one who had hosted the lunch where Fitzie had met four men like himself, obviously his competition. He was informed then that between the written part, which he had sent them months earlier from Germany, and the personal just completed, he had been evaluated at the "Excellent" level, but with a major reservation, shared by all the pipes, concerning his interest and "desire." Fitzie said they were probably right, come to think of it, and that he was sorry he had wasted their time and money, not to mention his own. The man said it didn't have to mean that at all. Fitzie said it did, and flew back to New York, feeling confused by the mixture of relief and disappointment in his stomach. He had failed, yet felt glad. That had never happened to him before. It happened several times right away after that, though, each time he interviewed with a company even resembling Interelectric, Inc. They all seemed like his memory of the Jesuits; like the Army but without the fun. Eventually, Fitzie accepted his reaction. He didn't understand what about them shut him off, but he realized they did and always would—which freed him to salvage what time he could by getting out as soon as he could after he discovered he was with one of "them." One save was the Blessed Mother Man, the television executive Fitzie would remember, and hate, forever: he was all blue and white. His hair was white, even his eyebrows; his suit, shirt, tie and socks were blue. He sat behind a white desk in the center of the blue rug that covered the entire floor of his white-walled corner office. The blotter on the desk was blue. The cuff links in his shirt were blue. By this time Fitzie had made his portfolio: ads, the book critiques, college stuff, some Army booklets, displayed under the acetate pages of the ten-dollar book he had invested in. It had a black leatherette cover and looked good there unopened on the blotter on the desk in front of the Blessed Mother Man. And it stayed looking good for fifty minutes of, "You know, I envy you. I really do. To be starting out again! I'd love that. Of course, in my day, it was a lot tougher. What I had to do—and you may look into this, Mr. Fitzpatrick, it's as good a way as any I know—look, go out to New Jersey or up to Connecticut. Maybe out on the Island, even. Get yourself on a paper or a radio station. Ten million things to do. You write the news, the obits, anything. You go to a meat market and sell them a minute—that *you'll* write for them. To this day I use what that taught me, and not that many have it, believe you me." Weeks before, twenty-odd interviews before, Fitzie would have sat there, legs asleep, making the eyes show interest, praying, hoping. Not anymore. Another big Protestant bullshitter keeping him from the next man, the one who might hire him. "Sir, are you going to look at my book?" he said, interrupting the blue and white memories, jamming the blue and white tape recorder.

The Blessed Mother Man looked at him as if he had just appeared there on the chair out of nowhere. "I guess I'll know the right time to get to that, huh young man? Let me tell you something about an interview."

Fitzie got up, picked his book off the desk and walked to the door. "I'm sorry," he said, "but I need a job, not advice."

"Well, let me tell you, forget it! With that attitude . . ."

"Your ass," Fitzie said and went out.

What kept him going was the other kind of men he met. The ones who didn't have jobs for him and said so and gave him something else: names. "Tell him I said to call him, okay?" It was a geometric progression that had Fitzie writing smaller and in the margins of his calendar book. One name became two and each of those had two or more names he could call, using theirs. Now he was not in Grand Central at all during the days, he was walking the streets, calling the numbers, finding the floors and the doors. Early enough, he had found the saint, the B.C. man who, again, couldn't take on anybody right now, but gave Fitzie . . . his secretary and telephone number! Now Fitzie could leave a number and didn't have to say, "Oh, no, uh, I'll call back later."

That August in New York had the feel and taste of bad, warm cantaloupe. The only air hid in the parks, behind the Public Library, Central Park, the U.N., but he could never afford to stay in these oases long enough. The hour or less spent in this air-conditioned building or that only made the outside that much more sour and heavy. One noontime toward the end, although he didn't know that, Fitzie stopped walking in the middle of a sidewalk. Something had snapped. He was the racehorse who abruptly, for no apparent cause and despite all spurring and whipping, quits and stops. He couldn't do it. He was kidding himself. It was no good. Someone yanked the valve in his navel and all his air whooshed out, leaving him a limp, used rubber on the Times Square sidewalk. The whip: *No, it's just the heat. I ought to get something to eat.* He had been skipping lunch; his face was starting to break out from the cheap, greasy food, and his money was growing lighter and lighter. He had to get out of the rancid, orange heat, had to sit down for a while. He paid his way into the first movie house he came to, the newsreel theater. Inside, the cool felt so good he wanted to drink it. The place was completely empty, except for a sleeping old woman in the last row, her arm around the brown paper shopping bag in the next seat. Fitzie walked halfway down the aisle and slid into a row, slumping heavily into a seat right in the center. Alone, he sat surrounded by empty seats, looking at the screen but not registering the pictures, feeling only the heat leaving his body. At last his body reinflated itself to a low, but sound, solidity. His mind, his spirit lay faint and still weak. He stayed there, slowly opening his head to the sounds and moving images reflecting off the screen. He held on to this hesitant peace, grateful for having found this limbo, this cool womb, waiting to be saved or to die.

When he first heard the footsteps he vaguely had them as the shufflings of the old woman stirring or leaving. But no, they were coming closer, someone plodding down the left aisle, the woman or some new soul come out of the heat. At the far edge of his vision the figure finally, slowly broke the emptiness. Now there were two of them among the empty seats in the front half of the movie house. Fitzie moved only his eyeballs to see the intruder. It was a man, maybe forty maybe ninety, featureless behind thick Army-issue, plastic-rimmed glasses and about four days of whiskers, and wearing a long, soiled, khaki-colored overcoat, like a World War I greatcoat. He stopped his plod at Fitzie's row. Fitzie couldn't accept what was happening: the man sidestepped heavily into the very same row, removing the coat. Fitzie held his head straight at the screen, gripping his portfolio on his lap tightly with both hands, tightening his bottom so as not to shit his pants. With a crash of the folding seat, without speaking, the man sat right next to him and spread the coat over both their laps.

Fitzie shot frantically out of the chair, out of the row and ran up the aisle and out into the fire outside. He walked up the sidewalk, crying openly, unable to pull his collapsed face together again. Nobody looked, nobody spoke, nobody stopped the young man in the neat suit carrying the black leather portfolio as he moved along through the people, weeping. And Fitzie was glad of that, at least. From the inside, he grabbed himself by the throat and shook himself until he stopped.

The hypodermic of anger shot coldly into him then and he was back. He wiped his face with his hands. From a cashier at her register inside an open restaurant door he bought a Milky Way and a Fruit 'n Nut Bar and ate them, warm and soft, as he walked instinctively back to Grand Central. There he sat on a long bench in the waiting room and talked to New York: *Okay, bitch, how much dues to pay? Your move. I'm going to screw you until your eyes pop.*

But that was all. He got off easy. On the Thrusday of his fifth week of crawling over the biggest Tank in the world, Fitzie made a Popsicle.

When he telephoned "his" secretary later in the afternoon, she had only one number for him, one name. Sheldon Horowitz. He went at five-thirty for his first, brief meeting. The next morning he went back and talked again, leaving with an appointment for a third interview, the following day, Thursday. That Wednesday afternoon he returned to an office he had visited two weeks earlier, a magazine publisher, and was offered fifty-five hundred to start as a researcher. He asked for a couple days to think it over.

Horowitz was a short, soft-voiced man making, Fitzie later found out, sixty-two thousand as a Creative Group Head in the big advertising agency that was to be Fitzie's first. He wore black suits, blue shirts and black ties. That Thursday he told Fitzie that he wanted to hire him because he liked his being twenty-six, married, traveled, experienced in management (Army officers are management), and because he thought there was good thinking and "flair" in the portfolio of print advertisements and television commercial scripts Fitzie had written as an assignment from one of the agencies that never got around to hiring him. Fitzie realized, though, what really got him his first job: it had been that quick, offhand exchange of his final interview with Horowitz. "By the way, whereabouts in Somerville are you from?"

"Tower Square."

"Oh, yeah," Horowitz had said, and the way he sounded the words told Fitzie that this man knew precisely what Tower Square was. After a second Horowitz smiled and said, "I'm from Malden, straight across the train yards from you."

"No kidding."

"Yeah. I've been down here seventeen years and you're number one I've met out of there. Isn't that something."

"Yeah," Fitzie said, trying to be cool. When Horowitz then offered him the writer trainee job it was for six thousand and Fitzie took it. The man in personnel, taking Fitzie through the Blue Cross insurance, withholding and other paperwork said, "You must come from some money, huh?"

"Are you kidding?" Fitzie said. "What do you mean, money?"

"Well, nothing. I mean it's none of my business, but with two kids you must be crazy. How are you going to live on six in New York? Why didn't you hold out for more?"

Because he was desperate for the job, because he had thought six thousand dollars was a lot, because he didn't know anything was the answer; but he just smiled and didn't speak. After that the man kept to his paperwork. High on success, Fitzie telephoned Janice in Boston.

That Sunday Janice went with Fitzie back to New York. They had a week to find a place to live, and another to get themselves and the children into it before Fitzie had to start work. Janice was elated and excited; for her it was clearly, at last, the beginning. For Fitzie, however, it was still more an end. He had done it. It was over. He couldn't yet think about what might be beyond that.

In looking for a place to rent in New York, as in everything else they had done and would do, they had no precedents, and so their first action was a mistake. Believing whoever it was who told them Manhattan was "impossible," they didn't look for an apartment in Greenwich Village, or in the East Village, or up along Central Park West, or on Riverside Drive, or the Lower East Side. They didn't look in the city at all. Nor in New Jersey. Nor in Brooklyn, because although the run of prices in the classifieds looked possible, Brooklyn to them was a bummy place, where the Dead End Kids were from, where, if you lived there and said it on the radio, everybody in the world laughed. Even the Dodgers and Chester Riley had left Brooklyn. So they spent their week of apartment hunting in just one area, the one that seemed most affordable and somehow less foreign and threatening to them. Queens. They answered ads and saw real estate agents in Flushing, Woodside, Jamaica; in Whitestone, Kew Gardens, Maspeth and Astoria and Bayside and Long Island City and Corona. On their last day, Friday, they signed a two-year lease, paying a month's rent of $135 in advance and another month's rent as security, on a set of four rooms in a long row of new, two-story connected brick apartments in a small area near where the East River meets the Sound. It seemed nice. There was a park, with trees and swings, at the end of their street. From there the Manhattan skyline could be seen on a clear day. The apartment's kitchen was modern, with a wall oven. The owners were a lady of fity or so, who worked, and her son in his early thirties. They lived upstairs on the second floor. It was as good as anything else Fitzie and Janice had been shown, and they had run out of time. The following Wednesday they left Boston at five in the morning, with their kids, to meet their furniture and belongings being delivered from Army storage in Brooklyn. They were in New York. Where their loneliness, or aloneness, didn't begin, but where they discovered it.

44

Fitzie had a fantasy about living in New York, a day-time, eyes-opened fantasy. He liked to pretend it was Paris; not the Paris he had seen really, but the Paris he had seen in French movies, the gray, where-to-live Paris, with some black and white filmed London suburbs thrown in. Hence, when he left Janice in the mornings at eight and walked to catch the bus for the Main Street Flushing subway station, and when he looked down at the crammed fields of flat, square, chimneyed housetops from the elevated, hurtling train, he was not Fitzie of New York, but the American in Paris. Not there on a leave now, but living there, working there! He watched the people around him, fascinated. How strangely they talked. What exotically foreign lives were they living? With him right there among them! The game ended by itself each day the moment the train would burrow under the river for its dark crawl underground to Grand Central, but that didn't matter. Fitzie in real New York was more than enough for his days. And as soon as he would come up again out of the tunnel each night, back on the Queens side, he could always turn his Paris-London suburb back on for the trip home. The only rip in the film was Janice, who had no fantasies, who lived in Queens, not Paris, and in the daytime, at that.

On his first morning at the agency, Fitzie was put into the office of a writer on vacation, instead of his assigned desk, phone and typewriter in the glass-walled cubicle in the "bullpen"—the lone writer among the lettering and mechanical men of the art department. How strange and exciting all the words sounded to him: comp, spread, logo, engraving, subhead, copy, spot, one-liner, a sixty, a thirty, an I.D., buckeye, weasel, mouse type, think-session, push, nice twist, reprise, zoom, tight close-up, windows, air, quick-and-dirty, a rough, a thumbnail, voice over, renderer, a hooker, slice-of-life, gestalt, schmuck, dub, supers, punch, grabber, answer print, interlock, story-board, serif, fey, pan, dolly, proofs, stand-up, savvy, demo, testimonial, factory-window, overlay, klutz, break bread, touch base, get back to you, the Coast, schtick, location, hack, wordsmith, schlock account, bullets, fly a little, a big shop, ciao, baby—words used as talk, filling the halls, flooding over Fitzie out of offices, in elevators, from every man and woman he found himself among from that first morning, words that sounded unique and alive to him even after he learned their meanings. He had, surely, come into a new and different world. He sat there, that morning, at the typewriter on the desk in the loaned

45

office. The office was an office, ordinary except for the cork bulletin board on one wall covered with colors and shapes he couldn't take his eyes off: two Volkswagen ads, several photographs having only the face of a birdish young man in common, presumably the rightful owner of the office; and vivid posters, drawn and photographed, for film houses, art shows, photographers; a line drawing of Charlie Chaplin, an "Observer" article torn from a *Times,* more—a collage, to Fitzie, of life on Venus or in Alexandria. He sat there, alone. In an hour the only people to come in were a secretary, to get him coffee, and two men, each to say hello and welcome him "aboard." He sat there and stared at the typewriter, a Smith-Corona portable with no paper in it. Somebody was paying him to hit those letters and make words. That's all. To think of things all day. To dream up his own Popsicles! They were going to give him money for doing that. Good God, how could he ever have told this to his granfather dying in the back yard by the B&M tracks, urging the P.O. on him!

As he had discovered in the Army, there was nothing much to learn; there was simply bad or good and few others around who knew the difference better than himself. Trying to learn how this new Tank worked, how it was to be run, he saw that any products, cars, liquors, cereals, soaps were really only things people used, objects, parts of their lives, and so there had to be some bell to be rung about practically anything, that people would hear, recognize and like. There was another discovery: like an insurance policy that he didn't know he had suddenly paying off, or an amnesiac conked into remembering, Fitzie, at twenty-six, woke up in this Horowitz world of words and pictures, full where he had thought himself empty, smart instead of a clod. His mother's, the nuns' and brothers' warnings had said Bum. New York was now saying Judge. Fitzie thought it hilarious. And he pushed it to the hilt. He *did* know what was good and what wasn't. He was the one who knew what the idea really ought to be. Why the hell not. After all, that's what he had been trained for. He had the education, the credentials for it, from the Strand, the Inman, the RKO, the Loew's, the Brattle, the Harvard, the old Laff Movie, the funny books, the radio.

Saturdays and Sundays and stolen weekdays. Years of them. Stopping on the way for Walnettos and Sky Bars and nigger babies and dill pickles, going to the balcony so when the dillies were half eaten they could be lobbed, wet and pulpy, green at the bottom, white near the eaten end,

46

high up through the dusty white projection beam then down to squash onto somebody's head or lap. Sometimes sending one kid in with a ticket, after the picture had started, to slip to an exit and slam down the bar, opening it to let the three, five, six shadows come running in, silhouetted against the blinding outside light. No more than two could be caught. The East Side Kids, Leo Gorcey, Huntz Hall. The Corsican Brothers. The Sullivan Brothers. Cagney. ("Made it, Ma, top of the world!") Lash La Rue. Bill Bendix belting the Nips on the head with his Brooklyn blackjack, first lifting their helmets off. Gregory Peck (Pecker) jumping her (who? Wanda Hendrix? Jennifer Jones.) on the moonlit barn floor. *The Killing*: Giant Sterling Hayden with the dumb tie down only to his second button, the bucks flying all over the airport, the bullet holes like spurting pimples on Elisha Cook, Jr.'s forehead. Boston Blackie and Mousie. Gene Kelly the sailor dancing on ash can covers. (Mm, wouncha like to get inna that Kathryn Grayson?) Jimmie Gleason. Ann Blyth. Regis Toomey. If somebody doesn't get in there and defuse that Jap fish this whole sub'll be blown to smithereens! Dan Duryea. John Hodiak. Dane Clark-slash-Richard Conte. Robert Lowery. Uh, oh, now he's going to plug in the toaster, but his hand's still in the sink! Ooo, Ollie.

No time for that now, Billie. Shredded Ralston for your breakfast starts the day off shining bright. Well, if it ain't ol' Waxy. Leee-Roi! Aw, Unc! With Agnes Moorehead as Merilie. Wally Ballou, here. Oh, Connie, that nice Mr. Boynton. And J. Carrol Naish as Luigi. But Uncle Remley said—lying on his parlor floor, the speaker at his ear, studying the whorls in the rug.

The universe, in the ears and eyeballs, of orange and green suits, of crashes and splats and aarghs; so much more real and alive than *Silas Marner* or even the Gospels: Easter Sunday was when they got to wear suits with jackets that had a pocket on the inside where DICK cap pistols could be carried in and whipped out of to shoot a crook coming around the end of a piazza on a three-decker. Fitzie's academy, his prep school. Rialto U. An education he never knew he had, turning out to be an honors course. And he realized that he had even gone on to graduate school: he remembered Uncle Miltie. And Jerry Lester's "Dagmar and Beanbag." And Ernie Kovacs. William Powell, the Ritz Brothers, Fatty Arbuckle, Chaplin, the Ziegfeld Follies, King Kong. Fitzie was fifty years old! Casey, Crime Photographer! Eartha Kitt as Wilde's Salome on "Omnibus"!

Fantastic. This advertising-Tank was where you got to do all those magic, wonderful, funny, beautiful, scary scenes and tricks, situations and exchanges your memory had been filled to the brim with. Fitzie thrived. "No, no. You know what it is? It's Jack Lemmon on the train in *Some Like It Hot*, you know, where he's supposed to be a broad and is in the bunk with Marilyn?"

"Remember the Slowly-I-Turned thing Abbott and Costello used to do? Well the kid can do that."

"Yeah, yeah. Only she has to feel like Gene Tierney when Laura's in her country place. It has to look like that."

He loved it, every day of it. Of course, at that first agency, in that first year, he was a failure, too. Very few of his Popsicles got sold. They had given him a Popsicle-making machine, and he had quickly, joyfully learned how to run it. But then they would come and be sourly troubled, worried and disappointed when they saw he hadn't made Social Tea biscuits, which was what they really wanted, it seemed. Not Horowitz or the writers, producers and other "creative" people Fitzie worked with, they kept feeding him with praise and encouragement; but the ones, it turned out, who actually owned the place, the account management men, the M.B.A.'s, the serious, pipe-smoking marketing majors who wanted to "just move product off the shelves, fella," the men in the hats, the fraternity brothers, the headshots in the *Times* and *Wall Street Journal*, businessmen, Babbitts, executives, Ivy League Protestants. Sometimes, Fitzie felt that he had left the Army only to become surrounded by more colonels. Civilian colonels. It was crazy. It was their place, all right, and they did reject nearly everything Fitzie did. Every time he offered them a Popsicle, they took a Social Tea. Yet they—not Horowitz alone, but they themselves—kept asking him to come up with a new *Popsicle* each time. So he finally said the hell with it and just kept making his Popsicles. He didn't understand, but at that point it didn't seem to matter much. He was still having so much fun doing the stuff, he didn't yet care whether any of it got produced or not.

In Queens, Fitzie and Janice were living lower than they had in the service. Once they got used to getting paid every two weeks instead of once a month they realized how little money Fitzie was making. Not that they didn't make it work for them; as they had traveled in Europe, they lived in Queens. Janice baked bread. She made chicken Tetrazzini, she fried rice and put together all kinds of casseroles and meals for them, wasting, like her mother, the Irish feeder of eleven, nothing. Fitzie would kid her. "You've done it. An eggless omelet!" He bought and drank only beer now, no hard stuff at all, and picked whatever brand was cheapest. Knowing nobody, they had no entertaining. Both cut down their smoking. Fitzie's one treat was his payday lunch, when he would accept one of the invitations to have a real lunch, with a drink. Every other day, he would be there with his quarters at the windows at the Automat on Forty-second Street and Lexington, a sandwich, milk and coffee. In Germany, they remembered with unfunny laughs, a Gasthaus meal of schnitzel, spaetzle and potatoes, including the wine and beer and coffee, was rarely more than four or five marks. A buck. And that cheap, great commissary steak. And the eight-ounce filet mignon at the club for a dollar fifty! "Well, at least we had it to talk about," Janice would say.

"Someday, lady. You watch me."

"Yeah, I know. Stick with you and I'll be wearing diamonds."

"True, true. One of the best little girls that ever walked the street."

"It may come to that yet."

"Shut up. More spaghetti."

Janice read labels, clipped coupons, watched the *Long Island Star-Journal* for sales. In uniform so long, Fitzie's school suits were still wearable. When winter hit he took the epaulets off his gray, belted officer's overcoat and wore it to work. It was very warm and looked awful. They had bought a good Pfaff in Germany and Janice made all of the children's clothes. They kicked themselves for not having rented nearer to the subway; the bus Fitzie had to take added twenty jerking minutes to his commute and fifty cents a day, two fifty a week, five dollars a pay period to their expenses. That was a bottle of scotch. Bottled here.

In October, they did it. They had scrounged enough money together and were going into the city! To see a play. And have a drink. And eat. Oh, God was good. Fitzie waited for her at the Vanderbilt Avenue exit of Grand Central. After work, he had gone and had about six beers and the free popcorn and hot-dog chunks at the

Cobb's Corner inside. It was a Friday and payday and he had skipped his lunch for this. Janice was late, ten minutes, twenty-five, forty. Janice was never late. Something had happened to her, she was waiting someplace else, she was raped in Corona. Then she came, up the stairs and through the doors, heels clicking, scooting haughtily between two cabs to come up to him, the eyes on high beam, the skin color up, the hair terrific in the french roll, the Copenhagen suede short coat turning them both into some other young couple, smart, with-it, doing everything all the time. It was Grand Central: he hugged her largely. "Jesus, I was worried about you!"

"Oh *you!*" she punched his back. They started, hurrying down Forty-third Street.

"What happened?"

"*You* left me the car without any goddamn *gas* in it."

"Oh, Christ."

"I ran out of gas! I *stopped* in the middle of Northern Boulevard!"

"Oh, lady. What'd you do? God, I'm sorry. I'm *stupid.*"

"This is great. This *guy.* He stopped behind me, you'll never believe this, and you know what he had in his trunk? A five gallon can of gas!"

"Nobody has gas in their trunk."

"He poured it in, he was about fifty, a truck driver or something, and said, 'There ya go, honey, do somebody a favor sometime!' and went off!"

"Holy mackerel, what luck. Jeez, you think there's nobody around like that anymore. You try to pay him for it?"

"With *what*? I was so embarrassed. I had one crummy token and some green stamps. You got paid didn't you?"

He loved her. She was flying. She wasn't really mad, she was loving it, telling it with swoops of her arms, making a great scene of it. They were late, almost, and had to run across Times Square and up two blocks, Janice moaning and laughing, running up on her toes over the sidewalk gratings. Trotting with her arm tight inside his, Fitzie was only then aware of how alive Janice could be, should be, used to be, and hadn't been since, since they had come to New York.

"To the left and upstairs," the ticket usher said.

About a minute before the curtain. Climbing, Fitzie saw two seats against the wall, the very last row in the one-balcony theater. They weren't his. His were right in front of them, the second last row. He helped Janice out of her coat and sat, feeling just a twinge of disappointment at

50

not being in those other two, pure seats. The lights went out, the play started. It was *A Thousand Clowns*. Jason Robards, Jr., Sandy Dennis. That was why Fitzie had picked it. He knew nothing about it, but he had been to only two real plays in his life, not counting London. One had been *Pajama Game* with John Raitt when he had come down to New York one weekend in his last year of high school; he and three other guys in one room at the Hotel Dixie, two going in with the suitcases, the other two filtering in later one at a time, the four sleeping head to toe in the twin beds. The other play had been in Boston, during college sometime, Eugene O'Neill's *Long Day's Journey into Night*. With Jason Robards, Jr., as one of the sons, the funny, sad drunk. And Fredric March as the father: Mr. Tyrone, Fitzie's other grandfather, his wonderful Rock Harbor suicide grandfather. But it was Robards Fitzie remembered and when he had seen the name in the *Times* he picked that play to be their first. For Fitzie and Janice that night, the play could have been what its name said. It killed them. Alone in the dark with the spirits on the stage, Fitzie and Janice collapsed and straightened, fell apart, came together again only to break apart all evening, like Punch and Judy. Everything hit them, the ukelele, the kid's names, the chewing out the next apartment house for its quality of garbage, the calling out the Park Avenue richies for volleyball, the squelching of the Chipmunk-man, the foiling of the social worker, Sandy's teeth, Jason's hat, the crazy, warm, womb-room set, the kid's window exits. They stayed in their seats during intermission, sweating and weak and happy, using the stupid words, the only ones that came, but sharing the joy nevertheless: "It's really good, isn't it?"

"Oh, yeah."

Afterwards, they left, shuffling downstairs in the crowd to the cold outside, humming, "Yessir, that's my baby, nossir, don't mean maybe."

They walked west and went to Jim Downey's: down the aisle between the booths of real faces below the picture faces on the wall above, being seated in the room at the back, trying to look like somebodies to look at, trying to look to see somebodies. Ordering drinks, her sour without fruit, his new find, a rob roy; reading Jim Downey's story on the cover then inside the menu for food, "I toldja he wuz a sport," Janice cracked to the empty chair between them. The two of them snug inside the smoke of the place, within the people talk and laughs and spoon-clanking and glass-tinging, the loud, crowded privacy of

51

the place. Fitzie shut the menu, slid it over to the table's edge and looked around: by the way, oh by the way . . .

"What are you going to have?" Janice said.

"I am going to have the scrambled eggs, and I'm going to have with the scrambled eggs the Irish bacon and I am going to have a very large, cold bottle of beer, and I am going to eat much bread, then I will have coffee. Four cups of coffee, and maybe a stinger."

"Go all the way back, you didn't say may I."

"What are you going to have?"

"God, eating out is such a waste. We could eat for a week for what this is going to cost us."

"Yeah, but what the hell, this is so great. Stop looking at the menu and talk to me. Tell me about yourself." The drinks came. "Ah, here's to us," he said and clinked his glass against hers. Janice put the menu down and drank some of her sour. "Mm, that's good. Give me one of your cigarettes, or buy me some. No, give me one of yours."

He got up and bought her Kents from the machine.

"What's the matter?"

"Nothing." She looked away.

"No, really."

"*Nothing.*"

"Talk about the play, huh?"

"Oh, I loved it. It was really good."

"Look, we've got this coming to us. And it'll be a helluva long time before we get to do it again, damn it, so why not . . ." The waiter came with his pad opened. Fitzie looked to her. "The same as you're getting," she said and he gave their order.

"I mean you were so *up* before."

"I know. I suppose it's really a waste not to enjoy it. I'm just so beat all of a sudden, I don't know."

"Well, it took a lot to get out of the house and in here, then you had that damn gas. That was my fault."

"Can I have another one of these?" she said, swooping down the foam.

"Thatta baby," Fitzie laughed, relieved, and called the waiter.

"Why weren't we born rich?" Janice said, a cliché of theirs, not serious.

"Give me time, will you? It's only been three months."

"Seems like three years."

"Does it? No, I mean, really? It doesn't for me. Hell, it takes this long to get used to anything. It's been a lot of bumping around since Germany, don't forget. Poor kids don't know where the hell they are."

"Yeah, I guess I just don't either. What a party-pooper I'm turning out to be."

"Ah, you're beautiful. Man, coming out through those cabs tonight."

"Oh, Fitzie, it's such a dumpy, shitty place."

"I thought you liked it!"

"No, the apartment's okay. But, oh, I don't know. Even the First National they've got. It's dark and dirty and boxes piled all over the aisles all the time."

"Is that right?" He didn't know. He had never been in any of the stores near them. When he thought of where they were living, there was no outside to his picture, just their rooms.

"And the people are all so yuck! Old and cheap. And there's nobody around where we are. *Nobody.*"

"Oh, there must be. We'll meet them. Did you ever get to see that one two doors down? With the baby?"

"Just today as a matter of fact. I was coming back from the park."

"Anybody home?"

"Yeah, I think she's all right. They're from upstate someplace, I forget where she said. But way up, near Canada. They're only here for a year. He's getting his master's in the city somewhere."

"In what?"

"Safety," she said.

"Safety!"

"I knew that'd get you!" she said.

"Je-sus Christ. *Safety?* How the hell do you get a master's in *safety,* for the love of God? Holy mother!" Fitzie made much of it. It had broken the blues that had come to their table.

"Oh, I'm sure it means something. You know, in factories. Or on railroads or something." She was trying to hold her mouth together.

They both busted then and after that the evening was fine again. The eggs and bacon were good. That was fair because there was no bacon for breakfast at home for the next two weeks.

The next morning, Saturday, he went with Janice down to the street where the stores and shops were, the post office and police station. That's what it was, a street. Not a town, or a square. And Janice was right. Driving through, it looked inoffensive enough. But up close, inside the stores and along the sidewalks, the place breathed a poorness. Not a money-poor, God knows there were enough new Galaxies and Imperials around and plenty of dollars moving about, and good clothes; but a people-poor, a vague sourness, a spiritual cruddiness that made the stores and windows and doors, even the parking meters, seem rundown and hopeless. Fitzie's own Craig Street and Tower Square had been dumpy and gray and he hated them, but this Queens place wasn't the same. This street of stores and people was slutty.

Then he checked out their own street. Very weird. It was a short street, quiet and safe, ending at the park grass. New, the trees were still gawky and meek but someday would probably be nice and full. So what the hell was it? Because there was something, all right. Ah! No kids, for one thing, no more than one or two bikes every now and then. So, no basketball hoop on the telephone pole, no stickball games in the street, no stone or chalk drawings to brighten the blacktop, no screaming, hollering, machine-gunning, no marbles, no chestnut fights, no yo-yos, no red rover, red rover. But so what. Fitzie's own two were still small enough to go around invisibly, nap-tied indoors half the time. Hell, maybe all these people were—, but *what* people? Christ, that was it. No wonder it was so quiet, as promised by the landlady's son Don. There was nobody there; let alone kids, there were no people. Bodies, yes. All the houses were occupied. Figures caught going off in cars, going in from cars, walking by, eyes averted. But none of the houses were lived in.

The back yard, small but grassy space, was off limits to them as tenants. That was too bad, it would have been good to let the kids out in, Janice could have kept her eye on them from the bedrooms and had a little time to herself without them up her skirts, but, well, live and let live. If Donny and his mommy loved the goddamn patch of dirt that much, let 'em. There was always the park. Fitzie had been there too, but, as with the "town" and the street, not really, not through Janice's day-in, day-out eyes. When the kids woke from their afternoon naps he bundled them up, and with Janice walked the half a block of quiet, and crossed the top of the T to the park. It was big. Pushing the boy in the low German carriage, Janice and the girl ahead on the uphill concrete path, Fitzie felt much better. The park was fine, the park was something else, unlike the street, the place. Up and over the hill, they could see the river on the left, then the wide, swirling intersection with the Sound; down and around, alongside the water, to the playground. They put the kids on the swings, the little one in one with a front bar, then sat on a bench and looked out at the river-Sound and smoked.

Straight across, the Bronx looked fine; a little farther up, the Whitestone Bridge clean and high and grand in the day's cloudy light. A tugboat pushed a barge full of something blue toward the East River. "You feel alone?" he said, looking still at the water.

"Yes."

"Me too. I like this, though, the park."

"After all these years."

"What?"

"You still say *pahk*."

"Sets me off. Kennedy's making it the in way to talk now."

"If we were home, you'd say *park* with nine r's, you phony."

"Damn right. Except we are home, aren't we."

"Yeah, I guess we are."

"Bitter, bitter. It's not that bad, is it, babe?"

"No. Maybe being alone is the way anyhow. I wish you were with me though. When I'm alone *alone*, it all gets so fuzzy and I get depressed. What a creature darling Janice is becoming. I am a darling, though." She pinched her own cheeks and they laughed. Maybe it was going to be all right.

But November that year was a bitch: hateful wind and ice on the sides of trees. Fitzie came home one evening, in the dark, from his Paris subway ride and his Queens bus. He was late, the kids were in bed asleep already. Janice was lying on the Macy's sofa watching television in a blanket off their bed. "Heat on the fritz?" he said.

"No, it's on, but it's still cold as a witch's here."

"Did you go upstairs?"

"I saw her but she says she doesn't know anything about it and the thermostat says seventy-eight and Donald won't be home until ten."

"Sewing class night, I suppose. It's the damn garage, you know. The shithead ought to have it insulated. To save dough, if nothing else." The garages in all the houses in the row were under the first floor, drive-downs.

"Dough, hell. I'm freezing."

"Well come into the kitchen and feed me. You can leave the oven door open."

Listening for it, when Fitzie heard Donald's key hit the front door lock he went out to catch him before he went upstairs. He was pretty sure Don wasn't actually a queer, but he was mincy, with long eyelashes, and Fitzie still had that old instinctive, unfair but there, distaste for the type. "Hey, Don, can you come in here for a minute?"

55

"Hi! Some night, isn't it? There's nothing wrong, is there? Hi, Janice."

"Don, it's freezing in here," Fitzie said.

"It doesn't feel bad."

"You just came in."

"Well, the heater's on, I can hear it."

"Yeah, and your mother says the temperature's up, but I don't care, the place is cold as a bastard."

"I'll go check." He went upstairs, they heard him going down cellar to the heater, then he was back. "Gee, everything's fine. I turned it up to eighty, that's much higher than I have to. And here, here's a thermometer."

"What's that for?"

"We'll leave it here," He put the stand-up thermometer on their Grundig. "Then you'll see. I've got it really way up."

"Don-o, that thing can say two hundred for all I care. All I know is I don't like coming home to find my wife wrapped in blankets to get warm."

"Well," Donald said with a TS shrug.

"Well, what are you going to do about it, is what I'm asking you!"

"Calm down, Fitzie, he's got the heat up," Janice said, trying to moderate, but only making him feel vaguely betrayed, hence meaner.

"It's your goddamn garage you know, it's sucking all the heat down. Your Riviera's probably sweating down there. The garage ought to be insulated."

"Well, I can't do that this year," Donald said. "You have no idea how much it takes to run a house like this." A pygmy dart to Fitzie's ego: at some level, and he knew it, Fitzie resented this sissified man for being only about four years older than he yet owning this house and the new Riviera and a black cashmere topcoat; resented his living with his mother, his not letting them use the back yard. Mostly he resented being suddenly where he was resenting things like this, piddly, petty mosquito things. "Do what you want," he snapped, "it's your money you're pouring through that floor, not mine."

"Mm. It's too bad you don't have a rug. Or carpets."

"Well we don't! We *like* wood floors. We like *warm* wood floors even better!"

Donald insulated his garage ceiling about two weeks later. And Fitzie and he were never more polite with each other after that, although Janice couldn't bring herself to put him down as vehemently as Fitzie did. He knew how Janice felt. She pitied Don. He didn't seem to have any friends. Only rarely would he get dressed up and go off on his gorgeous wheels. He lived, in fact, much like they did. Worse, because he owned the place, he had to stay there. They didn't. The idea, the possibility of getting out, had begun, way back in Fitzie's mind, a tic, before the heating scene. But he had covered it quickly, and kept burying it whenever it would poke through. Christ, they had barely moved in, were still all up in the air, it wasn't that bad; anyhow, they had a lease, and you didn't go *from,* you moved *to.* Still, Janice was down more often than up now, week after week, discouraged by nothing, by everything. At work, Fitzie was thinking of her more often, her on that zombie street every day. Christmas came just in time. They drove home to Boston. It was a good break. The kids wallowed in the attention and the goodies. Being reconnected to the mother ship seemed to refuel Janice nicely. And Fitzie was rather a hit at his own house, at theirs, at Janice's married brothers' houses: everyone loved talking about advertising, and he was now an embodiment of the New York they all were so curious about, and he lied humbly.

They drove back, down the Wilbur Cross and the Merritt. They let the kids fool around with their Christmas gifts for a while then put them, bushed, to bed early. It was New Year's Eve. They had a quart bottle of Schlitz and a bag of potato chips, and sat on the floor, listening to their old Eddie Calvert, Bobby Darin, and Stanley Black records. Near twelve, Fitzie filled two of their German crystal champagne glasses with the end of the Schlitz and turned on the television to Times Square. Hooray. They tipped glasses and sipped 1963 in with their beer, and kissed lightly, there on the floor. Then he shut off the set. "Not like last year, huh?" he said.

"No. Right now you'd have your tongue in that aviation major's wife."

"Oh, come on. She *was* a piece, though. You did pretty well yourself."

"That was always the best party of the year. All the dress blues and the gowns."

"And the free champagne and African lobster tails."

"Ha! Then the general's reception the next day. All of us green and ill."

"But then starting in again!"

"Yeah, remember Duke? 'It's only pain!' "

"Seems like a hundred years ago," Fitzie said, then he sighed. "Goddamn it."

Three weeks after that, they moved. Blindly, after not even five months, and having to hit the last of their savings to do it, but also with hope, with the excitement of convicts over the wall, they fled that street, that part of Queens. To another. Just to go. They may have done it anyway, but an excuse came along, a physical justification: Donald's basement. When they had taken the place, because it was so small, Donald had agreed that they could have storage space down there, beneath the stairs, as well as Janice's Maytag wringer. In December, he had told them sorry, but he was having the basement finished. Fitzie lugged the stuff up. The suitcases he squashed, upright, into the closets. Their three old "pirate" trunks became tables and hassocks in the living room. He squeezed the washer into the efficiency kitchen, but it had to be hauled into the passageway whenever they used the kitchen table. In three weeks the workers left. The basement was beautiful. They had tiled the concrete floor with a Spanish Armstrong design Fitzie had seen on an inside cover of *Life*. They lowered the ceiling a little and installed some stuccolike, acoustical stuff, and paneled the walls in imitation teak. Where the Maytag had been went a little john, and beside it a tidy bar. Donald then put in some modernistic floor lamps and spotlights, some low Japanese-style tables and cushions, a Sony on a high stand and, the pièce de résistance, a great, white leather reclining chair with about two hundred positions. Each night for five nights, they would hear Donald come in, go upstairs to eat, then, padding in his stocking-slippers, slip downstairs by their door to sit in his white reclining chair, drink his Schenley, and watch his Sony—alone. On the fifth night, around ten, Fitzie put down his *Sports Illustrated*, lit a Pall Mall and went out the door. Janice, on the couch, said, "Where are you going?" Fitzie didn't answer. He thumped down the cellar stairs, turned the corner, walked past the plastic trash cans, past the john and the bar and up to Donald, half-prone in his chair. Donald didn't look away from the television when he said, lowly, "Hi, Fitzie."

Fitzie dropped his cigarette onto the Armstrong and stepped on it.

"Donald," he said to the man's profile, "we're getting out. Just as soon as I can find another place."

"You can't," Donald said, still not moving his head.

From the time Fitzie came until he left, Donald never moved his head, never looked at him.

"Why not?"

"You've got a *lease*. You know that."

"Stick it. I'm moving."

"I'll take you to court. I'll have my lawyer take you to court."

"Go ahead. I've already seen mine," Fitzie lied. "You changed the conditions under which I signed it."

"How?" Still low, a sleepy whine, sounding bored.

"You promised me storage space. And the washing machine."

"Is it in writing?"

"No, it's not in writing."

"Then it doesn't count."

"All right, Don-o. You know what counts then? What counts is I'm telling you I'm getting out and you can stick your lease up your ass. *And* your lawyer's ass."

"I'll sue you."

"And I'll beat the shit out of you."

"That's a threat. I can call the police on you."

"But not in time, cutie. So you decide. I've told you, now I'm getting out. You've got my security. Fuck you, Donald."

Fighting the push inside him to wreck the place, Fitzie turned and walked back upstairs, sweating. He told Janice. She said only, "You did?" surprised, then nothing more, sitting there staring at him with a little smile on her mouth as he picked up his magazine, sat down and lit a fresh cigarette.

That Sunday, they drove across Queens to answer an ad: 6 rms, $110 mo. They looked at no others; they took it. More room less money. Again, it was a row house, but old, not new. An old house, yellow brick, on an old street off Jamaica Avenue, Queens, down near the Brooklyn line. They went through it all as if hypnotized. To save money, Fitzie loaded and unloaded the Opel six times, making three trips on a Saturday, three on Sunday. Monday, Mayflower came and took their beds and refrigerator and what trunks and furniture he hadn't been able to fit into or onto the Opel, with Fitzie, on sick day, following behind now carrying only Janice and the bewildered kids. By nighttime they were in. The lights hadn't been turned on, so he took them all to an Italian bar and grill for supper, which made it an adventure, then bought a box of plain white candles in a corner variety store on the way home.

The candles winking around the place heightened the truth that they were now living in another cave within a cliff of caves, flats called apartments. This new one had high ceilings, covered with tin, and its doors were old and scarred but solid, not hollow. There was linoleum on every floor, even the living room, and all kinds of wallpaper—from monster rose to weeping willow Dixie, with top-hatted Rhetts and gowned Scarletts in silhouette. But maybe it was the candles that also made them not care: they were someplace new, and it felt good. "The poor things," Janice said, closing the children's bedroom door, "they probably think it's always going to be candles."

"Maybe it should be. It's nice. Sort of like the grotto at Lourdes."

"Twenty years from now some psychiatrist will be telling us we never should have done this to them. Very traumatic."

"Yeah, well, where's *he* living right now? Tell me that."

"Oh, I'm only kidding. It's funny. Such an old place. We never should have lived in a new place. We aren't meant for new places."

"So now we know. I think we better go to bed before we burn this new old place down."

Most of their weekends that spring went to fixing the place up. They painted over the paper with cheap paint from Sears, hung bamboo and beaded curtains in the doorways, tried to hide the linoleum under scatter rugs and mats. Janice made drapes of burlap from Macy's and dyed them in the Maytag. The sixth room, the bonus, a tiny room in the front off the living room, they didn't touch. They left its walls their blossom pink and told the kids to feel free. All their toys and tables and chairs and animals and blackboards went in there. After a month of finger painting and crayon scrawling and Scotch-taping up pictures and pages from coloring books, the room looked hideously delightful. With some green he had left over from the kitchen Fitzie brought the top half of the walls together with the kids' bottom half by painting a gigantic flower in a pot on one, a curvy ladder on another and a floor-to-ceiling door on the third. He and Janice loved it as much as the children, but anytime one of the landlords would come up from downstairs, they would discreetly keep its door tightly closed.

The landlords were an Italian family, Pop and Mama in their late sixties, unmarried Angelo around thirty-eight, and single daughter Rose about thirty-five. The Bertocchis. The meek of the earth. They had only bought the

60

house a year before, after a lifetime in East New York, and were scared and leery of being property owners. At every encounter—on the front stoop at night, in a store on Jamaica Avenue—whichever one of them it was would again announce how "nice" Fitzie and Janice and their children were. Nice. So nice. Begging for reassurance that it was true, petrified that it might not be, that these strange-talking people with the foreign car, this sharpie who went off in a suit and tie in the morning and didn't come back until dark, this swift-eyed Irish girl who never stayed home, who walked, walked, walked every morning, every afternoon with those poor little angels—weren't really nice. They were tenants. They weren't their kind. They might gyp you, hurt your house, steal from you, blow up the oven, drive you broke with water and electricity, be gone in the night without paying the rent.

Gun-shy after their Donald experience, Fitzie and Janice sensed the Bertocchis' fear and tried, whenever confronted by one or more of them, to prove how nice they were, what a good choice they had been. Mostly, they avoided them. They were bowled over one Saturday morning in June when they came out onto the stoop and saw the Bertocchis there waiting on the concrete inside the iron fence, ablaze in frilly dresses and tuxedos! They were going to a wedding. Taking turns recording the event with Angelo's Instamatic. Fitzie took the camera and snapped them all together. The sight of them made him feel as gay and excited as they, giggling, were. Mama was a mountain of spumoni under a pink, ribboned kite of a hat. Rose lovely, happily self-conscious, in a dress, too long, the color of her name. Angelo was Baby Huey in a tux, and Pop . . . Jesus, Fitzie couldn't believe it. Above his brown shoes and white socks, the old man's black trousers came to mid-shin, exposing two inches of white hairless bone. Fitzie felt angry. Did the poor old guy think he had to accept wrong-size pants from the renter? What was the matter with the rest of them, with Angelo, for letting him out like that! Then he looked closer and saw that the pants weren't short, they were hiked up to his ribs. Oh God, the poor bastard had probably thrown away the cummerbund or hadn't got one, and wanted to have black show above the V of the white jacket. Then he caught Pop's cuffs. Nobody had told him french cuffs folded up: he was wearing two sets of cuff links on each arm, the rented ones in the bottom holes and big, yellow ones in the top holes. Holy Mother. Embarrassed for him, wanting to fix him, Fitzie, talking, all smiles, worked his way close to Angelo, thinking to take him aside and nicely put him straight. But when he saw Angelo was wearing his shirt studs wide, dull, metal end out he chose to say nothing. After the car had come for them and carried them off and he was driving his own toward Rockaway Beach and Janice had not mentioned it, he knew he had been the only one to notice. Slowing the car because his eyes were tearing from laughing as he told Janice, he prayed the old man would get through the day safely.

They went to Rockaway Beach every weekend that summer, not knowing it was supposed to be shabby and tough. Only a half-hour away, it had a boardwalk: no Massachusetts beaches had boardwalks. Long, narrow, worn boards in V's and arrowheads, wide enough for a parade. The sand wasn't white Cape Cod dune sand, but it wasn't dirt, and the water was real Atlantic, with tides and breakers in rock and wooden eddies. When it rained, they would still go out someplace, in the Opel. Sometimes just to drive: to Rockaway to see the wind in the waves and the rain on the sand, out to cruise the dripping-treed lanes of Forest Hills and look at the houses; or the other way, into Brooklyn, or out to Idlewild; and into Manhattan by one of the bridges to avoid the tunnel toll, sometimes to simply crawl in and out of an area like Wall Street or Chinatown or the Village, sometimes, when the money was there, to take the kids to a children's theater show, or a movie. Their Bertocchi place was fine, only for them then it was more like a tent than a cave. It didn't seem to be for staying in, except at night. So they never, that summer, stayed in it very much.

From the very beginning, of course, Fitzie, the man, got to leave it every weekday morning. Away to go do his job of work for them, although he still was not thinking of it as a job like *a job*, nor of his daily subway commute as that. Since the move, his Paris-London fantasy had taken an exotic twist, adding a dash of Alexandria, for his route now took him through Williamsburg, where the Jewish men in their beards and hats and overcoats and always cruddy shoes would board his train on their way to the diamond district. And now, too, he would cross over the East River by bridge, the best bridge, the Williamsburg Bridge, a marvelous bridge, for from it Fitzie could see three other great bridges, the Manhattan and the Brooklyn close down the strong, wide water, and the 59th Street

Bridge, to the other side, dim, farther away up the disappearing East Side Drive.

On his train, he would do his waking up, his pocketbook reading, his future-success-wealth-fame-dreaming and his praying—if that's what it was. Long out of the morning Hail Mary, Our Father, Glory Be and Morning Offering school years habit, Fitzie had met Franny Glass one day in his first week on the new subway, Franny and her Jesus Prayer. The Jesus Prayer stopped him. It zonked him. The idea! The idea that, regardless of what words you used, if you *believed*, blindly, irrationally, with held breath *believed* that what you asked God for would happen, it would. What balls! Oh, it was already in there someplace, in Fitzie down under a layer of sheets or towels somewhere, either from the Jesuits or the Dominicans, one of them or all: "Whatsoever you ask for in prayer, believe that you will receive it and it shall be done unto you." But they had never said *really*. Never let on they believed it themselves. Holy shit, what if? One gorgeous, quick push into space, out of the explainable, ordered bubble, out into weird, no-reasonville. What a push. What a beautiful, secret tool to have. What a guts-ball thing, to be brave enough, to be dialed-out enough to try it. Fitzie did. Hanging from the white enamel subway train hand ring, he tried it one morning, clenching his back molars, closing his eyes, he pushed out, a toe in the water only, out and right back in again, "Christ, let me make it." Wow! He *knew*! Right out of his mind he shoved it then, as if he hadn't done it, so he couldn't doubt it. After that, he did it every morning. He never pinned it down, either, never spelled it out. He let it just mean *make it*. Be good. Do well. Work, wife, kids, life. Whatever that meant, that was what he wanted, and was asking for. Sometimes it wouldn't come, the feeling, the knowing, the quickening in his chest and head. When it didn't happen, he wouldn't push it, wouldn't try it again. He somehow sensed that that hole in his mind could be opened, quick as a camera shutter, only once; a second exposure would let in only a flood of doubt and embarrassment and cynicism. He would just go on with his train ride into the city, on with his day, hoping only that the next morning it would work and he would feel it, the sharp, icicle *yes*. When it happened he would, afterwards, go on. When it failed, he would go on, back to his book or to his window or to his thinking.

He had made a plan, and it was for February. He would be at the agency for six months then, and would ask for money. Soon after the move from new Queens to

63

old Queens, the time came and he asked for the money in a note to Horowitz, who endorsed it and sent it up. They said no. Sorry, but things are tight, be patient, keep up the good work. Mad, Fitzie typed out a list of his monthly expenses, food, clothing, rent, transportation, an embarrassingly complete list, added them up, typed his income beside the sum, attached Horowitz's endorsement of his first request with a staple, and sent it directly to the agency's Creative Director, whom Fitzie had seen, at a distance, twice. The month inched by. Then two weeks of March. During this slow-moving time, the purge took place, Fitzie's first agency bloodbath. Of Horowitz's original group, Fitzie and one other survivor, a twelve-year veteran of the place, good, and a favorite with a big, solid account, were absorbed into another group and Fitzie was given a fifteen-hundred-dollar raise, effective March 15, to be in his April 1 paycheck. April Fool's Day. Fitzie took Janice that night to eat at the Palm, then to the eleven o'clock show at Plaza Nine, then for a nightcap at the Cattleman, to celebrate.

She had a stinger and said, "Poor Mr. Horowitz."

"I don't know, he's pretty cool about it."

"Have you seen him?"

"Yeah. They give guys at that level a desk and a phone and a secretary off in some corner until they can get placed somewhere."

"That's big of them."

"I go see him a couple of times a week."

"It's scary isn't it. That poor guy."

"Ah! He's got a fantastic house in Rye someplace and no kids. Shit, they're loaded."

"Still, how old is he? That must be pretty hard."

"Well, I suppose. But he told me he can stay on the beach a year if he has to, and there are plenty of guys who've done it. Except it does get pretty touchy if you go that long, you start to look like a real loser and places are scared of you."

"Be good, baby, be *good*."

"That doesn't have much to do with it. Horowitz is good."

"Then why?"

"He's a Jew, for one thing."

"Oh, come on. I can't believe that. You yourself told me how *open* advertising is compared to other businesses."

"Well, yeah, in general."

"No. It can't be just that."

64

"Well, it didn't help him any. No, I guess he stepped on the wrong toes, didn't kiss the right ass, all that. One good thing came out of it, though. He gave me a big speech the other day, about the 'Inc.' I should have after my name. I think he's right. If they screwed him they can screw me someday, too. He was funny. He said that if the right job came along, the *president* of the agency would take it."

"That's awfully cynical."

"Yeah, but it's also the ball game, I think. What the hell, you do basically the same thing at one place as you would at another. So if you move, it's not like moving from General Motors to like Du Pont, you're just sort of shifting from one department to another in the same place."

"I'll take your word for it, but it sounds pretty weird to me. You aren't really thinking of moving, are you?"

He smiled. "Horowitz said he gave my name to a body snatcher. Ought to be calling me next week."

"A *what*?"

"A body snatcher. A flesh peddler. An employment agency. You know, a guy who knows who's looking and what's open."

"Well, I don't know. I think they've been damned nice to you. Horowitz's problems aren't yours."

"Oh, don't sweat it. I know they have. They could have started me higher, though."

"You didn't know that *then*. We were damned glad to get it. Listen, let's have one little Irish coffee, then go, okay?"

"Beautiful. Money's a fantastic thing, isn't it?" Fitzie laughed and ordered.

"We really had it good, didn't we," Janice said.

"What?"

"In the Army. Thinking about it, *that* seems like home now."

"Do you miss it?"

"Yes. Do you?"

"I don't know," Fitzie said. "That's hard. I do and I don't. If we didn't get out, I never would have *known*, you know? I think I'd always be wondering. We should stop thinking about the past."

"Whether you could make it or not?"

"Yeah. Of course I still don't know. But it feels good." He caught the quick side-glance of her eye. "You love New York too, don't you?" Fitzie said, a gentle probe.

"In June. How about you?"

"No, though, how are you? Really."

"I'm fine. This minute, anyhow. I'll get with it, just give me some time."

Fitzie stayed through the summer. By fall, he had begun to care. He was making better and better Popsicles, they were still buying Social Teas. It was beginning to burn him. He sat back and took a look. There had to be a better way to clean the vats. He saw it and began working it: it has to be in *their* terms; get a copy of their goddamn, i.e.-filled, ergo-loaded strategies, and read them. He did. It was difficult for him. Two inches of mimeographed words and charts, in blue leatherette with an acetate peephole on the cover, on an orange juice that really wasn't, so it had to be called orange *drink*. Christ Almighty. Still, he got through it and after that always had a hand on their throat. *Their* terms. Never say something's great or terriffic or funny or a takeoff. Say only how everything serves the strategy, gets the point over, registers the flavor story, underlines the efficacy claim, implies the convenience benefit. It worked for him. Suddenly although usually the junior at a copy meeting, and generally the one with the nuttiest or most ambitious commercials and ads, Fitzie would become the only one who was speaking the language. His Popsicles were being received as Social Teas! He started working later nights. Not that late but the thing was, Fitzie, caring now, no longer shut off on the Queens-Paris-Subway. He carried it around with him, around the house. He loved it, was excited by it, was involved in it.

Then John Kennedy's head was smashed apart in Dallas. The agency, the city dizzy, shut down and went home. *No! Oh, yes*. The television weekend, then: the weekend of a country, millions of people being told they had cancer. For that one weekend, Fitzie and Janice weren't alone. A part, temporarily, of society, they watched the television, saw Ruby shoot Oswald, saw the empty horse, saw Jackie and Caroline and John-John, about the same ages as their own girl and boy. Oh, man, what's it all *about*? He was beautiful. She was beautiful. He was *funny*. He never said, "What's more," in speeches. He was us, not them. Oh, Jesus. Oh, God. Tuesday, everybody left the blank Westinghouses and Philcos still warm and went back to work and so did Fitzie. But he didn't, either. The reality of his grandfather lying dead and gone, never to get on the P.O. payroll—he was back in that, with white deer running, and he couldn't get out. He was nobody again, or somebody in the wrong place at the wrong time. With no idea of where he ought to be.

It passed, Fitzie did come out of it, but not in time to help Janice. Before the Kennedy leech, she had already been being drained—by him, really, becoming a separate cell all of a sudden. Not that that was the way he first saw it. All he could know was, there was something wrong, in him, in her, in them. When he would get home at night, in the chill November dark, the only one coming home as late as six-thirty or seven, he had begun to feel not dread, but a tangible absence of anticipation. Home had turned into where he was to stop doing things, where he didn't know what there was to do, where every word he spoke, every move he made seemed to be somebody else talking, walking, eating, sitting, reading. Fitzie at home felt like an actor. When the day ended he didn't want to stay at work, did want to go away to Janice and the children in their place, but when he would get there, a lull would come over him, and he found himself not feeling anything with her, faking everything: *business as usual. Glad to be home. Hi, how's it going? Tell me what kind of day you had. Oh, really? Isn't that something, though.* Her only defense against him was no-talk. The screaming silences. Her internal combustion, rags in a closet, whose heat traveled to him invisibly, but burned him just the same. At supper, later in the night, in bed; once during a week at first, then more and more often; over after an hour or so, or not there in the morning, but then lasting for days, for whole no-Rockaway Saturdays and Sundays: "What's the matter?"

"Nothing."

"Well, you're pretty quiet."

"I don't mean to be. No, I'm not."

"Come on, what is it, Janice?"

Something he did? Something he said? Something he didn't do? Didn't say?

"Nothing. Really."

"What happened? Did anything happen?"

"No."

"Then what? You're so down. Want a drink?"

"No."

"I don't want you to be down. Tell me."

"You want everything to be fine. Well, everything's fine."

"Well, what's wrong with that?"

67

"Nothing, goddamn it, nothing. It's my fault, don't worry."

"Jesus, *what's* your fault?" Wishing it would go away.

"I do a lot you know."

"I know you do, baby, I know you do." *What is she talking about?*

"Balls."

"Said the king."

"You bastard."

"No, no, I'm sorry. I just hate like hell to see you down like this."

"Hate. You're just sorry this is during the week. Sorry I'm spoiling things."

Women! Sigh, chuckle-chuckle, sigh. This was Fitzie's father's word, Spider's answer, comment, thought, and Fitzie would now use it against Janice. *Women!* sigh, chuckle-chuckle, sigh, he would say to himself, in his father's voice, and resign himself to the evening, night, or days of silent estrangement she would then inevitably, unfairly, punish him with.

Fitzie found himself leaving the agency. He hadn't decided to, he had simply been called one morning by Dwight Ferris, of Dwight Ferris, Inc., Personnel, who had recently placed Horowitz as creative director of a big drug agency and who thought it time for him and Fitzie to meet. Fitzie felt absolutely no pulls within him to consider not saying yes. He was in New York to move, it was about time he moved. That was what it was all about? Terrific. Let's get the show on the road. If he were more satisfied, happier, making it, Janice would be too. And more money would mean less pressure on her, less worry, more things they could do together. On that December 8, he took an early subway into the city, to stash his black leather portfolio in a Grand Central twenty-five-cent locker. And to go to Mass across Lexington at Saint Agnes Church on Forty-third. Then he went to work, as usual. At noon he returned the yellow-headed key to its slot to redeem his portfolio and kept his appointment with Dwight Ferris at his office, a hurried adjutant's walk ten blocks uptown, off Madison, seven floors up in a dark, creaky automatic elevator that, like a chilly cellar, left Fitzie needing to go to the toilet. He found it at the end of the empty, ammonia-smelling hallway. When he got to the Ferris-marked, opaque glass door and went in, a voice from the single room beyond the one-coffee table waiting area told him he could have taken longer in the men's room, could have combed his hair after all. Dwight Ferris had a "few moments more" with another client. He lit a cigarette. Feeling the smoke suck into him, he had a peculiar thought. It was, *Right this second, nobody else in the world is doing exactly what I'm doing, right here, except me. Janice. Dishing out tuna fish sandwiches. Dad. Down a hold or up a mast in the yard, no, in an engine room, a pure silver wrench in his greaseblack hands. His grandfather. Oh, God, he's still dead. Funny. When you're away, everybody you know could be dead or alive and it wouldn't matter until you thought of them. Duke, McGregor. Both out by now. God knows where. Somebody at my desk, in my files at the Detachment, or on the road to the border? Somebody running the Tank. Somebody cleaning the vats. Somebody inside, listening to Ferris. Somebody moving along the hallway, footsteps outside. What if I'm not supposed to be here? Is somebody waiting for me to show up someplace where I won't?* The inner door opened, the other book carrier passed by Fitzie without looking and Fitzie was inside, shaking hands with Dwight Ferris, both of them descending into chairs during the shake. Ferris was older than Fitzie had expected, heavier and duller-eyed. He looked and spoke like the nonstar men who report the news on television. Fitzie didn't trust him. He paged through Fitzie's portfolio gravely, with few remarks other than, "Hmn, cute. Cute," and, "Did this run?" Fitzie sensed it was an act, for effect, and played statue in the chair, smoking, giving the man no clues. He wanted not to be there, yet had to have the events happen. Finally, Ferris shut the book and leaned back in his swivel chair. "You're getting rather a late start, aren't you," he said to the air. Fitzie watched Ferris's hands, knowing they'd be tented together, finger to finger over his convex vest at any moment. When they were, Fitzie nearly laughed. "Well, I'm twenty-six, if that's what you mean. I was in the Army."

"Yes. Well, I don't know. The work is fine. Good, sound stuff. A little too much flipness, I should think, but over all quite good."

"It's called humanity," Fitzie smiled. Ferris smiled back: Jack Webb looking into a mirror.

"Trouble is," Ferris announced, "you're up against the kids. Twenty. Twenty-one. The young turks. Fresh out of school, right off the streets. That's what the business is now, and you have to face it, keeping up with them. A

69

whole new ball game. They're fresh and brash and brilliant. Nobody told them there are rules. They don't know enough not to be original every time out. They think film. It's their literary form. The *now* form. And graphics. They think graphics. And they speak today. Sometimes I wish I was back in, back at the top in the biggest, hottest shops in the business. But no. Not seriously. There, you're confined. Here, you deal with them all, see the patterns, help shift them, help control, direct their growth. You have to know not what happened, but what's *happening*. You have to stay with-it, young, hep, You have to know how to bring them together, educate both sides. There are a lot of old-timers, old *stallions* still kicking around, you know, and they're in charge. The pioneers of the profession. They have to be helped to adjust, to take in these young tigers and put their brilliance where it'll do the most good." The man stopped and turned slowly back to face Fitzie, letting his line of silence reel out and out.

"Fuck 'em," Fitzie said quietly.

Ferris made a noise in his throat.

"Mr. Ferris, all I want is a better job and more money. I don't mean to be rude, but I have to be back at work in twenty minutes. I'm not twenty-one, but for Christ's sake, I'm not fifty-one, either! I'm as good as anybody I've seen, whether you think so or not. What's flip to you and what's fresh and brilliant, anyway? And for God's sake, it's *hip*, not hep!"

Ferris was beautiful. He nodded, his chin curled and his lower lip pushed out in total agreement and approval like a teacher hearing his own theories played back. "Good," he said, shifting over for the weather forecast, "I knew we could do business together. You have to think of me as your agent, young man, as your business manager. We're in a people business, mind you, where we have to help each other. Now." He slipped a sheet of notepaper out from beneath his bronzed railroad spike paperweight and pushed it across to Fitzie. It's all sounds, Fitzie thought. You make some sounds, then I'll make some sounds. "At this point," Ferris reported, "you belong either at F and F or at WFB. Here are the names and numbers. Give me this afternoon to make first contact, then you call tomorrow. I'll call you in the morning to touch base, just in case somebody's out of town or something. Oh, by the way, fill this out before you leave, will you?" It was the registration agreement clearing Ferris for a fee and Fitzie filled it out at the coffee table, then left.

Fitzie's first interview was after five Monday in the next

week with Linda Holt, personnel "gal" in the creative department of F&F—large, a few huge accounts, venerable, WASP; in the same category as the agency Fitzie was leaving but a little more solid, a little slicker. She wore no wedding ring, but Linda's nose and cheekbones said she was either married or had changed her name from Papadopolous or something. She was pretty. She smelled pretty at her polished oval desk. She looked pretty amid her pewter mugs bursting with red and orange rockets and her seven, variously sized, variously framed watercolors prettily half lit by the one lamp in the corner. And she told Fitzie she didn't think he was "heavy" enough yet for F&F. Fitzie left, having no idea of what she was talking about. He had surprised himself by reacting to her and her setting so quietly, politely. The only words not replies to her questions came as he was walking out: "What's that anyway?" he asked her, sniffing aloud, smiling and looking at her ears.

"Joy," she smiled.

"Oh," Fitzie said. "And they all jumped for, huh?"

That night, he told Janice. "Oh, yeah. It's very expensive," she said.

"Well, I'm going to get you some anyhow. It's really wild! You know, she had powder in her armpits."

"I'm glad you didn't get the job, the more I hear."

"What I can't get over is, I don't *care*. I don't feel disappointed or mad or anything. It's as if I wasn't there, practically. I went in and out as if I were in a daze."

"Let's have some tea," Janice said. They were sitting at the table in their narrow kitchen, looking out at the gardens and back yards in the quadrangle behind the block of row houses. Wash lines ran from windows to poles in the fenced rectangles and a few sheets here and there had been left out to flap, stiff and eerie, in the winter night. She clanked the red kettle over the blue gas. It was past nine. "I don't understand," Janice said, "how come nobody creative saw you."

"I didn't even think of that. Hey, what kind is this? I guess she must screen everybody, you must have to get through her first."

"It's mint. Mint tea, if my mother could see me now."

"Well, we'll drink it out of the saucer."

She poured them cups and they smoked and sipped the tea in the light from the fluorescent circles in the tin ceiling. The feeling between them was close and easy and warm. "Well, the hell with them, then. They don't deserve

71

you. Joy or no Joy," Janice said, her mouth near the cup rim, into the soft steam rising.

"Thanks," Fitzie smiled. "You look good, you know it, lady?"

"Even without powder in my armpits?"

"Hair is nice too."

"Irmgard."

"Brunhilda. Really, though. The purple bags are gone. And you've got nice color in your cheeks."

"That's from hauling my little friends through the snow all day long."

They were back together again and they both knew it. They both knew too that it was because they felt transient again. In between. Loose. Expecting. Neither did, but they could have traced back and seen that the Silences had begun petering out at the same time or shortly following the moment Fitzie had mentally left the agency. They had never quit their lovemaking, it was their plasma, their generator, but this night it spun a softness about them they knew was loving and were glad to have it back. In the dark Janice giggled about going out tomorrow to buy a ton of mint tea and Fitzie punched her in the rump, but they both knew the other knew. They were like the coastal birds that fly as one solid wing but break into pieces when they land.

Their first two children were two years apart, without help. The boy was approaching his second birthday, and Fitzie and Janice were beginning to worry. Nothing was happening, and they wanted something to, Fitzie because he had had only the one sister, fourteen years younger than he, hence each an only child; Janice, because she had been the fourth in a close, surging arm-locked Irish clan of eleven. Janice got the name of the specialist by calling the head of the nursing school where she had trained. On a snowy Saturday, Fitzie chugged the Opel around the Harkness Pavilion block seventeen times, waiting for her to come out, unable to find a parking space in the snowbanks, the kids in the back being kept fairly sane by finger-drawing the steamed windows. Janice finally appeared at the entrance, beaming through the sooty blizzard. Sliding back across Manhattan to the 59th Street Bridge, she told him. There was something. "An infection," she announced like a sweepstakes winner. "He says

I've probably had at least one 'mis' already and didn't know it."

"Hmm. At your cervix, madam?"

"Yeah. That goddamn kraut doctor bastard, I knew he was a quack."

"Honest to God? Is that it, really? Goddamn them!"

"Well, maybe. He said possibly. It's hard to tell."

"So now what?"

"Well, we have to get some stuff at the drugstore that I'll use, then he'll do it in three weeks. I'm afraid you'll have to go through all this again."

"Do what?"

"Blast, sweetie, blast! That's what he called it, he was funny. I really liked him. Man, there's nothing like the best."

"I'll have to go through this again. Poor me."

"Poor car."

"Little did this little Green Hornet know what it was getting into. From sunny Madrid to this."

"Ssh, it'll hear us. One thing we don't need now is car troubles."

That third Saturday was one of those rare, once-a-winter Aspen-Stowe days, dry, cold and clear. Fitzie drove in earlier this time and parked. While Janice was up in the Pavilion, he let the skipping, bundled children lead him up and down the west, white half of upper Broadway and slurped hot chocolates with Marshmallow Fluff in the sticky Liggett's booth. He had the Opel breathing thinly in the pickup zone ten minutes before Janice came, small, through the black, cold shadow. Inside the car's warmth and pecking along, she remained pulled in and tight. "Was it very bad?" Fitzie asked, holding his cigarette so the smoke pulled out through the butterfly window.

"No." Even her voice came thinly.

"No, just a gang-bang, huh? At least they didn't shave your head."

She forced a weak laugh. "Just get me to your sleeping bag, okay, señor?"

"Okay."

The boy and the girl, usually two craning, yacking heads between them, standing on the back floor, sat back the whole way quietly, fiddling with their mittens and boots. "I just feel so drained. He said I would, though."

"Did it work, did he say?"

"He was sweet. He said I'm built to drop 'em in the fields without missing a potato."

"Did he say that nice? You want a drag?"

73

"Yeah, thanks. Yes, he said it nice."

"You tell him how you delivered in like a half-hour both times before?"

"Shut up now, okay?"

Fitzie propped up the pillows behind her and tucked the bedclothes and quilt puff around her and lugged in the TV from the living room to the top of the bureau. Then he dressed the kids again and walked them to the avenue in the after-six dark freeze and got two large pepperoni pizzas to take out. He brought the kids' table and chair set from the Crazy Room and put it beside the bed near Janice. He turned out the lights and they ate by candles and remembered moving in. Janice couldn't finish one slice and at the end a whole half was left over. "Will it keep?" he asked her.

"No, throw it out."

He switched the ceiling light on and put the children into their Doctor Dentons and perched them on his side of the bed to watch Gleason. When he finished jamming the pizza boxes into the barrels on the sidewalk outside, he came back to get the kids into bed. He clicked off the set and got booed. "Come on, now, go get one story each and I'll read to you in your own beds."

"Fitz?" Janice said. The night wind building up outside turned then to rattle the glass storm windows and whistle through the cracks, stirring the thin drapes amd making the room feel chillier than it was. Janice began to rise stiffly off the pillows. "Help me into the bathroom. I think I have to go."

The children stopped and stood at the foot of the bed, watching. Fitzie said, "Get moving," as he went to Janice, but they stayed. He pulled the covers away from her as she swung her feet to the floor. "Good God!" he swore: bright red came pulsating out from the bed. The bottom sheet was covered with blood, with more picked up by the top sheet, and it ran loudly down the back of Janice's nightgown. The color hit like a scream in the room. "Oh, baby," he said, putting his arm around her shoulders; the touch shut her off and she crumpled toward the floor, out. He swung his bare right arm under her legs and lifted her up and across his middle, the wet coming warm to his arm. "Mumma!" the girl shrieked, bringing the boy's mouth open to let out an immediate siren of crying. He lay Janice back down onto the bed over the spread of blood and steered the horrified, screaming children swiftly into their room, hitting the light switch and pulling shut the door. "You get stories, Mama's okay, I'll call you out in a minute." Back, Janice's eyes were open. "Towels," she whispered. He ran to the bathroom and grabbed the whole pile. She had her gown up and he pushed two large bath towels between her legs, opening a third one and tucking it up beneath her back tightly, pulling the front end up her front and holding it taut with his fist at her throat. He held it, hearing his own breathing, hearing her breathing. He found himself counting his own heartbeats; at forty-eight, Janice opened her eyes. His nose was almost touching hers and she smiled. "I think it's stopping," she breathed.

"Can you hold this?" he said.

She grabbed the towel at her waist and nodded. He pushed up off the bed and lunged heavily into the kitchen, tearing the doctor's card from his wallet. He got an answering service and told them. His "Goddamn it!" and the bam of receiver onto cradle struck the air at the same time. He went back to her. The inner towel, white, was coming pink. He lifted the outer towel from her grip, and replaced the inside one with a fresh towel from the pile, then pulled up on the outer one again, sitting next to her on the bed, up near her shoulders. With his free arm he reached and pulled the covers over her. She seemed to be sleeping. He could hear the children's crying, their springs unwound now, coming through the door: mewing cats. He began counting the throbs in his chest again, wishing they weren't so loud. He tried to stare through the wall at the complacent phone, to will it to ring. But it remained still. He reached to the night table and tore a cigarette from the pack, twisting it, and lit a match one-handed. Janice remained still. He tightened his pull on the outer towel. He pulled the smoke from the cigarette, trying to hurt it with his tight lips. He noticed that the smoke, when he silent-whistled it out, seemed to hit something in the air that turned it back on itself. A draft: the wind outside had come full around and was now hitting the back walls straight on, rattling the windows louder, lifting the drape curls now, not merely stirring them. His eyes dropped and he saw that Janice's right leg hadn't been reached by the covers, and was lying out flat and straight, bare to the hip. He couldn't move the gnarled bedclothes to cover it. In the smoke-graying light of the tin-ceilinged bedroom he sat there smoking, pulling the towel, and looked at the delicate blond, nearly white hairs that ran along her thigh, thin little arches in a row, drawn in yellow pencil on ivory paper. A little girl's leg hairs. They looked so helpless to him, so open to be blown away, like dandelion fluff. He

75

stretched and opened another bath towel and smoothed it gently over her leg.

Janice woke. She looked up at Fitzie and he could see her remembering slowly. She looked down at the towel-cinch he held at her breasts. "Oh, darling," she moaned.

"Are you all right, do you think?" he said.

"Like a wet mop. Where are they?"

"In their room."

"I don't feel any running. How long?"

"I'm not sure. Ten years. About a half an hour, I guess."

Her hand lifted from the bed and went into the towels. "Let loose a second," she said. "I think it's stopped. You can let go. Go up on the top shelf in the closet."

He stood and walked, legs pins-and-needles, across the room and reached down the blue box. "Are there many in there?" she said from the bed.

"No, about half full." He stopped at the bureau and got the belt from the top drawer. "Aren't you smart," she smiled. Her face against the mahogany headboard was gray. "Know what we used to call these in the stockroom at Woolworths?" he smiled, taking out a white pad.

"I can imagine. What?"

"Fanny farmers."

"Ho, ho."

"And manhole covers, that's right too."

"Nice kids. No, let me do it."

"That's all right, just lie there."

"No, please. I don't want to disillusion you."

"The gynecologist's sex life, you mean? Don't worry, miss, I never let business interfere with pleasure. Lift up a little, can you?"

"My, my, aren't we capable all of a sudden."

Fitzie laughed, feeling more relieved, still waiting for the phone. "It's really pretty nice," he said, finishing, "when you look into it." He looked up. "Hey! You're blushing, you're actually blushing."

"Such a hood. You'll always be a hood." She shut her eyes, easing back.

"Wait, just a second now, up a little, that's all," he whispered, pulling the nightie off over her head. He dropped it on the floor and got another from the bureau and slipped it onto her. "Just bear with it a couple more minutes." He yanked the red sheet out from beneath her, supporting her with his arm under her bottom, and threw it, too, onto the floor. "Let me get up. It'll make it easier."

"Sure you can? I don't want you keeling over again."

"No, I have to go anyhow. And I smell."

He walked her to the bathroom, then came back and stripped the bed. He made it fresh, then went back and stuffed the bloody towels, sheets and nightgown into the hamper. After Janice washed, Fitzie propped her up in bed again. "Stay like that just for a little while," he said, "then you can sleep." He opened the door to the other bedroom. They were huddled together, both on the girl's bed, curled and touching. Flopsy and Mopsy. The boy sucked his thumb. The girl's eyes were dirt-streaked. He woke them and carried them in to Janice. She clutched and kissed them and he kept them there until they were fully awake, until he felt sure the image of Janice, pretty and happy, was washing into their heads. When the little boy wandered, giggling finished, toward his clucking-hen pull toy in the corner, and the girl began to launch into the latest episode in the adventures of Lilly-Bille, her invisible but not nonexistent chum, the naughty one who said *shit* and *God's sake* all the time, Fitzie figured the mind prints had taken and swooped them up and back into their beds. Then the doctor called, finally reached at a house party in Mamaroneck. Fitzie spoke quietly into the black mouthpiece, walking back and forth along the axis of the narrow kitchen. None of the angry words from before were to be found, he shook physically, he felt glad to hear the older voice in his ear: Not that unusual. In fact, only to be expected. Perhaps should have warned her of it. No, no hospital trip necessary. Call if heavy flow happens again. Shouldn't. All not fine by morning, call again. Don't worry, good-night. Fitzie hung up, sealing himself alone in the flat with his sleeping Janice, his sleeping children. He sat at the kitchen table, not smoking, his hands folded, and thought, for the first time, of God and mentally said Thanks. But, since He seemed the doctor who didn't arrive until after the fever had broken, Who, in fact, had only happened to drop by, unnotified, Fitzie couldn't see either how he had forgotten to call Him, or why he should be thanking Him for anything. He got up, dropping the whole thought. Deliciously weary, he undressed and legged gingerly into the bed beside his warm, thickly breathing wife—only he didn't think *wife*, he thought *girl*. Fitzie slept. He didn't wake again until nearly ten the next morning and it was to the smell of the bacon frying under Janice's fork and to the sound of her voice yapping at the kids who were in the living room fighting at the TV over the cartoons or Sonny Fox.

After pretty Joy lady Linda, for whom he hadn't seemed heavy enough, Fitzie had met the other Ferris name. Davy Toto, copy chief of WFB. It was a name Fitzie had heard, a splinter story here and there, long before Ferris had scribbled it on the paper: not really old, mid-forties, but around for a long time. One of the *characters*. Fired from every major agency in New York advertising. For wearing sneakers all the time at one old Venerable—in the early fifties. For coldcocking the chairman of the board at another. Another chopped him for being a Red when McCarthy was on television. Canned once, perhaps the same place, for attempting to organize a copywriters union. So the tales went. The most recurrent: on the beach for over a year—blackballed, they said— Toto walked into the office one day of the president-creative head of one of the giant places he hadn't worked for, and said, "Give me your worst problem, and a week. No money. If you don't like what I do, goodbye. If you do, you hire me for fifteen." They did it, they liked it, he started, and in one year had vaulted himself back up into the fifty-thousand-dollar class. Six months after that he was out again, nobody could say why, and into a period of anonymity as a group head for several years at one of the second-layer, great gray middle, agencies. It was boredom, they said, that finally pushed Toto to take the copy chief job at The Meatgrinder, the Revolving Door, WFB. The night Fitzie met him, Toto had had the job for slightly more than a year—the longest it had ever been held.

Fitzie's appointment was after-hours, for six-thirty on a Tuesday. He stayed at his desk, appearing to be working, but merely listening to the stillness wash rapidly through the halls and emptying offices. At WFB, it could have been ten in the morning. Toto's secretary walked him in from the reception area. Lights were full on, people were running about, phones were ringing and typewriters chattering. In three minutes Fitzie decided that Toto was a schizophrenic, paranoid, manic-depressive, magnetic, egotistical psychopath and that he liked him. He sat in a corner office at a large desk clear of everything but a typewriter lit by a Tensor lamp and a shallow fruit basket heaped with about fifteen packs of Camels and a dozen or more pharmacy bottles—green, brown and clear—of pills and capsules. Toto was a handsome man in the Dean Martin manner, with black hair curly and cut long. Toto

78

wore, as Fitzie came to learn he *always* did, a blue denim shirt, collar open, black tie pulled down: ascot knot. Yet from the blue denim came an alarmingly feminine, sweet scent of some kind of cologne. And he spoke in a weird mixture of Al Capone-Little Italy shipfitter street slang and an artificially swank, actor-British accent. He would drift from one to the other constantly, with no apparent common denominator other than a vague lisp. He started out with Fitzie in the soft Peter Lawford: "Mr. Fitzpatrick, how do you do."

"How do you do."

Toto flipped through Fitzie's portfolio quickly, grunting indifferently at each page. "Fine, fine," he said. "Do you smoke?"

"Yeah. Thanks." Fitzie accepted a Camel and a light from Toto's Zippo.

"So. You fancy yourself quite a toughie, huh?"

Shook, Fitzie reddened. "Who told you that? That's not true."

"You tell me that," Toto said.

"Oh. Ferris said that, I suppose."

"Dwight Ferris is a whoremaster!" Toto exploded. "A leper who deals in men's souls. Yet a kind man, a gentle man, an honest man. We are very old friends. That's why darkies are born, as they say. Ferris performs a necessary and valuable service. And what do you think of Horowitz?"

"What can I say? He took me off the street. Gave me my first job."

"You don't like him."

"As a person I like him. I found out he was out of date, that's all."

"He is. He should get onto the management side before he gets killed for good. So you're also seeing F and F, I understand?"

"Ferris talks a lot, doesn't he."

"What did they tell you? Where are you with them?"

"They loved me. I'm waiting to hear their offer."

Toto smiled. Front-lit by the Tensor, he made Fitzie think of Vincent Price. "You think you're lying," he said, "but that happens to be true. Marv Silver will be calling you soon."

"Who's Marv Silver?" Fitzie asked, mouth dry as dirt.

"For Jesus sake, he's the creative director over there! We started out together years ago. The first Jew to get accepted into the lovely F and F fraternity. Still can't play tennis with them, though."

"All I saw was a broad."

"Darling Linda, of course. She was quite taken by you."

"That's not what she said."

"Play, play, play. To make you think they're doing you a favor and get you for less! Come now, Mr. Fitz, naive men cannot survive in the jungle. Some tough!"

"*I* didn't say I was tough, *you* said it. Or Ferris or somebody. Ferris did say you needed somebody, so do you or don't you, I'm late for supper."

"*Dinner,* dum-dum, *dinner.* You're playing with the big boys now so you'd better start acting it. *Yes,* I need you. I need ten of you. Do you know how many people I've got on staff here? None, that's how many. Zero. They're all free lance. Moonlighters. Mercenaries. That's how this place has been running for years. And I am the first, numero uno, to be able to prove myself to Mr. Nemo, to convince him that with a core of loyalists, with *esprit de corps,* with a legitimate, baptized, circumcised creative *department* under me, I can take his WFB and cut through every F and F on the street like a hot knife in lemon meringue pie! What do you know about Abraham Nemo, Mr. Fitzpatrick?"

"I hear he's a prick. I hear he stole some big accounts for himself, then lifted the place from whoever W, F, and B were."

"Lies! You wouldn't be here if you believed that."

"Listen, what do I care."

"Abraham Nemo is a giant. A man among pansies. A have-not among the haves. A one-man agency, maybe the last. What a chance for you, what is it, *John?*"

"Fitzie."

"You go to an F and F. Go ahead. Lean across desks all day with the fags and talk about T. S. Eliot. Get soft and fat. Or join the guerillas. Abraham Nemo is a *Hun.* Come and drive the great Roman legions crazy from the trees, from behind rocks."

"Oh, God, Ann Rand."

"*Ayn* Rand, Fitzie, *Ayn* Rand. Ignorant people shouldn't try to be smartass. And you will have *me.* Do you know what I do? I take the beatings. I go to Abraham Nemo with your work, with what he needs but doesn't know it, and he whips me. He *crucifies* me. Not you, me. Bloodied, humiliated, I wait and I win. For you. For him. It's *alive* here, Fitzie. A big newspaper city room, not a salon. We'll run and fight and *work.* How much?"

Sweating, Fitzie said, "How much what?"

"How much are you getting, how much do you want?"

"I'm making nine, I want twelve."

"Balls. You make seven, I'll give you nine."

"Nine, twelve."

"Ten."

"Ten thousand?"

"Ten thousand dollars, start in two weeks unless you can get out quicker."

"Okay."

"Good. Smart move. You won't regret it. Good-night, Fitzie, I have a meeting."

At the door, Fitzie turned and muttered a confused, "Uh, thank you."

Toto looked up. "Just so you know, Fitzie. F and F would have gone for the twelve. But I may have to take two out of my own to give it to you."

Fitzie laughed. "What do you mean, would have? Aren't they going to call me?"

"They'll call, but you can't go with them now."

"Why the hell not?"

"Because you're morally obligated to us."

Fitzie stared at him through the Tensor's light splotch.

"Aren't you?" Toto asked, not in British: *arncha?*

"Yeah," Fitzie said and walked out through the running people. Toto's secretary seemed to have gone. He called Janice and she got all excited, then he took the slow night subway home.

The Joy lady did call to say Mr. Silver had decided that they would like to see him, heavy enough or not. There came Fitzie's first tickle of pleasure. He told her sorry, but they were too late, he had taken a job for fourteen as, "Well, Davy's calling it sort of his protégé." She said they'd keep in touch. The other satisfaction Fitzie scraped up for himself was the fee victory. Fitzie called Toto the next morning "to double-check one thing. You'll be picking up Ferris's fee, won't you? I know that's common practice at F and F, and it slipped my mind last night." Toto called back in the late afternoon and said they would, but not to mention it to anybody. On his first day at WFB, Fitzie was given the usual personnel paperwork to fill out. In between Blue Cross and the biography sheet, he found a brief, typed letter on WFB stationery. He read it. It said that he agreed to repay the Ferris fee, should he leave the agency employ on his own accord anytime prior to one full year. In a way, he saw that it was pretty shitty, smalltime thing, yet in another way it seemed fairly legitimate; besides, being caught in the new-job psychology at the moment, and his basic instincts being to find a home, a good steady job anyway, it looked very unlikely that he would not be there forever, so, considering it all as very moot he signed the letter, forgot it and went to work.

There was no time for first-day fluffing off at WFB, no break-in period. Fitzie was officially assigned to the booze account and the rent-a-car account, but it was made known to all hands from the start that everybody was on every account. There was panic in the air, a constant state of urgency and push, as unremitting and as physically felt as the heat from the wall ducts. This pressure was one element in the very positively designed atmosphere and attitude of the place, as created by Abraham Nemo and enforced by Davy Toto. It was forbidden to open any office window at any time or for any reason. There would be no personalizing of working areas, no pictures on the walls, no rugs on the floor, no radios, phonographs or like equipment to be brought into one's office, or, as in Fitzie's case, one's cubicle: he shared an office with another writer, as yet unhired, and was separated from him by a portable partition, metal on the bottom half, opaque glass on the top. Fitzie's instincts pouted at all this. At the first agency, once he got moved out of the bullpen, he had followed custom and fixed up his office until it was Classical Creative, practically a study or den, with books in a glass-brick and shelves unit, prints and posters on the walls, transparencies on the windows, all lights out except the one desk lamp; it had felt very intellectual and comfortable. Yet Fitzie's newer, developing instincts accepted the WFB standards with relief and approval. They made for a feeling of impermanence and independence, and he recognized it as related to the no-ties, transcience-freedom that had refreshingly come into his and Janice's lives. As the strain between them, and the Silences, had diminished when he had gone job hunting and they had begun talking of moving again, so Fitzie began to feel, at work, a sense of himself as his own man, as the phrase used to go, as the unattached, self-sufficient, C.O.D., solo-operative. This Gun For Hire.

His was also Leslie Montague's first day, but it took two weeks before Fitzie got put into Montague's new group, two weeks of wartime frenzy all day and then, at least four days a week, beyond and into the night, until eleven or midnight. From nine until five, Fitzie would do the daily work on his own accounts; each generated a lot of small-space newspaper and trade messages, radio announcements, promotional posters and folders in addition to the never-ending quest for *the* national campaign grail. Then Toto would be at the door, never asking it simply as, "Can you stay?" but always with the dart, the sell: "Need some trouble-shooting, up to it?" and, "Hey, man, very hot project. Save my life, huh?" Sure that it had to be eventually somehow rewarded, Fitzie would say okay. He would call Janice and talk to her for a while, saying awkward "How are ya's" to the mute or giggling kids. Janice was always disappointed, but these not-coming-homes didn't seem to infect their life as poisonously as had his prior mental bringing-work-home. There were usually at least five of them on those "crack teams," mostly writers, sometimes one or two art directors. Toto was always there to run the night, which invariably began with drinks and dinner, on the agency's tab at the Top of the Sixes on the roof of the Tishman Building on Fifth. They would knock off one or two, sometimes more, rounds of gibsons, bloody marys, rob roys, Toto's scotch and sweet vermouth, at the same window table, talking and looking down at the million lighted night New York; they'd eat, then go back to the agency, lightheaded and giddy or morose, for the hour of brainstorming in the conference room before splitting to their solitary stalls to rant and rave or ramble stream-of-consciously on yellow copy paper about a new perfume or an old hairdressing, how do you symbolize cleaning power, which will make bigness a positive, can we find the way to preempt mildness? Like a proctor at final exams, Toto would eventually come around and pick up their work and let them go home. Fitzie asked Toto one night why they couldn't just get right at it at five and skip the Top of the Sixes to knock off at eight or nine? He was told no, it wouldn't work so well, and besides, this was how Mr. Nemo wanted it. Which ended that.

Montague was older, over thirty-four to Fitzie's over twenty-seven, and had been around; WFB was his fourth agency. Fitzie couldn't get over him: he was tall, with extremely long hair, and stood and moved with noticeable grace and the straight-backed poise of a dancer, which he had been. It was still 1963, nearly 1964, and Montague wore Pierre Cardin suits, low trousers with huge belts, striped ties on striped and checked shirts and large soft hankies of coordinated colors in his breast pockets, buckled-and-strapped Foreign Intrigue raincoats and Italian slipper-shoes. When Toto told him that he was to be assigned to the group he was letting Montague form,

Fitzie stiffened inside: the word said he was a raving fag, or at least a fey weirdo. He went anyway, of course, and found in Montague the first friend, besides Janice, he had really ever had. At first, though, Fitzie was merely bowled over by his first exposure to personal style. On his first morning as Montague's writer, Fitzie came into his office-half to find five new ties draped across his blotter, with a slip of paper saying only, "Welcome. L. Montague." Fitzie picked them up. Each was five dollars anyway: three vivid stripes, two bright paisleys, all wide, all silk. He carried them into Montague's office. Montague was watering an orange tree in a pot on his desk. Fitzie said, "Hi, I'm Fitzpatrick. What are these for?"

"Fitzie, how do you do." Montague shook his hand and went back to his tree. "They are for you, of course. Please wear them, will you? Do you mind?"

"No, I guess not. I don't know what to say, actually. Thank you?"

"Will you let me tell you something about yourself—without getting embarrassed or offended?"

"Go ahead."

"If appearance isn't everything, it's at least the one thing in life one does have some control over. Tell me, do you like looking like a cop? Why do you wear those dark suits and dark ties and white shirts all the time?"

"I don't know," Fitzie looked down at himself sheepishly, "I don't really think about clothes that much."

"I don't think that's true. I think you fear standing out. You think it's safer to be as inconspicuous as you can. Am I wrong?"

"I'll think about it and let you know," Fitzie said straightly. There was nothing in Montague's manner to raise any defenses.

"Good. In the meantime, you'll wear those ties, won't you? It's a good start. And listen, will you let your hair grow longer? I understand you've spent quite a ghastly length of time in the service, but that should be far behind you by now. You could have rather a good look if you help it, you know, sort of the later Frank Sinatra, I'd say."

"Boy, that's a helluva thing to tell an Irishman, you're really something else."

"Which brings us to me, at last. But enough about you."

They both laughed.

Fitzie lit a cigarette and sat in a chair. "Okay. You."

"What do you have to tell me?"

84

"Nothing. But I'd like to ask you something."

Montague finished with the orange tree and sat at his desk opposite Fitzie. "Very well, what?"

"Are you homosexual?"

"Would it matter?" Montague asked right away, smiling.

"I don't think so," Fitzie said.

"Then are you heterosexual? I am a ballet dancer. A male ballet dancer. I was also a lieutenant j.g. on a destroyer for three years. I am an elegant person, I am an alone person. You are a very direct person."

"Well, so are you."

"Tell me, how talented are you?"

"You tell me in a month or so."

"No, answer it."

"I think I'm very good. I also think I need to get some kind of a point of view on things."

"That I can give you. That was a very good answer."

"You know, for a dude, I think you're probably a pretty good shit."

Montague whooped laughing.

"We will devastate them with looks, talent, elegance and vulgarity!" Montague said. "What do you think of this place so far?"

"It's got my head spinning. I think Toto's really wild. The nights are starting to get to me, though."

"Well, let me tell you you've made a mistake. Nobody should be here. Ever. It's a very evil place."

"Then what are you doing here?"

"I'm a pragmatist. My reputation is entirely in fashion. I need television and package goods if I am going to go as far as I want to go, which is very, very. Also, this dump was desperate enough the meet my outlandish salary demands."

"Why is it so bad for me?"

"I was speaking pre-Montague. WFB is a notorious concentration camp. This *renaissance* they're claiming now is about their two-hundredth. It's all very Freudian. Abraham Nemo is a sadist. All beneath him, including us, are supposed to be masochists. A perfect relationship."

"Well, screw that, if it's true."

Montague ordered coffee by phone. "This night work orgy," he went on. "It's so silly. You must have noticed how fake it all is."

"I was beginning to wonder what happened to all the stuff I've been turning out."

"Forget it. It's all futile, and all quite deliberate on their part. It gives those shells who hate to go home at night

85

the Great American Excuse: my job. So when someday somebody comes along and says Hey, how come you were such a rotten husband and lousy father, they can say My Work!"

Montague's secretary brought in the brown Schrafft's bag and took the cardboard cups from it, pulled off the lids, ripped the bags of sugar into each, stirred them with wooden sticks, then placed them on napkins in front of Montague and Fitzie. "There," she said, proud of herself.

"Miss Sweeney, Pattie, this is Mr. Fitzpatrick," Montague announced formally, after watching the coffee ceremony silently, approvingly. "You may call him Fitzie and you will be very nice to him, won't you? And you will not maul her, Fitzie, will you? At least not all the time."

"Only when she asks me," Fitzie said. Miss Sweeney blushed and left. She had perfect, large breasts which she carried as if they might spill. She wore fluffy, angora sweaters, men's shirts and no stockings, even in the winter. "Marone!" Fitzie grunted when she was gone. "Does she type, too?"

"With one finger, slowly. But she knows *I* hired her and she's more stunning than any other female in the place, including Mr. Nemo's."

"Everything part of the act, huh? You are a calculating bastard."

"Mm, but also, have you never thought, Fitzie, why shouldn't everything be as nice as possible? If we have to spend our life every day doing stupid things for stupid people, does everything have to *look* dreary too?"

"All *right!*" Fitzie laughed. "I'll *wear* the damn ties."

They sipped the hot coffee. "Okay," Fitzie said, "but what good are we going to be able to do—not being masochists?"

"Well, we shall be very grown-up about it, I think. We will make for ourselves the best portfolios in the city. For every assignment, we will create an *original* every time out. Something new, something nobody's ever seen before, something the poor public will sit up and not despise, for a change. Then, when the fools reject it, we will place it into our books and calmly do whatever drivel *they* want. And nights we will eat, drink and drive them mad with endless reams of foolishness, always laughing, never complaining."

"And look terrific."

"And say funny things. You know what I'd like to do?" Montague said, pushing his hair back over his ears with his long, thin hand, "I think I'll have a hospital cot put over there near the window."

"And have Miss Sweeney dress all in white every day."

"Oh, yes, yes. And when we hear Toto or someone coming, one of us can fall prostrate onto it and moan weakly."

"And say, 'More work, more work'!"

They roared. In the following month, Montague hired his new group. Every day a stream of portfolio-carrying creatures poured endlessly through his office. Out of some fifty or more, Montague chose four. Anthony Bruce was a short bearded man of thirty-eight who looked more like twenty because he had a child's crinkling blue eyes. Montague said later that he'd picked Anthony because of "those little socks he wore; teeny, short socks sticking up out of those wonderful boots." Anthony was put in with Fitzie on the other side of the divider. The first day they said hello it wasn't just Pleased to Meet You, it was Great to See You *Again*, as if they had known each other well long ago, in some earlier life, and were now getting back together again as they had always known they would. Anthony was an Englishman, had deserted his child-wife and scooted off to South Africa twenty years before. He had been a newspaper man, then high up in an advertising agency in Durban before he left it all to buy a white-washed little house on the water in the south of Spain— "See? That's my face there in the window. A goatherder took the photo for me"—which he still owned but had to leave "because of the foot-itch, you know," to emigrate first to Canada for a summer, then, illegally, down into the States to New York. He lived down on Avenue B in a railroad flat with a small-breasted woman of thirty and grew marijuana in flowerpots on glass window shelves and spent most evenings, when not at the agency, away from her in ancient McSorley's men-only beer joint. He lent Fitzie all of his Lawrence Durrell books. One morning during his first week, Anthony came into their office, said, "Morning, mate" to Fitzie, sat on his chair, and ripped the right leg of his trousers right along the crease from the shin, over the knee, to his pocket. *Schhht!* They were thin, worn trousers a thousand years old. Fitzie, with the base of a stapler, reached under the middle drawer of the metal desk and forced down one steel edge. Then he had Anthony call the office manager and verified the story that Anthony had simply pushed the chair back, to rise, when the nasty, negligent edge had caught and torn his practically new pants. Anthony got a new suit at De Pinna for a hundred dollars. A hundred WFB dollars. He told Fitzie to keep all the Durrell.

Fitzie, in a gang again for the first time since the Army, felt brand-new. Montague also hired Richard Fletcher, Athenia Tree and Johnny LePage. Fletcher and Anthenia shared a two-cubicle office next to Fitzie's and Anthony's. They soon found they both played the recorder, so into the WFB impersonal, push-air soon came, each day, an on-and-off concert of eerie, lonely, tootles and hootings. Fletcher was as old as Anthony but looked it. Fletcher had founded, with a friend, an improvisational theater that caught on quickly and began drawing young would-be actors from everywhere. The theater grew and began to move, to Chicago, San Francisco, New York. It was a Thing, and it had been Fletcher's but at some junction, at some unmanned, bell-clanging crossing in the night some-where off a map, the Thing went on, only Fletcher wasn't with it anymore. Sometimes he would be right in the middle of a recorder piece, or in mid-sentence talking to someone, when he would suddenly reach his arm out, almost as a separate, living being, and began to dial the phone on his desk. Fitzie never saw him look up a num-ber: his fingers must have known every number he could ever call. His fingers must have memorized Fitzie's num-ber when they had first shaken hands, for, not a full month after Fletcher came, he began calling Fitzie at home on the weekends or nights when they didn't work at the agency. He would have nothing specific to say, just hello, what are you doing? Montague's theory was that Fletcher was never sure the world was still out there and kept calling to check up on it. Athenia, his cubicle mate and recorder partner, was very good for Fletcher. She was very good to him. Tiny, dark-eyed, bobbling-boobed Athenia, already strung out herself in little pieces all over the countryside, seeing her shrink three hours a week, smoking five packs of Old Golds a day, drinking vodka but not eating food, living with Herbie-the-brilliant, AC-DC sculptor on Fourteenth Street in the crusade to make him DC once more; Athenia, the rest of them sensed, seemed to derive some semblance of self-unity from being with silent, gaping-mouthed Fletcher. Athenia had left her Chicago family of some wealth and taken an honest to God freighter from Newark to Tangier. "Just so I could send the cable to Bryn Mawr, I guess." She, in the better part of a year, bummed her way to Italy, to Paris. In London she was introduced to full orgasm and to the Arriflex camera by an Irish film-maker hustling there, trying to get to New York or Hollywood. So she, too, made Fitzie feel thirteen idiot years old.

Johnny LePage was the last to get picked by Montague for the gang. He among them was the most experienced and proven professional, had had several good jobs and rather a name around town for his high quality level of performance. In looks and dress he seemed an ordinary man, about Montague's age. Not so. Johnny got an office for himself on account of his seniority, and, adhering to the Nemo ban on decorating walls and floors, obediently did not hang his twenty-foot bullwhip on a wall, merely coiled it atop his desk. "What's the bullwhip for?" Fitzie asked him.

"For whipping bulls," Johnny answered with his large-toothed smile. He still had a slight Texas drawl and when he spoke his voice broke slightly, wetly, down in his throat. "No," he laughed, "that's what I said to Toto when he asked and he didn't blink an eye. That's because he can't really believe it's there. He thinks he's the only one who sees it."

"Which is why you put it there?" Fitzie laughed.

"Put what there?"

They busted. Johnny's unique contribution to The Montague Plot was his ability—when it came, as it inevitably always did, to giving *them* their mediocrity—to do bad well. He knew how to write a bad ad correctly so that no Toto, no Nemo could tell it was a fake. But then the morning would come when Johnny wouldn't be there. Johnny was an incurable assman. He couldn't quit. And, while you might now spot Johnny at Upstairs at the Downstairs with an Audrey Hepburn, if you trailed him for enough nights you'd catch him sooner or later with his arm up a hog's skirt on barstools in some switchblade sty on Eighth Avenue. He would always make it back though, as freshly showered-looking as ever.

From the night Fitzie brought home the Montague neckties, and Janice cried "Terrific!" Janice seemed to Fitzie like an extension of them, the member only he knew, the one who stayed home and was there waiting, even after midnight, to hear and cheer the day's doings. Janice told Fitzie she hated Nemo, hated Toto, hated WFB, hated the too-long days and the nights alone without him. At the same time, she liked him there, liked his arriving, bright-tied and long-haired, full of laughter and stories to give to her. And she liked the others, long before she met them. She would ask, "Has Johnny come back yet?" Or, "Fletcher called me today."

89

"Today!" Fitzie would yell. "The bastard! I was probably sitting beside him and he was talking to *you*! What'd
he want?"

"Nothing. He was sweet. He just wanted to know how I
was feeling and how the kids were. We talked about the
War on Poverty for a while."

"Jesus Christ. What a beaut."

To Janice, Fitzie's group was like their daughter's Lilly-
Belle, unseen but real and *somebody*: She did get to see
them all, but not then, not until later than she would have
if she and Fitzie hadn't been in the process of moving
again.

Moving!—again—felt wonderful; it felt a part of
Fitzie's new job, new money, new friends. The world felt
new again, and younger, faster, brighter. The newness in
fact speeded up their moving, made living in old
Queens over the Bertocchis, the state of *waiting* it always
seemed, less tolerable by the day. When Fitzie told
Montague where they were living, he said they had to
be out and into the city *within* the hour and Janice
reacted to him later with that *just as I suspected* flounce
of her mouth that always made Fitzie feel like her kid
brother. December's Saturdays and Sundays, interrupted
by another Christmas in Boston (speaking of Fitzie's move
but not daring to mention *their* picking-up again) to
chasing *Times* ads around the Village, up in the East
streets, Central Park West, Riverside Drive. Zilch: Gone.
Too much money. Too small. Area rape-ville. No kids.
Present tenants will *sell* the privilege of paying the landlord
the security, the month's rent in advance, the rent. Okay,
fair enough, how much? Eight hundred. Good God. But
it's rent controlled. Still too much, goodbye. We don't
know what to do. Well, the way is, let the missus here hit
the supers during the week. Slip 'em a fin, they'll let you
know. Can't do that, we live far away. Oh. Too bad. But
then the Saturday that somehow always comes, this one a
bleak January Saturday, when he chugged the Opel away
from the curb yet again, cracking out of the frozen brown
slush to drive down their list of addresses Janice-scrawled
on a pink napkin. The first stop an off-chance, just out of
curiosity place, not in the city but close-by, maybe something, maybe nothing.

They forced the Opel across the width of Brooklyn,
through the lead-gray air that was spitting snow now,

through the *Daily News* names of Bedford-Stuyvesant, Brownsville, East New York, all looking like Dorchester and Roxbury and Roslindale to Fitzie and Janice there inside the steamed windows. Then past the Piel beer factory and the Ex-Lax plant and along Atlantic Avenue toward the water, nearing the harbor, going west. Syrian restaurants and spice stores and bakeries and Jewish delicatessens, Italian pizza parlors, Irish barrooms, Puerto Rican record shops: smoked by the January day, all looked tough, poor and dirty. Their directions said to go to the other side of Atlantic Avenue, down toward Red Hook but not that far, watch for the Long Island General Hospital. The street was one-way the wrong way so Fitzie had to turn the humming Opel down the next, down toward the Japanese freighters prow to prow at the docks there, then around and up again. "It looks like Charlestown, for Chrissake," Fitzie said when they were below and could see the whole area, steep streets with no trees, climbing up away from the water. The houses were long pink dominoes of old brick undefended against the years of use and the salt winds of the harbor. Steps rose to each doorway like gray, concrete gangplanks from the cracked and heaving sidewalks. "There it is, eighty-seven, the fourth one up from the end, the black door," Janice said.

"You don't mean, by chance, the one *right next* to the one with the VFW Post sign on the front?" Fitzie pulled the Opel over but didn't shut it off. "It's like Brick-Bottom in Somerville, let's get out of here."

"Oh, we can't," Janice said, "I said we'd come." *Why doesn't she sound disappointed like me? What is she seeing? Damn it, she does. She knows something again. But I'll be damned if I do!* He killed the engine and set the brake, twisting the wheels to an out-angle.

"Daddy!" The boy and the girl yelled as they got out, "Look! The Statue of Liberty!"

And there she was, all right, way out there in the muck, waving. "Hey, yeah," Fitzie said. "Well, that's something." And scanning across the cold-bound water, he saw downtown New York, looming up as a single enormous iceberg with windows, like some preposterous Egyptian king's palace shouldering the sky. A nice thing to look at. They crossed and climbed the eleven steps to the double black doors and stepped into the foyer to the bank of brass mailboxes and the second set of doors, this set locked. Through the glass they peered at the first-floor hallway: waxed black linoleum floor shining in the clear-bulb light from the simple chandelier that dropped from

91

the very high ceiling; a marble mantel beneath a wall mirror, and on it a flowerbox with artificial greens. The floor radiator was painted dull silver and looked like pop art. "Well, I'll be damned," Fitzie said, leaving breath on the windowpane.

"It's well kept up," Janice said beside him, as if she had said it before and was now repeating it. "Three blank, that must be it. Two, Singer. One, Roberts. Basement, Stevenson. That's her," Janice read and pressed the last bell button. "Yes? Hello!" The voice came from behind them, outside. "Hi, I meant to tell you to ring down here." They trooped down the steps to the sidewalk and went in, pushing the children, through the iron gate of the front fence. The girl was standing, shivering in white Levi's and a sweater at the opened gate to the doorway beneath the staircase. "I'm Betsy Stevenson, come in and meet the Cellar People." Behind her, holding the china-red door open, stood the others. Fitzie couldn't believe it: this Betsy was Janice's height, her shape, her age; the guy in the sweat shirt and dungarees had a different face than Fitzie, but was otherwise his double; they had two kids there, a girl and a boy, the same ages, it looked, as their own. Jesus Christ, they'd run into themselves in a cellar in Brooklyn.

"Oh, wow," Janice said.

"This is a fabulous apartment," Fitzie said to the guy as Betsy was saying, "Sit down, we're still having coffee. A *bad* Friday night," and they sat at the dining table and took their coffee from crockery mugs.

"Uh, I'm *Bob* Stevenson, by the way," he said. "They call me Buck." He and Fitzie shook hands again.

"Oh! I'm sorry, darling," Betsy said, "I thought we did all that in the hall."

"Well, I'm John Fitzpatrick, called Fitzie, and this is Janice. Whom we call Flame."

"Really?" they all laughed.

"No," Fitzie and Janice said as one.

"He thinks he's funny," Janice explained. "Isn't that weird. *I* thought we had done the introductions, too."

Fitzie and Buck both dropped their packs on the table at the same time and both packs were Pall Malls. "Oh, no," Fitzie said. "This is too much," Buck said. They didn't laugh.

"How long have you been here?" Fitzie asked him.

Buck answered, "Two years. Just."

"Well, that's a little more than us," Janice said.

"Hold it, now," Buck smiled. "We can blow it, you know? Listen, Fitzie, you rather have a beer?"

"I sure would."

Janice made a face. "At ten in the morning?"

The kids by now were exploding land mines and having a hell of a time in the bedroom.

Fitzie raised the wet, brown bottle and said, "Here's to . . ."

"The reunion," Betsy finished it. They laughed a little. The men drank the beer. The four smoked and talked for about a half-hour, biography swapping. It wasn't Janice or Fitzie who finally remembered, it was Betsy: "The apartment!" she sang. "You have to see the apartment!"

"We'll take it," Janice smiled.

"I don't know if you will, though," Buck grumbled. "Where are the keys, Bets? It's pretty rancid right now, probably. God knows how many people they had living up there, they were there long before us and they'd always slip the rent in the mailbox so we never got inside. Fourteen Puerto Ricans and a goat, I think."

"Do you own the place, by the way?" Fitzie asked.

"God, no, wish we did," Betsy said, digging into her massive pocketbook. "No, the landlady lives in Florida. Whoever lives in this apartment gets to be the caretakers. We collect the rent, put out the trash, call the plumbers, you know. It's easy, really, and we get a nice rake-off on our rent."

"Great. Did you do this place yourselves?" Janice asked.

"No. Isn't it neat? A young architect had it before us and they conveniently had a fire, no big thing I don't think, but she let him knock out walls and everything afterwards."

"Yeah, I'm sorry you're seeeing this place first. I don't know what the hell we're going to find up there."

Buck and Fitzie climbed the three flights; the key fit but didn't move the lock. They returned to the basement. "Why don't you bring the kids up to the landing?" Buck told Betsy and Janice, "I'm going to try to get in from the roof, I know there's a skylight up there. Then I'll let you in from the inside." Fitzie followed Buck up the cold, slippery fire escape on the rear wall of the building and climbed onto the snow-crusted tarred roof. "Man, this is wild," he said.

"Yeah. I've never come up here before," Buck said. From the slightly canted roof they could see the whole harbor picking through the snow-gray air; the entire height of the Statue; across to the Jersey waterfront, black, square heads and eyes poking up through the choppy waters.

At the skylight, it took the two of them to pull off the tarpaper box-lid frozen over the square opening. Buck reached in and yanked the window open. "Oh Christ, is that what I think it is down there?"

"The bathtub," Fitzie laughed. "With the showerhead pipe right in the middle. We'll have very high voices if we don't miss that."

Buck snickered. "Shit, no sense both of us breaking our balls. I'll go."

"Okay, you go."

"Huh. How much of a drop would you say that is?"

"Hard to tell, looking straight down like this."

Buck said, "Ah, what the fuck," and went over the side, feet-first into the hole in the roof, and hung there, his hands hooked over the frame, his feet dangling past the showerhead. Fitzie knelt and fumbled to get as tight a grip as possible on Buck's wrists.

"So long, GI," he laughed and took Buck's hanging weight into his arms, then started to lower him. "Try not to swing. Say when and drop straight as you can."

"When."

Fitzie let go of Buck's arms and watched the top of his head plunge away. The landing thud took a lot longer to come than Fitzie thought it would. Buck was sitting in the tub. "Make it?" Fitzie called down.

"My entire body is broken. Je-sus Christ!" the voice came up. Fitzie climbed down the fire escape and watched Buck let the women and kids in from the hall, then come and open the window for him.

"Bugs! Bugs!" the four kids were yelling, and they ran around the stained linoleum floor stamping their feet to get the cockroaches scampering madly in all directions to escape. It looked as if somebody had spilled a bushel basket full of raisins onto the spacious floor. Their bodies *cracked* when a foot landed on them. The kids were having the time of their lives and made a wild Mexican dance scene in the large room empty of everything but a sink and an elderly refrigerator in a corner. The children's gleeful murder cries echoed loudly in the outsized kitchen.

Betsy was obviously embarrassed. "Oh, this is disgusting. I'm awfully sorry."

"They can be gotten rid of," Janice said quickly. "You have any downstairs?"

"No, the guy comes once a month."

94

"Now we know where's he's been sending them," Buck said.

"Well, you have to keep the place *clean* to keep them out!" Betsy snapped.

"Don't yell at me, I live down with you, remember?"

Fitzie watched them and laughed. "Hey, cut it out," he said, "it's keeping the tigers happy isn't it?"

The four of them explored the flat. "It could be just great," Janice said.

"You know, it could be *really* great," Fitzie planned aloud, "like if somebody would knock out this wall, put the kitchen in the middle of the house, that would be a back bedroom and you'd have a huge living room then."

Buck said, "Yeah. If you owned one of these old houses and put some money into them, you could really make them fantastic."

"Well, that's what the Heights is."

"Well, how's the rest of the block?" Janice asked.

"Counting the Spanish whorehouse down the end?" Buck said.

"Really?" Fitzie asked.

Buck's "Yeah!" was covered by Betsy answering, "This is really the only building in the street with young people renting. With *outsiders*, like us. The rest are all old neighborhood types. Pay about forty a month still, some of them. They sort of ignore us."

"We know what that is," Janice winked.

Back in the Stevensons' apartment, Buck said, "You guys as hungry as I am?" Janice said, "Oh, no, we have to go" to Fitzie, while Betsy was saying, "Oh, yes, let's have lunch. Your kids must be starved," so Betsy didn't hear her, or did and ignored it, and hopped into the kitchen. They all followed. Janice started buttering bread. Fitzie and Buck stood at the garden windows with their beers and looked out. The snow had started again and was whitewashing the old snow gently and evenly. "Must be nice in the summer," Fitzie said.

"Well, even now the kids get thrown out there. But it's great in the good weather. It's theoretically ours, but the rest usually hear the ice cubes and come down the fire escape."

"Nice." Fitzie watched his word hit the windowpane, then turned his head back to the girls making sandwiches on the counter. "Goddamn it," he announced.

"What?" Buck said.

"It has just occurred to me. Well, first, we're going to do this all wrong, all dumb. No dicking around, no feelers

95

or any of that shit. We're going to take the apartment, you know that."

Janice looked up from the Velveeta and smiled at him.

Betsy sang, "Oh, great! Oh, I'm so glad."

And Buck said, "Roaches and all," and swigged from the Black Label.

"But no, that's not what I mean," Fitzie had already begun to say, "that's almost beside the point and *that's* what I want to say. It *is* beside the point, it's *obvious* that we'll move in here. Christ, we have to, we'd be losing our bloody minds. I mean, isn't it just great, isn't it just super-terrific to be in New York, all grown-up and on your way; where everything's at, where it's *happening!* Balls. You live like, like wolves, for shit's sake."

"Have another beer," Janice said.

"No," Buck said to the garden snow, to himself, "wolves go in packs. But I don't know what we're like. Like nothing else, I suppose."

"Oh, bitch-bitch," Betsy said. She and Janice carried trays into the kids now back in the bedroom. "Move in tomorrow and we'll start a colony. A *commune*."

In the Opel going east, Fitzie said, "I hope we're not being foolish. I mean they seem really great, but first impressions and all that. I don't know. The place is going to be a lot of work, it's really a crap-hole."

"It'll be good," Janice said. Her words came over "crap-hole." She lighted two cigarettes and put one between his lips. "I think they'll be fine, too. But it doesn't make any difference, does it. It's the place. It's a good place for us."

"I hope so."

"Well, it's still *us*. I mean it's going to be us one way or the other anyhow."

"Yeah."

Oh, the drums went bang that year and the cymbals clanged and the horns of Fitzie's Tank blazed away.

Fitzie and Janice were flying. A comma, not a period, would likely be coming after Brooklyn in their Boston, Baltimore, Germany, Queens, Queens, list—but the list itself was no longer one of the things that automatically went up on a new wall like Janice's spice rack. Keeping score had ceased; they weren't, suddenly, thinking that way anymore; they had moved into a railroad station, into an airport where the lights and sounds were always on,

96

where people could come or go or stay as they pleased or were able to manage and there were always people doing all of it. They felt comfortable there. They liked it.

Buck and Betsy Stevenson had been themselves that beer and skylight Saturday; no pockmarks or scars or other bad surprises showed up in the long close-up that followed Fitzie and Janice's moving in. Like Fitzie and Janice, they were a unit, didn't *have to have* any outside help—not in the real way, anyhow. It happened to be that the other kind of help was the one personal zone where the Stevensons and the Fitzpatricks did, and would forever, unalterably, differ: they had it, Fitzie and Janice didn't. Material help. Money. Not just getting it, but knowing it was there, not being able to imagine its *not* being there. Buck and Betsy would admit they wished they didn't have it, would confess they felt it an under-cutting of their confidence, their strength, their inde-pendence. But. They were unable to mean what they said; Fitzie and Janice were unable to believe they could mean what they said. But it wasn't important anyway: Fitzie and Janice had each other, really had each other and neither wanted or needed anyone from the outside. They were making love all the time. He was in her and they were balling and rolling and holding and coming tight every minute they were together, even while they were fighting or not speaking or having dinner out with other people or talking in an A&P about the price of bing cherries.

So this was New York. You did finally get some people, friends in a way, but mostly just people with some con-nection to you that you liked; and these people were invisible things, Lilly-Belles, out there somewhere in the big limbo. To get to them you called to them or you went out into limbo to where they were; or they called, for you were their invisible people. They came, then, or you went, by arrangement, in the car or by subway or bus or taxicab. For dinner. Oh, sometimes to meet for a drink or to see something, a play, a film, or to eat out; every now and then a party, but mostly you had people for dinner and went to where they were, for dinner. Janice thrived. Fletcher came with his blond wife, just returned from her third separation from him. Fletcher made only two phone calls. Anthony came from Avenue B with his woman on bicycles across the bridge and brought Spanish wine. They had the Stevensons up when Athenia came with her fierce Herbie, and when Johnny came he brought a tall English girl who seemed bored but who helped Janice serve and do the dishes and had long, tanned bare legs that she crossed and recrossed as she sat listening to them until Fitzie, silly from the flash-shots of her aqua panties all evening, began making bombs. He and Johnny started to drop glasses and spill ashtrays. Finally dizzy, then stoned mute, Fitzie careened to bed and went out, dressed, with visions of aqua pubic hair dancing in his head. Johnny and the girl stayed the night, she on the couch, he on the floor, had Sunday breakfast with them, then left. Johnny wasn't seen until Thursday and Fitzie crawled morosely through guilt for the three days.

These dinners with Fitzie's new people were spaced over months; in between, he and Janice were called by them and went out into limbo, for dinner. Real contact, as they had with Buck and Betsy, was never made with any of them. This was not disappointing, for it wasn't people being cold or locked off. It was people keeping to themselves. Montague was outside of this. They saw him more often than the others, and in a different way—except for the first night, when he arrived at their landing in turtleneck, tweeds and boots, bearing two dozen daffodils swathed in green florist's paper for Janice, a doll and toy from Design Research for the children—whom he insisted on seeing, asleep in their beds—and sangria for Fitzie. That night he was like the others, with his own elegance, of course—the Gentleman Dinner Guest, creating topics, providing transitions, listening with straight eyes, remembering charming anecdotes, forbidding, for Janice's sake, any mention of the agency or work. He came by cab and, at fifteen past midnight sharp, went away by cab, leaving them liking him and saying what a great evening, but leaving also an after-image of himself as wispy and elusive as a television show seen the night before. Within the week, however, Montague thanked them for the evening by a note which invited them to his apartment for the next Friday. He didn't mention it at all to Fitzie in the office.

Montague lived in an old, polished-wood, one-bedroom flat over Sheridan Square. "Come see my treetops," the note had said. "It's lovely." They brought Pernod, which delighted him. "You *are* listening, then!" he said to Fitzie, but looked, smiling to Janice. He had prepared the meal himself, a soufflé, and the three of them washed the dishes. They went outside for coffee, walking MacDougal Street, ablaze with color and pounding with the music smoking up through the gypsy crowds from the Cafe Wha?, having espresso at a table on the café side of the

Fat Black Pussycat. The coffee was milky, "The worst Postum in the world," Montague boasted, but the entertainment was worth it that night. Singers, comics, anything would step up onto the small platform into the lights and do their thing in front of the postered brick wall for nothing more than what the passed hat picked up. Tiny Tim came in that night, still in the obscurity of his Village-places fame, with the Hedy Lamarr hair to his shoulders, blowing his kisses, rolling his eyes high away from the Steinberg nose, to plunk his little ukelele and do his snicker-quelling, wonderful MacDonald-Eddy solo duets.

"I think he *means* it," Janice whispered, applauding, maternal.

"He'd *better*," Montague laughed. A big-shouldered Negro with two teeth took the stool and sang "Misty." A young, clean-cut chubby man then impersonated the Empire State Building. Fitzie said he wanted a drink, so they walked to Marie's Crisis. The woman singing "Kansas City" at the piano in the doorway to the bar lifted a hand from the keys in a quick hello to Montague. Then they went up the stairs and next door to Arthur's—"the fabulous Club Arthur," Montague announced, holding open the door for Janice. They sat in the dark on the side wall of the narrow, small place, toward the rear to be near the three-piece combo working around the elevated piano. Dated jazz, heavy bass, but it was nice. It let them talk and listen. They stopped, though, when the caramel girl in the beige sweater slid from her stool at the bar and stood facing the room at the piano, on the floor and close to Fitzie, sitting on the aisle chair. "Good to see ya, Jeannie," a voice from the dark said low. She sang "Frankie and Johnny" in her own mixture of Sarah Vaughan and something else, blue but up. Her tight dungarees bisected her box with their seam, making it bulge as she rocked it smoothly and slowly in and out, never quite making a bump, simply stopping her pelvis on the back-pull when she finished the words. The people asked for more, but she only smiled and returned to her solitary stool to talk to the bartender.

"You like that, huh?" Janice laughed softly to Fitzie and gave him a light punch on the arm.

They were drinking beer. "This is a very favorite place of mine," Montague said, not acting. "I come here a lot of nights during the week when it's not crowded."

Fitzie could see past Janice's wide eyes to her inner

snapshot of poor Montague alone and lonely near the silent piano and covered drums. His own picture had somebody else in it, maybe two other men dressed as richly as Montague. He didn't like either picture, didn't think that either was true, but couldn't imagine what was. They stayed there together until three and their talk took on the pattern it was always to have. They talked of the Self, never really calling it that. They got together carefully often. A few times Janice drove over the bridge early on a Friday evening to meet them after work at Sweet's at the Fulton Fish Market, to crowd up the creaky stairs and eat lobster and sole and swordfish from the gray steel trays of the old Negro waiters, some looking as if they could have been there against the dull yellow walls, in the sea smells, since 1845. And, in the summer, Fitzie would "rent" Buck and Betsy's garden and Montague would climb down the fire escape with him while Janice carried the gin and bitter lemon and Rose's lime juice and ice through the Stevenson's back bedroom. But they loved the Village, so often they would eat from the blackboard menu at the Blue Mill or in the Charles IV, nearly always ending up at the Club Arthur. At first, it seemed that Montague was trying to tell them something, but the dialogue passed beyond that; and while Montague's age and uniqueness tended to set him as teacher and giver, he would just as often release his feet to give them the control end of the seesaw, seeming to feel there was something he could learn from them. He had left his Wisconsin home ten years before, for the Navy and San Francisco, after which he came to New York, as planned, to try to make it in Dance. "When I finally saw I wasn't going to be a star, that was it."

"Did you drop it altogether?" Janice asked.

"I tried to go back after a year in advertising. But I was right the first time. Then I tried to manage a company for a while, but that's sheer agony, so I came back into advertising again. I still work out though, twice a week."

"It must be good, to have something *else* in your life, like that," Fitzie said.

"It is. As long as you don't let it be a reminder of your failure. Then it could be your downfall."

"So you don't look at it like that," Janice said. "I sometimes wish I had dancing or acting or painting or something to occupy me."

"But don't you have your hands full with the children and the cooking and all that?" Montague asked.

"Of course, but that's what I do. What I have to do. I

don't know, I mean it seems there should be something away from everything else, that I could go to."

"Well, you can make something," Montague said. "It doesn't have to be something you've already had. For instance, I've started to take French lessons. I have a wonderful little old lady who comes wheezing up the stairs every Thursday night. I *have* to learn, now, just to know what she *hurls* at me when I open the door."

They laughed. "Why French?" Fitzie asked.

"For a thing," Montague said, "like what Janice is after. It's ... well, I think you've got to run your life, don't you? You have to fill it with whatever *you* want. If you don't, then it doesn't run at all and can just crumble. Or, you can just go on doing what all the fools say you should be doing, whatever *that* is, and be one of the robots. Unhappy and screwed up, with no idea why. But I also think I might like to go and live in Paris someday. I was there a year ago and went around, to *Elle* and *Paris Match* and some of the agencies."

"Oh? How great."

"It was. They have no idea what they're doing, of course, and their stuff is something ghastly. They *loved* me. I know I could go there and be a smash. But I'd have to know French, no question about that."

"God, I think that's terrific," Janice said."

"Please, don't leave now," Fitzie said. "Nemo and Toto will kill me."

"Do you think it would really be different, living over there, I mean after the newness wore off?" Janice asked him. "Do you think you'll really go? Did Fitzie tell you how we were going to do that? He tried to get a job there for when we got out of the service."

"I could have separated over there and still got a free trip home when I wanted it."

"He tried the *Herald Tribune* and A.F.N. and all sorts of things, but nothing came. Then we were going to take an apartment and just live there for the month of August. We even had one all ready, you know how everybody gets out of there in August, well we were going *in*! Then we got curtailed and had to come home in July."

"Yeah," Fitzie said, "I wasn't that disappointed at the time, but I've wondered a lot since, what would have happened to us if we had done it."

Montague took it in, in his intense, drinking way of listening. "It's really a shame you didn't," he said, "but I try to never regret what *didn't* happen. That can kill you. But," he sighed, "I don't really know if I ever will or not.

The lessons are fun anyway, and it's something ahead, a future possibility."

"Man, I've been coming to that lately," Fitzie said. "That's really a thing, isn't it?"

"What?" Montague and Janice asked.

"Well, I'm starting to feel like I'm in sophomore year, you know? I've been here say, roughly, two years. And okay, it's fine, it's fun, but I know that all of a sudden I'll be *there*. And then what? I mean you like to think there's something up ahead. And as long as you play it like that, it's no sweat; but when you stop and think, you know, is this it? Am I here for the next twenty years, for the rest of my *life*? That's very hard to take. Nothing, like *nothing*, seems worth that."

"No," Montague frowned, "not even when you're in something that isn't stagnant, where you *can* go up, can go to the top relatively quickly."

"As we are," both Montague and Fitzie said, only a syllable out of unison, making the three laugh, but shortly.

"I have no idea," Fitzie said, "what it would be like if you worked for a bank, or IBM or GE or something like that."

"Some *real* business," Janice said.

"Maybe then there's no problem," Montague said.

Fitzie said, "I think they could kill me, really. Could make me into whatever they wanted me to be. I'm just not that strong. Or I don't know what I want clearly enough to know what I don't want."

"Also," Janice patted his hand, "you want to win so badly."

"Well, what's wrong with that? You want me to lose?"

"See what I mean?" she smiled to Montague and raised her thumb at Fitzie, then to him said, "I just want you to know what you're winning, my sweet middle-class Catholic hubby."

"Ah, shit," Fitzie said.

"Wouldn't it be a gas, though," Janice said to them, "to *pretend* you had that kind of faith? And made that your life, telling everybody to shove it?"

"We're really too old, kids, to drop out," Montague said. "Besides, we haven't had the training for it. Wrong backgrounds."

"Yeah, but we're too young, on the other hand, to buy the program. Just too much Protestant-Catholic-Puritan bullshit. Layers and layers," Fitzie said.

"Yay," Montague said, "the Silent Generation speaks out."

"Fuck *Life* magazine anyway," Fitzie said.

"Okay," Janice said, "but if we *are* in the middle, maybe we're the only ones left around who can *do* anything."

"Call me in a couple of years, when I can *afford* to make my own life," Fitzie said.

"Don't you ever stop hinting for a raise?" Montague said.

"No, he doesn't and don't, Fitzie," Janice answered.

"Well, in the meantime, you two can at least take French lessons. Or go to Arthur Murray's."

"Or join Jehovah's Witnesses," Janice said.

"Or pound sand," Fitzie said. That was what the three of them talked about. And they saw Montague so frequently because they liked being with him—for precisely the opposite reasons they liked being with Buck and Betsy: Montague was nothing like them, lived a life that bore absolutely no resemblance to theirs, was older, single, childless, mobile, refined, and, in one consistent way, enigmatic. He did, once, speak to them from this shadowed corner of himself—or at least they thought he did.

It had been the end of May, Janice's birthday and a holiday weekend. Work, the apartment, their newfound people, the snare drums, horns and flutes were blasting full away down the street at quickstep. Janice was even pregnant. She had told Fitzie the first night they slept in the new Brooklyn apartment. Montague had a girl friend, a pretty, divorced ex-dancer named Susan. Susan appeared and then didn't, off and on; they never knew when Montague would include her. For Janice's birthday, for the hell of it, the four of them were to go to Fire Island for four days. Montague made the arrangements.

The plan was for them to all go together in the Opel, but Montague called the evening before to say a ridiculous conflict had arisen, and why wouldn't Fitzie and Janice go out alone for the first two days, then he and Susan would come and spend the second two days with them? It was fine with Fitzie and Janice; in fact, a boon, a surprise chance to be by themselves, away, for two whole days. Not since Spain! Before eight, they were on the Shore Parkway going sixty-five along Brooklyn's bottom. As they passed Fort Hamilton, Fitzie gave it the finger. They hummed past Kennedy and ran out into Long Island, onto the Montauk Highway and into the town of Sayville.

"Look at this, and not much more than an hour away," Fitzie said as they slowed for the town streets, looking for signs to the ferry.

"I know. I had no idea. We really have to start getting out and see where we're living," Janice said.

"Not that we could live here. I doubt if anybody commutes this far."

"No. It is America, though, and so close!"

"God, it really reminds me of Rock Harbor."

"I'll keep an eye out for your grandmother."

"I wonder if there's a hospital. You could nurse and I could dig clams."

"And help out at the bean suppers."

"And become members of the community. Roots, baby, *roots*!"

"Sure. It wouldn't take more than forty years."

"Let's do it, huh? We could drink and kill ourselves."

Janice laughed. "We're being mean, you know."

"Defensive, anyway," Fitzie muttered. They finally cleared the elm-ceilinged, chirping, picket-fenced lanes and were near the water. "Maah! Smell that."

Gulls squawked and swooped or spread-hung silently in the pale green winds above the low white-painted buildings bunched small around the empty ferry slip. Fitzie paid their fare to the boy in the glass booth and left their suitcase on the shelf at the gate. "We've got about a half-hour," Fitzie said. "He said there's a coffee shop back here."

"Oh, we walked right past it. That's where the noise is coming from."

Inside the screen door with the COME ALIVE! PEPSI sign on it, the place was jammed dark with people perched on stools at the looped counter and standing squashed together on the small floor, ordering, talking, eating. The thin space overhead was filled with cigarette and fried eggs smoke and rock radio music. Trying to catch the eye of the counterman, they became aware that it wasn't quite people cramming the diner; besides Janice, there were only two other girls, straight-haired young city types together. All the rest were men and dogs. All the dogs were small, expensive-looking dogs, a few looking up their leashes from the floor, but most cradled in upbent arms. And none of the men were alone, rather in pairs and groups of three or four. Fitzie and Janice were behind the seated girls and the broad back of a man in a Canada Dry uniform. Fitzie's "Two blacks!" finally got a nod. They stood, their heads close but not looking at each other.

What grouped the men most immediately was their clothes, not their faces. The clothes, the clothes, the beautiful clothes, *those* clothes in the color spreads of *Playboy, Esquire,* sometimes the Sunday *Times* magazine. Checkered, close-fitting trousers. Italian silk shirts. Marlboro Country jackets. Double-breasted blazers from Onassis's yachts. Fur-soft pull-overs. James Bond turtlenecks. Navy bellbottoms. Fitzie caught Janice's eyes seeking his once, and whispered, "C.Y.O. marching band. Must be a competition someplace." A new gang burst in through the screen door, pushing into more space than there was. They appeared the way a troupe of clowns had appeared in a circus Fitzie and Janice had seen in Germany. The German clowns had come through a curtain tumbling and orating to the crowds around the single ring; these came, five of them, through the screen door jostling and squealing to the crowded coffee shop. In their mid-twenties, they were arms and hips, teeth and eyes and tight behinds in lavender slacks and imitation-silk vests, white and powder-blue striped polo shirts, flowered suitcoats and a single, gold-band earring. Their giggling ran to the edge of hysteria before it turned back and began again. "Let's go," Fitzie said. A vague chill had come into his skin, with his memory of old school's-end warnings of cellars and the cars of strangers. As he passed one of the clowns, a voice said, "Purr, purr."

Fitzie and Janice joined the line close to the front and it grew behind them with the others from the coffee shop. A true people-ferry, it was a boat of seats, long wooden benches fore and aft, with a belt of glass windows around all sides except at the prow. Aboard, they sat on the rearmost bench to have windows behind and to both sides. The men, dogs and girls followed, carrying radios and cardboard boxes and toasters. The Canada Dry man and the clowns were not among them. The ferry took a long breath, gliding backwards, then leaned forward to write a wide, straight line though its own curve and on, getting faster, over the solid, smooth channel's surface. The marsh grass started to blow past them faster and faster until it ran itself out and they were into Great South Bay. Just sky closing tightly onto water, until they passed the other boat and saw themselves going the other way, except their mirror image had no faces at the windows and said Cherry Grove instead of Fire Island Pines on the sign at the wheelhouse. Fitzie and Janice now knew why the clowns hadn't joined them. The old fairy-boat joke. Their boat tacked slightly and let them watch the razorline between sky and water rapidly get blacker and thicker, rising up—the creation of earth filmed in stop-motion— until it was a wide grease pencil blacking between the blue and the blue. Fire Island. Fitzie and Janice were expecting Cape Cod, but that wasn't what they got.

They were the last down the steps to the Pines landing. Their suitcase stood blue and alone in the white sun now full and unslanted on the wooden dock. Their hotel was the only one and it was right above the landing, overlooking the small harbor the bay made into the land. They changed, followed the nearest bleached-wooded walkway away from the harbor and reached the beach in about two minutes. The Atlantic was so close it appeared to be a high, blue wall. As they went closer, the top of the wall fell back and stretched out flat. Fitzie ran straight in, head-diving into a third row wave still mounting its rise, shoulders just beginning to curl forward. Hot ice! Frog-kicking, he pulled the painful cold apart with his arms. Done, stung, he kicked up, Pall Mall lungs pulling, to dolphin through the upper crust and wait for Janice. He caught only the tight-together soles of her feet going down white. He side-stroked toward the beach to where she would come up. Gasping, spluttering, they grabbed each other for their victorious babble of kicking legs and sneak feels. The unfamiliar bumping of his belly reminded him. "Hey, lady, is it okay for you to be in? Old flubadub there might not like the water."

"It's too goddamn cold to stay in anyhow." They swam the waves back, then walked inshore to where the small, green-haired dunes made free backrests. From here they could see the look of the Pines, the jungle-thick covering of pine trees that grew out of sand, hard and gnarled and entwined together no higher than a porch roof. Along the dunes there were houses with the smoothness, the angles, the canniness of driftwood, decked and roofed like a spread of Lego combinations.

Janice wore a peach colored one-piece suit cut like a toga that hid her without yelling pregnant! "Damn!" she said.

"What's the matter?"

"I didn't get one look!"

"Oh. Coming up, you mean? From the boys?"

"The suit did. *You* did. I didn't get one eye!"

"Ah, you're a fat old pregnant mother, what do ya want?"

Her slap on his crotch brought him straight up. He took the Coppertone from her bag. "Do that again," he said, "and you'll start a riot." She opened her eyes to him quizzically, but said nothing. They took an hour of it, of the surrendering to the warm, thick needles. Sun-wise, they grudgingly forced themselves full awake and walked back to their room of light, whitewashed stucco walls and frosted glass door, with only the bed, a rickety Salvation Army bureau, two canvas director chairs and lamps scrounged from somewhere. Janice pulled down the faded yellow bed throw and stretched herself out on the white steet. "Mm," he said, "strawberry and vanilla." Her legs, face and arms had taken a little pink heat, and she had powdered after her shower. He flattened his ear against her belly under the button and said, "Hey you! How's it goin' in there? You okay?"

Janice grabbed his head and pulled. "For not answering his daddy, he ought to get a good poke in the eye."

"Poke him, I gonna wail the bejeezus out o' him, dat's what ah's gonna do ta dat dere tar baby."

When they woke the room had been painted light blue. Janice picked the pillows up from the floor, pulled the sheet up over them. Fitzie lit cigarettes. "That was good," he said. The words cracked and made him cough. "Was it for you?"

"Yes. It was. For a start, of course," she laughed sleepily.

"Maybe we shouldn't have any kids. Then we could do it in the daytime all the time."

"Well, you'd still be away. And then we'd have to go away to do it nights."

"That's it, isn't it. The being away. Christ, it's been a long time."

"It's that, but you know what it is? It's being alone."

"That's good?"

"That's good."

"Yeah. It is good. Except we're always alone."

"Not like this."

"I know. Wow, it's six-thirty. You hungry?"

"Starved," she said. "Where you going?"

"To get . . ."

"Oh. You meant food?"

"Oh. Ho."

The sun hadn't gone, it had only left their side of the building. It was low now, but still lighting and heating when they found it at the restaurant-bar attached to the hotel above the harbor wall. They sat at one of the wooden tables on the deck connecting the hotel to the low, glass-walled "Hermitcrab" bar. The waiter closed down the umbrella over the table. "Turn your chairs," he said to them, "and get the bennies before they go."

"The what?" Fitzie said.

"The beneficial rays of the sun," the kid laughed.

They laughed and turned the chairs and ordered gimlets. There were several women around now, but still most of the tables had the men at them. Further down along the quay toward the bay was the Pines' market-shop combination, so there was continuous traffic on the boardwalk beneath the deck, of couples and groups of men and dogs, going to and from the market, many pulling the red children's wagons used on roadless Fire Island for carrying luggage, groceries, everything. Fitzie and Janice drank the first gimlets quickly and ordered more. As the sun got closer to leaving, blue came into the air with its chill, and the dimmer lights of the inside room of the Hermitcrab began coming on. Janice sucked the lime from her drink and puckered. "God, they are beautiful, every one of them."

"Who?"

"All these *guys*."

"I know it, it's unbelievable. They must all be models and actors. Except they're all not, I just saw a guy I met once, and he's an account man someplace or other."

"Did he see you?"

"No, but he probably wouldn't remember me anyhow."

"He good-looking?"

"Oh, yeah. But, you know, he dresses very conservatively, very Brooks Brothers. At least when I met him. A lot are bankers and salesmen, not just interior decorators."

"It is weird, though, so many *men* together."

Fitzie laughed. "Who knows? Maybe it's just a Holy Name convention. Or a bowling league."

"A seminary."

"The Jaycees."

"The Elks." Janice giggled and held her glass up to him, rattling its cubes.

"Oh bad," he smiled and signaled the waiter.

"Do you feel funny?" she asked.

"A little, but nobody's bothering us are they?" Their third round came. When the boy was gone, Janice said, "He's so nice. Do you think he's . . . I mean, he looks like he's in *college*."

"Christ, don't start playing *that* game, love. What difference does it make. Listen, if it were all mixed couples,

108

there'd be some jerks wanting to *get together* with us, right? Wouldn't that be terrific."

"Right. Yes. That's right." Seeing his face, she blushed a little. "What are you all chuckles about?"

"You," he laughed. "I'll buy you a book when we get home, okay?"

"All right, all right. But it's just so ..." People were leaving their tables, some to bunch into the bar inside, carrying their drinks, most going off toward the pines and the houses. Newcomers, sweatered or jacketed for the evening, were arriving to take the tables or go inside. A large, white Chris-Craft made a slow-moving wall along the walkway, then stopped in front of the hotel. Music floated up from its cabin. Girls came out onto the aft deck, splattering vivid colors against the dark water in their short shifts and silk pajama outfits. Five of them, young and flushed and laughing, with five bright-moving men. They stayed on the boat, hauling a drink-wagon up from below. Fitzie grinned, "Feel better?"

She snickered. "Yes."

"Hee, hee, hee," he imitated Duke as he used to do, knowing it delighted her. She leaned to him then and whispered, "All right, but I just want to know how *you* know so much about it."

"I don't really. But we did a lot of it in Germany. Not me, but McGregor, hell, half his cases had to do with it, and he told me a lot. In fact it was why he volunteered for Korea way back."

"*Volunteered*! I didn't know that. Did Dorothy know that?"

"Probably. But he'd been in D.C. for two years, in the Pentagon. Chasing queers. And he just couldn't take it anymore. It sounded very grim, I wouldn't tell you half of it. Messy deals like staking out some poor bastard of a colonel or a cryptographer for months at a time, bugging houses, two-way mirrors, cameras, all that shit."

"My God. Why?"

"Security. The commies could compromise a homo and get all our precious secrets."

"That's disgusting. But can't they get somebody with a girl? *That's* what always happened in the spy movies."

"You mean do they chase cockhounds, too? Of course not. That's okay. That's *natural*, you see. The American way. And I will announce that I am now totally depressed, that I am going to my room and assume the fetal position in the closet for the rest of this wonderful weekend alone on Fire Island with my mistress, and will then kill myself, after breakfast Sunday."

Janice laughed and took his hand in both of hers and kissed it. "Dah-link?'"

"Eva? Zsa Zsa, is it you?"

"Yess, my dah-link. Ve will go now to my room. Ve vill fool around and ve vill get dressed up *splendidly* and you vill take me to dinner."

" 'Ve vill fool around?' Jesus Christ, some vamp." They went, they fooled around, then they dressed and went back outside. The moon was out. "You want to go see the water first?" Fitzie said.

"No. I have to eat or I'll die."

They sat and drank martinis straight up, then they ate. And ate. Real clam chowder, with cream not tomatoes. Sole and swordfish, hot french bread, baked potatoes with sour cream, vinegar-clean salad, cheesecake. Espresso nearly solid. Then Galliano on ice cut with lime wedges. They hardly spoke a word during the eating, but kept looking up at each other to roll eyes or grin, Huck and Tom on their raft. Over the Galliano and cigarettes, Janice said, "I wonder what the poor people are doing tonight."

"Or," he laughed, "what was the cartoon, the generals on the hill? 'I hope the enlisted men have a sunset like this.' "

From the jukebox, the Beatles had done a set and the Rolling Stones were up now and the drinker-edged dance floor was covered by sandals, shoes and bare feet moving. The five Chris-Craft girls rocking in the crowd were flames that had jumped from the fire. The new dancing. The hands-talking, introverted, no-touch, Sound-digging, new dancing. Holy Roller meeting gone Cool.

Cool.

Up.

This wasn't kids, swinging and flailing and humping.

This was Older.

Cool.

Which made it work. Which didn't merely absorb shock, it smothered shock in its sleep, with a pillow of Cool:

Men were dancing. Together. Pairs, all right. Definite couples. But parallel. Geometrically apart forever through the outer space of Beat. Crowded, but room enough made for more people in through the door and for Fitzie and Janice up from their table and for whoever else felt like

110

it. It exuded a peace, this rock. If dogs had felt like dancing, space would have been made. For the dish to run away with the spoon. For green eggs and ham. For Fitzie and Janice to give their bodies a swim in the mystical body of yay-yay. They stayed until after two in the morning.

Their children-set alarm clocks went off at seven, beginning their second day with the pleasure of waking to know they were sleeping and could sleep forever. They came back to full light and life, together, at eleven-thirty. They stretched and turned in the sheets until it ceased being exquisite and became merely stretching and turning. They smiled thickly at each other. Neither spoke. They went to the bathroom in turns, returning to the bed. Lying there looking up at the slight shiftings of the sunlight through the glass doors on the whitewash ceiling; then, with no play, no speaking, Fitzie rose and made the unity actual, not moving, just breathing, until it started itself without them and went, as they watched then at the last moment caught up and joined the line of skaters across the ice. The whip was cracked, sending them sprawling, breathless, into the snowbanks of sheets.

"Fitzie?"

"Yeah?"

"You awake?"

"No."

"Do you feel as good as I do?"

"I feel beautiful."

"How?"

"I don't know. Free. Young. Strong. Tough."

"And *different* you know?" Janice said.

"Different. Alone?"

"Alone-good, not alone-bad though."

"Scared."

"Why? Of what?"

"Of, well, not scared exactly. Confused, anxious. About ahead, next. Future."

"Oh, why can't it be like this all the time?"

"Because you have to work," Fitzie said, "you have to pay bills and rent and make the money it takes to go someplace like this so it can be like this."

"I suppose so. 'Life *isn't* a fountain?' "

They laughed weakly.

"Still," she said, "it seems dumb. I mean, when you're back doing all that, working, *living* I guess, it seems to go and go in some kind of *unawareness*. Like we don't know

111

what we're doing. It's been better, lately. Since we moved to Brooklyn and you went with Montague—it's not that. I mean it's not an unhappiness, it's vaguer than that."

"Then the thing for us to do is get rid of the unawareness, huh?"

"Easy to say."

"Yeah," It was gone. For a while, he was getting it, glimpsing what she meant, realizing that *was* the trouble, the gnawing there even when things were going well, the suspicion that there was something else he ought to be digging out and considering. Some elusive alternative. *Unawareness*, she said. Close. Come on: sounds like? No. Mercurial, it had run. Why couldn't he push her, ask her to help? Because he was ashamed of his being maddeningly able to go along ignoring it. He knew he had a valve inside him somewhere, run by the nun in his ear most likely, that automatically shut off bothersome and unpleasant thoughts. But if something kept rapping at the window as persistently as this, maybe it wasn't merely some distraction, some temptation to be resisted; maybe it was the truth. And maybe, then, what he did wasn't discipline or single-mindedness at all, maybe it was *unawareness*. But goddamn. Why wouldn't it hold still, yell louder? In the sunlit silence there, hearing only Janice's feet scraping softly against the sheets, he thought, *Poor Janice. She thinks I'm the one who knows things.* So he couldn't ask her to go after it, get it and give it to him. Ego wouldn't let him; but also he knew she wouldn't be able to do it, wouldn't have the confidence, would think he was kidding her. *But she is so much closer to it than I am.* She had managed to get one thing across to him anyway: it wasn't nothing out there; there was, sure as anything, *something*.

Crack rattle! Crack, rattle! Janice went taut. Fitzie opened his eyes and shot them at the door. The black shadow knocked again. "Mr. Fitzpatrick?" it said. "Telephone message."

"My God, the kids," Janice gasped.

"Slip it under, can you?" Fitzie called and jumped to the cold floor to pick up the slip of yellow paper.

"What?"

Fitzie chuckled. " 'Plans snafu. Gone back to city. Explain Monday, Montague.' "

"Oh, thank God. That was scary."

"Yeah," he laughed.

Janice lay back. "You getting back in here or not?"

When they were getting into their bathing suits, Janice said, "I wonder what happened to Montague? That's too bad."

"Yeah, he would have been fun. But your heart's not broken is it? Mine's not. I'm getting to like you."

"Mm. I wonder if he ever intended to come."

"Big Daddy plays marriage counselor? Gets us off alone?"

"Well, that *is* possible. It's not what I was thinking, though."

"Oh. The Hermitcrab? Yeah, that could be. You think he cares that much what we think?"

"I hope he does," Janice said.

"Me too."

"This would be his way of telling us."

"Assuming he is, of course," Fitzie grinned at her.

"I was doing that, wasn't I."

"Well, who knows. Who cares. Come on, let's go hit the beach. It doesn't matter one way or the other, that's what I hope he knows."

"Yeah."

For the rest of that afternoon and evening they played the same album side as the day before, except they stayed long in the sun and not so long dancing in the Hermitcrab. The sound didn't sour any. Saturday they slept late again. In the afternoon they took a beach taxi along the surf edge for the skidding, chortling half-hour or so to Ocean Beach, to get a bigger look at Fire Island. The kid driver said, "I can get you down there, but I can't come back for you till like eight tonight, on account of the tide's on its way in and'll cut me off." They said that would be all right, figuring there would be enough to do there, and took the number to call that night. At Ocean Beach, they dropped to the sand out of the roller-coaster car and walked through the blankets of people to the dunes. Families. Two-and-three-kid families, Daddy milk-white and bellied reading the *Daily News* in his green plastic, silver aluminum chair, Mama in curlers sitting large-crotched near the umbrella yelling to Jimmy and the others did they want their Yoo-Hoo now and put that space gun down it doesn't belong to you. When they reached the top of the dunes there were roofs for as far as they could see, all the same one-story height and so close they looked connected. They went down the stairs to the wide concrete walk that ran away from the beach. "Christ, it's like Revere Beach," Fitzie muttered.

"No, it's Queens," Janice said.

"Right. Queens by the sea."

They had come to the bay side of Ocean Beach. "Good place for a shopping center," he said.

"What else is it?" And it was, only done in Seaside Village style. Packs of teen-agers hung bored and surly outside a community hall. A crowded, busy place. Sunglassed and sportshirted people, with baby strollers and shopping pull-carts, bustled in and out of stationery-souvenir shops, supermarkets, drugstores, sportswear stores with toy alcoves and five revolving paperback book stands. "Must be terrific in August," Janice grumbled.

"Hey, great idea. Let's rent a place for the summer, it's only a couple of grand. You can move out with the kids, meet a lot of swell *folks,* families like ourselves, and I'll come out weekends, 'kay?"

"Listen, what are we going to do? We can't stay here until eight tonight."

"We can't stay here another two minutes. We're going to walk back. A thousand miles."

"Okay. Let's see how far we can get. It'll be a good way to get a look at some more of it."

They found the concrete walk that left Ocean Beach, following the bay. Wood planks began at Seaview, wood floating in sand. They passed into Ocean Bay Park. More open, the salt winds from the bay mussed them up into better humor. They walked, stepping apart a few times to let a cyclist pedal through. Then they came to the high, steel Cyclone Fence with the gate in it at the walkway, bearing the sign PRIVATE PROPERTY. "Point O'Woods," Fitzie said. "Must be Irish." The gate stood open, but they stopped before it. Within, it was all trees, but not like the sea-creatures at the Pines; it seemed that someone had uprooted all the tidy landscaping from some suburban Scarsdale or Darien and filled this one part of Fire Island with the clipped firs and pines and groomed bushes. The houses were old, high, and big, two and three stories with gables and shutters and attics and sweeping, screened porches. "Don't move," Janice said. "There's an electric eye."

"Okay," he said. "We can either go in and get shot or go have vodka and bitter lemon in that place out there."

"Oh. I didn't see that. Great."

A long wooden building ran out into the bay like a pier.

They walked the length of it and went into the restaurant end. Inside, a vast basketball court with polished floors. Young girls perched on high stools along the bar drinking and staring out across the tables to the bay. Fitzie and Janice took a window table and sat in the yellow heat. There were another twenty or so girls, in flocks of two or four, at the tables, helping the stool girls watch the water. "I've died and gone to heaven, right?"

"I can't believe it," she said, "all the men at the Pines and all them here."

"All that poontang going to waste!"

"This isn't fair, you're winning both ways." A waiter brought them their drinks. "Getting much?" Fitzie asked him.

Embarrassed in front of Janice, the kid couldn't answer.

Janice said, "I mean, they don't look the same as the men at the Pines, you know? I mean that would balance it, anyway, if they were all dikes."

"That they're not."

"Well, they're not all *that* great, but all them here and all the men by themselves at the Pines!"

"Ah, I'm sure the boys are on their way. Looks like a big pickup joint."

"Then where are they?"

"Christ, how do I know? It's a freak weekend, everybody decided to skip it or something."

"There's nothing more pathetic than groups of girls alone."

Fitzie spotted the pool table in the dark beyond the bar. "Ah! Come on and I'll complete your education." He put a quarter into the slot and released the balls, racked them up, then picked two cue sticks from the wall. "You ever play?"

"Just that time I did my psychiatric at Worcester State, with the patients. But it was just fooling around."

He showed her how.

"The cue is the white," she said.

"Right."

"If you lose you'll cry, won't you?"

"I won't lose, baby. You want to play for something," he waggled one eyebrow, "interesting?"

"That's no fair," she said, "I'll lose that anyway."

"Mmm."

"No, we'll play for who drives the sitter to the Bronx when we get back tomorrow."

They played. Janice began getting it, he started to get it

115

back. They both kept checking the scene back on the other side of the bar. The yellow there was dimming as the sun drifted away.

"It *is* weird," he said.

"It's sick."

"Like Army wives waiting for the troop ships to come in."

"They should have it so good."

He laughed as she missed the cue ball. "Yeah," he smiled, bending to go for the Eight. She pushed the end of his stick behind him. "Bitch," he whispered.

"I guess you have to feel sorry for them."

"Ah, there's probably all kinds of guys out here, gone fishing for the day or something."

"They probably came out all excited, too. Bought new clothes, made reservations."

"Just to get laid? Come on, we going to shoot pool or bullshit?"

"To find a *man*," she said. They played five games, then walked back and had dinner with their reflections in the window.

She let her hand fall over his on the table. "I like you, you know that? I just thought I'd tell you."

"That's nice. That's good to know."

"Let's go back," she said.

"Hey, it's after eight. Let me go call."

The voice said to wait down on the sea beach at Ocean Bay Park. "Be about twenty minutes."

The air by the clomping night surf had no chill in it. They stood and waited for the lights they sought. When they walked their heels sent back blue sparks. "Ooo, do that again," Janice said.

"Phosphorous in the sand."

"Wild."

"Getting eerie, wish he'd come."

"Adam and Eve and Pinch Me."

"How's old Pinch Me?"

"Nice and warm."

"Where is that bastard? He said he was leaving then."

They waited for another fifteen minutes.

"Listen," Fitzie said, "this is dumb. Let's start walking and we'll hail him down when he comes."

"What the hell."

They began walking along the beach, kicking up sparks in the night. Still no lights. Then: "Christ," Fitzie muttered, "we're running out of beach. That's water up there." He stopped them, looking ahead. The sand was

116

disappearing. The dunes, about five feet high where they were rose ahead in an upward push into black sky. "Come on, we'll take the high road." They walked the top of the rising sand cliff. Struggling over much wind-crushed red snow fencing, they passed about nine Sherlock Holmes houses, dark and empty-looking. Janice said, "This is getting scary."

They stumbled on. "Wouldn't the kids love this," he said once.

"I can't talk," her voice said, "I'm afraid I'm going to step off into the ocean."

"We're too far to go back." The straight, flat thing he had been watching began to come out of the dark, a walkway across the dunes. He pulled her up after him. They looked down the steep stairs to the whipping, dark water. "That's what you call your high tide," Fitzie said. He felt panicked now, too: the dunes were ending a little further along, quitting halfway up in the black sky. A small bell tingled from somewhere down in the woods and frightened them. It tingled again. "Great. Now we're going to be arrested," he whispered.

"Thank God."

He lit a match. Sure enough, a small figure came toward them, a young girl of about fifteen. "Oh!" she let out, startled, spun and started to squirrel away.

"Miss? Could you help us?" Janice called and the girl turned back. "Are you guests? This is private property, you know," she said, scared and frosty. Also *caught*, Fitzie knew, looking for her boy friend in the night. So she won't be too snotty, won't go calling Daddy too fast. Janice explained their predicament. Still cool but visibly relieved, the kid directed them to the public phone "at the post office Simply go left at the second streetlamp and walk straight. I'm sure it's open all night."

"It better be open," Fitzie side-talked as she bicycled away into the dark, "or I'll rape you. And so will my wife."

They walked close together through the thickest, darkest part of Point O'Woods, and came to the post office, in darkness except for a small room open to the side with two telephone booths in it. Four directories were chained to the wall and lying open on a shelf. On the wall the words FUCK YOU and PRICK and EAT ME and a heart were scrawled in vivid orange lipstick. "Hurry, or we'll get blamed for it," Janice said and went out to wait in the dark.

Fitzie made the call and came out. "Well?" she said,

"Oh, you know. First he had a flat. Then he heard the tides were óff, said he's been waiting for me to call back."

"I'll bet. Well, is he coming *now*?"

"Well, he's going to come as far as he can and wait for us."

"We have to walk?"

"Yeah, he says we can make it okay."

They walked back and went down the staircase that dropped into the sea. When the water receded, they jumped, turned and ran back to the dune wall. The waves lunged through the air after them. They hugged the dune wall, and ran-froze-ran through the lunging until they didn't have to stop anymore. They slowed to a fast walk and covered fifteen minutes of wider beach beyond the reach of the clawing ocean. Finally, the taxi eyes peeked up over the round earth ahead of them. Fitzie yelled, and tugged Janice forward into a run.

"Man, look at that!" The water was between them and the fierce double beams now and its huge soaring through the lights dazzled Fitzie. It was inevitable. And irresistible. Fitzie caught her. "Oh, Christ," she said.

He laughed. "You're about to get your uh-uh wet yet. Want me to carry you?"

"No," she said. "Let's go and get it over with."

"Thatta babe, come on, it'll be great. Look at those waves in the light!"

Janice began to laugh, but Fitzie had started to run so couldn't ask her why. It hit them no higher than the hips. They waded through, holding hands. Janice kept laughing, interrupted only by a shriek each time the waves struck. They finally broke away from the heavy, lapping water and ran up to the chugging taxi. The kid inside, all teeth, pushed open the side door. "You really got it, didn't you!" They crawled into the back seat, soaking it, gasping, "Oh, God. Oh, Jesus." The kid backed the jeep around, then ground forward into his own ruts, back toward the Pines. His breath back, Fitzie asked her, "Now what the hell are you still laughing about?"

"You. We're *drowning* and you tell me how great the waves look in the lights."

"Well, they did."

"If you don't mind my saying," the driver yelled back to them, "you looked terrific coming through those waves in the lights. Like an escape from Russia or something."

"Yeah, well, if you don't mind, I'm so pissed off at you I'm not going to talk to you, okay? And I *know* you're a different guy."

The kid laughed. "Okay."

They slogged straight through the crowds in the Hermitcrab to stand next to the fire. Janice drank a double bullshot. Fitzie had a boilermaker.

Sunday, they woke to the tick-tick of rain against the glass door, and rolled over until one. They ate bacon and eggs inside the Hermitcrab full of people in Windbreakers and ponchos, waiting with their luggage for the ferry. They were back in Brooklyn by six. Although he had won at pool, Fitzie drove the sitter to the Bronx. When he got back, instead of reading the usual Seuss to the children, he told them of his and Janice's Great Adventure in the Sea at Night, making only one lie, that he had carried their scared mama through the waves. The kids razzed her for it and her laughing turned into that giggle and Fitzie knew what she was remembering.

Four

"I'M GLAD, I really am," Montague said very straight that Monday morning when Fitzie said how much they had liked Fire Island Pines. Fitzie felt, and sensed that Montague also felt, that he had actually joined them there as planned, had shared the weekend with them, had experienced with them—not their private, recaptured loving, but their first clear glimpse of what different conditions of living were possible: the estranged Pines Cool, which they saw that they could live with because it seemed to make room for them without terms; and the respectable Ocean Beach, or the more respectable Point O'Woods, which they saw that, for the moment, they couldn't live with because the one seemed to have no room worth taking, while the other seemed not only out of reach but too cloistered for their blood. They did share that weekend with Montague, as they shared so many hours and evenings with him that summer, and it brought them all closer together. Toto asked for night work that first evening. Both Montague and Fitzie said no, and Fitzie brought Montague home for supper. At the door, Janice was visibly delighted to see Fitzie home, to hear Montague's flattery for her tan, to be getting an unexpected, extra night of not being alone, before their normal timetable resumed. The next night it did resume. Fitzie said yes to Toto and worked until near midnight and it was fine. Weeks passed. Fletcher would call. Johnny would drop out of sight. Janice's womb filled. When Fitzie came home, late or early, he came open not closed, *up* with recorder tootings, with rantings against Toto and Nemo and the Top of the Sixes, but with roman candle excitement over Montague's heroics and his own growing portfolio of "fantastic" and "fabulous"—though unshown or unsold —new work. They went out for dinner, had people in. Riis Park with Buck and Betsy for weekends, down the fire escape for gin in the garden during the week.

When the Tank in Powell's back in Boston shut down at summer's end, it was done smoothly and gradually.

120

First a slowing down, then a cutoff of one side, cleaning all parts; finally, the closing down of the last side, the dismantling, draining and cleaning. Neat. Fitzie's personal Tank also shut down at the end of that summer, but not neatly at all. With valves bursting, gears stripping, a snarling confusion of movement in all directions. In fact, it wasn't at all clear for a while that it was indeed blowing apart. Seemingly good things overlapping seemingly bad things. In late August Toto fired Fletcher, over Montague's protests, for the phone calls, the recorder concerts, the once-too-often no to night work, the thin trickle of output. The others ignited like a book of matches and flared for a week. Then Toto told Johnny LePage he was through, too. WFB had no two-week notice policy. It was Get Out. Again Montague played Mr. Smith in Washington. Again it was no use. Toto was getting Johnny for the disappearances. What they all knew, what was truly sending jolts of despair through them was that Toto was really getting Montague. It was Montague's power, and hence their safety, their free life, that was being taken away. Montague may have been able to make a comeback, may have been able to prevent what was left of his patrol from being called back to garrison duty, if little Athenia Tree hadn't quit. But she did, the day after Fletcher got it. She had to. They understood. She was good, they were all good, so she got a job right away at another agency; but they all knew that she simply couldn't live around that empty desk and still phone as if Fletcher had never been there. Montague was nice to her. "Well, really!" he said, "we couldn't stand the sound of *one* recorder all day." Athenia laughed, grateful, and Fitzie, Anthony and Montague laughed, too, but fake as television laugh tracks: the three of them had been given raises that week.

"The bastards!" Fitzie stormed guiltily the first morning it was just the three of them. "What are we supposed to do? Christ, it's *Here, divide their money among you.*"

"I think I see me ship looming on the horizon," Anthony said softly through his beard.

"No," Montague said, "not yet." They were at a table in the Dogwood Room for lunch. Fitzie and Anthony were drinking martinis and eating hot corn bread morosely. Montague sat cool, elegant and straight, smoking Fitzie's Pall Malls and Anthony's Gauloises—the only sign he was ruffled.

"Well, if I have to go to work, it can't be for a bleeding asylum like this," Anthony said.

"No. I don't mean we won't all go. We will. That's quite clear now," Montague said calmly. "But I do think we shouldn't be childish about it. The least we can do is benefit from all this. There are the three of us, after all. And Toto has agreed we can keep all the same accounts without taking in any of his cretins. I mean, what *can't* we take?"

"*The Lost Patrol*, huh?" Fitzie said. "Well, I'm not being McLaglen. Just shove my saber into my grave, will you?"

"Where *are* you, Fitzie?" Anthony asked.

Fitzie shrank from the direct question. He couldn't answer yet. He needed more time to think it out, it had all happened so fast. Montague had just said it was clear that they all had to go. It hadn't been that clear to Fitzie. On one level, he had felt sure it was going to turn out fine and was waiting for Montague to tell them his plan for making things as they had been. But on another level a nagging voice had been clucking, "See? I told you so. It couldn't last. Who do you think you are? Now will you come in and get to work?" And this voice had an outside extension, a tangible mouthpiece. The Joy lady. She had been calling him, had, in fact, called him once a month ever since he had gone to WFB. Each time he had said, *No, thanks just the same, but I'm very happy*. Now, he wasn't sure. The voice was so persistent that maybe it had to be right. Maybe he had been merely playing hooky all this time. In a way it would be a relief to admit he was Henry Aldrich and say *Coming, Mother*, once and for all. To Anthony now he just muttered, "I don't know, buddy, I'm too depressed to even think about it."

"Now, listen, kids," Montague said with forced lightness, "do you realize what we're doing? We are letting them get to us. If they thought they could actually *depress* us, there'd never be an end to it! No. We must mark time. We must go on as if nothing whatsoever has happened. In the meantime, I shall go and become creative director of some small or middle-sized place, bringing the two of you with me, and there will be no Toto, no Nemo. Just us!"

The half of him that wanted it let Fitzie believe and take hope. "And what we do will run for a change," he said.

"Yes!" Montague, fed, added. "Because *we* will set the policies."

But Anthony didn't chip in. "Ah, mates," he sighed, "I've heard that tale before. Not that you maybe can't do it, Monty, but usually the only time it works is when you open your own shop. Else, there's always a Nemo in the

122

woodwork somewhere." And to this, of course, Fitzie's other half, his older, Henry-half whined an immediate *He's right. That's true. Forget it, you're dreaming. Grow up!*

They went back to work. For almost two months. In these same weeks, things happened to Fitzie that took his mind off the daily question mark of work. Two major things almost concurrently: first the move, then the baby. The move was their fourth, counting the return from Germany, in little more than two years. Except it was really only a half-move, because it was within the same building in Brooklyn. Buck and Betsy came up one night and offered Fitzie and Janice their garden apartment: they were leaving. "Betsy!" Janice yelped. "You can't do this to me."

Buck and Betsy acted pleased and excited, but somehow self-conscious and embarrassed as well. "Oh, it won't be that far," Betsy said. "And I've really had the slum-dwelling bit, to tell you the truth. Wait'll you're here as long as we've been. And, you know. The kids are getting up pretty near to schooltime, and where the hell do you send them. Private school in the Heights for a zillion bucks a year? I mean you guys have the parochial school, but we can't send ours into that hellhole of a public school, they'll get knifed! Anyway, we're just not city folk to begin with." Her soliloquy went on, and it sounded so tight that Fitzie knew they were listening to a speech worked over and honed for a long time between themselves. To Buck, chugalugging his Ballantine from the cans quietly, he said, "Croton, huh? You going to be near Cheever?"

"Huh, no, I don't think so."

"It's pretty nice, though? Old?"

"Oh, yeah, like over a hundred. Two acres. It's an old farmhouse, wait till you see it."

"I don't know. Can you see the Statue of Liberty from the roof?"

Buck laughed. "No. No more boat horns in the night, goddamn it."

"I didn't even know you were looking!" Janice said. "You sneaks."

"We weren't really," Betsy said, low, played out. "In fact you might say we didn't. We never really went house hunting. This was the first place we saw."

"Phew," Fitzie whistled, "brave people."

"Oh, but it's *gorgeous*," Betsy answered. "There's a fireplace in every bedroom, and one in the living room you can *walk* into! I mean you couldn't build a house like

123

it now for a hundred thousand. It's a steal, really. Buck's mother found it, wouldn't you know. Heard about it all the way upstate somehow."

"They're giving us the down payment," Buck admitted.

"Fantastic," Fitzie covered it. "You lucky bastards, that's really great."

"But what are we going to do without you?" Janice pleaded.

"You've got wheels," Buck said, "we've got wheels. Come up every weekend."

"And bring our sickles," Fitzie laughed.

"Yes, it isn't the ends of the earth," Betsy said. "You don't think we'll let you get away, do you?"

"Still, it won't ever be like this again, right in the same house," Janice said.

There was nothing to do but accept it. Buck and Betsy moved out and Fitzie and Janice moved down.

Betsy had left the apartment Ajaxed and gleaming, so their only chore was sliding their furniture out of one pattern into another, gleefully, until the right combination happened. For the first time they were in a place that excited them. It didn't cover them with that air of transience they had come to like but neither did it make demands. They could just wake up there and move around there and live there, free to stay, free to leave, very much at ease in the meantime. In a week it seemed they had lived there always.

While they lived on the top floor, they had come awake each morning to a certain sound. The Baby Ben rang and the kids squawked but they awoke to neither, rather to the gentle rumble, outside, in the air of the back yards, the smooth humming of many men milling close together—the longshoremen who gathered every morning early on the street in front of a low, one-story concrete building on the cross street below, to get their day's work orders. *On the Waterfront* men, the same scene without the malice or the disappointment: this was the sixties so all of these men got work each morning except when they were out on strike. The sound was the mixing, the blending, the stirring together of sleep-thick talk, dry-mouthed laughter, workshoes from Sears scuffing gutter trash, all over the steady roll of names and numbers. Now, sleeping beneath the window that opened to their new garden, they were reached by the underbelly of that sound overhead, making

124

it seem farther away; but they woke to it still. Fitzie's eyes opened to it that morning, a week after they had moved down.

Something was different.

Not the sound's change; he had got used to its new pitch after two mornings.

Not the window. The screen stretched unripped.

It was Janice. Her eyes were already opened, before his—that was different. He turned his head on the pillow to see if he was right. She was looking at the wall, her hands up on the hill of her stomach. "Hey," he said.

"This is it, kid," she smiled.

"Since?"

"About five."

Bingo. He was legs through the tucked sheets and blankets, onto the icy linoleum-on-cement floor. "You call Moscarella?" he asked, pulling a shirt on.

"Yes, he'll be there. Take the kids upstairs now."

"How far apart?"

"Close. It's time. Go ahead. I'll get dressed."

The hospital was on the very next block behind them. Walking was the fastest way. Holding her arm with one hand and her suitcase in the other, Fitzie walked Janice down their sidewalk, past the Spanish whorehouse, and around the corner, stopping every ten or fifteen steps to let her turn into a half-knot, then untie. Around the corner and blam, right into their fifty-voice alarm clock. "One side, Mac, lady with a baby. Scuse me, coming through." A face would begin to laugh, or scowl, then see it was true and back away and help. "Good luck, girlie! Hey, make way there. Baby comin'! Below! Hey, Angelo, move your ass, will ya?" Janice was laughing, but it made her knots come faster so she bit it off. Cold and shaking, Fitzie could only keep saying, "We're there now. We made it. Here we are," over and over to her as they poked along, praying it was true. Going uphill on the next street, the high hospital seemed to take a step away every time they took one toward it. Finally it stopped and they gained on it, then were inside, then on the elevator, then Fitzie was by himself with her coat and her suitcase in the waiting room. Immediately a nurse came and took them, too.

Then another nurse came and led him to a desk and he showed his Blue Cross and Blue Shield cards and answered her questions, having to sit down and strain into his hands to recall the birth dates of his daughter and son. Back in the waiting room, he stood at the window smoking and staring down at his own bedroom window across the way and down. He tried to see upstairs into the first floor to catch a look, maybe, at his girl or boy in there, but he couldn't. All their blinds were drawn. Weird, to be up inside a high building looking out at where he lived, as if he himself might come through that door down there to sit on that white iron lawn chair or sweep the soot from the brick patio. If Fitzie had appeared then way down in the garden there, he wouldn't have been surprised. It all seemed so bizarre. And suddenly, knowing that his own girl and boy *were*, right now, inside those upper windows behind those beige venetian blinds, hit him hard: he had two children. A girl named Loretta and a boy named Joey. Holy God. It was true. It had to be true because he could feel the coldness of the metal lock in the middle of the window he was looking through. *Hey guys!* he yelled inside his head. *It's me! I'm up here. It's okay. I'll see ya later.*

The poor little bastards. Did they have any idea that he was only now becoming aware that they *were*? After what, five years, six? Four and two? Five and three? What did he tell the nurse? He couldn't remember. Ah, bull. I've known they were there, I've been very good to them. Very good *with* them, people have said that. Christ, I don't remember when *you* two were born? Like hell. Both at Bad Cannstatt. Both at night. Seven dollars and fifty cents and five dollars and fifty cents, respectively, and extra day in with the first, the girl, Loretta, the tiny redhead. Born in the middle of an alert, damn right, lights out, sirens wailing, kraut interns running down the halls with stretchers, me pulling down long black shades for the fat old nurse-major, "Yes, ma'am!" And old Joey, hair yellow as lemon, fat and happy from day one, springing Janice a day early, saving me two bucks. Nothing alike, a redhead and a blond, nothing like me or Janice, leaving me open to all the jokes. Wish this one was eight bucks; man, the Army was the place to have babies. Yeah, and stitches that infect, too, you pricks. Mother of God, I'm having another baby! No. No? Then what the hell am I doing up here at this goddamn window? Fitzie looked at his watch. It had been only fifteen minutes since they had come through the street door. He turned and saw where he was. A small room, two leather sofas, old, two stuffed easy chairs, a coffee table with its glass cracked, five floor ashtrays, their bowls cleaned. No cute signs. No cartoons of pacing, smoking daddies. Just one bleached Currier and Ives print in a frame and a stack of *Lifes* and *Looks*.

126

Thank God. Must be a good, no-fooling-around place. He went back to the window. The blinds were still down and closed, still hiding Loretta and Joey from him.

Oh, Janice, baby, do it, don't hurt, be all right.

In six minutes, twenty-one total, Millie—or the little girl they later named Mildred—was squeaking at the doorway behind him, her mouse sounds sneaking out the crevasses of the white blanket she was wrapped in, tucked into the arm of the grinning young Puerto Rican nurse. Beside her, Doctor Moscarella looking bored. "Here you go, Mister Fitzpatrick, a nice girl, just under six pounds."

Fitzie went to the bundle. The nurse opened a hole at the top. "Look at that," Fitzie said. Her face was the size of an apple, with a mouth open and moving around in all directions. They hadn't got all the red cleaned off her skin, but it was the black that slayed Fitzie. Her eyes were black, under black eyebrows, under the blackest beanie of hair imaginable. "I'll be damned." He couldn't hold it, his laugh came right out into her squeaking. "She's beautiful. Thank you. How's my wife?"

"Fine. She was terrific," the doctor came alive, "she's still out for a while, but just fine. You tell her, though, that was too close. She was too smart aleck."

Fitzie laughed, proud, elated.

"I'm too old for that kinda stuff," Moscarella winked.

Fitzie went in by her bed, leaned on the side gate and looked at her pale, closed face. She murmured and opened her eyes once, but she was still someplace else. His laugh, on its own, kept coming out. He couldn't feel it. He could only feel that delicious blaze down inside him, looking down at the sleeping Janice. He left and took another look at the black-haired apple before walking back to the house. All the longshoremen were gone. The street was still and empty. He put their suitcases into the Opel's trunk at the curb, then retrieved Loretta and Joey. In the car he told them and got them all excited. He bought them lunch at La Guardia, then flew with them on the Eastern shuttle to Logan, taking a taxi to Janice's parents' house. All the time he kept feeling an urge to squeeze them and mug them up, but held it back until he said goodbye to them. They were confused enough without that. He was back in New York and at the hospital with flowers and candy and magazines before visiting hours started. Janice was propped up waiting for him in her new nightie, hair brushed and face made up, looking fifteen years old. When they embraced he whispered, "Thank

127

you," into her hair. Then, sitting on the bed, opening the Candy Cupboards, he grinned and said, "How's baldie?"

She flushed pink and laughed, "I think I'll have to stay off the motorcycle for a while."

"All right, who's the guy this time? Buck? The roach man?"

"Oh, my God, did you ever see such black hair?"

Having fetched Loretta and Joey from Boston as swiftly as he had dropped them, Fitzie took a week off when Janice was released and stayed home with them in their new apartment with their new child. Millie. The Black Sparrow. The Brooklyn Baby. For that week, she let him put his job, his *career* anguish out of his mind. Her pinpoint reality woke him to the reality of the older ones; it was as if he had brought three home from the hospital, had overnight become the father of three, and now had to figure what he was going to do with all of them. For them. It didn't make him feel older. It made him feel younger, tougher, more pressed to go grab his piece, stake out his claim.

The charge he had got from Millie's birth jazzing through his arteries, he took the D train back to Manhattan with a knife between his teeth. He threw down his shot of Franny Prayer for extra push and tore into WFB that week kidney-punching both Toto and Montague. To Toto: he was sick of the bullshit, they *had* to start getting his stuff through and they weren't getting any more eye-wash, make-work out of him. If he had to do this it might as well be good, and he was fed up with putting his good ideas into his portfolio and seeing the dreck running in the papers and on the television. Not only that. To Montague: they *had* to give him more money, idiots all over town were taking down more than he was.

"Fitzie, they just gave you two thousand," Montague said, leery.

"Balls. Blood money, and not enough anyway."

"Why push it now, though? Let's concentrate on getting out of here."

"Ahh!" he spat—the first show of his doubt, even to himself, of Montague's plan. He backed away from it quickly, into anger. "Because I want it now, that's why," he said and walked out.

The Joy lady called that Thursday and he heard himself saying, "Your timing's right this time, sweetie. Yeah, I can talk." He said no to Toto Friday because his interview at F&F was for six o'clock. He pushed them to sixteen and when they offered it he said he had to think about it.

"I don't know, Fitzie," Janice said. "It sounds so, I don't know, *cutthroat*."

"Why? To hold them up? Shit. God helps those, you know. Haven't I been working to midnight for nothing? *Welders* get time and a half." He couldn't stop. He plunked the offer onto Toto's basket full of pills and Camels. In a day, Toto came back with fourteen. "That's really the best we can do now, Fitz. Hang in, will you? If we land this new account we're pitching, there'll be more loose bucks around." And he might have hung in. He might have snapped out of it then, taken the fourteen and thrown his dice with Montague and the way of life, the freedom-to-live that it meant, if Toto had not added, "Anyhow, kiddo, you split now and you owe us money."

"What does that mean?"

"You know. But never mind, anyway. You're too much of a stickball player to go for the F and F crap."

"Come on, Davy, what do you mean?" Fitzie demanded because then he did know. He remembered the letter.

Sure enough. Turning British, Toto arched his eyebrows and lisped softly, "Very well, there is the little matter of the fee we paid for you. And if you care to recall, there is a letter on file in which you promise to repay us should you take your leave short of one full year. Some eight or nine hundred dollars, if my memory serves me correctly."

"You can't hold me to that," Fitzie said. "You yourself just had to pay it on a descending scale. If I quit after six months, you wouldn't have been out zilch."

"Well. Apparently you have learned something this year. Perhaps that itself is worth some money. Unfortunately, the letter alters matters considerably. Should I send for a copy of it? You were a farmer to sign it, of course, but I'm sure you know that now, too. The fact remains that you did sign it."

It gave Fitzie the red cape he needed. Already kicking up dust and stomping his hoofs under cover of his new-father-fighter drunkenness, he now had a target outside himself to zero in on, an excuse to charge. He told Toto he would have to think about it. Then he called the Joy lady and accepted the F&F offer. He gave Toto two weeks' notice, and knowing this was more than he would have received from them increased his sense of righteousness. When confronted with the fee, he simply stated that he would not pay because he didn't believe that he owed

129

it, letter or no letter. For two weeks, Toto not only never asked Fitzie to stay late, he ignored him entirely. Janice was confused and said nothing. Anthony resigned; he had been right and Fitzie's move only proved it. Montague worried. It didn't reach inside to their friendship, but Fitzie knew Montague thought his move shortsighted and probably harmful; more than that, he had taken it as a desertion, a breach of loyalty if not promise. The worst part was, Fitzie sensed that he had unwittingly punctured Montague's own confidence. No hope or optimism leaked out, but a weariness did seep in. But Fitzie saw this only vaguely. For one brief moment in the Friday morning of his last day, it seemed that he had lost.

When he stepped out of the elevator at nine o'clock, the receptionist said that Toto was waiting to see him. Frigidly British, Toto asked him if he had decided to pay the fee, adding that they were now prepared to let him do it in installments, so much a month, in consideration of his new child and so forth. When Fitzie said no, Toto calmly informed him that they had no other recourse, then, but to withhold the two weeks' salary owed him, and sue him for the remainder. Electrocuted, Fitzie asked once again for some time to think about it. Toto gave him until noon, saying he would be free to leave anytime after that, one way or another. Fitzie walked straight back to the elevators and went down one floor to payroll. It he had learned anything from the Army, he had learned the wisdom of befriending the powerful. The mess sergeant, the supply sergeant, the company clerk, the motor pool mechanic. Their counterparts in the civilian world included the Golden Eagle, the person who distributed the paychecks. At WFB, this was a spinster in her late thirties whose legs draped flesh, who stared silently out at the world through trifocals. Fitzie had never fawned over her, any more than he had over the librarian, the head of the mailroom or the girl who pushed the Schrafft's wagon. He had simply spoken to her, twice a month, or when he might pass her in a hall. *How are ya? How's it going? Nice day, huh? Oh, got a cold?* This day, he went straight into her lair, startling her slightly as she sat arranging envelopes in empty typing paper boxes. "Hi. Thought I'd save you a trip. I'm also going to be away for the rest of the day, so I'd like to get it a little early, if that's no trouble."

"Oh! Mister Fitzpatrick! Surely. Let me see now . . ."

He didn't know it would be there. Any thought at all would have made him doubt it too much to try. But he hadn't thought. He had gone directly to it as the first obvious possibility. It was there. She had it, unflagged, and she fluttered it up to him. "Here we are. There. Have a nice weekend if I don't see you," she smiled. "You too," Fitzie said and left, feeling guilty for what she was now doomed to endure when her phone rang. Back in the elevator, he plummeted nonstop to the ground floor and entered the bank right there off the lobby. He cashed the check, unnecessarily but satisfyingly, into nothing larger than singles and fives—a wad! Then, from a phone booth in the same lobby he called upstairs to Anthony, who four minutes later stepped out of the elevator carrying Fitzie's few personal belongings: his London Fog, his five-dollar Scripto, the German leather beer bag he used as a briefcase. When Fitzie told him, Anthony spluttered "Marvelous!" down the front of his beard, then grew very nervous and pushed Fitzie out of the building. They shook hands. Anthony said, "Cheerio, mate. Keep an eye out for a spot for me up there if you like it. Call me when you're settled." They were on the street. Fitzie said he would, yanked Anthony's beard and crossed Madison to drop out of sight down the hole to an F train that would connect to a D, which would take him home to Brooklyn and safety. All the way his heart kept pounding with a mixture of fear and hilarity. Hustling along Clinton Street in the harbor air, he let out a loud laugh that made an old woman sweeping her stoop stop and smile after him. He hurried to get home. This would tickle Janice and color the whole move nice and bright. He would call Montague at home tonight.

It was something they didn't call Boston about. Boston could take the going from six thousand to sixteen so quickly, all right. They'd flip over that and drop it at wakes and in barrooms. *Well. Janice's John is doing very well for himself, let me tell you.*

You call that dough? Listen, I got this brother-in-law, see. Naw. Janice. Fitzie Fitzpatrick from Tower Square, you know him? B.C.?

But the moving from one job to another and then to still another in less than three years. That was something else. No sticktoitiveness. Somebody see that on your record, it won't look good. The tortoise and the hare, don't forget. Johnny Come Lately, tsk, tsk. *I don't care, you can't learn anything unless you stay on it long enough!*

As if there were anything outside of surgery and bomb-making not learnable in a month.

As if there were a record.

So Fitzie went to F&F and was there before anybody at home got wind of it, dropped into one of Janice's letters, "Ever since Jack went to F&F, his new agency . . ." Then the rebound, "By the way, did you mention John is in a new job? We . . ." And so on, until it was an accepted fact, and since it had already happened and there hadn't been a depression or a hurricane, it must have been for the best. Ironic, because as risky and dubious as they knew it would seem to Boston, to Fitzie, and gradually to Janice, it was just the opposite. It seemed a return from insane to sane, from loose to tight, from sloppy to neat, from notorious to respectable. And it was a long time before they realized that it *was* a bad move, although hardly for any Boston reason.

From the beginning, Fitzie was sure it was going to work. This was it. F&F had everything that appealed to him. It was big-league, Blue Chip, polite, rich—and soft. Meringue begging for a hot knife. Just as the hippies and the kids and the Negroes were now beginning to raise hell with the country, shaking up all the old farts and making them doubt themselves, advertising as a business was getting noise from the furnace room that it couldn't shut off any longer. It had to change. In the first weeks he drank it all in, sitting in quietly at meetings, auditing conferences, all eyes and ears and no tongue with other writers, group heads, associate creative directors. He felt like an espionage agent, a spy, and he loved it. Leaving at five, as all the other gentlemen did, he would report his day's findings to Janice, passing on to her his estimates of trouble spots, weak spots, general terrain. "It does sound great," Janice said, "but isn't it sort of stuffy?"

"That's just it. At a good place, I'd be just another sharp guy. Here I can be *it*."

"I suppose. Anyhow, it looks like you won't have to be giving them your whole life."

"What do you mean by that?" he said seriously.

"What? Nothing, I didn't say anything." They were finishing some wine after dinner, at the counter in the kitchen alcove, half watching the gray turning to night outside in the garden. "Oh, if you're going to be like that I'm going to watch television."

"Maybe I ought to still be working until midnight!" he dropped in the air at her back, and felt ashamed before it was all out. She kept moving into the main room and

132

didn't answer. From the crib in the hallway outside their bedroom the baby started her ack-ack squeaking. Fitzie went and picked her up, hearing the television set come on. He thumped and hand-wide, hot back until Millie delivered the *erp* into the space between his neck and shirt collar. *Give her time,* he thought. *Too bad she couldn't come with me every day and see how easy and great it's going to be. That's okay. She'll get with it, she'll love it.*

As Millie's birth had pushed Fitzie to move, it also, that Thanksgiving, brought Janice's parents down from Boston to Brooklyn. The first entrance of Family into their life since their marriage. When they got up early Thanksgiving morning and saw the snow falling so wet and heavy out of no-sky, they worried. Janice's mother and father were in their late sixties. This was to be their first time in an airplane. Fitzie called La Guardia. Planes were landing. Janice called Boston. They were coming, they had called Logan Airport and everything was fine. Fitzie left early in the Opel to be sure he made La Guardia before the plane from Boston. He chugged to the Eastern terminal way at the end of the long boomerang and parked at a meter. Inside was assembly at the asylum. The floor was invisible beneath the grim, frustrated holiday people unable to get to Washington and Boston or waiting for people who hadn't arrived from those cities. The green letters above on the TV screen said that their plane was on schedule, due in fifteen minutes. He didn't believe it. Not with all these bodies thronged in failure. Not with that sticky snow falling outside through the fogged glass doors. He waited at the edge of the mob. The bar was closed. The green letters stuck to their lie five, ten minutes past the landing time. He called Janice to see if she had had word. No. He went back and stared at the green letters. *This is a recording, nothing can go wrong, go wrong, go*

They were up there someplace, up in the sky, in stormy space, like Mel Brooks's astronaut, *above buildings!* He could see her lips moving in the calm face and the fingers below desperately feeding the rosary beads into the lap like bullets into a fifty caliber; and the old man, cursing them, the damn tinkers, if they lived where they belonged we'd be into the Paddy's now and snug! Fitzie, the longer he stood, grew chillier with dread. Finally the voice through the address speakers from a million miles away. Their plane had been rerouted and would land at Kennedy in ten minutes. Jesus Christ. Buses would carry them back to La Guardia, those who wished. Oh, man. They'll die there. They won't know what to do. He called Janice, upsetting her. "Listen, they'll probably call. Tell them to stay put and I'll be there as fast as I can."

Into the outside row of honking, angry roaches filing slowly along through the increasing snow on the Grand Central Parkway, east. Thousands of exhaust pipes smoking, windshield wipers hacking relentlessly away. All of the people from La Guardia times ten, hence ten times more hostile, furious and forlorn, looked away, hiding their faces as Fitzie walked into the bigger Kennedy terminal. He looked and looked. He called Janice. "Hi, look, I'm afraid they're on their way back to La Guardia."

"They're here!" she said, and he looked at her through the mouthpiece. "They took a cab and got here about twenty minutes ago. Are you coming? Hurry, we're all starving."

It used to happen when they would visit Boston. He'd lose her. She'd revert and become theirs, not his, and he would shrink and sit reading in chairs feeling alone. The longer they were married and the more seldom they visited, the less keenly it would strike Fitzie, until it had stopped happening, until it was They coming, They staying, They going, with Their kiddoes, and Janice stayed his, even in her own, old house. Until this. He found the Opel shivering and afraid between an Impala and a Buick and got in, his toes cold and numb inside his soaking shoes. He wanted to be there quick before any of them started wondering what was keeping him, he wanted to beat the taxi's time, so he sped, yet glumly considered poking along slowly. Acting like a kid with his feelings hurt had a certain sweetness to it. *Damn.* The thing was, the one sure point he knew the old man gave him was *smart.* Only now he had blown it. Things were supposed to happen without a hitch, period. They should have stepped from the plane into his car. Anything less was dumb. And this had been everything less. *Up his,* Fitzie shrugged and passed a Corvette.

Janice's tiny mother turned from the oven, wiping her man's hands on the borrowed apron, smiling rosily at Fitzie as he came through the hall door. Fitzie smiled to see her in their closet of a kitchen acting as if she were in her own. "Well, you made it," he said down to her as they touched cheeks swiftly and awkwardly. The Mooneys were not kissers. "You look terrific, Mrs. Mooney," he said. "Too bad the trip got so messed up." She was Mrs. Mooney to him, the old man Mister, not Mom or Dad Mooney, not Kathleen or Pat or any other cute in-law title and Fitzie had always liked it this way.

134

"Oh, John, you poor lad," she sang, flustered, "making you go out in all this."

The old man came out of the front kids' bedroom carrying Millie. Janice, Loretta and Joey trailed behind. "Good God, you're here already?" the old man hailed, stomping forward with his huge hand stuck out ahead of him. Fitzie took it, saying, "Hey, there you are. Welcome to the big city."

"And what do you make of this one?" the old man boomed, jouncing the baby on his shoulder. "The image of Janice when a baby I was saying."

"Yeah, she's the hot one," Fitzie laughed. Janice's eyes told him everything was going fine. She took Millie from her father and said to Fitzie, "You must be freezing after being out in all this so long." Which translated to, the old man wants a drink.

"What do you say?" Fitzie said to him, "little taste of the mop?" and got the bottle of Jameson's from the teak highboy. Pouring it, he called in, "Sorry I missed you at Kennedy. I was afraid you took the bus."

"Oh, the bleeding fools," he bounced off the low ceiling. "If it was left to her you know we'd be in Baltimore or hell and gone. As if the Lord didn't put tongues in our heads to use."

Fitzie brought in the drinks. "Slainte," he said, raising his glass.

"Slainte," the old man winked. They drank the Irish, standing beneath the ceiling spotlights that illuminated the huge *Toledo* print Fitzie had bought at the Metropolitan. "Aah!" the old man coughed. "A little more water in there I think, Jackie boy." Fitzie fixed it and came back. "Sit down," he said, indicating the large black Danish bear chair. He himself eased down to the edge of the flat, backless sofa. "So how's everything at home?"

"Ha!" he wheezed, filling his Peterson. "For one thing, the bastids'll all be having to cook their own gobblers this day, good enough for 'em." Janice and her mother clucked from the kitchen. He drew on the pipe then leaned back into the chair. "It's a comfortable old thing," he said surprised.

"Mm. We bought it in Denmark."

"Did you. They know what to do with wood, all right."

"You'll have to come down in spring, you know," Fitzie said. "In this soup you can't see the harbor or anything. Makes everything look pretty bleak, this time of year."

"I was saying. Put me in mind of a part of Cork City, coming in the cab."

Uh, oh. Fitzie knew the old man considered Cork City the depths of poverty. In his whiskey Fitzie saw the Mooney house on the outskirts of Cambridge. Huge and venerable, set back from the street, surrounded by trees and grass; not lace-curtain, but the immigrant's self-made castle. To come from that to this. He knew the old man must be struggling to put the two together: his and Janice's storied success, and the Cork City street. "Of course, city living is a different thing than, like, up around home," Fitzie felt he had to say. "You know, people are more concerned with the insides down here."

"Ay," the old man puffed and sipped, "still, I snooped a bit and these old houses must've been a grand thing in their time."

"Yeah. You should see the first floor in this place. Marble fireplace and twenty-foot ceilings. And farther up the hill it's called Brooklyn Heights and the houses have all been kept up better. This area is just starting to come back."

"And do people live in the whole house up there?"

"Well, the really rich. But most are broken up into apartments."

"I see. More money, the scoundrels." Fitzie had to laugh at this, for the old man had made his by buying two houses with mattress money during the depression and turning them into apartments—right on the border of Harvard. He had three more now. He liked to say how Harvard had put his brood through Boston College. "Janice tells us you've got yourself an advancement, you're in a new job?"

"Yeah. It's a crazy business. You move around a lot."

"Good," the old man said, meaning it sounds very strange indeed to me but you must know what you're doing. In this, Fitzie felt less defensive with the old man, who himself was a body of conflicting forces: on the one hand he damn well disapproved of their not having a tent on his reservation, yet in doing what they were doing they were being more like himself than any of his other children, and he had to give it to them. He had come to America only because he couldn't make it to Australia, and had settled in Boston only because his plans for New York had gone amiss. To this day he held an awe for New York and Fitzie realized that it was this, as well as the basic recognition of himself in them, that had left them free of any interference by him over the years. Fitzie made them two more whiskeys and wished they hadn't come. The old man couldn't see or comprehend Fitzie's

136

job, his work, so that remained good and safe; but he was damn well seeing where and how they lived and Fitzie could tell that it had to be less, worse than he had imagined. It was inevitable. So be it. Sorry, old man, but this is it. This is how things are. Hope you can live with it because we sure as hell can. She's your daughter, but I am not your son. I am you, thirty-five years ago.

The old man said nothing.

When they sat to eat, Fitzie said grace. He got a drumstick, the old man got a drumstick. Throughout the meal, the old man was all laughs and poetry. He directed some attention to the children, but it was simply his presence that made them behave so humbly and well. He declared the butterball "better than Kate ever come near making in all the years." Mrs. Mooney had brought a plum pudding still wrapped in its butter-soaked cheese-cloth and a dark fruitcake she had baked a year before. Fitzie ate some of each, the old man taking a wedge of Janice's pecan pie. "I've never had the likes of this before," he said.

"I learned it in the Army," Janice said. "It's a southern dish." He didn't finish it.

After tea, he asked Fitzie to check the condition of the roads. They were clear now, the weather was letting up. He wondered if Fitzie would mind taking him for a little drive. Fitzie said he could use the air. In the Opel, Fitzie drove without saying much, expecting a speech, a *smart* or *dumb* from the old man and possibly a lock of horns, depending. But the old man simply wanted to see Wall Street. Reprieved, Fitzie sped across the bridge and down into the financial district. He pointed out the exchanges, the banks, the steep, close cliffs where the brokerages lived. The old man, looming huge in the small car nearly pushed his head through the front and side windows, eating the buildings with his eyes. "The money of the world, here," was all he said clearly enough for Fitzie to understand.

Fitzie put them on the nine o'clock shuttle, luckily, without a hitch. When he got back to Brooklyn the children were already asleep. He and Janice ate cold turkey sandwiches inside on the coffee table, with the Black Cat wine they hadn't served that afternoon.

"Hope we're that full of it when we're their age," Fitzie said.

"Aren't they great? Imagine flying for the first time at their age."

137

"Everybody should be so young." Was anything coming?

"They couldn't get over the kids," she said.

"How so?"

"Oh, they thought they were so grown-up."

"Even Millie?"

"That one. Did you see the way he flipped for her? I think it was really Bridget she reminded them of, not me."

"Oh! The one they lost. I forgot all about that."

"I guess you can get through anything," Janice said.

"Mm. She was older than you, right? That was a long time ago. You can't ever forget, though, I guess."

There was something, and then it came. "My mother said he thinks it's terrible for us to bringing up the kids in a cellar," Janice said.

"When the hell did he say that?"

"I don't know."

"Well, I mean did he say that or was it just her?" As if it made any difference, as if that would unsay it.

"She was delivering a message," Janice said without tone.

"It's not a cellar, for Christ's sake, it's a garden apartment."

"That crap doesn't mean anything to him."

"What do you mean, crap?"

"Oh, nothing. I mean to him it's a cellar, that's all. You know, they've never seen anything like this. What do they know about it. I told him how much you're making now. He couldn't get over it. He'll go back now and kick all their asses. They'll hate you."

"All the better to *move* with, my dear?" Fitzie said.

"I didn't mean that at all and you know it. Why? Do you want to move?"

"No, I do not want to move."

"Well, I don't either so why are we talking about it? I was just trying to tell you how sharp he thinks you are, that's all."

"Okay. I'm sorry."

"Just for the sake of argument, though," Janice said, "can you see us staying here forever?"

"The thing is, it never crossed my mind. I'm crazy about the place, the house, the whole scene here. *You* certainly seem happier here than anyplace else we've been."

"I am, I love it. I was just asking. But you're right.

138

into concept. Now he could stand, no longer one of
Now he could get funny and speak of Loony Ty
Merrie Melodies, Sonny Fox, Disney, Dr. Seus
Captain Kangaroo, fantasy, reality, Gulliver,
—and bring out his commercials, their new c
ing up no pictures, eating a candy bar as
bit and that, playing the dialogue fro
music from his tape recorder.

They laughed. One guy clapped
lulls. Run *their* half of the meeti
answer. No, we can't do it tha
to the drawing board, Tho
that you don't have to go
Heh-heh, from the
kiss-ass here, either.
How much? We
here. Let's see n
Sold. Go. G
over there a
Fitzie
in his
satisfa
hea

to do is wear a grown-up suit. And today
tague-suited: striped shirt, polka-dotted tie, black boots.
Then, in the office of the guy—he was just a guy, Fitzie
could see that— pushing the button that brought the Tank
to life, and cutting short Thornton's long, Latin soliloquy
to do it. "Okay," he said, "are you ready for greatness?"—
and waited, insisting they react one way or another. When
they did, half smile, cough, look away, he changed abruptly. *Think I'm another kook, huh? Uh, uh. Watch yourself,
buddies, here comes your life story.* Not ignoring the
others with the guy, never ignoring the underlings, but
arrowing it all into the eyes of the guy at the head of the
table, the only one who could say yes, Fitzie didn't talk
about his little movies. Not yet. He talked, instead, about
sales figures. About market reports. Competition's status,
their sales, the concepts, reach and frequency of their
campaigns. Then into their own position, their past
Nielsens, their strategy, how it had been executed (which
they knew but had to know he knew) and finally, what
they should be doing now. There. Now they were all even.
He had shown that he was fully aware of everything they
knew. Now he could go where only he knew anything,

them.
nes and
Peanuts,
Mark Twain
ampaign, hold-
he acted out this
memory over the

Quick now, push it. No
g. Say no when that's the
way. No, we can't go back
nton, because it's my board
ack to.
uy at the head. Doesn't like little
ood.
l, I happen to have an estimate right
w ...
eat to see we're being taken care of finally
F&F.
ade the sale on a Friday. On Monday, he was
office early, still high on the feeling. Self-
ction. So sweet and filling. *I* did it. *Me*! The group
's name was Paul, he was around thirty, and he came
to Fitzie's office around ten but the grin wasn't there,
nor the handshake. He carried a container of coffee and
stirred it with a wooden stick. "Hey," Fitzie said, "you
hear?"

"Yeah," Paul said thinly, "very good." He sat down.
Glasses. Teeth. Rep tie. Rogers Peet suit.

"Well let's hear it!" Fitzie laughed.

"I'm delighted, I think it's great. Really," Paul said.

Shy? Is he a shy person, is that it? "Well, what are you
doing, saving the applause for the end?" Fitzie grinned.
What the hell *is* this!

Paul laughed a little, then stopped. "Look, ah, I have to
say something to you. I've had sort of a complaint about
you."

"Who? About what?"

"Take it easy. It doesn't matter who."

"Thornton?"

"I guess you came on pretty strong, huh? He's pretty
upset. I mean there's a certain way things are done. And,
well, he says you were awfully flip and smartass out there.
Now, I don't want you to worry, Fitzie, he says it won't
go any further than me."

Fitzie was halfway across his desk, elbows on the blotter.
"Flip! Jesus Christ, man, we *sold* it! That's a thirty-

thousand-dollar package you're talking about and I got them to go with it, or didn't he mention that while he was at it?"

"We can do without all the Irish, huh?" Paul said. "This isn't the first thing anyone ever sold, you know, and the thing is we don't go beating up clients around here."

"Beating up, shit," Fitzie said. His neck hurt. He sat back into his chair and picked up the phone. "Listen, if you think I'm here to be trained, you can blow it out your ass." His finger stopped at the dial. He didn't know the number. Still holding the receiver, he slammed open the directory and scraped through the pages. He found the number and dialed it. "Thornton?" he said. "Fitzpatrick. You stay right where you are. I'm coming up." Then he hung up and stood, pushing the swivel chair back, rolling it to the window behind him.

"Come on, Fitzie, simmer down," Paul said, and Fitzie saw that he was a good person who was right now very confused and worried. He stood still, looking down at him. He lit a cigarette. Evenly, he said, "Paul? I didn't beat up anybody. Those are guys out there, and that's how I talked to them. I didn't lie to them. But I didn't suck their ass, either. I did what I do. I sang and I tap-danced and they paid for the show. To me, that's what it's all about. I'll see you later," and left him there in the chair with his coffee. As he went toward the elevators the anger came back. He had to wait for the elevator, then he had to go up five floors, then he had to walk another hallway to Thornton's office. At first his thoughts were simple and of the surface things. *I'm right. The stuff is good. It's for their good. I sold it to them. That's all there is to it. Anything else is horseshit.* But as he went and the anger rose and he started to picture Thornton's face, his clothes, his voice, Fitzie thought of Harvard Square. Walking nights from Somerville to sit next to them at the long tables in Widener's reading room, printing a phony name and Cambridge address on the cards ot take their books out. Their long scarves, their tweed jackets, their dirty white sneakers, rumpled khakis, Volkswagens, eating clubs, frisbee games on the grass beside the Charles. Talking in tongues at the next tables in Albiani's, in Hayes-Bickford's, in Cronin's. *Christ, is that what it is? Me getting them. Ach, who needs it? Who cares?*

I do. I must.

It must be in there. Yeah. Kill a WASP a day for Christ. Terrific. Some motive. He stepped through the doorway of Thornton's office. Thornton sat behind his desk. He was one of them, all right.

As Fitzie closed the black metal door, Thornton opened his eyes a little wider. Fitzie sat opposite him, and in the act of it he learned something he had never before realized: his mind didn't run him at all. There was another sense operating here, a step ahead of his reasoning. His mind didn't know what to say, had no idea how it was going to go, but the sense, the *thing*, had it already figured out. Fitzie lit a cigarette, without offering one. "Hi," he smiled.

"Hi," Thornton said. He had an extremely strong, low-pitched voice, much stronger than his slender, sharp face, much older-sounding than his age.

"I understand from Paul that you and I don't seem to understand each other," Fitzie said, smiling.

Thornton's head dropped from its stiff point, his shoulders visibly relaxed. "Oh, hell," he chuckled, "I must say you surprised me as much as you did them. You're quite a pitchman. The only, well, qualification I'd have to put on . . ."

"It was a good meeting, wouldn't you say?"

"Uh, well, yes. Sure! As far as the actual . . ."

Fitzie came up over the desk and took Thornton's necktie in his fist at the knot, and whispered, "Then now hear this, Shirley, you ever have anything to say to me, you say it to me. You hear that? You pull this chain of command shit behind my back again, you mess with me at all, ever again, and I'll *physically* kick your face in for you." Thornton's left hand came up and grabbed Fitzie's wrist. Fitzie pulled on the tie, raising Thornton's body forward in the chair and releasing the hand. He held him there for a breath then pushed him down, hard, into the chair. He let go of the knot and straightened up. Rust red with blood, Thornton's face and neck faded to clamshell gray as Fitzie stood looking down at him.

Fitzie knew that if he stayed, he hadn't done what he did—he couldn't have. Nobody acted that way, not here. He stayed. He sat again and smiled again, smoking the cigarette still in his left hand. He spoke as he had before, not in a whisper, explaining to Thornton the solid objects, the details, concerning the production of their commercials: which film houses should be called to bid, what talent should be auditioned, when this would be done, how long it would take to prepare, to shoot, to edit, to mix, to show. He offered Thornton a cigarette and lit it for him, talking with the smile. *There, there, take it easy. You'll be*

142

all right. It's over now. You've been coldcocked, that's all. Scream or anything and you might get really hurt. When Thornton finally spoke it was to ask a specific question, about the job, and then Fitzie knew it was over and he could safely leave the man. He answered Thornton's weak, irrelevant question, "No, no location. It all can be done in a studio," and got out, free to spend the next month performing the acutal work involved without having to look over his shoulder or listen for any knife whistle. He knew there wouldn't be any. The job came in on time, on budget and was fine.

That was the beginning, and it held the answers.

Fitzie didn't dwell much over that first run. He inched the speed up on his tunnels carefully and began playing this big, new Tank. People saw. He knew people saw: See the Tank run. See Fitzie make Popsicles. Big ones, small ones, some as big ... that didn't come yet. That's what he was after now. He had to have the big one. He needed it to show Janice she was wrong, wrong to be starting those goddamn Silences again. Women, sigh, chuckle-chuckle, sigh. They wanted it every way. They wanted you to work and make money and be happy at it—and be home all day, or at least full of piss and vinegar when you got home at night. Go, stay. Love work, hate it. Let's go out a lot, let's not, it isn't much fun anymore. Be good at work but don't think about it, don't talk about it, don't care about it. Talk to me, shut up. Come alive, drop dead. Christ, he had to show her.

The big one did come. He didn't have to wait so long for it, either. Nor was it any kind of a lucky break. That was the thing about New York—fast, one flight up, no waiting. Buried in among the big-spender accounts he had a little one that nobody paid much attention to. It was a classy, small New York store without much money to spend on advertising. As his predecessors had done, Fitzie wrote a trickle of ads with his left hand and would bring them to the old white-haired man who, among his other titles, was the advertising department for the store. He knew what he wanted to say but nothing about how and didn't pretend to. He placed himself entirely in the hands of whomever the agency assigned him at the time. He and Fitzie liked each other and had lunch together more often than the store's billings required. On his own, Fitzie got an idea. Instead of writing about the store and go barely

143

noticed, swamped by the giants, why not start a fire? Talk about who uses the store—and go on television with it. Fitzie created an idealized person, a composite of who everybody wants to be, tied it to the store, found a well-known fashion photographer who was trying to cross into filmmaking, and a rock composer who would do an original score for the publicity that might come from it. Because it stayed a lark and never a major project, the job was done without snags. When it hit, Fitzie was as surprised as anyone—not at how original and beautiful it was, he had known that every step of the way, it being his own fantasies he was indulging; but at the splash it made.

His picture poem ran only in New York and New York loved it. Within a month, more people were going into the store. But more important for Fitzie, the business saw it. He began getting calls. From other agencies. From the better headhunters. From strangers who just wanted to say "great." This was it. He was flying and even Janice got swept up into the bright glare of it. He began taking a few of the choicer interviews. F&F knew it and brought him to twenty thousand. Fitzie stopped the interviews; some offers were for more than that, but he sensed that he had snatched more than the four thousand from F&F, he had crashed out of the controlled line of satellites and now had his own orbit. He was the only one they had.

The night Montague announced that he had landed his creative director spot and could start bringing the old group back together, it was easy for Fitzie to say, "I think I'll take a rain check, Monty." His charge of satisfaction was so apparent and Janice's face and talk echoed it so clearly, that Montague was able to decide he was right. "There always seems to be one spot at those big places," he said, "and it looks as if you might be it. I guess you should stay with it and see. You can maybe rescue me when I flop in a year."

The awards dinner was held in the new Hilton that spring. Fitzie bought a dinner jacket and Janice wore a silk pants-formal that, with her new boy's haircut, made him call her Zelda all night. He even introduced her as that to everyone they met during the crowded, tinkling hour of cocktails outside the ballroom. Inside they sat at a grand round table with the director, composer, producer, art director and others who had been involved, drinking Mumm's and eating veal while they watched the mammoth screen above them reel off that year's winning commercial films. Fitzie's intense happiness had only one slight hole in it, and that was his not being the one to weave, beaming

144

but suave, through the glittering faces to the stage to accept the Oscar-like, shining gold statue. An agency official did that. But this puncture was sealed when Marv Silver, the creative director, brought the trophy over and set it down next to Fitzie's water goblet. "Come on, Zelda, up on the table," was all Fitzie could think to say when the others rose and toasted him. Instead of breaking up afterwards, their group moved outside together and walked along the midnight sidewalks to Cheetah on Times Square. The director's bearded rep paid their way through the ultraviolet foyer and once they were seated within the immense furnace of shock-treatment sound and lights-swirling, he produced a fresh fifth of Johnny Walker Red in a brown paper bag. *Zang, zang, zang, zang.* They tried to speak but couldn't hear, could barely see each other, so they all laughed and passed the bag from mouth to mouth—the only medium possible for communication, except for the inevitable one calling them irresistibly from the floor below. So they danced. The epileptic kids made room and gave silver-toothed approval to the cascade of tuxedos and gowns that streamed like falling dimes out of the darkness and into the bubbling caldron of liquid poster paints and sparklies. Fitzie and Janice sank smiling into the thickness of the electric sea bed. It was just after four when they slid out of the cab in front of their apartment.

"Zelda, Zelda, you should see yourself," he smiled drunkenly. She had made them whiskey sours and they were flopped over the kitchen table sipping them. He switched off the ceiling tubes so that the only light came, soft and blue, from the ignited four gas burners of the stove.

"Oh, I'm dead," she sighed. "That was great."

"Mm. I wish we were just arriving last night. So we could do it all again."

"Boy, that Ted Cochran is a beautiful man, he's Bronson's agent, huh?"

"Yeah, they call it rep. Ted's got a couple others, too, both still-photographers. That's why he was so generous, this gets him into film. No. He's just a good person. What'd you think of his date?"

Janice was still a little high. She straightened up in the chair and waved her bare arms in the blue light. "The most gorgeous, perfect woman in the world!" she declared.

"You hated her," Fitzie laughed softly. He couldn't look away from the gaslight.

"No. You can't hate that. You can't even envy that.

145

The most beautiful girl I've ever seen up close. What is she, like Egyptian or something?"

"Uh, uh. Mulatto. A creamy Milky Way candy bar."

"Gee, that was wild. The whole thing. My hero. Yours was really special, wasn't it. I mean they were all great, but ... It's funny, you hardly ever see *them* on the tube. You just see the crap."

"Yeah. Well, it's getting better all the time," Fitzie said and, kneeling, lit a cigarette quickly from the fire.

"Now, will you see Ted and Bronson a lot, and the rest?" She took the cigarette from his hand on the shadow-flickering table between them.

"Well, I see the agency people all the time. I don't know. If I give them another job, I guess. Otherwise, a lunch or something every now and then."

"Oh," She too now stared into the firelight on the stove. "Wouldn't it be great if you could keep people?"

"Hunh?"

"I mean, it's depressing. They come and then go away forever. Too bad you can't, when you meet a Montague or Anthony or like the ones tonight, and Buck and Betsy, you know, people who've got something, why can't you just see *them* all the time?"

"Zelda. I'll buy a villa on the Riviera and we'll move there with all the good people."

"Fitz?"

"Yeah?"

"You know what?"

"No, what?"

"You should get out."

"You want another sour?"

"No."

"Well, I do," he said and made a new drink at the counter in the gaslight, shaking it in a Cheez Whiz jar. "Get out of what?"

"I don't know, I thought about this tonight. Last night. You really ought to get out, now. I mean, you've done it."

Fitzie turned to her with his drink, leaning against the counter. "Hey, it's nice and warm up here. What do you mean, darling? You're juiced, right?"

"Oh, maybe. It sounded right when I thought it, though. That you should go do something else."

"That's crazy. What else do I know how to do? And I'm just really making it now. Man, I'll have them by the ying-yang now! Did you see Silver come over tonight?"

"No, I know, I know. That's not what I'm saying, I'm just saying you've done it, you've really done it, so maybe

146

you ought to go try something else now, that's all. Oh, I don't know what I mean, my head's going around. Don't you see?"

"Jesus, lady. I'm pushing thirty, you know. We've got three kids and we're just starting to get somewhere and you want me to go start something else. Give me a break, will you? How many times do you get to start before you're just another loser playing with yourself?"

She had her eyes closed, her head resting against the kitchen wall behind her. "All right, all right," she sighed, "I'm sorry I brought it up. I'm sorry I said anything. You're right. What the hell do I know about anything." All with her eyes closed, her lips barely parted, as if talking in her sleep.

"Ah, come on," Fitzie said, trying to sound gentle. "Don't . . ."

"I'm going to bed," she said and was up and gone past him, out of sight into the blackness at the edge of the kitchen alcove, a silk spirit vanishing faster than his breath could turn around inside him and come out. He stood, stunned.

"Goddamn it!" he shouted out loud and flung the empty glass out of his hand to smash with the sound of a whole window shattering against the kitchen floor. He decided he was drunk. He snapped the switch and the fluorescent ceiling rods plinked instant cold whiteness into the room. The eerie blue light from the gas burners was gone. They were now merely four rings of gas flame he could see where making a black smoke in the air that would stain the white wall and cabinets overhead. He shut them off, click, click, click, click, and got the dustpan and brush out from beneath the sink. The kids would be up in a couple of hours. He and Janice would be exhausted and hung over. They would have headaches and be impatient and hard with the children. They would strike each other with Silence and not speak of the great time they had had the night before.

"Slow down, Fitz," Janice said.

Snapped out of his stare, Fitzie looked at the speedometer. She was right, he was going too fast for the Hutchinson River Parkway's rain-sprayed surface. Too fast for the health of the aging Opel. If, as he suspected, they were going to be buying a house, there'd be no new-car thinking possible for a while. He lifted his foot on the gas pedal. A

147

house. That was why he had been speeding; he had gone into a daze over the house they had left less than an hour before. It was a November Sunday afternoon. It wasn't that he didn't like it. It was a big, sixty-odd-year-old colonial on a corner with a gigantic beech tree, nearly finished shedding its copper leaves. Fitzie had seen the duck-prints earlier leaves had left on the sidewalk. A fine house, not too far from the Sound in the town of Merrimac, not too far from Connecticut, not too far from Manhattan either. The best of the seemingly hundreds of houses they had looked at since August. The first Janice had fallen for. "Got a quarter?" he said at the toll.

"Here." She reached it around Millie, gurgling in her lap. Loretta and Joey were in the back. He could feel it in her fingers as they brushed his: she wanted that house. That should have been that. He liked it fine, she loved it. But. For one thing, they hadn't ever openly decided that they wanted a house at all. They had started looking, for something to do on sweltering Sunday afternoons, and to just get better acquainted with what was available where: if they ever were to buy a house, they should know what they were doing. *If*, of course. Just if. The Whitestone Bridge swayed in the wind and he felt the eerie shift in his wheels as he edged to the right. Sometimes Manhattan was a wispy graph in the sky to the west, but today there were only thick clouds over the Queens houses below the bridge, near where they had lived for their first few months in New York. Fitzie skimmed down and along through Flushing, to undercut to the Brooklyn-Queens Expressway after La Guardia, racing night for home.

The house hunting had been fun, so they had kept it up past the summer and into the fall. Fitzie himself had become bored with it by October, after the foliage had disappeared, but he had hidden his disinterest: Janice loved doing it, and their life together had warmed up since they had begun the house-hunting game. It even got so that he could mention the unmentionable, work, to her at dinner or reading at night. She seemed now to no longer resent it. As if she had changed her mind and no longer wanted him to go try something else, something more open to the noninvolved, laughing looseness they had had with Montague at the terrible agency. Or perhaps it was just that she had walked away from it as he had, letting it clot like a cobweb in a corner, not looking at it, simply living with it. Whatever had happened, she seemed to be back up there with him. He liked that and didn't care what had caused it. At the same time, he couldn't help

148

linking Janice's apparent return to cheer with their house-hunting Sundays. So, now what? One out he knew he had was money. They had about four thousand, but that wouldn't be enough. That wouldn't be an out, either, he knew, if Janice really set her head on getting the place. The thing was, he didn't really know where her head was, nor did he know why he was automatically searching for *outs*. Maybe she didn't want it. Maybe he didn't not want it.

"Daddy's work!" It was Joey seeing downtown out the back window. To the boy, Fitzie worked in every skyscraper in Manhattan. He stopped at their stoop, set the brake against the hill and helped Janice unload them all through the grating and into the apartment under the stairs. Then he went back and pulled the Opel across the street. Locking it up, he wondered whether Merrimac-near-Connecticut was plagued with alternate side of the street parking regulations. Then he remembered: the house had a garage. Two car.

"We need bread and you-know," Janice said from the kitchen. He started back down the hall.

"Okay." He moved again toward the outside door. This time another voice stopped him: the montage on the hallway wall dividing their apartment from the VFW clubroom next door. With Joey on tape and Loretta on razor blade, Fitzie had covered the wall with *Réalités* pictures—a Provence girl clutching an orange, a third full breast, against her coarse, red sweater, her eyes lemon-and-lime green; the Berlin Wall in grainy black and grays, spotlighted at night in the rain; the Acropolis in corny Kodak colors; an autumn-mottled path in a Paris park, dotted with white-stockinged children stooped forever over never-reached leaves; the green-marble, glistening meat of a just-shucked oyster—nearly a hundred flaring pictures from baseboard to ceiling and from door to staircase, so bright it virtually screamed *Yawee*! Fitzie paused before it. *Now where the hell in a house could you do something like that!* But maybe you could. In his nearly thirty years, he had never lived in a house.

Out through the iron grating and up onto the sidewalk again, pulling up the collar of his Army fatigue jacket. His sudden reappearance seemed to pull down the salty dark of night over the street and harbor. He looked down the hill and saw, fuzzy, the square-eyed sparkle of a Battery-bound ferryboat through the fog, but then the night-lights on a docked Japanese freighter strung up a blinding net of glare across his vision and he lost it. He turned away to

149

climb the block to Mac's. Sunday night. He was going for supper stuff. What was strange about that. Nothing, except that he was thinking about it in that memory-storing way of noticing things that he soon wouldn't be doing or seeing anymore. He walked up the wavy-slabbed sidewalk, looking across at the uphill cliff of brick fronts and brownstones, splotchy, tacky, chipping pink or beige. Her old man had been right Thanksgiving Day. It was a filthy place. It was Cork City. Shabby. Cobble Hill, what a laugh. Sounds like a quaint ad in the back of *Holiday*, but it was black soot all over the cracked concrete and the parked cars; bent beer cans, smashed bottles, dog shit, ripped Spanish comic books and torn newspaper pages wet in the gutters or sucking against fences. And no trees, not even a dead one; only flaking fire hydrants. So how come he loved it. Why this grabbing on to it all of a sudden, holding on for dear life, afraid she's going to want to take him away from it?

He reached the corner and waited for the traffic throttling down from Atlantic Avenue. He considered walking up there to hear the noise and maybe have a beer in one of the pizza places. No, Janice was waiting. Across the street, Mac's yellow light reached out into the street and showed up the clusters of raised, round bumps stuck into the hardtop like bunkers on a night battlefield. Son of a gun. How had he never noticed them before? Soda bottle caps sunk into the street. Ha! Coke, Pepsi, Dr. Pepper, Seven-Up, about twenty of them, many too rusted to read, Canada Dry, cream soda. *Soda*. That always hit Fitzie funny. Back in Boston they called it tonic. He could remember collecting tonic caps, prying out the cork liners to press them onto sweaters for badges. And waiting for the city men to leave their paving or patching, then running out to kneel and push the caps into the soft tar. Sometimes the summer sun would get so hot it would melt the street enough to do it then. They never just shoved them in, as these in front of Mac's; they made hearts and swastikas and arrows and kids' names and *fuck you*s and crosses. The next time he went home he'd have to see if Craig Street, his street, was still the mosaic of tonic caps it used to be. In the few times he had gone to Craig Street since he'd left nearly ten years before, he'd hardly looked at the houses, let alone the street itself. Just in and out, wham-bam, hi, goodbye, he hated it so much. Christ, could that be in it, too? After all the jumping around Queens had he latched on to this piece of Brooklyn because it was so hip and alive and free, as he and Janice

150

had told themselves? Or was it just him all the time, him simply going back to Craig Street, where he knew where he was and what to do? Wouldn't that be a laugh. Jesus.

He crossed and went into Mac's, clinking the bell at the top of the door, glad to see Pete behind the counter jammed with Hostess cupcakes and doughnuts in racks, in front of the glass-faced freezer case. There was no Mac. Fitzie bought his paper from Pete mornings and played an occasional number from him. Tonight he was eating a slice of salami from his hand and gave Fitzie his loaf of Wonder, bag of potato chips and two quarts of Schlitz with his usual swiftness but no talk of the rain or the Giants. "There ya go, Mister F., enjoy 'em." Fitzie took his bag and left, feeling that he was doing it all for the last time and not liking that feeling. Bald, tee-shirted Pete had seemed so sad. Did he know something Fitzie didn't? Had Janice told everyone but him? Was that a Mayflower van on the street in front of their building? Hey, pal, pull yourself together.

He took the chips out of the bag and left them in the hall bookcase, then went into the apartment. Loretta and Joey were eating grilled cheese sandwiches and Bosco at the kitchen table in their pajamas, which made him tiptoe across the dining area floor. "Too late to kiss her nibs?" he whispered.

Janice took the bag from him. "Yes, she went out like a light." Fitzie put the beer into the refrigerator. "Aren't you going to have one?" she said, taking the bread away.

"No, I need something stronger. It's gittin' *col* out dere." The kids were being quiet and inconspicuous, eating as slowly as their hunger would let them, trying to stretch it. Sunday was go to bed early night, no TV, and either songs or a story, not both. Sunday night was also don't bug Mama and Daddy, they want to read their big fat paper—although Fitzie feared this Sunday's *Times* wouldn't be opened until tomorrow. He swished the martini around in the ice-filled measuring cup with the blade of a kitchen knife, poured it into a wine glass and sipped, smelling juniper and grinning at Janice.

"Daddy?" Loretta said, making Joey say "Daddy?" one syllable late.

"What—sweetie?" Fitzie gave the girl first go.

"Daddy!" Joey wouldn't buy it.

"Okay, what Joey?"

"Is that water?"

"No."

"Can I taste it?"

"No. It's whiskey."

"You can drink it when you're in college," Loretta said.

"Shut up," Joey said. "Come on, Dad."

"No. Eat, now, and knock it off. Now, Loret, what is it?"

"Daddy, are we going to buy that house?"

To himself: Oh Christ. Nice kid. Five going on twenty.

To Janice, silently, a look: Did you have her say that? Her look: No!

To Loretta: "I don't know. Why, did you like it?"

"Yes. It had a room with pink wallpaper that I could have. By my*self*," the last pointed to her brother.

So. The goddamn house had done something to everybody. It must be haunted, for Chrissake. He smiled at the child. "I don't know. We'll see," he said. *We'll see.* What his father had always said. What he'd vowed he'd never say to his own children, and what he was always saying to them. "Come on, now," he said, "finish up and go to the bathroom and I'll put you to bed." Unreliable, neither Joey nor Loretta even attempted to con him into an extra story so he had to tuck them in and kiss them good-night. Even Joey's Teddy was there, unlost. Janice came to kiss them and put out the light.

She was always glad to leave him alone in the kitchen Sunday nights, happy for the break and knowing how he loved to play short-order cook. But tonight she came in behind him, ducking through his arm to rinse a glass and fix herself a drink. "Out of my way, now, woman," he said and worked one-handed while he drank from his martini. "Go get the chips and be quiet or they'll hear the bag."

She came back with them and sat at the table with her drink. She didn't say anything, so he didn't. She hummed. Forking bacon onto lettuce, Fitzie had to admit it was stupid. All the times, the nights when he would *pray* for her to speak, to snap out of her blackness, to be happy—and now here he was, irritated and up tight because she was on and humming. Janice waited until he had the tray balanced, then put out the kitchen light. He sat in the bear chair, she on the sofa and they each ate two triple-decker BLT halves before speaking.

"Nice, isn't it?" he said.

"Mm. Wish we had some Drambruie?"

"Yeah. And a fireplace."

"That was a nice one today. She said it worked, too."

"Oh yeah," Fitzie said, "it was. That was a nice house."

"Oh, it really was," she said. "It was a great house."

"I knew you flipped for it."

152

"It'd be a great family house. Couldn't you see Joey out in that yard?"

"Yeah."

"Well," Janice said and stood up, "I'll get the coffee." She came back with the coffee but didn't sit. She went back and got the *Times*. She put it on the sofa beside her, dug out the magazine section and pushed the rest over to him. He sipped his coffee, watching her. "It kind of reminded me of Elmwood Road, didn't it you?"

Janice looked up at him, smiling. "I know what you mean. Not the outside, but the rooms." Then she looked back into the magazine. Elmwood Road was the name of the house Janice's family had grown up in. Not the Mooney house: "Elmwood Road." She had to be thinking of it; that house today had been too obvious, it could have had a SOUVENIR OF sign on it. Picking her up there in college, Fitzie had envied them that house, although he never said it to Janice. An inn, a ship, it was unquestionably a good place to live. Had it been he, he thought, and he had just found his Elmwood Road near Connecticut, not too far from Manhattan, wouldn't he be crawling all over her to get it? He couldn't tell. He let the newspaper crumple down into his lap and looked across the coffee table at her. After a moment, she felt it and looked up. He didn't know what to say, so he yawned. "Too bad we're not loaded."

"Do you really want to talk about the house, Fitz? I didn't think you would."

"Well, hell. Yes and no."

"Well what do you think?" she asked softly. "*Should* we move to a house?"

"Christ, don't ask me, I like it here."

"So do I, you know that. The thing is, we *do* have to start thinking about what we're going to do; this place is getting pretty tight with three kids."

"All right, we can get a bigger apartment, then. Or maybe buy one of these old houses around here. Pick one up for around twenty-five and fix it up. What's the matter with that?"

"To be honest, I don't think the city is any place to bring up kids in. That's why nobody here has any. Or one, maybe, big deal. So you go to the park. In daylight. And not by themselves. Terrific."

"Aw, come on, now. I'm sure there's a lot of people doing it and making out fine."

"With summer houses and nurses, maybe!" The blood was up in Janice's cheeks now. "Shit. You get a choice.

153

Bring them up fags or sissies or watch them get mugged. Not me."

"Well, what the hell is Merrimac going to be? Christ, you read how great the kids are turning out in Darien? I'm not so sure the streets are that bad."

"Oh!" Her eyes narrowed. "Let's hear it, Fitzie. How you smoked and threw rocks at trains and hopped trucks and stole junk out of cellars and sold it to the ragman. You snuck into movies and put your hands up sweaters and skirts. Wow. Since when is fucking Craig Street so wonderful? That's not what I've heard all these years."

He whistled. One long, light whistle. *Man, this ain't worth it. What the hell do I care where I live?* "You finished?" he said, "or've you got some more words to put in my mouth?"

"That *is* what you're thinking. Don't say it isn't."

"Don't tell me what I'm thinking, huh lady? All I know is, we aren't Buck and Betsy Stevenson. They were from that to begin with, the whole house, town, community thing. They never did really dig the city the way we do."

"The way who does?"

"I do. Don't you?"

"I'm out *here* all day, remember?"

"I can't help that, can I. And it'd be nice if I could say I hate it, but I don't. Sorry."

"Oh, let's not get into that."

"No, let's not." Fitzie went to the radio. Soft music came into the room. "But from what you say, we ought to *live* in there, so you *would* be there all day."

"From what I say. Jesuit logic wins again. Wonderful."

"Thank you." He sat down again. The kids had left stuff on the floor; he picked up a plastic ukelele and plunked the one string left on it. *Boong.*

"Was that logic or epistemology?"

"Ha-ha," he said. *Boong.* "He's your old man, not mine. You should have gone to college, not nursing. You should have been a boy. What's new."

"Define your terms, isn't that it? How cute. Well how about *reality* terms, Fitz? How about three kids, because we do have them, you know, and how about I come from a house just as much as Betsy Stevenson!"

Boong. She twisted her head away. *Oh Christ,* he thought, *what are we doing?* He dropped the ukelele. "Boy. We just had to find that fucking house today, didn't we, Jan?"

"What?"

"Want a drink?"

154

"God, yes I want a drink."

He went to the kitchen and made them bourbon and water. He set the glasses down on the magazine section and sat on the floor, his back against the wall.

"We're always getting ourselves into things like this," he said. "It must be easier if you don't have to question everything you do. You know—have certain things you don't have to worry about."

"Like where you live?"

"Exactly. Like everyone we know up around Boston. No two ways about it. You eventually buy a house. Period."

"Well, we're not in Boston."

"That's what I'm saying."

"Oh."

"Listen, Christ, I'm not *against* the house, I just feel we'll be better off here for a while, that's all."

"That's you. What about me?"

"You want to move out to a house? We'll move out to a house."

"Don't do me any favors."

"Oh, Christ." He reached under his knee and pulled out the thing he had been leaning on. It was a musical clock. He wound the back handle and its childish melody began tinkling out.

"If you're going to keep playing with all the toys," she said, "I'll shut the radio off."

He dropped the clock back onto the floor.

Oh! Capital, O, capital H, bang. Light bulb over the head. That was it! He had got his, she simply now wanted hers. Aha! I keep the job? She gets a house. Fair enough. Easy, in fact. Because I don't care that much. Careful now, though. She'll want me to want it too, or it won't be any good.

He laughed: heh-heh, dumb old lovable me. "To tell you the truth, I still can't get over the kind of *loot* we're talking."

"Look at the money we give away every year in rent. A house is your own."

"I guess it would be great, to have a place that was all yours. Dig a moat around it. Joey could piss right off that porch and nobody could say a word."

She snickered. "He would, too."

"Hell, so would I. Every Saturday I'd get up at six and drink beer all morning. Say, what's that great, yellow thing in the sky, a rainbow? No, that's the new people. They're Irish, I'm afraid." He picked up Loretta's old

Easter straw hat and sat it on his head. "Could I chop wood?"

"Yes, you could chop wood."

"Could I burn leaves?"

"Yes, you could burn leaves."

"Could I get a dog?"

"Maybe if you're good."

"And have horseshoes? And plant flowers and take walks and sleep out and nail you in front of the fireplace every night?"

"Stop it!" She was laughing. "And take off that silly hat." He skimmed the hat up onto her lap.

"It might make us feel, you know, *us* again, wouldn't it?" she said.

"I guess," he said. "And you know, I always used to think how fantastic it would be to have *stairs*. Every house in all the movies always had *stairs* for people to go up. Go *up* to your room! Or, just a minute, I think I left it *upstairs*. That would be great." He drank his bourbon and tried to think of more things he liked about houses.

"Of course you'd have to commute to work," she said, "Would that be awful?"

"Hell, I used to take the Boston and Maine from North Station to Rock Harbor when I was seven years old. All by myself. The Boy Commando on a trip. You'd go by the huge yellow mountains of sulphur in the Monsanto yards in Everett, then whip across the Lynn marshes and look down on the water and boats, and this immense depot in Salem used to hang fake, green snakes from the beams to scare the pigeons out. Jesus, I haven't thought of that in years."

"You never told me all that," she said, and he could tell the bourbon was warming her, he was warming her. He was warming himself, too.

"Hey, what am I talking about? I *have* lived in a house! Jesus Christ, my grandmother's! You've *been* there! How the hell could I forget that? The oldest house in the world and *stairs*—steep narrow stairs up the ass! I loved it there."

"So commuting might not be all that horrendous, huh?"

"Hell no."

"Good."

Fitzie rolled his eyes up to the twin spotlights in the ceiling above him and thought, *A four-story building on top of me, people sleeping and screwing piled up on my head, Man, we've come a long way from Saint Louie. And*

156

*the farther the better. This is getting to be a lot of bullshit.
Merrimac. She-it. Anyplace I hang my hat. Sing it, baby.*

He pulled his legs out from under the table and crossed
them. "Now!" he said loudly, to break the silence they had
settled into. "There is still the little matter of bread." This
was going to be the hard part.

"I read you the letter," Janice said quietly.

"Aw, hell, Jan."

"Well, it's ours, Fitz. I still don't see why you can't see
that."

"It's your father's. Which he would like to give to us.
Which would make us just like every soft jerk I know in
New York. Getting help from homesie."

"You can't tell people what not to give you."

"You don't have to take it."

"It isn't as if it's for us anyway. You know it's for the
kids, really."

"Let him open an account for them." Fitzie's hand was
on the floor, finger-drumming. It suddenly touched something brittle that made a clackle-sound against the wood.
He picked it up: a white Casper the Friendly Ghost face
from Halloween, with round eyes and the smile of an
angel cut into it. He put it on his head like a hat, the thin
elastic cord under his chin.

"What if he died, Fitz?" she said, "and left it to us in
his will?"

"I guess there wouldn't be much you could do about
that." He nearly laughed.

"Then what's the difference, if you're going to get it
anyway? Isn't it better to have it now, when we need it?"
Janice slid off the chair and knelt next to his hip, sitting
back on her ankles. The elastic cord was hurting the skin
under his jaw. He pulled it off and snapped it around his
head, making Casper's face zip in to cover his. "You ass,"
she laughed and dropped her hand over his bent knee.

Fitzie adjusted Casper so he could see out through the
eyeholes and stuck his tongue out at her through the
grin-curve. "Okay," he said, "but don't ever forget who's
the one making the *payments* on your damn old house."

She came forward onto him. He brought his legs up
reflexively. She leaned in the valley between his thighs
and his belly, her face at his chest. "*Our* house, huh? Say
our house, Fitzie."

"Our house, Fitzie," he said through Casper's smile.

Five

———◆———

IT WAS TOO JACK LEMMON, too Tony Randall, too years
ago Bob Cummings, and Fitzie hated finding himself in
the role and being unable to get out of it. He was thirty
and it was tearing him apart. *Oh, yeah. Heh-heh. Poor
bastard. That's funny.* It wasn't like him at all. He had
never, since he made twenty-one, been age conscious. He
could get up on an August morning, be told it was his
birthday, and have to think to know which one. Maybe
that was it; had he paid his years more attention perhaps
he would have seen this one coming and got ready for it—
instead of being ambushed by it, hit by its careening chrome
front bumper. His body had been caught staring. He had
a tough face, scarred from early fights and acne, that he
knew hadn't changed much since the Army, and knew
from his father and pictures of his grandfather, wouldn't
change all that much in the next twenty years. He walked
the twenty minutes every morning from his house in Merrimac to the station for the commuter train to New York.
And before breakfast he did the same number of sit-ups
and leg-lifts he had done since, oh God, in college. He
smoked too much, over two packs of Pall Malls a day, but
he always had. He always figured that two weeks after he
quit he'd be killed by a truck. And his middle tended to
grow its roll more frequently lately, but he knew that was
from the two—rob roy lunches at the Brasserie or Sardi's
or Mike Manuche's every noon and the two homemade
martinis with Janice every night. As soon as he'd catch
sight of it, looking down his front, or begin to feel the flab,
he'd cut it all down for a week and that would take care
of it. There had been no loose hair, no new wrinkles, no
slowing down that might have tipped him that his sky was
falling.

If anything, Janice's own arrival at thirty, two months
before in May, had pushed Fitzie's head deeper into its
unwary hole. She threw her arms around thirty and
danced with it. To her, it was a great beginning impatiently earned and Fitzie didn't have to look back in their

photo album to know she was better looking now than she had ever been. Since Marilyn Monroe died and Barbra Streisand came in and all the clothes began to really forget the war, hardly any woman could look plain except from some private perversity. Janice benefited from this but it was much more with her: the great eyes had always been there and the legs and the skin. The beauty Fitzie had always seen was now ready for the public. She made her dazzling debut at thirty. Fitzie basked in her glory, proud and possessive: she wore his brand, the thin, tiny blue tattoo of leg veins, one for each of his three babies, which didn't show even in bare legs, but which he and she both knew were there. The year before, they had gone to San Juan for her birthday. This year, because of having just bought the house in January, their money was tighter, even though he'd been raised to twenty-four thousand that spring. So he bought her an antique brooch at Henri Bendel's. When he gave it to her he said, "It's no weekend of sin, I mean I know you'd rather do than have, but at least it's sort of more *yours,* personally."

"It's beautiful," Janice said. "I love it. It's so unusual, it's *today* perfectly."

She was right, the brooch was her magical day. She wore it, blue, green, gold, metal and stones in a long, tapering finger, on the breast of her short white dress that night when he took her to dinner, and Janice was the brooch, strong, delicate, gleaming. Fitzie looked at nothing else, saw only Janice and her birthday brooch all evening; and if he had ever, in thought, connected her thirty-day with his own—which he didn't—he could have felt only *fine, terrific, up, new,* and perhaps have been struck even harder by it when it came on two wheels around the blind curve at him that August.

Even the day itself was unlike his usual days. He came downstairs at seven-thirty for breakfast, made the turn into the kitchen and ran into *yays!* and *Happy Birthday to You!* sung by Loretta, Joey and Millie, all mouths and tonsils at the table, led by Janice grinning at the stove. "Hey, very good," he said sheepishly when they had finished and were clapping.

Janice kissed him and said, "Cake and presents when you get home."

"No, now!" the children protested.

"Wait'll you see what I gotcha," four-year-old Joey said.

"What?" Fitzie said.

"He can't tell you," Loretta said threateningly into

Joey's face. "They're a surprise, you have to wait until tonight."

"Come on, Joe, tell me," Fitzie whispered loudly to the boy, who swept his eyes from Loretta to Janice and said, "Nope."

"Aw, come on."

"Nope."

Fitzie grabbed and raised him by the shirt neck, "Schweinhund. You vill tell me or *helse!*"

"Okay! It's . . ." the boy began, laughing, but Loretta clamped her hand over his mouth and Janice made a show of rescuing him from the Nazi.

Two or three cars would always slow down alongside Fitzie in the road to offer him a lift to the station, and he would smile and wave them on. In a good mood, he would think, *That was nice of them.* In a down, he would think, *Lazy bastards, wouldn't hurt you to try walking sometimes.* This morning neither up nor down, not thinking at all, he found himself trotting to reach the green Volkswagen that had squeaked to a quivering stand ahead of him. Fitzie remembered his name, Herb Munro, from the lawn party where they had been introduced earlier that summer. A statistician who worked down Wall Street, a few years older than Fitzie. "Thanks a lot," Fitzie said and slammed the door shut from the front seat. Munro had already begun to clutch-ease the car forward. "Car laid up?" he said.

"No, I always walk," Fitzie said, "the only exercise I get."

"I used to," Munro said. He had the Volks up to forty, which seemed sixty through the quiet, sleepy streets. "I wonder now how I ever made it."

"How long you been out here?"

"Six years. Damn. This is the latest I've been in a long time, I'll never find a space."

"What train do you usually get?"

"Seven fifty-five," Munro said as fiercely as he downshifted.

"Oh. Then you have to go down from Grand Central, don't you. How long's that?"

"Another twenty minutes. When's the next one now?"

"Eight twenty-four," Fitzie said. "Plenty of time." He was sorry he had taken the ride. No air, now. No walking. No looking at trees and chimneys. Now he'd have to stand with the others on the platform, waiting instead of running up and jumping on the step, the last one aboard. Maybe he'd even have to buy a paper and hold it up to his

160

face to look more like the others, to feel less like Labor at a Management meeting than he did anyhow.

"Yeah, but God knows what I'll do with the car," Munro frowned. "God, I'm the world's worst commuter. You wouldn't believe yesterday. I was late, as usual. Not this late, but late. I did four complete circles around the station, not a space. Finally, I just pulled up in front of the cop that directs traffic there and I said, 'Hey, where the hell am I supposed to park this anyway?'—figuring, you know, maybe he knows some side street or something. And you know what the thick mick says to me?"

Dear God, Fitzie thought, *I've lost my face. I must not look like me anymore!*

"He says, 'Why don't you put it there, at one of the meters?'"

"And I says, 'But they're only good for about three hours, aren't they?'"

"And he says, 'Well, that's all there is, now, and the worst that can happen is you get a ticket, and who knows? Maybe you won't.'"

"Anyway, I did. I pulled into the meter lot, got on the train and you know what the last thing I saw was from the train window?"

"No, what?" Fitzie said, aching for the answer to be what he thought.

"The same son of a bitch was standing at my car writing me out a goddamn ticket!"

Fitzie coughed out a laugh so loud Munro slammed on the brakes and Fitzie's forehead came to within an inch of the windshield. He was about to try to apologize, but saw that it was only a stop sign. They had reached the station, a quaint, slate-roofed little building with pointed arms reaching out, as in exercises, to both sides. Like the one Mrs. Miniver got off at, where the railroad man grew roses and named one for her. "Fifteen bucks!" Munro cursed. "Listen, you'd better jump here, this'll probably take me all day."

Fitzie felt soft for the man now. "Naw," he said, "listen, I'm good luck. Go ahead and take a swing through the lot and, oh! Hey, look! I see one. Honest to God. See it? Beside that Triumph?"

"Yowza!" Munro bellowed. "By God, you're right! I don't believe it!" He shot the Volkswagen into a sharp left and fairly flew up and into the dirt parking lot; a tight squeeze, but the car fit. Fitzie felt good. He felt that he had given the man something nice, to pay for the ride. "Oh, wow," Munro laughed as they walked together along

161

the concrete platform toward the station house. "I can't get over it. Ha-ha! Listen, partner, you *have* to ride in with me every morning now. What luck! You know, anything can happen now today and I won't care, know what I mean? When something great happens like that?"

Fitzie wished he could have stopped Munro from saying that. He saw the cop ahead of them at the Seagram's 7 poster and knew the other hadn't. "Which one of you is driving the green VW?" the cop said, stepping slightly in front of them, stopping them.

"I am," Munro said, astonished.

"Let's see your license and registration," the cop said. He wasn't the traffic cop. He was a motorcycle cop, with boots, sunglasses and a helmet.

"What'd we do?" Fitzie asked, as friendly as he could, keeping hidden the old hatred inserted by the kick of a cop's shoe when he was ten.

"There's no left turn there," the cop said impatiently: *Everyone knows that!*

"My license," Munro said feebly, handing it over. "Registration must be back in the car."

"Let's go," the cop said, and he and Munro began walking back toward the lot. Fitzie said, "I have to get a paper. I'll come back and wait for you," but Munro didn't turn. *Let's go.* Jesus Christ. Anne Frank! He watched them go. If he puts his hand on his shoulder I'll jump him. He went to the station, got at the end of the long line of clay suits filing past the newsstand, took a *Daily News* and was back outside again. There was still a good ten minutes before train time. He saw Munro and the cop walking back from the lot and he headed toward them. As they reached the motorcycle, they came apart. Munro stood, visibly sagging, and waited as the cop talked into his small radio. The town of Merrimac, New York, was small. The police station was near the train station. Before Fitzie was within even shouting distance of Munro, who wasn't looking in his direction anyway, only staring at the motorcycle, the police car had pulled up and sucked Munro into its front seat. Fitzie stopped. The insigniaed door was slammed shut by the motorcycle cop and the car pulled away with Munro inside it. Fitzie watched until the police car turned out of sight. He must have left his registration at home. He's going to pull up in front of his house in a police car. Maybe he'll just stay home for the rest of the day. But he'll have to come and get his car. They'll probably drive him back. He'll catch the what? The ten-something, for Christ's sake, and be late as hell for work.

Fitzie turned and walked away. He flung the *Daily News* out of his hand against a *Hello Dolly!* billboard. It fell down onto the platform as a piece; it hadn't come apart. Fitzie felt the cop's pistol pointing hotly at his back. He went back and picked up the newspaper and pitched it down into a wire litter basket.

His body faced the tracks but his head and face looked back to the cop standing at the Seagram's 7. He wasn't pointing his pistol. He had his arms folded above his black patent leather Sam Browne belt and he was looking at Fitzie. Fitzie stood staring back at him. The longer they stood the closer they seemed to come to each other. He felt that he could now see the cop's eyes behind his green Polaroids. *Oh, my God*, Fitzie thought, *I may go and hit him. It is possible. I may. I may be going to do it—now. No, I didn't. I may in another minute, then. Now? No. Now, then?* The train hurtled in then, too fast, spraying the platform and the station and the people with its blast of dust and soot and metallic air. The gush of the train broke the eye barrier between Fitzie and the cop with an audible pow! Fitzie looked away from the cop to look at the train, sending the cop down into the earthquake crack of nonexistence. He looked up toward the first car, holding his body back until the last attaché case swung out of sight up the stairs. Then he fell into a run, past the station house, to the other side, grabbing the worn handrail and leaping to the stair just as the train whistled its *Feet-Feet* and began to roll. He made it. Just as if he had walked. As if he hadn't taken the ride from Munro. But he had. Which was why he now felt as if he had eaten something too heavy for breakfast. And felt so distracted that he let himself slip into a two-seater, on the left, where the sun would backlight the solid filth on the window and where he would have to cross his legs and shrink so as not to touch the cord or cotton edge of the banker or the broker or the lawyer that would soon press into the seat next to him. He usually went to the shaded window of a three-seater on the right side, where the chances were good that the seat space between him and whatever executive took the aisle seat would stay open all the way; even if a third commuter took the middle, the three-seaters were wide enough to spread in without touching.

He lit a cigarette while the conductor punched his red ten-trip ticket, then rode staring at his jaundiced reflection in the dirt on the window glass. If the comptroller, the executive vice president, the head of sales did come and sit beside him, and if he had a *Times*, he could infuriate or at least distress him with the *Times* trick a cameraman friend had taught him; he could open the paper to the Daily Crossword Puzzle, fold the page with enough flourish to ensure the man was paying him attention, then whip out his ballpoint—better than an erased pencil—and fill in every single square without a second's hesitation with letters, any letters, then, bored, push the whole paper down the hole between his legs to the floor and look out the window or up at the ads with a sigh. That opened their ulcers. But he didn't have a *Times*, and he had fired his *News* away unopened. It wouldn't work with the *News* anyway. Fortunately, at New Rochelle, the last express stop, a young Negro secretary got on and took the seat beside him, so Fitzie didn't have to shrink himself, but let his side touch hers—no pressing, just naturally—for the last half-hour to Manhattan. She smelled nice, very female, and by the time he got to Grand Central, he was feeling better.

It was as if Janice and the kids hadn't tipped him off an hour before. Fitzie entered his office, saw the lone white envelope waiting on the top of his desk, the only object there besides the single lamp, and was totally surprised to find that it was a birthday card. It was from the company and was signed by the president—personally, not by his stamp. He turned it over. Hallmark. Twenty-five cents. Simple, tasteful. Hmm. There must be somebody in personnel who has to do it; keep a list of birthdays, check it, buy cards, have the man sign them, and send them. It shouldn't be striking him so sharply: it was perfectly in character with F&F, it was that kind of agency—blood drives, Secretary Day, Christmas parties for employees' children, profit sharing, flowers and matches in the reception areas, so why not birthday cards. Thoughtful. Benevolent. His secretary, Pam, entered the doorframe. "Good morning, boobie, happy birthday," she said.

"How the hell did *you* know?" Fitzie said.

"The card came last night, for me to put there this morning."

"Oh. Terrific. That why you're all dolled up?" She wore an extremely short black-leather skirt and black-leather bolero.

"Silly. I have a date."

"You going to whip him or what?" Fitzie laughed as the girl came in, closed his venetian blinds halfway against the sun and hit the base switch on his desk lamp.

"Don't you like it? It's Paraphernalia and I can't eat for six months!"

"It's great, very hip. I love it. You going to get me coffee or not?"

"Okay. Why don't you have a Danish or something too? I'll put a candle on it."

"Ha-ha. No."

"How many, anyway?"

"How many what?"

"Candles. Twenty-six, like? Twenty-eight?"

"Twenty! Come on, go get the coffee, will you?"

"Jeez, some birthday boy," she said, hurt.

"I'm sorry," Fitzie said. "Let me wake up, huh?" What's the matter with me? Why didn't I just say thirty? It's the truth. It cannot be that I don't want to seem old to young girls. It cannot be that. Goddamn it, it is not that!

His phone rang. It was Marv Silver, the creative director, who must have been the only person in the world who didn't know it was his birthday. At least he didn't mention it. "Hey, that's great," Fitzie said when Silver delivered his news, "Jesus, that's really terrific. Thank you very much, man, really. Aah, come on, yeah, yeah, the board of directors—I know it was you. No, not today. I've got a recording at United from twelve to two, rain check huh? Right. And thanks again." He pushed the cradle button down with his finger, keeping the receiver in his hand. He felt like a robot, obeying control signals from some remote source. With as little thought as he had had when he said words to Silver, Fitzie dialed home. Janice answered.

"Hey, it's me, he said. "Guess what.

"What?

"They just made me a vice president."

"Oh!" she gasped, "that's fantastic. That's fabulous! Oh, wait'll Boston hears this!"

"Christ, don't tell them. They'll think Hubert Humphrey died."

"Ha! Oh, God, this is great. You must be flying!"

"Yeah," he said. "Well, I kind of had an idea. I mean, hell, it's just another thing to keep me here. There's nothing dumb about them that way, you know."

"Oh, listen to the toughie," Janice said.

"No, listen, really, what is it? It's not any more money, you know. It's just a rug and some stationery, it's just something it's better to have than not to have, that's all. Just because there's already four thousand other idiots who have it."

"Yeah, and fifty million who don't," Janice said. She wasn't taking him seriously. "They made you it on your birthday, did you think of that? Oh, this makes everything perfect. Do you think they knew?"

Jesus God, she's right. "Well, they know it's my birthday. They sent a card."

"Really?"

"Yuh. But, no, this is separate. This was Silver. In fact it won't be announced for another week or so."

"Boy, I'm so excited. Will you be on time tonight?"

"I don't know."

"You should have drinks with somebody, to celebrate."

"Goodbye, Janice."

"Oh, okay, see you tonight."

Fitzie hung up. Pam brought in his coffee, all sugared and stirred, and walked back out without saying anything. Still in a little huff, Fitzie thought vaguely. He felt drugged. Maybe he should go home to bed and get up again, start again. Everything seemed weird. Even Janice. "You should have drinks." Yeah, and get hit in the mouth when I come in late. Or get the Silence for a week. Anyhow, he had done the vice president thing nice and quickly, passed it straight from them to her without getting any on his fingers. No, wait, there was a little sticking there. Christ, he felt lost. The house was supposed to be hers, the job his. Why had he put the V.P. over onto her side? Janice was obviously delighted; he felt nothing. Man. The transmission's starting to come in garbled. It must be this goddamned birthday gig. So I'm thirty. So the hell what? And it cannot be the frigging kids either, with their *Don't trust anyone over* noise. What do they know. Because I am not thirty *thirty,* for Christ's sake, because thirty *thirty* means old, fifty, dead, stupid, corrupt, fat. Listen, buddy, *you* go do almost four years in the Army. Well, no, not Vietnam, that's different. But *you* come start in New York at twenty-six, goddamn it, then talk to me. Oh, it wasn't canteen coffee. She went out to Schrafft's. Well, that was nice of her. That was something, at least.

Then. Right then, right away; not later, not even a half-hour for Fitzie to drink his coffee, get his head straight, start things going, make some calls, see some people, do some work. No, right then, the Local button lit up and sounded, *bizzt-bizzt.* "Yeah?"

"It's a Sheldon Horowitz?" Pam said. "Who's that? He says you know him."

He not only knew Horowitz, he knew exactly why he was calling; although the two hadn't seen or spoken to each other for what, now, three years? Over that. Fitzie had heard on the street that Horowitz was out again. This time for a shitty fifteen-grand job in some little dump, instead of from the eighty or a hundred-grand spot he'd had before that. Or from the sixty-grand job he'd had when he had hired Fitzie. Christ, that had been an August, too. "Should I put him off?" Pam said.

"God, no. Let me speak to him."

Click. "Fitzie?" the voice came in its boyish littleness, its tiny lisp. Fitzie could see the face, the cigar, the black suit, black tie, blue shirt.

"Hey, Mr. Horowitz, how the hell are you?" Fitzie said not over-heartily; Horowitz was not simple. There was an unexpected pause. Disconnected? No, the little voice was still there and now it said, "Well, isn't that nice."

"What?"

"Hello, Fitzie."

"Hi,"

"You called me *Mister* Horowitz, you know that?"

"Yeah?"

"Nothing, it just hit me funny, that's all."

"Well, hell, I still call my father Daddy, too. You know. And I've been bigger than him since I was twelve," Fitzie laughed. *Oh, no. You prick. Why'd you say that? Bigger than him! God. Now you going to tell him you're a V.P.? And isn't it tough that he's on the beach? Nice. Real nice.* "No, you know what I mean, I guess I'll just always see you as the boss and me as the trainee," Fitzie said, and the way it sounded made him sick.

Horowitz laughed faintly. "Well, I'm not going to ask you how you're doing because I know. I hear nothing but very good things about you, Fitz, and it makes me feel proud."

Oh, please don't do that. Not that. "Aah, well, you know," Fitzie put it down.

But Horowitz wasn't doing that. "What I called you for, Fitzie, is this," he said. "Look. I saw Marv Silver yesterday afternoon. And I'm seeing the big man tomorrow, huh? Now, they may call you about me. They shouldn't have to, but they might just the same. So I thought I'd call you and ask you this. Just this. *If* they ask you, I'd appreciate it if you'll think back to that time, and if you can remember anything nice about me, about me— well, just tell them that, would you? Now, if you'd rather not, all you have to say is you didn't really know me that well. You know, too many people between you and me and all that. That's legitimate." Pause. Then: "There. Well, that all I wanted to say. You know it's too bad we haven't seen each other. That's my fault. But I'm not

167

going to say let's get together for lunch or something, 'cause we won't, will we. But I don't think that necessarily means anything bad, do you?"

"No, I don't," Fitzie said. He cleared his throat.

"And we always get your Christmas cards," Horowitz added.

"Yours too."

"Well, okay, then, Fitzie, keep it up and I'll . . ."

"No, wait, listen," Fitzie stopped him. He was too beautiful. He had to be told something. "Mr. Horowitz? You're asking me not to say anything bad about you. Okay. But I want you to know something—I don't have to try to remember anything. I remember. And there was nothing bad. Not as far as I'm concerned. It was all good. I'm sorry, I have to go now, goodbye." Fitzie hung up. He lit a cigarette and sipped coffee. *Wow, what a way to come on to me. What a beautiful way to come on. Ingenious, too, the old bastard. He'll make it back, he really will.* Because if he hadn't called, Fitzie wasn't sure what he might have said to Silver, if asked. That F&F should be getting rid of all the Horowitzes they had instead of bringing any more in? Maybe. Fitzie believed that. Or that Sheldon Horowitz was a smart, savvy pro who ought to realize he doesn't know how to write ads and commercials anymore? Probably. Fitzie believed that, too. But now. Now he knew exactly what he would say, if asked. He'd lie. He'd say, yes, you should hire him, he's terrific. Because Horowitz had been the man who had hired him, and he owed him that. And because a company is only a company. Birthday cards or not.

Although it meant leaving the air-conditioned cool for the muggy noon heat, he was glad to be out of his office, out of his building and on the street. This was new, too, this getting cramped at his desk, itching to be on the move all the time. He walked up Madison, smelling the delicatessens filled for lunch take-outs, watching the cars and cabs curse the yellow Con Edison pens around the idle generators and jackhammers. He watched himself coming along the blocks in the store windows. He was a young guy, that's all, who knows how old. They called him *sir* in restaurants and such, but hell, they called him *sir* in the Army when he was only twenty-two. He got looked at, but that shouldn't bother him. He ought to be used to that. He had the tough face and he wore colors, which made him not one of the ubiquitous New York midtown men, so he got looked at.

Today it was four singers, already rehearsing beyond

the glass wall when he arrived at the recording studio. Women with the voice of Peggy Lee or Lena Horne, but no face, or a dumpy body or a farina personality. Men who could sing like Tony Bennett or Andy Williams, but were too short, too homely, too lanky, too unsexy, too something or not enough something else. Sometimes it depressed Fitzie, seeing them up in a room like this at microphones anonymously singing ad words. Other times—depending on his own condition at the time—they reassured him. After all, they were working, weren't they? At something they liked doing, too—not in a car wash or laundry or bank window. Today, they depressed him. Luckily, they were only in for a half-hour re-record; the rest of the session would be a rock group—which never depressed him. He wouldn't open his head to them today, that's all. He wouldn't listen. His producer was there already, talking to the engineer at the control board, speaking through the switch on the timer box to the voices. It was Trevor Williamson, so Fitzie could trust him. He seemed to be always linking up with Englishmen; what would Janice's old man say to *that*. "Hello, mate," Trevor said.

"Hi," Fitzie said, "you looked pretty." Blue denim shirt, black bellbottoms.

"Glad you like it."

"They all right?"

"Mm. We're about ready to put one down." He nodded to the sound man and told the singers, "Okay, lads, let's do one now."

"Get us anything to eat?" Fitzie said.

"I beg your pardon," Trevor said and pointed to the deli box filled with aluminum foil mounds and lidded cups.

"Sorry, I'll never doubt you again," Fitzie said and took a burger and a cup with an *R* on the lid and sat on the metal chair against the back wall. He ate slowly, looking at the floor, only dimly aware of the voices and music. When he did look up, Trevor was looking at him quizzically. "Thing I hate about you, Fitz, you're on my back all the time."

Fitzie smiled. He suddenly felt drowsy. "Was that a take?" he asked.

"It was. I've let them go. What, your mum not keep her promise last night?"

Fitzie gave him the finger.

Trevor laughed and took a burger. "Oh, my," he said. "We're going to be fun to be with, aren't we."

Fitzie threw his foil ball into the basket, stood and lit a

cigarette. "Aah," he stretched, trying to come out of it, "if I hear that song again I'll puke. When are the kids due?"

"Half twelve. They'll start drifting in shortly, I expect."

"Well, *that* should be fun."

"When are you going to write something that'll *take* us someplace?"

"Ha. Everything I do lately starts with 'Open on full shot. Eiffel Tower.' "

"Good. As it should be. Heat got you?"

"No, I don't know. Just the wrong side of the bed, that's all," Fitzie said and thought, Trevor is good. Janice hasn't even met him after all this time. We'll have to have him out. We have to start seeing more people like Trevor again, more kooks.

Fitzie and Trevor waved back at the new group through the glass as they unpacked. Five boys, two still in their teens, all with the Jesus hair and the shades. "Hope the account men come fortified, our loveniks there will scare them to death."

"There won't be any account men," Fitzie said.

"Not told?"

"Told that I'd break their faces if they even phone."

"What I hate about you, Fitz."

It was Fitzie's lyrics and their music and on Trevor's cue they began laying it down. Layer by layer. Hard rock. More than an hour of this, adding, adding, and they were still far from ready to pour in any singing. "We won't make it, man," Fitzie said at the clock.

"Booked the afternoon."

"Very good."

They took a break for coffee and Trevor passed around the forms for them to sign. When they began again, it was there. They were soon ready to begin building the tiers of words. The lead asked if they could hear their music back. Trevor had them wait while the engineer did a rough mix, then amplified it, loud, into their half of the studio. Smiling, nodding, they began to sing, three grouped at a boom mike, the drummer and organist staying back. It was hard. Take five, six, seven, eight. Take fourteen. Fitzie by now was feeling like one of them. Like Trevor's, his fingers and legs and head couldn't help moving. The beat, the sound moved down through them like air. "How old are you, Trev?" He asked right in the middle of it all. He didn't know he was going to say it. His words under the noise surprised him. Trevor showed no reaction. He just answered, "Twenty-four," and didn't add "Why?"

Fitzie was confused. He wanted Trevor to return the

170

question so he could see what "thirty" would bring to his face. And he didn't want Trevor to return the question.

Then the group did their freak-out. They screamed and wailed and pushed it to a frenzy, then let it thin and thin and finally fade out. It was wild. Fitzie and Trevor applauded into the sudden silence and the group lifted their arms tiredly and smiled. The engineer had been mixing all along with his third hand, tapes spinning on three Ampexes, stopping, reversing horizontally and vertically, so he needed only another ten minutes to overdub the last few takes. When he finally had it and played it back, Trevor wanted something cut out, and the lead had problems somewhere near the end, but Fitzie had no idea what they were talking about. He was overwhelmed by it. It was out by itself somewhere and extremely hard, which was good because he was going to lay it over milky, watercolor-soft film pictures. He loved it. When they were ready to play it again, Trevor came back from the engineer and said, "Now, this'll be close to it."

It played again. The group was smiling at each other, Trevor was all teeth, hitting Fitzie on the arm, and Fitzie felt himself sinking. The coming-to-be of the music had drawn him higher and higher up to lightness and excitement, and just as he was feeling up and happy he went right over the top and down again, barrel-assing straight back to the bottom. "Oh, no, man! You don't like it?" Trevor groaned, seeing Fitzie's face.

Fitzie sank into the chair and covered his face with his hands, pressing his fingers hard against his eyes, trapping his breath warm on his skin. Then he took his hands away. "No, it's beautiful. It's fantastic. It's *too* good, you know?"

"Oh," Trevor said.

It made him feel sleepy and heavy to think about it. "It'll be agony," he said more to himself than to Trevor. "They'll hate it."

"They won't understand it, you think?"

"Ah, it'll be too loud. Too hard. Too raucous. Not *clear* enough. Not *nice*. You know. We want it to be new and all that, but. I just dread what I'll have to go through to get them to buy it, that's all."

"Well, look, Fitz. You want to fix it, then? I can bring it all down easy enough. And I can bring the words up. You want to maybe put the whole line out in the clear once? Would that help?"

Fitzie smiled. "Yes, that would help. No, we won't

change it. Up theirs. This is the way it's supposed to be and this is the way we'll go with it."

"Okay, but if it's going to be all that bloody hard on you."

"Ah, maybe it won't. I'm out of it, today. I'll feel better when the time comes. We'll sell the mother." Fitzie winked and stood up: no sense in pulling everyone down with you—cut the rope.

They crossed back to Madison on Fifty-second Street. It was after five. At the doorway to the Barberry Room Fitzie stopped on an impulse and pulled Trevor inside with him. By God, he would stop for a drink with someone. They stood at the bar and had two gin and tonics each, talking the recording. Fitzie thought birthday and vice president and kept quiet about them. He left Trevor at Forty-ninth to bring the tape to the agency and went on alone toward Grand Central. The DONT WALK pushed him back up onto the curbstone at the corner of Forty-eighth.

The first car on the starting line was a dull blue, beat-up Falcon and was slow to move out. The frantic honks of the furious cars behind snapped the Falcon out of its daze and it finally turtled out into Madison, a two-way street then. As the Falcon reached the middle of the intersection, a gleaming yellow Chrysler taxicab roared up from behind on its right, then incredibly hooked a left in front of it, burning rubber to go down Madison. It didn't make it. The Falcon hit it in the left rear fender. Both cars froze like a snapshot. That bastard, Fitzie thought. As he watched, the cab driver came out cursing. A gorilla, twenty-two or -three, the neck of an ox, khakis, tight white tee shirt, sleeves torn off at the shoulders to show the horse-leg arms. He covered the Falcon driver's face with *fuggin' assholes*, then swaggered back to his wheel, horse-arms ordering him to pull over to the curb. The onlookers began to continue on their way, but Fitzie stepped off the curb. *What the hell. I saw it. I'll tell him. Screw that wop.* He took two steps and stopped. As the cabbie's door slammed shut, the Falcon's flew open. *Oh, Christ, he's juiced.* One second before, the man was innocent victim. Now he was merely a little less guilty than the outlaw cabbie. The man had *thirty* scrawled all over him. High school football player gone beer-fat, cheap summer suit open over transparent cotton shirt, skinny Tie City tie. He was a slob; he was his car. He lumbered up to the cab. The ox looked up, knowing the words. But no words came, the slob's fist came, landing flatly on the cabbie's

172

cheek. The ox couldn't believe it. Fitzie's bowels rolled over sickly. More people stopped now. The cabbie, of course, was out again; he hit him, *chuk!* The slob bled immediately, down onto the white shirt. He grabbed the cabbie's neck, the wrestler's start, but then just ripped the tee shirt, *sshhitt!* A worried groan came out of the crowd. The cabbie punched the fat, boozed Falcon driver. Fitzie tightened his stomach to prevent the man from bursting into tears. He wanted to yell Stop! But the fight seemed too sordid to be stopped. It had to go on, and he had to stay watching it. But something was wrong inside him. The fight turned sadder and yet funnier now, as the Falcon driver began bouncing delicate karate chops off the ox's shoulders and arms. *Oh, my God, he's pretending he's a black belt! Swish, swish,* the open hands flashing down to land like masseuse taps. *Chop! Slash!* Fitzie knew it was funny but his body turned female on him and was disgusted. His stomach shrank with nausea as if he, not Fat, had taken the knee in his balls, and his legs shivered. The traffic screamed at the top of its lungs. Heads began looking for the cop that had to arrive but never did. In worse shape than he looked, the cabbie was stumbling around as stiffly and tiredly as the Falcon driver. Desperately, he began swinging his arms like softball bats, clubbing Fat against the ears. And when the ass finally went down, it looked for a second that the ox himself might pass out, but he didn't; he just hung there on the edge of gravity, coughing. Now Fitzie could leave. He walked unseeing to Grand Central and onto the train, feeling his stomach still cringing and hating it. He tried to remember exactly when he had last fought anyone, but couldn't decide whether it had been in college or even longer ago, in high school. What had happened to him, that he couldn't take a fight? What had turned him into the ensign who faints at the floggings? Oh, my God. A mad scientist had drugged him and operated on him without his knowing it and had removed something. Something he needed, and didn't want to lose! But when? How? Had Janice been in on it? No, no.

On the train, unexplainably halted for fifteen minutes, fans off, in the Bronx, the gin and tonics helped Fitzie slip behind a thin sleep. When did they take it out of him, his spinal fluid, his appendix of tough? Long ago? Just this morning? Or it's the heat. Or it's this foolish birthday thing bugging me. Or it's nothing and I need a drink and shower and some TLC.

173

It was eighty-six degrees and six forty-five at the Merri-mac station, but Fitzie didn't call Janice for a ride and didn't hop the bus. He walked. Before he was halfway, his crotch and his armpits were soaking. He didn't care. He wanted to turn red and pour sweat all over. Hep, toop, threep, fo. Go, baby. Maybe all this damned depression could go out through his pores and get sucked into his suit, which he could take off when he got home. Aah. Even on good days, he would start tightening up and feeling down right along here, by the little lake, anyway. And he could never manage to throw that grim sense of The End that dropped over him every night. Why couldn't getting home be just the second half of his busy, interest-ing, fast day—instead of the leaden, postgame vacuum it seemed every night? The spirit in him all day—funny, bright, excited—could never seem to make the trip from Manhattan to Merrimac. It fell out over the Harlem River, he guessed, if it made the train at all. It was as if he didn't know who he was at home or what he was supposed to do or say. Even when the children weren't aggravating, cruel animals but Loretta, Joey and Millie all fed and washed and ready for bed, running around or busy at something or watching TV; and Janice wasn't harassed but chipper with lipstick on and her hair brushed and life seemed as it should be, under control, chugging forward, glad to see him—even on those evenings he couldn't seem to catch the beat and get in with them. He wasn't sure which chair was supposed to be his. He didn't feel there at all. He was still coming up the stairs behind him or still on the train or back in the city or back in Brooklyn or the Army or working in the ice cream plant or pushing the carpet sweeper over his mother's rug. Someplace back there, all the time. Someplace else. He kept hoping that one night *he* would catch up with *him* and it would be Fitzie himself who walked in the door.

Janice. Janice. How crazy. It seemed now almost that he had to go away from her to be with her. During the day, at work, he'd think of her and miss her and love her. Yet when they were together, they weren't. Before, they would lapse every now and then into Silences or squab-bles. Now they would lapse into happiness. They had to go along and wait for it to happen again, praying it would, afraid it wouldn't. Before *what*, though? Fitzie had origi-nally blamed it on the house. It had started then, he would decide, when they had moved out to the house, and he would play with the conceit that he hadn't really moved out with them. That was it. Sure. It was like hell. It had entered their lives before that, right in their wonderful Brooklyn apartment. He was past the lake and the pines, nearing home. He wore a mustache of water now and his sideburns were darker than the rest of his hair. As he always did, he checked himself, like taking his pulse, like reaching over in his pants' pocket to see if his cock was there. No different than any other day. He was, as usual, back behind himself somewhere, swimming in the Harlem River: he dreaded reaching the house, where he wanted to be more than anywhere else in the world. When he finally slogged around the corner of his street the teacher was there on his chaise lounge again. Fitzie knew he had been there all afternoon. "Hiya, Fitz," the teacher waved and grinned. "How was Fun City today?" Fitzie wanted to go stomp him, but he laughed. "Watch it or I'll buy your school and fire you." The teacher was a decoy. When Fitzie's foot struck the first brick step, the front door sailed open and there was Janice in a pink cocktail dress with feathers all over it, tanned legs down, tanned chest and shoulders up, her face a match flame. "Surprise!"

He could only look up at her radiating there and laugh and look shocked.

"We're going to have a party!" Janice sang, coming forward to reveal her silver shoes—also new—as she clicked down to meet him, kiss him and hand him one of the filled German crystal wine goblets she carried. She clinked her glass against his, "Happy birthday," she whispered, "congratulations, I love you, and everything."

He sipped—martini!—as she did, then kissed her in return, still having no words to say except, "You didn't. You hussy!" At the doorway, he said, "I've never *had* a birthday party!" He felt happy.

Janice stopped, her arm in his. "Really?"

"One. When I was seven. Billy Chadwick peed his pants and had to go home."

"Oh, that makes it all the better. Now stay right here. Close your eyes and don't move until I tell you." He obeyed and felt her leave him. He stood there in the dark. "Now!" Janice called from inside, from the living room to the left of the front foyer. He opened his eyes and walked forward. When he turned, the music from a flaming Wurlitzer started and Janice and the children sang "Happy Birthday to You!" from their places in front of it, although the machine was filling the room with "Piano Roll Blues." He caught Loretta slip in a ". . . dear *Fitzie*,"

175

and made "I heard that" with his mouth. They repeated the chorus a couple of times so they could end when the Wurlitzer did, then all roared laughing. Fitzie played the whole thing for them, keeping his mouth and eyes wide open in astonishment, rocking his head back and forth in his hands, then finally clutched his heart and fell to the floor in ecstasy. Joey pounced on his belly, then they all hauled him up like Gulliver. "We're having *two* parties," Janice said.

"Where the hell did you get this, it's fantastic!" Fitzie asked, rubbing his hands over the round, smooth top of the machine, swirling lollipop colors inside its head.

"I rented it."

"Aw, I thought it was for me, it looks beautiful in here."

"It's thirty dollars for the night," Janice said. "I don't know if they'd sell it."

Fitzie sat on the floor with them around the cake on the coffee table and opened his presents. One of his own ties from Millie, wrapped in aluminum foil. A paperback *Moll Flanders* from Joey. "He liked the cover," Janice grinned. And a frozen orange juice can transformed by Loretta, with silver gilt paint and elbow macaroni and glue into a pen and pencil holder for his desk. He blew the candles, ate the cake and some M&M's and drank a little orangeade, exlaiming his surprise and pleasure repeatedly until it seemed their party and not his. Then Janice said, "Now you have to hurry. Everybody'll be here in about fifteen minutes. Have your shower, and I left you clothes on the bed."

"Everybody who?"

"Everybody I could think of."

"Honest to God?"

"Yes! I got carried away after a while and even told people they could bring someone if they wanted to."

"Beautiful! You're too much. I still don't know how to react. Hey!" He had looked into the kitchen from the stairs and saw the six-foot hero sandwich and the table-size platter of hors d'oeuvres under green cellophane. "Will you look at all this! And the booze! Good God, lady, you get a second mortgage or what?"

Janice laughed and pinched his side. "The dress alone will keep you poor and mine for the rest of your life. Like it? It's your birthday present."

"I can't get over it. Any of it!"

"Well, I thought maybe poor Daddy could use a good blast," she smiled, but looked away quickly as she said it.

176

"Daddy?" he said. They had long ago agreed never to do that, call each other Mum and Dad, even though their children were at the ages where it was easy to slip into.

"Oh, you know what I mean," she said. "Come on now, go get handsome."

Fitzie started up the stairs, but had to turn back. It was the closest they had ever come to saying anything about it. "Hey. That bad? A real drag?" he asked her.

Janice shrugged. "No. Serious? Aloof? Discontented? I don't know." Then, the power back on, the lights up again, the teeth: "A hoss's arse!" she said, mocking her own accent. "Now get going, will you? We're having a *party!*"

"Fantastic," he laughed, "okay," and went on up the stairs. Again, he had known it, but had to hear it to really know it: she had been suffering. He had been hurting her. Without wanting to. Without being able to stop, to change it. He put on her flowered shower cap and laughed at himself in the mirror. This was great. He couldn't believe it was happening, right in his own house and in just a little while. He hadn't been surprised in a hundred years, in fact he wasn't sure if he had ever been surprised the way Janice had just surprised him. He showered. When his cock began to awake he thought of doing it, the lather like female come, but didn't—it would take the edge off his feelings and tonight his feelings were happy and excited and hopeful. He scrubbed dry with the coarse towel, picked the martini from the sink ledge, threw it down, went into the bedroom and dressed. The Wurlitzer sounded up through the floorboards.

The children filed past him up the stairs, visibly mad but *being good*. He turned and went back up, telling them each that the best party was over, then went down again feeling young and lean, Errol Flynn checking the game tables. He felt like flipping a half dollar. The teacher and his wife were the first there and Fitzie accepted their greetings Flynn-smoothly, making the talk-talk, putting his arm around Janice's waist. They had their drinks, so Fitzie went to the kitchen for himself and damn! if she hadn't hired a bartender, somebody's graduate student son. Perfect. Then they came, the Party, people he and Janice knew and didn't know, some bearing bottles, some funny birthday presents: the toilet paper printed like dollar bills, the unspillable drink, the legitimate Ronson lighter, the Bogart poster. Like farmers to church, the closest arrived earliest, with few exceptions. Montague came early, although from Sheridan Square, having changed from work-elegant to night-chic, bearing a wide brown belt for Fitzie that buckled like a saddle cinch. Fitzie put it right on and wore it for the rest of the night. Montague was the only one of the old bunch who made it. Until very late, the party was a crowded, milling, dancing scene; chattering, drinking, dancing, laughing. Tall, Montague weaved through them seemingly a part of it but aloof as a fashion model hired to mingle. Janice and Fitzie were too busy to stop long with anybody, but were still both surprised and disappointed when Montague said goodbye a little before midnight. It was all right because he was one they would be seeing again, yet it seemed somehow also too bad, like running into someone you want to see at the wrong time, late for an appointment.

Buck and Betsy Stevenson arrived separately, she early from Croton, he later from the city—half-smashed from killing time in Charlie Brown's at Grand Central. Like Montague, they were real to Fitzie and Janice but also got cut off by the neighbors and other quasi-strangers making the Wurlitzer Room a dream scene. Buck and Betsy, however, stayed. About fifty people made the party. Fitzie's secretary Pam and her date, a junior something at Chase Manhattan. Then a lot of other people who existed for Janice as only names-from-work, or at the most as faces Fitzie had introduced to her at other parties, plays, occasions. She had simply looked them up in Fitzie's address book and called them—and only the Sunday before, when he'd taken the children to the Statue of Liberty. That was part of what made it more happy hour at a cocktail lounge than a house party: they had been given very short notice; it was the middle of the week; it was a surprise party. Walking into a house with a Wurlitzer helped. So did Janice's Army maneuvers: the bartender, the more-than-enough liquor supply. When she brought out the food around ten, she set it up far from the bar, to keep everyone up and moving. Fitzie avoided the men and moved all night from wife to wife. Primarily, he danced and drank. Once, late, he pulled Janice into the tiny john off the kitchen and mugged her up. He wanted to say something to her but nothing came out that meant anything. Not realizing his dribble of words were anything but pleased gin sounds, she abruptly dropped down onto the toilet pulling up the feathers. Slightly put down, but mostly angry at his own tongue, Fitzie slipped out and decided to get some air.

On the back porch, he stood on the edge of the top

wooden step and breathed the warm night air, trying to make out the swings in the rear of the yard. Then he looked down and saw the mound on the bottom step. It was Buck. "Hey, what's the matter?" He went down and squatted beside him.

"Hi, Fitz," Buck said after looking up and straining to identify him—his movements, his words, all thick and slow motion.

"Uh, oh. Past the point, old buddy?"

"Yup."

"Going to puke?"

"Already did."

"No help?"

"No."

"Still dizzy?"

"Fitzie, I love you but goddamn I hate all the fucking phonies you got in there."

"Ah, they're okay," Fitzie said. But he didn't know if they were at all. He hadn't noticed, one way or the other. They had all just been his Party. "Somebody get to you?"

"They all did. Their smartass word games and all that shit. They think they're so sophisti-cated, they don't know what it is."

Oh. Not the neighbors, then, the work people, the writers and producers. "What, they playing trivia on you?"

"Thassit. But they don't think they are. Warhol, my ass. Oh, Fitz," he put his hand on Fitzie's knee, "I think I'm gonna barf again." Fitzie rose and helped him to his feet. "Come on, Buck, let's make it around the block." They walked, stopping to let Buck empty, hard, into the teacher's hedgerow.

"And that big bastard and all the *ass* he gets on *location*."

"That's Ralph. I guess he does," Fitzie said, baffled. Was all that going on? He was glad now that he hadn't been paying attention. "Come on, though, don't let them get to you."

Buck's head was up now and he was walking without Fitzie's help. He kept spitting into the curb and breathing loudly.

"I think I'll go home, Fitz."

"Now, no, you don't want to go home! Besty's having a helluva time. No, we'll walk it off, you don't want to leave me alone with all the phonies anyhow, do you?"

"Ah, maybe they're not so phony, it's probably me."

"Hey, remember the roof in Brooklyn? First day we met

you guys? Cold as a bastard, Statue out in the harbor? Seems like we were ten years old, now."

"Yeah. Not so long ago, either. Almost lost the family jewels that day."

"Ha! Going down that skylight into the tub! Christ."

"Maybe I should have."

"What?"

"Lost it."

"Hey, what the hell is bugging you, babe?"

"Oh, all the talk. You know there's some guy back there telling me how he knocked his wife up ten years ago and that's why he's married to her but he's glad because she's made him what he is today."

Fitzie had no idea who that could have been. "So?"

"So, shit. So nothing. Fitzie, I'm involved with another woman."

"Oh, Jesus." But then, Army training: halt! No questions. Just listen. "I'm sorry to hear that, Buck."

"Why sorry for Christ's sake?"

"Because I love you and I love Betsy. And you don't seem very damned happy about it, do you." *And you think it's a mortal sin, too, you hypocrite, why don't you tell him that?*

"I'm *drunk*, that's why!"

"Okay."

"It's not that simple, Fitz, you know?"

"Yeah, I know." Pig's ass. Is she a nice girl? Do you love her? Don't you love Betsy anymore? Are you *screwing* her? How did it start? What are you going to do? No! No questions. He was sober now; at least he had walked off that overhigh daze and returned to the level where thought and talk and driving a car were possible. Handling Buck's thing was not possible at all, however. He stored it away for tomorrow, for sometime. "Hey, know what we need?"

"A drink," Buck said.

"Exactly." They were coming up to Fitzie's house. A car was pulling away, another starting and turning its lights on. "Let's go in the back way. Hate to be coming in when people are leaving."

"Christ, we should see you guys more often," Buck said, meaning it.

They paused on the stairs. "Why haven't we?" Fitzie said. "What the hell happens? We're not that far away. Not in the same building, but, shit, what?"

"I don't know. We just don't, I guess, that's all."

❁

As Fitzie opened the door to the kitchen, the glass hit
the wall directly above the jamb and he got glass, ice cubes
and watered liquor down over his hair and forehead.
"Hey!" he yelled, his arms coming up too late. He backed
into Buck and knocked him against a wall coat hook,
"Yow!" A female back left the kitchen for the living room
as they came in from the hall a second time. It was Tru
Wade, her husband Eddie—tall, bearded, young, owner of
a film house Fitzie sometimes worked with—close behind
her, following, pleading with his arms. Fitzie looked at the
four or five faces hung around the kitchen. He didn't
know any of them. The bartender was gone. "What happened?" he asked, wiping his face and head with a pink
paper towel from the rack.

"We don't know," a girl said. "They were talking together at the table and I guess they were having a fight or
something. She just let the drink go over her head."

"She never even looked,'" the man beside her said, "just
threw it straight back and took off."

Fitzie balled the towel into the wastebasket and went
into the living room. The Wades were opening the front
door, alone. There was almost no one there anymore.
Janice was sitting in the sole remaining group on and
around the couch in earnest discussion: Betsy Stevenson,
the Rubens from up the street—the only Merrimac people
Fitzie and Janice had made contact with—and Jerome
and Trixy Buffington. Jerome worked with Fitzie. None of
them looked up. When Fitzie passed them and reached the
Wades, Tru was already going down the stairs. "Hey,
Ed?"

Ed turned, "Oh, hey, that was great. Happy birthday,
Fitz."

"You guys okay? Tru going to be all right?"

"Oh, yeah. She's, you know. I'll see ya, huh, man?"

"Okay, Ed. Say good-night to her for me. Drive safe.
Thanks for making it." He went back into the living
room. The Wurlitzer was still turning its colors but was
silent. Quiet music was coming from the stereo. Buck,
with a fresh drink, was in the group now and they were
going at it. Snips bounced off Fitzie's ear as he passed
through: *Malcolm X, Bobby Kennedy, military-industry
conspiracy, violence, busing.* Vaguely, summer thunder
way out in the Sound, Fitzie snagged a tremor in Janice's
voice, a little hostile, cutting off Sarah Ruben's calm
words. But he ignored it and went back to the kitchen.

181

The strange people were still there, two young couples and a single guy, all in mid-twenties except the single, who was closer to Fitzie's own new age, thirtyish. They had full drinks and were sitting at the kitchen table and leaning against the stove and dishwasher. The single guy was perched up on the counter next to the sink. "Watch the splash," Fitzie smiled as he dropped a handful of machine cubes from the plastic sack into his fresh inch of Cutty Sark. "Everybody got what they want?"

"Fine."

"All set."

"Terrific," Fitzie said and turned to them, pulling on the scotch. Who the hell are they? he wondered, and was dimly surprised to find himself staying there with them.

"Your friends kiss and make up?" the single guy said from above.

"Oh yeah," Fitzie snuffed. "I guess they'll be okay."

The two couples tittered generally. *Oh Lord, newlyweds? Engaged?* The scotch going down felt far away and impotent. "Too bad, though," he heard himself saying, "I hate to see people go at each other like that. Especially them. Ed is Christ, he really is."

"With that beard!" one of the girls squeaked. Fitzie looked. White blouse, plaid skirt a little long, nylons, ratty hair, heavy forearms, a tiny blue Immaculate Conception medal hooked to her silver wristwatch. Oh dear. Twenty-two going on forty-four.

"Not just that," Fitzie said. "He's really the world's most gentle man. Really a *good* person. Incredibly successful."

"What's he do?" one of the young husbands asked. Probably the Immaculate's. Crew cut, white shirt, low ankle socks, madras sports jacket, smoking Raleighs.

"He started as a cameraman, then he became a director and started a film house. Ed's like thirty-five or thirty-six and if he isn't a millionaire he's close to it. They're building a house in Connecticut someplace that I hear is like the Dalai Lama's palace."

"Doesn't sound very *Christ*-like," the single guy said. "Do they have any children?"

Hmm. Ah, ha! I know what *you* are! "Three," Fitzie answered. He had met so many in Boston he could smell a priest a mile away. "One by his first wife, two theirs."

"Ah," the single said.

"What do you mean 'ah'?"

"Nothing. There's just always something."

Fitzie sensed a current pass through the others behind him. "Always something what?"

The man smiled down. "Well, all I know is two people had a fight ending up with a full glass being thrown against a wall, he's been married before, and you say he's Christ. I'm not saying anything." He smiled again. This time, an actual sound from the others, the rustle of breaths. And there it was suddenly inside him, the old thumb of anger jammed up his windpipe.

"If I say he's Christ, he is. I know him. And his first wife *died*. In a car accident. When she was twenty-six. Ed's still got a bum hip from it. Okay? But I think you were figuring divorce and I say so what?"

"You better tell him, Al," the Raleigh smoker grinned.

Fitzie looked as the guy eased down from the counter. Damn. He was over six feet. "What," Fitzie said, "that you're a priest?" He was pleased with himself; he had taken the fun out of it for them.

"Yes. Father Al Cronin," the priest said and put out his hand. Fitzie shook it and looked around, admitting he didn't know the others. They all gave names and shook his hand. He kept only Munroney and Coogan. The Raleigh guy was with the frumpy girl; he left the other two in their invisibility. But how the hell did they get here? As if she heard him, the medal girl said, "I knew Janice from P.T.A. at Saint Raphael's last spring. I met her at the Grand Union this morning and she invited us and said to bring friends."

"You're kinda young to have a kid in school."

She blushed. "I'm a teacher in the kindergarten. A lay teacher."

"How do you teach that?" No response from any of them. He turned back to the priest. "Where's your collar?"

"He only wears his blacks when he has to, right, Al?" the Raleigh smoker said.

"I find they build a wall," the priest explained.

"I don't know, I've always thought there was something sneaky about plainclothesmen," Fitzie said and knew he was going to go after him. But why? Because he was thirty and because he was unhappy and because he felt like it and because Ed Wade was very goddamn Christlike and because Buck was having an affair and because he was on his twelfth scotch and had passed the point where he could get drunk and leave it all. Father Al. *"In mufti,* right?"

183

"That's right!" the priest said. "I haven't heard that in a long time, though."

"What are you, a Latin scholar or something?" Raleigh asked Fitzie.

"Oh, sure. Tantum ergo makes your hair grow, Agnus dei puts out, all that."

"No, really, did you have Latin, did you go to Catholic schools?" the priest asked.

"Six years of it. And two of Greek! The *Ratio Studiorum*. Terrific."

"Ah, the Jebbies, then. By that accent, I'd say Holy Cross, right?" The priest started to fix himself a new drink.

"No, B.C. The same thing without dough," Fitzie said, and his body, in spite of him, had already begun obeying ancient stimuli and was reaching down the bottle of Pinch from its hiding place. "Here," he had to say, "saving the best wine until last."

The group laughed.

To retaliate, Fitzie added, "See what you can turn it into. Make it blush."

The priest wiped the quick squint away from his eyes. "When did you get out?" he asked.

"Fifty-eight," Fitzie answered.

"Me too."

"Where'd you go?"

"Saint John's."

"Father Al did two years in the service before he went in the sem," Raleigh put in. Meaning he's really a man, Fitzie understood, he's been around, he really knows, you know? Wow. Holy cow.

"Enlisted man?" Fitzie asked, trying to get it back to the fight he wanted.

"Yes, you?"

"Missed captain by a month."

"Why'd you get out?" the priest asked. At least he had known enough not to add any water to the Pinch, Fitzie noticed.

"Money."

The priest smiled. "And are you making it?"

"No, the Pinch was a gift from the Holy Name Society." There. Just in case you didn't know before, *Father Al, buddy, chum.*

They smiled at each other.

"Father Al and St. Raphael's Holy Name aren't what you might call the best of friends, either," Raleigh chuckled from the sink. Touch that Pinch and I'll break your

184

fingers, Fitzie thought. The clod didn't take it; he poured gallons of the Cutty into his glass and said, "I guess you haven't heard Father Al on the pulpit."

"No, I haven't." That's it, let them think I don't go. "You pretty hot stuff, Father? Am I missing something?"

"Mass, maybe?" the priest said and the gallery glowed. "I say the eleven-thirty and the five every Sunday."

"Well, I say the eight. The working people go early. Fitzie winked. "Maybe I'll sleep in though, and stroll down later, if you're really worth it. You say hell and balls for the nice people, that it?"

"Phew, you've really got a chip on there don't you, fella," the priest said, the squint in his eyes tight.

"Shouldn't I? You've had your say for decades, and you didn't do shit. I'm sick of you."

"Then why do you go?"

"To Mass? That's my movie, not yours. You're just the hired man there, buddy. Read the book, lift the chalice. That's what we pay you for." Fitzie made himself a fresh drink, from the Pinch. "Okay, Father, come on, say something in Young Rebel. Then say someting in Vatican Two. Then we'll mourn the assassination of Pope John."

"I will if you'll say something constructive. It's easy to throw stones, but change takes work, and getting involved. What are you involved in, Mr. Fitzpatrick?"

"With Mrs. Fitzpatrick and all the little Fitzpatricks. But you can call me Fitzie."

"Well, that's not enough, my friend. The Church needs more people like you. Why aren't you sounding off where you can do something?"

"Like where?"

"The parish has all kinds of things going."

"The parish, Father, is a dead fish. I can hardly see myself as a sheep in Monsignor Whatsisname's flock. We aren't immigrants."

"But you have your children in St. Raphael's," the kindergarten teacher said, trying to be nice.

"We took them out in June."

"Oh."

"Why?" her husband said to defend her.

"Because it can only pay its teachers about three grand a year and that has to make for pisspoor teachers, and because most nuns still think a lily grew out of Saint Joseph's staff, and because parochial schools don't teach faith anyhow."

"Oh, come *on*," Raleigh said, incensed.

185

"He's right," the priest said. "But when are you going to say something I don't agree with?"

"I couldn't care less what you agree with or don't."

"Nevertheless . . . ."

"Nevertheless whaleshit."

The priest laughed. "You're too much," he said. "We need more piss and vinegar like that."

"Know when you'll get it?"

"When?"

"When you go to Harlem," Fitzie said. He needed blood. *You.* Not some priests, *you.* In your blacks."

"How can *you* tell *me?*"

"Because you have the collar on. On your forehead. You go help somebody, and I'll come and listen to your daring sermons. I'll even sit beside old Irving here."

Irving lit a Raleigh, eyes behind gauze.

"What's he tell you, Irving, that makes you and your lay teacher think he's so wunnerful? Huh? The Pill? He make all the old ladies gasp when he says it's up to you? You like that, Irving? You take the Pill every day, Irving?" His own laughter stopped him, then Janice stopped the whole thing for a while. She came through the door with three empty glasses. She had had an empty kitchen in her mind, and Fitzie saw the sight of them take the tight frown off her face. "Oh! What's this, another party?" A bell rang in Fitzie's mind: she's loaded and looks all up tight. What's she into in there?

"Janice," he said, "meet Father Cronin. You can call him Al. And these are the Munroneys and these are the Coogans. Or vice versa."

"Oh, shut up," she laughed. "Hi, Francine, and this must be Jimmy." She shook Raleigh's hand, who grinned to tell the world he was sober. The others said their names to her, but Fitzie missed them again. "Is he telling you filthy stories?"

"We're talking religion," Fitzie smiled at the priest.

All dutifully ho-hoed. Fitzie was trying to catch Immaculate Conception's eye. *Hey, dummy, see how you oughta look?*

"Listen, why don't you all come in and break up the goddamned gloom in there?" Janice said.

The *goddamned* tipped it. Something had its teeth in her, all right.

"Here, let me," the priest took the glasses from her.

"Oh, thank you, Father, I have to go to the little girl's very badly."

"What'll it be?"

186

"A bourbon on the rocks, scotch and water, and a sour. They're in the refrigerator in a jar."

"The Cutty, the Cutty," Fitzie whispered loudly to him and went after Janice, heading for the toilet. "Hey, lady, how you doin'?"

"Oh, that damned Sarah and her esthetics dreck again. I've really had it!" Not good, Fitzie saw. She's really bombed. Ah, it was probably nothing to sweat.

The priest had the drinks ready, and was pouring new Pinch now into his and Fitzie's glasses. "Well," he smiled to all, "now that we've got me in Harlem, what'll we talk about?"

Fitzie had lost interest. Now he wanted it to change. He wanted Montague to be there, or somebody who would insist that everybody be laughing. It was his birthday and he was supposed to be having a blast. And, oh my God, now they were silent. Maybe they'd follow Janice and join the other group and then maybe there'd be a realy party again. No such luck. Janice emerged to the cheers of rushing water, picked up the priest-made drinks, said, "Come join us when you feel like it," and was gone again and none of them made a move. He felt the priest near him and knew that he, too, was moving his toes around inside his shoes. Poor bastard, what's he hang around with creatures like these for? Must not have anybody else. Empty room, single bed. All the more reason for getting off his ass and doing something.

"You were discussing the Pill before with Jimmy," the priest said, lips tight. "You're not *against a* new ruling on artificial contraception?"

"God, no," Fitzie said, glad for the sounds. "I just think you're all running around as if the world's waiting for Rome to *proclaim* something—when really nobody gives a rat's ass *what* the big stone Church says."

"Then why have a Church at all?" Raleigh demanded.

"You asked it, you answer it."

"You *are* oversimplifying," the priest warned, "careful now."

"Careful your ordained ass. You guys are really hung up on sex, you know it? Those guinea cardinals with their frigging rhythm. They have no idea that the one time in the month you *can't,* is when even the most frigid chick in the parish really wants it. That's natural, right? And when Rome says okay, kids, sexual intercourse each other, you don't want to. The guys got a soft on . . ." Fitzie stopped. " 'Soft on!' You hear that?" he guffawed. The others

187

laughed, a little; even the other husband rose from the dead and snickered.

But the priest was speaking and his sounds brought Fitzie's guard back up. Uh, oh, we've touched a nerve. "What you don't know," he was saying, a little quivery, "is how difficult it is for *us*. How would you like to be inside that confessional and hear people *bleeding* and not be able to help them? Do you know how that feels? Who do *I* go to? Who cares about me?"

"What's a mother to do," Fitzie cut him off coldly. Not me, Father. Some other time. I'm sorry, but there's a time for truth and there's a time for bullshit. No truth tonight, thank you. Raleigh came out of his anesthesia just in time, ready to strafe Fitzie at last. "I know guys like you," he began, with such animosity in his voice that Fitzie wanted to hug him. "You Madison Avenue bassids!"

Fitzie welled up with love for him. Say advertising, say advertising! We'll get on that, and I'll hand you your ears. My father, monsieur, was the best swordsman in France!

"You're full of shit. That's what you are, fulla*shit!*"

"Jimmy . . ." Immaculate Conception cautioned.

"Naw, somebody's gota let him have it," Raleigh said, "you guys gimme a swift pain in the ass. Anything goes, that's you. All the hippie pigs. Somebody tries to be good and he's a square. I know. And nobody's supposed to love their country anymore. If you don't like it here, get out! That's what I say. And get out of the Church, too, if you can't take it. Bullshit to all of ya." He was wearing down. Fitzie wanted to feed him, get him going again.

"Well, the Knights of Columbus *are* a bunch of fags," he said sincerely.

"Ah, screw yourself!" Raleigh stared down at his empty glass. Fitzie poured some Pinch into it for him. There might be somebody home in there after all.

" 'Fags,' *You're* all fags, your fruity clothes. Big belts. But that's okay, too. Anything you want. Run away. Don't work. Picket the colleges. Jesus Christ."

Up boy, up. Okay. "Well, look, everybody in Washington *isn't* rotten? Come on, who do you think killed Jack Kennedy?"

"The Commies! goddamn it. And you know it. And they're behind the hippies and the niggers and all of it!"

"Tell us about the *niggers,* Jimbo. What's the Church say about that, huh?"

"Kiss my ass, fella. You phony bassids." Raleigh drank his Pinch.

"We ought to be put in freight cars and gassed."

"Yeah!"

Fitzie roared.

"Oh, Jimmy," Raleigh's wife said.

"Okay, come on, Jim, that's enough," the priest said.

"You're a pain in the ass, you know that?" Jimmy said again to Fitzie. "I know. I don't care. These guys want everything to fall apart. Let the kids go crazy, hair like girls. Girls going around with nothin' on."

"It's great, ain't it?" Fitzie winked.

"Great, shit. Everything's crappy and these guys say it's great. People goin' crazy on LSD. Addicts everyplace, for Chrissake. Kids smoking pot."

Oh, Christ, how to end it? It's all getting too stupid, I feel like going to bed and I don't want to feel like going to bed. He looked at the shadow couple now for the first time and said, "Hey, Father, can't you put something on their tongues, give 'em the power of speech?" He had pegged them as more of Raleigh and wife, only quiet, but he hadn't been sure. Maybe they were alive and open and simply content to listen. But no. Addressed by Fitzie at last, the other-Raleigh answered and in one quick gesture told him what he was and what he thought, and provided him the jolt he needed to escape from them, from his day. The kid, leaning against the refrigerator, lazily dropped his left hand across the middle of his extended right arm. "Hey," Fitzie said, "do you know what you just did? Did you mean that?"

"Mean *what?*" the guy said. He could have been leaning against the window of a pizzeria at night, with the boys. That's how he said it.

"You cross-armed me."

"So?"

"So that means fuck you," Fitzie said. Hit him. He's the cop at the station, the cab driver, the board of directors, the priest, the New Haven Railroad. Hit him. "Get out," Fitzie said.

Nobody moved. A photograph. The priest's face made a grin, You're kidding. "Didn't you hear me?" Fitzie said to the priest "I said get out. All of you. Right now."

"Who do you think you are?" Raleigh said, not believing it yet either.

"I'm the one who just kicked you out of here. Now, move."

Immaculate Conception believed him and got up. Fear on her face, she stepped toward the door to the living room, toward the voices of the others in there. "No," Fitzie stopped her, "out the back way."

"Hey, listen, Fitzie, nobody . . ." the priest began.

"You too. Out!" Fitzie said. Errol Flynn.

"Damn right I'll get outa here," Raleigh said and moosed through the door to the back porch. Fitzie smiled. He wouldn't have to say it again. They were leaving. The priest was the last and turned his face to him, sure Fitzie was going to take it back. He stood at his screen door and watched them go, heading for a Rambler station wagon. For him they were gone already. He walked back inside. He had to get back to his party.

The empty kitchen surprised him. My God, I did it. I booted them the hell out of here. Well, I'll be damned. He rehid the Pinch and sauntered into the living room, feeling numb and removed. The Wurlitzer was asleep, quiet and dark; someone had unplugged it. Three on the sofa: Buck, Jerome's wife Trixy, blond and all legs, either listening or sound asleep with her eyes open, and Sarah Ruben but with her face and talk directed away and to Janice perched on the old piano stool. Fitzie plunked himself down onto the floor behind and between Jerome and Betsy Stevenson. Leonard Ruben sat in front of Sarah but was in the bigger conversation.

"Where are your friends?" Betsy whispered.

"I kicked them out," he grinned.

"Oh," she smiled and returned her gaze to Jerome. There it is again. I make sounds, you make sounds. I said I kicked them out, you think I don't mean that. He looked around at the silent movie. Wonder what they're talking about? Looks awful. Janice's eyes have turned to marbles. "Fitzie!" Trixy had just seen him, no rest for the wicked. "Trix! It can't be you with all these scholars. What have they done to you!" She got off the sofa and pulled him to his feet. He took her to the stereo.

"Now we'll have a damn party," she gushed, squeezing his hand. She had been asleep; she was smashed. Fitzie rejected the plain gelatin music and racked up a Rolling Stones record under his cherished *Dave Brubeck Quartet in Europe*. The talkers hardly looked up. He and Trixy faced and began dancing. Trixy, Trixy. Female. Janice couldn't stand her. Fitzie liked her. She was thirty-eight and reminded everyone of it often to hear the surprise, the disbelief, the flattery; that's how unhappy she was about it. She might have made it as a singer, dancer, actress. But she hadn't. The stories had her in twenty beds at the same time, but Fitzie liked her and Jerome too much to consider their possible truth. He preferred to regard Trixy's relentless sexuality as another defense against her name, her failure, her living these many years. She had wonderfully full breasts and did everything, short of showing them, to make people notice how perfect they were. Trixy could really dance, and now Fitzie watched her go and tried to learn from her, feeling alone with her and the music. Buck passed through his vision once, then came back through the fog carrying a tray of fresh drinks. He and Trixy covered a lot of the room. When they came close to the group, Betsy and Leonard smiled up, but Sarah and Janice could have been alone out in the yard. He and Trixy fell into a laughing embrace when the rock record ended, then broke apart to sip liquor while the Brubeck fluttered down. "The Wright Groove": easy, piano, horn, sweet but up enough for them to just slow down the hips and jerks and improvise. But then "Like Someone in Love," and they had to go together and dance body-to-body, her head on his shoulder for a while. As the piece built they broke apart, laughed to each other and began to jitterbug. This was good; when they had been love-dancing, he had started to worry about what he had done in the kitchen. Trixy wore a sheer minidress of summer pastels swirled together like oil globs on a palette. Moving frenetically yet in patterns, she turned into something else in his head: Wurlitzer lights against some slender kiosk covered with bright posters. After the music stopped, it took her body a few seconds to come back together and stop moving, and she had just about made it when "Watusi Drums" began and caught hold of her. Like nursing a near-still yo-yo back into its spin, the rustle of applause then the taste of drums, slow-starting, then the delicate peck of the piano sent pulse after pulse out and down into Trixy the round puppet. Then it was all Joe Morello and leather heads on hollowed rain forest logs. Trixy's eyes lost Fitzie's face and turned down inside herself. The drums sent waves of shock into her body, coursing from her shoulders to her hips and pelvis. Her blond head hit the air and made the sounds. East Baltimore Street, Fitzie thought. Jesus Christ. He took his drink from the fireplace mantel and watched her go, looking over to the others with a grin. At least one of them had to look up now and see he was innocent. Luckily, Betsy did and said, "Oh, there goes Trixy!"

Trixy's husband Jerome turned his head, smiled, and turned back.

Buck's eyes cleared long enough for him to say, "Ooo, go, baby."

Sarah and Janice looked at her the way mothers notice a child. *That's nice, dear.* Then they went back, *Now go away, Mama's talking.*

Leonard Ruben watched Trixy's ass—Marilyn Monroe in *The Asphalt Jungle*—rolled his eyes at Fitzie, then incredibly returned to Jerome and Buck.

Leaving only Besty Stevenson, sitting, and Fitzie, standing, to watch Trixy dance her all-alone erotic dance. She was humping. Please stop, Fitzie thought, but she didn't. She went down to the floor. *For Christ's sake!* Fitzie begged. Trixy was being fucked, for all to see. Her dress climbed like crumpled paper, revealing her thighs fine and tanned. Fitzie looked but Betsy had turned away! *You bastards.* He could see her panties now, a lilac bikini that her hair showed dark through, and she was rocking her mound hard and up. *Goddamn it, that's Trixy Buffington's pussy right there and you're all just sitting there!* His penis had gone rigid. *Jesus, I think I could drop down and knock her off and they'd step over us to go get drinks. Janice!* He drank big swallows of his scotch. *Aw, come on, Trix, gimme a break. What did I ever do to you?* The skin of her lower belly now, above the panty top, now her navel. Just in time, Trixy made a mistake. Morello was going like ten warriors now and Trixy tried to stay with him but it was too much, too rapid, and she lost the beat altogether. She stopped the banging. She opened her eyes and laughed, "Phew!" and got up from the floor. She stood there breathing hard, straightening her dress. Sweat shone on her forehead, and, as if she had merely just given a yoga demonstration, she turned all exuberant and out of breath. "Where's my drink? Oh, thank you," she laughed loudly as Fitzie handed her her glass.

The others were faces-up, smiling and applauding her. Under cover of the noise, Fitzie hissed to her, "You cunt." "Mm, you're a hunk," she said and walked back to her place in the middle of the sofa. "That was great!" "Terrific!" "Atta girl," they were saying to her. As if they had been watching. As if she hadn't lain on the floor on her back, pulled up her dress and dry-humped Mr. Air on Fitzie's living room floor, at his birthday party, to his Brubeck record! Which he had had since Germany. He stood there with his drink in his hand and his cock sinking back to sleep. *Holy Mother of God, I'm losing my mind.*

I'm not even here. Nobody's here. We're up in bed asleep and we're somebody else, somebody very young and not in anything, living someplace else all by ourselves. "Anybody need a refill?" he said to the group. Maybe now they would all go home. Jesus, it was three o'clock. Or at least maybe he could sit in and it would be light and funny. That's what he wanted now. "Jan?" he called over Leonard's head. "How you doing? You want one? Sarah?"

He stepped past Betsy's back and stood near them. "What's the big fight about?" he chuckled, too loud. He looked at Janice. She was waiting for him to leave.

"There's no fight," Sarah smiled in her lush, cello voice. "Your wife is playing Babbitt, that's all," she said.

"That's what I mean," Janice bit, her face nearly blank. "What does that *mean?"* You don't talk in anybody's language, even."

"Explain to her, will you, Fitzie?" Sarah sighed.

Thanks a lot, Fitzie looked at her. "She means," he said to Janice, "that you're what, too literal?"

"Well, why doesn't she say that then! And I am not. I'm just trying to wake her up to the fact that people are just people that are very damn real. And her whole cute little *esthetics* bit is a lot of phony crap!"

"Maybe you're both right," Fitzie smiled. Light, funny. "Maybe you do run away in your own world, Sarah, and maybe you could give an inch or two, babe; abstract doesn't have to be unreal." He didn't know what he was saying, he just wanted to brighten them up. Janice's look sent a shiver across his back. Oh, man, she's crossed the line. And pretty drunk himself, he left her. It couldn't mean anything. Nothing could happen. Trixy hadn't really done what he thought she had, he hadn't really ordered strangers, invited guests, out of his house. He rejoined the couch-floor circle. Leonard was speaking now, telling his Jewish Father stories. They were funny, Leonard doing the dialect perfectly. So Fitzie couldn't be Bob Hope, then. All right, he'd have to be The Shadow again. He made himself invisible and sat down beside Betsy.

He couldn't have passed out. But something had happened, the room and the people in it were oozing around him. Had he smoked grass somewhere along the line and didn't remember? Whatever, here he was, watching a weird flick. Human voices on the soundtrack; the figures floating beautifully through all the thick liquid glass. Whee! Wup, the pink. The pink feathers in the round corner rising up and drifting away. Lost it. Aw, so pretty too and now it's gone. The lookout in the crow's nest yelled *It's Janice!* But the voices seemed too sweet, too important to listen to anything else. Something sharper and louder then. A slam. A door slammed. The pink left? He shut his eyes, drawing back across the slow-motion fire; a quick implosion that gave him a headache, then he opend his lids again and could see. Nothing had changed, except Janice wasn't there. Everything was standing still again. Invisible, he went out to the kitchen.

She wasn't in the toilet. He saw them on the table then and had to concentrate to make them out clearly: a claim ticket for shoes. Two dry-cleaning slips. His Diner's Club card. What in hell were they doing there, in their little row? He lit a cigarette from the gas flame on the stove and the new sound reached his bent ears. In the garage. She was trying to start the Opel and it wouldn't start. *Ha, that's my little old buddy, the Green Hornet won't go for anyone but its master!* It usually went for Janice, though. He suddenly remembered the others inside and felt embarrassed. They have no right to see us like this. He floated into the circle of people, hoping his Invisible Man switch wouldn't go on automatically. He sat, visible and listening. He didn't look when he heard Janice back in the kitchen, but when he heard the phone dial clicking he sneaked a glance over his shoulder. Her suede coat on. *The one I bought her in Copenhagen; looks fantastic still, after all these years.* She hung up and disappeared from the doorway again. Buck was talking, the rest smiling; good. Light and funny. The door slammed again. Listen to Buck!

He didn't snap sober completely until the growl of the cab's engine and the short squeal of its brakes came to him from the night outside. When they did, he put his glass onto the floor, rose and walked swiftly to the front door, out and down the steps. Running under the beech tree he yelled, "Hey!" but the rear door slammed anyway, enveloping Janice within its darkness. He ran back inside. The conversation went on. He softly called, "Hey, Betsy?" as he passed through to the kitchen. She came out behind him. "Listen, love, I'll be back in a little while. Keep an ear open for the kids, will you? And don't say anything."

"Fitzie, what's the matter! Where's Jan?"

"It's okay. Nothing. I'll be back." The Opel smelled of gas. Flooded. *Chigger-vrum.* The engine turned over and held steady. He flew back out to the street and whipped off. There were three lights between him and the Merrimac station. He stopped at the first and imagined the cop from the morning coming up to him now. He jumped the next light and the last one turned green for him. He rubbed the hard, smooth steering wheel with both thumbs. *I am here. She did go. Us. Now.* The station roof and arms black against the faint silver of first light easing up in the east. He leaped from the car, not shutting it. Nothing. Nobody on the platform. The station house shut and dark. The timetable taped to the window, read in the match light. The last one was a half hour ago, she couldn't have made that. She's not here. Jesus, she didn't even come here, she went to La Guardia! Back into the Opel. Nothing. It had stalled. "Come on!" he said aloud. "Come on, baby. You bastard, come on!" No go. He switched the key, eased the choke, pumped the gas but he only flooded it again and the whirr of the ignition started to slow and sour. He shut off the key and sat there in the still dark, rubbing his palm roughly back and forth beside him on the straw seat cover. He pulled back the sweet-sweet push to pee. Of course! He hammered the shift into reverse and released the handbrake. It started to roll. There was enough of a grade. Moving, he switched on the ignition and jumped the clutch. It caught. He would have to go back to the house for money. Oh, Christ. He fired the little old car nearly into the air, speeding back the way he had come. At his sidewalk he set the choke to hold the engine at its eggbeater shiver and ran up the front stairs. He stopped at the top. No, go around the back, get in and out, don't make a big thing of it with them. He jumped from the fourth step to the walk and vaulted the hedge to run along the side. Just past the dining room window he stopped.

Running, he had thrown a quick look into the house, to make sure they were all still there and okay—not pacing around calling the FBI or anything. And they were still there, but they didn't look the way he had left them, rather the way they had looked before: Janice was back on her piano stool talking with Sarah! He walked back to the Opel, reached in and shut it off. It quit with a shudder. He went into the kitchen through the back door and walked into the living room. Not looking at her, he went and sat down beside Betsy, who smiled worriedly at him. He told her everything was all right and thank you, with a smile and a wink, his heart banging in his whole body. He looked around. Still talking. *Nothing, right people? I haven't moved. You didn't notice a goddamned thing.* Well, to be fair, they couldn't have left, could they. They had to stay. You can't just up and scoot when your host and hostess have just stormed out—you have to stay and wait. For a while anyway. Still, Fitzie wondered if

195

one word, one glance had been passed. He looked across, past Leonard's ear and Sarah's knees, at Janice's face. The knot was gone. She looked tired, but sober. Sarah was saying something but Janice wasn't listening. He was alone with her. Fitzie suddenly laughed, inside. *Man. She didn't give a shit if the Queen and Prince Philip were here. She split! She had to take off for some reason, so she went. Son of a bitch, if she isn't something.*

In less than fifteen minutes the party broke up, easily, the way parties end. When he and Janice spoke, their fatigue let it be without anger. He locked up the downstairs. When he went up, she was in bed and nearly out. "Take some Alka-Seltzer?" he said, undressing.

"Yes."

"Where did you go?"

"La Guardia. Only we just got to the Hutch and I had him come back."

"Why did you go?"

"I don't know. I just had to get away from here."

"The booze? Or Sarah, was she really that bad?"

"No. The booze, I guess. I can't drink anymore."

"You were leaving *me*, though."

"I know."

"At least you left me the shoe ticket."

"Yeah. It's a good thing the car wouldn't start. I would have killed myself."

"Do you want to leave me, Janice?"

"I don't know," she said into the pillow, rolling under the covers to face away. "I just want to go to sleep."

He collapsed into the bed on his side and pulled up the sheet. Then he reached and snapped off the light and when he brought his arm back the pain burst in his head, as it had been waiting to do. Running into the sightless cave of sleep he knew he was moving in the opposite direction from Janice. She had gone that way, he was going, swiftly, this way. He knew, yet he didn't somehow care.

The alarm rang like an ax. He squeezed it dead quiet immediately and lay there. Guilt, guilt, guilt-guilt-guilt, guiltguiltguiltguilt—the sound of internal bleeding. *Oh, God, let me lie here and be still asleep. If I wake up, it all happened and if it happened, I don't know what I'll do.* Jesus, Moses, Moon, anybody! I'm living this dumb little life, nobody, doing nothing, just eating and earning enough, thinking tiny thoughts, never making the newspaper. Every day is so short and quick, only our years are quicker, why don't you lay off—whoever the hell I'm talking to. Get off my back. What did we ever do? It's so little, so fucking ordinary, it ought to be easier and simpler, happier and it's not. And it's getting worse all the time and I'm over thirty. When I open my eyes I'll be in my thirty-first year and I don't know any more than I ever did. I thought you said I'd reach a point where I would know. What ever happened to that, huh? You bastard, you cocksucker, I wish I knew the worst word in the world. Get out. Like them last night. Get out! Leave us alone. It's going bad, it's rotting! And the thing is, you dope, you clod, you meathead, you've arrested the wrong guy. This is me. I'm clean. I'm nobody. I can't do it, I can't fake it anymore. Look. Please. When I open my eyes, let it be yesterday, okay? The only thing I ever asked for before was just to let us be okay, let us make it, and the only way you can come through on that now is to make it yesterday and not today. How about it? Give us a break.

The ceiling. White and wide. Smooth, not a map, only faintly gridded. Fitzie looked up at the bedroom ceiling and suddenly his mind did the somersault. This hadn't happened in years. The ceiling became a floor and he walked around on it, and the best part was stepping over the thresholds, which were two feet high. Up and over the little wall and into the next room to walk over the plaster to the light standing up straight on its chain and look into it like a water bubbler, only there was a bulb there looking back instead of a drain. From there on the pillow, Fitzie couldn't tell which ceiling it was; was it his mother's, his grandmother's, the one in Germany? Genies and time machines were always fucking up. Maybe he had been sent years back instead of just the day he had pleaded for. You never get exactly what you order. He'd have to check. He switched on the rest of his body, his nerves, his hands. Ah. His right hand. He was flat on his back, his right arm was out and lying on Janice's belly. His right hand covered her cunt, his middle finger nestled a little deeper than the others, down in the hair, almost in the warm opening. But it meant nothing, no hope there, it had gone there on its own, neither sent nor invited. He turned a quarter inch on the pillow. She too was awake, lying there. Then he knew. It hadn't worked. It was today. Their hips were nearly touching, they were awake, but they hadn't come back, the distances covered by their night sleep-running hadn't diminished or disappeared; his hand was on her mound but it was as if his arm were ten miles long. Plasticman! Here, but very far away at the same time.

"Hung over?" he said quietly.

Silence.

"I'm dead," she said. She wasn't describing her hangover, she meant she was dead. The *sadness!*

His hemorrhage began spurting, guiltguiltguiltguilt, again deep inside him. "God, it's only seven-fifteen," he moaned. If he talked to her maybe her soul wouldn't leave.

"Are you going to work?" Her voice was without tone.

"No. I could never make it."

"I hear the kids."

"Yeah. I'll get up. I wonder what it is to sleep late, like until eight?" he said. Talk. Talk!

Janice didn't answer.

I bet that priest knows what it's like, he thought and forced his body, in pain, out of the bed. He went and booze-pissed, long, making much foam. Back in the bedroom, he pulled on white Levi's and a loose polo shirt over no underwear and went barefoot to feed the children yelping now down in the kitchen. He looked at Janice from the door before closing it. She had pulled the sheet up to her chin and closed her eyes. A little more and the sheet would be over her face and head. Is that her, Mister Fitzpatrick? *Yes. That's her. That was her. I did it. I must have. Nobody else could have.* Leaning down on the glass knob of the old heavy door so it wouldn't jam at the top, Fitzie pulled it closed tightly. Downstairs, he poured Rice Krispies into bowls, quieting the three pajamaed children gently. "Hi. Ssh, now, keep it down, Mama's . . . your mother's trying to sleep, okay?" Millie pointed her finger at him, turning in her highchair, and yelled, "Joot!"

"Huh? What's the matter?"

"She wants juice," Joey laughed.

"Us, too," Loretta added, "when you get the chance." Christ, she was being sympathetic.

"Oh, all right. Sorry." Luckily, it was already made, so he had only to pour it into glasses for them. He made coffee, lit a cigarette, picked up the wastebasket and walked through the house emptying ashtrays. His house was now a place where a party had been, an empty cocktail lounge in the morning. Ashes. That's what everything seemed to him. In a corner of the dining room he spotted the pile of glass. Christ, it was another piece of their German lead crystal, gone. Janice's suede coat was there, thrown across the teak table. The furniture, the

198

coat—he had bought both in Copenhagen that time. It was the coat Janice had worn to disappear into the cab in, to go to La Guardia in. Now in the light he noticed that the cuffs were fraying badly at the edges. He carried it to the hall closet and put it on a wooden hanger. It seemed so much thinner, so much lighter than it had been. Then he remembered the car.

There it was through the window, still on the street, out all night. He stepped through the front door into the morning August air, and went across the mildewed grass to the Opel. The keys were still in it. He turned the ignition. *Click.* He turned it again. *Click.* Poor little Opel, the Green Hornet, it had taken them everywhere they had been. *Click.* It was no use. She was dead. He removed the key and stepped out of the car, shutting the door. Very still at the grass crub, there was a sheer layer of white over the Opel's green chassis, white top and chrome bumpers; her windows and headlights were opaque and wet. He walked away and into the house to call Texaco, saddened but also vaguely irritated; so far as he knew he had always taken the right care of the car, drove it well, followed all the instructions in the operator's manual. It wasn't *that* old. Why the hell should it flake out on him, then? Well, he'd have to do something. He couldn't just leave it where it was forever. Maybe he could just roll her into the garage and leave her for, say, the winter, and maybe after that, well, he'd see. Sure. He would do that.

Six

HE WAS CARRYING his green B-4 bag through the automatic-eye glass IN door to the TWA terminal at Kennedy and it made him feel back in the service again, on his way somewhere, loose, free and tough. It was December and he was flying to California and he was going out of his mind with excitement. Cool, he was concealing his childish glee by disguising it, for the cabbie, the porter, the ticket girl, the boarding steward, as energy. Now there's a guy with a lot of balls in the air. See how he runs. Run, guy, run. *Look, I do this all the time and I'm in a hurry to get to my seat because my producer's waiting and we've got a lot of work to do so let's not have any little mix-ups or anything to annoy me, huh? Okay, let's get the show on the road, that's a good kid.*

The ping in the green eyes of the Welcome Aboard stewardess standing inside the plane at the end of the boarding tube: he didn't believe it. She gives that to old fatsos and kids and ladies; they taught her that in stewardess school. Trevor was there, saving the window seat for him as requested. "Hey, mate, there you are. Thought you weren't going to make it," he said in his British, getting up to let Fitzie slide in. Fitzie sat and was about to answer but when he looked up there she was with the eyes still going ping-ping. She was blondish, she was tanned and her teeth were so white and perfect his throat went dry looking at her. "Wouldn't you like to have me hang up your coat?" she said.

"Yes, I would like to have you," Fitzie said. He slid his suede jacket off and handed it up to her. "Thank you."

"Thank you," she said. "I'll be serving drinks as soon as we're airborne." She went off down the aisle holding his jacket to her wonderful chest.

"Jesus Christ," Trevor said. "What's this? Her *mother* took *my* coat!"

"I think she thinks she knows me," Fitzie said.

"Hot pants, it looks to me," Trevor said.

Fitzie turned and looked out the double glass window at

the coveralled men breathing white, running around doing things to the wings and great jet engines of this magical silver machine that was soon to carry him three thousand miles in a direction, west! he had never been. He knew Trevor wanted to start talking, but he stayed looking away out the window because he didn't want the taste of self-confidence and ego to go away.

"Your first, Fitzie?" Trevor said.

He turned, "No, I've flown to Europe and back, but never to the Coast before."

"I meant the Coast. But when did you go to Europe, on holiday?"

"With the Army." And so it should have begun, the exchange of personal histories, had he been simply traveling, as it seemed, with a person with whom he had worked amicably for about a year but with whom he hadn't ever really made contact. This trip, however, was happening at a point in Fitzie's line of time when it had to be more than itself for him. It had a beginning—the explosion of engines, the eerie lurch into movement, rolling out into the open runways for the incredible, stomach-pulling *up* off the solid earth into air, the plane-crosses, trucks, people, hangars, highways, house-clumps, white surf line of ocean all falling down and away into smallness below. To Fitzie the trip also had, possibly, no end to it. It wasn't the flying part, he had no thought of the plane crashing. It was the *going*. He was *going away* and he might not be *coming back*. It frightened him; he denied it. It pleasured him; he affirmed it.

He ordered—the green eyes pinging again, sweet—and got his first martini, his little paper plate of snacks. He ate and drank, listening to Trevor. It was better, he decided, to be chatting pleasantly like this with his friend. Then, if there should ever be any questioning of the crew or other passengers at some future time, it couldn't be reported that he had sat there silently, chin in hand, staring out the window, looking very much a brooding, calculating man—probably a confidence man or CIA agent. *Deserted his wife and family, hey? Doesn't surprise me a bit.* He would have to quit the flirting with Green Eyes, though. That would sound bad. Even if it was a *plan*, which it wasn't, yet, turning cockhound was certainly not part of it in any way. In fact, that was one weird thing about it; he had always thought that if he and Janice ever did run into trouble, it would be on account of that. He would somehow get involved in an affair. Or Janice would. And that would be it, *kerplooie!* That was what it always was with people. That or insanity, or something. But sex or paranoia would have been simpler to comprehend and handle than what had happened. Even if they had merely fallen out of love, he might now be actually following a careful, reasonable strategy of flight and escape, instead of only being dazzled and hypnotized by the sheer, unexpected yet real possibility of it. But they hadn't fallen out of love. What had happened to them, Goddamn it to hell, was *nothing!* And that was very damned hard to comprehend and handle.

Yes, Janice had taken off in the middle of the night that time in August, left his birthday party, got into a cab and told the driver to take her to La Guardia. But she had come back. And it had never been made clear that it was *him* she had left. They talked about it together. Not right away, but in the days and weeks afterward, at home after work at night in their living room, up in bed in the dark, calmly, seriously. She had had a terrific amount to drink. Maybe, like her father, she couldn't really take it. She had got into it with Sarah Ruben that night. Perhaps that was what she had run out on. She wasn't sure. Their life seemed normal enough, happy, thriving. Well, all right, maybe kind of dull and pointless relative to the distance and danger of the trail they had climbed to get there. And, okay, maybe he did work too long and did come home too tired, too indifferent. He'd try to change. But shit, who was any different? That was, after all, life, you know, sweetie. And hell, they were making it a lot faster and better than most, damn it. Which wasn't easy. Don't forget that. What the hell's the matter, anyway? Maybe we're making our own problems, huh?

"Maybe," Janice had sighed, "I don't know, it just all seems like a big drag."

"Oh, come off it. What'd you think it was going to be? Christ. I'm thirty, I'm a vice president and I like what I do and it makes us a lot of bread. How many people can say that?"

"Everybody we know. But that's not what I'm talking about anyway."

"Then what are you talking about?"

"I don't know! All right?"

"Well, if you want it to be all lousy, it'll be all lousy. Maybe we're just talking too much about it anyhow. Too hung up on ourselves, and our frigging *condition* all the time."

"Then let's stop. Doesn't seem to be helping anything anyway."

202

"No, really," he had said, "that may be it. Maybe we ought to start paying more attention to other things. See more plays, for instance."

"That's a thing. You know we did as much on six grand in Queens as we do now?"

"I know it, and that has to be dumb. And maybe we could take some courses or something together. And you could start sewing again. You used to love that, and God knows you were good at it. And how about the piano?"

"We don't have a piano."

"I'll buy you a piano. Why not? Hell, you haven't played in years. That's awful. You really had it. You can get good lessons, and the kids can take, too. I love piano music in a house."

So they had talked themselves into not talking so much about themselves anymore. Fitzie did buy her a piano. Janice did take lessons and began making clothes again, too. And they did start going to plays and movies and the ballet and museums. It worked. In the three or more months after Janice's walkout, their life settled. Settled. Settled. Slowly. Surely. Fitzie and Janice's life settled a little too far once, sometime in late September. It dropped, a foot through the ice, from calm to Janice's old Silence: "What's the matter?" he said, ninety times. "Nothing," she answered. On the third night he came home a little boozed. The Silence was still there. For dinner they had swiss steak, with a lot of tomatoes. From his place at the kitchen table Fitzie threw his plate through the doorway into the living room. *Pakeesch!* It smashed on the tile hearth of the fireplace, the meat flopping into some ash near the screen, the tomatoes splattering out red. Rising to go clean up the mess, he turned and punched the refrigerator door with his fist.

"What happened?" Loretta called down in her nightgown from the top of the stairs.

"It's okay, love," Fitzie assured her, "Mama just dropped something." The intern in the emergency room at Merrimac Hospital x-rayed Fitzie's hand and bound up his middle finger to ease the pain, but nothing had broken. Except Janice's Silence, which went away. Nothing much happened from then on. Nothing. Certainly nothing negative. Everything seemed to relax nicely, properly. In fact, on that one October evening when they found themselves breaking their vow and talking about themselves, taking a sort of inventory, they decided they had a going concern. Despite who they were and how little they knew, they decided they were adjusting quite neatly to their affluence, their grown-up, mature, responsible and decent status in such a complex, troubled nineteen-sixties world.

"I guess," Fitzie had said, "that it's just a matter of going with it."

Janice had agreed. "And you know what else? I was thinking. It was harder for us because it all happened so fast. You know, I mean, I think most people spend their whole *thirties* trying to make it. Striving. So it's all much more gradual for them, they've got too much to worry about just getting along. It must be easier that way. But *us*—New York, advertising—we did it practically overnight, so we didn't know what to do with it."

"That's very good. I think you're right," Fitzie had said. Agreeable. Their life became very agreeable. Fitzie and Janice lived agreeably with each other, with their children, with the people who came to dinner or for drinks. November followed, gray and mean-tempered as ever. But it didn't faze them; their house was well insulated, with Fiberglas. Steady, steady. Thanksgiving Day took pity and cut the gloom with a dose of sun, wintry-pale but reminiscent enough of Indian summer to warm the blood and bones. Which Fitzie needed badly. Not because he had been down but because he had been extremely up and hadn't let himself show it for fear of rocking their steady, settled, agreeable routine. Two days before, he had learned it was definite: he was going to California, to Los Angeles, to *Hollywood! Yahoo!* But he couldn't let on; my God, what would she think?

"Oh, that's great," Janice had beamed. "Aren't you excited?"

"Oh, I don't know, not really," *California, here I come!* "It'll just be for a few days, and it's work, and to tell you the truth I feel funny about leaving you and the little people here alone." *Toot, toot, tootsie, Goodbye!*

"Don't be silly, we'll be fine."

"Well, I hope so." *Oh, we're off on the road to Morocco!* "Still, this'll be the first place we haven't seen together, and that takes a lot of good out of it." *Westward ho!*

"I know. But it's so much money and I'd have to get a sitter, and I really couldn't leave the kids for that long now."

"Yeah. And we probably couldn't be together that much anyhow. I have no idea how its going to work or what I'll have to do." *Open up those golden gates! Oh, give me land, lots of land, under starry skies above! If you don't get a letter then you'll know I'm in jail . . .* He kept it in until Thanksgiving Day, when he was able to go dancing around the place laughing, silly and chipper, letting some of the happy gas escape.

Then, actually, it was no more than his old on-the-go juices running again after too long a quarantine. It hadn't become more, really, until the Merrimac cab let him out with his old B-4 bag at Kennedy. Only then did it gradually start to dawn on him that he was every minute, every cigarette drag, moving really and physically away, not from her personally—he couldn't think of it that way—but from all of it, the house, the street, the town, the county, the life, the *past*. And if he was moving away literally, why not then spiritually? If temporarily, why not for good? He put it down at first. But it wouldn't stay away. Until, with the slam of the cab door in his ears and the sudden weight of his bag on his arm, it abruptly took hold in his head. Men had done it; he could *split!* And personal agonies would be diluted by time, by distance, by their own ink and fleshless writing paper and stamps, and would pass, suppressed in thought as the unfortunate but unfatal dues to be paid for what he wanted so badly now—freedom, the new start, Life-Phase II. That part could all be taken care of. It could. The second, of course, that the possibility became that real to him, he shuddered and hit it with a *No!* But it had indeed, irrevocably become real, and kept slithering back to him, forcing him to look at its *Yes?* and even its *Yes!*

And sure enough, that giant silver flying thing with him in it had unquestionably powered him away from the ground. It had shrunk everything down to toy size and simply rolled it all away. And it was still doing so. He was already farther west than he had ever been, somewhere beyond Pennsylvania or maybe Ohio now, he couldn't tell. He tuned back in to check what Trevor had been saying. It was pretty interesting: he had been an amateur magician at twelve and into films by the time he was sixteen, which had brought him to New York, first for a documentary production house, then into advertising. F&F was his first agency. He was twenty-four, Fitzie knew.

"I'll be damned," Fitzie said. "My apologies. I had you down as just another kid producer. *Good*, but just starting out. God, I envy you your experience, and you're still only nine years old. Our college bit slows us up over here."

"You should talk," Trevor said, offering an Oval. Fitzie took it. "I wouldn't mind being where you are, with the power. Doing the only good stuff in the place."

"Older than you think, though, baby," Fitzie said.

"Oh, rot. How long has it taken you, ten years?"

"God, no. Less than three at F and F."

"Where were you before?"

So Fitzie told him, but in a new way, a way he himself had never heard. Four years in Military Intelligence, mostly in Europe; then New York, agency one, two, three, V.P. at thirty. The truth, but not the reality. Yet why not see it compressed that way? It sound pretty good, a little flashy, even. It sounded *new*, that was it. The pilot came on to tell them they were passing over the Mississippi. They looked out and down. "There she is," Trevor said. Fitzie said, "Yeah." That was all there was to say about the long, wiry, dark-brown line down there. Still, the idea excited him. He was now on the other side of America! Where nobody knew his reality, so would naturally accept the truth. How do you do, I'm John Fitzpatrick. Jack Fitzpatrick? Jock Fitzpatrick. Jay Fitzpatrick. Ah, they'd all come back to Fitzie, anyway. The name didn't matter, the name was okay.

"And what next?" Trevor said.

"What do you mean?"

"I guess you could own the place in a couple of years the way you're going, but I was just wondering what plans you might have. Uh, oh, tough luck, stud, Mother's pushing the drink wagon this time."

Fitzie got another martini. "No, I can't own it. The Episcopals have it forever."

"Careful, lad," Trevor smiled.

"I forgot. Make it Republican. Or WASP."

"Will you be opening your own then, do you think?"

"Ad agency? I've never really thought about it."

"You'd have to turn Italian or Jewish."

"They get all the publicity, but there's a lot of us micks around doing the same thing, and don't you forget it."

"A few limeys, too."

"True. But you, you're not going to stay in ad-land."

"Why not? No, I want to direct. Features. But commercials at first, I suspect. You know in England it's all of a piece. A man'll finish a feature one day, and go on a commercial the next. No difference to them, film's film."

"Not here, though."

"No, here the commercials are better than most of the films."

Fitzie laughed. "And a hell of a lot better than the English commercials, so figure that out."

"That's no puzzle. It's the writing here. America's way ahead."

"America, yes. F and F, no."

"F and F, no. Fitzie, yes. Lord, man, you must be thinking of doing films!"

"Oh, yeah, just putting you on," Fitzie winked and pulled the martini to his mouth for protection. Hmm. It seems you drag your own reality with you. Or you have to make up a new one fast. He hadn't been thinking of doing films. He hadn't been thinking of doing anything except what he had been doing. But maybe he ought to start thinking about getting out. *Getting out.* Hell, he was getting out right now. New place, new face, new reality—why not a new profession, too? *Getting out. Get out.* That was what he had said to those couples with the priest at the party the night Janice got out. *Got out.* Christ, she had. And so had they, what a weird scene. *Get out. You ought to get out.* Oh, Jesus, that was Janice. She'd told him to get out then. When? God, in Brooklyn that was, the night he got the Festival award and they went to Cheetah. *What do you mean, get out? I'm just getting in.* He was still not sure what she had been talking about, or what Trevor was talking about now—or what he was thinking about, really. She must know. *If she had said it that long ago she must still know.* Oh, that was terrific. *Dear Janice: I'm getting out. Of everything, including you. There's just one thing. Would you do me a favor and tell me what I ought to get out to? I'll really appreciate it. Waiting to hear from you, I remain, Sincerely yours, Fitzie. No. Sincerely, Fitzie.*

"Well who knows?" Trevor said. "Maybe Hollywood will discover us."

"Yeah. In that drugstore, what is it? Lana Turner and all?"

"Schwab's."

"Right. Or we could just go and stand on Hollywood and Vine and look terrific. You know I can't say Hollywood and Vine without hearing Bob Hope's voice."

"How's that?" Trevor asked.

"On the radio, when I was a kid. My whole picture of Hollywood comes from him. He was always talking about *Pasadena.* And the *San Diego Freeway.* And *Santa Ana.* And *Santa Monica Boulevard.*"

"Would you be open to something, Fitz? I'm only half joking, you know."

"What do you mean?"

"Well, it *is* out here you know. There are a lot of things to be had. If we wanted to sneak a week after the job's done. I've got a few names. We could probably get to see a lot of people."

"In advertising, you mean?"

"Hoot, you'd be snapped up by that! From New York? With your credits? But this is the telly, man! Everything's done out here, don't forget."

"You're right. I guess the Hollywood in my head is all gone."

"Well, what do you say? Shall we give it a whirl?"

"Jesus, I don't know," Fitzie laughed. Now he felt scared. "No, wait. You're damned right we will, why the hell not? All they can say is no," he said. He had to: he was thirty thousand feet in the air going about six hundred miles an hour over *Kansas* or someplace. Someplace on the other side of the Mississippi! Maybe there wouldn't have to ask Janice. Maybe he could find out for himself.

"What'll we tell the agency, though?" Trevor said.

"Frig them. I'll call and say the job's screwed up or something."

"Beautiful. What I hate about you, Fitz."

Then they laughed.

The stewardess came with their meals and Fitzie forgot his vow to quit playing eyes with her. "And what would you have for dessert, sir?" Trevor said slyly. They took the champagne. "Jesus, it's really a flying drunk, isn't it?" Fitzie said.

"Enjoy, enjoy," Trevor said.

Later, the screen was swung out and pulled down. "What's the movie?" Fitzie said.

"A Disney thing, one of the historical jobbies."

"You going to watch it?"

"Sure. Or sleep. You?"

"No. I think I'll go up to the lounge and watch the country go by."

He ducked beneath the screen and slid into the hot, yellow sun spreading itself over the lounge table. He looked down. Still flat. For miles, flatness cut by straight lines of roads, barely dotted by barns and houses. So much *middle*, how had his thoughts always jumped it all? The East, the West, period. Not so, it turned out. That would be something to do. *Get out*, and spend your years just moving over all of that down there. Just seeing it. What would be wrong with that? Unproductive, but as opposed to what? What would they live on? *They? He!* But, *they* had been thought first.

"Like more coffee? Oh, did I startled you? I'm sorry."

Fitzie looked up. "I was daydreaming I guess." It was her. She was there now, as he knew she would be—with the two solid Jell-O molds under her blouse.

"I would," he said. "I left my cup back there, though."

"Cups we've got." She stepped into the galley. What teeth! He couldn't minimize her. What a *girl*. How lucky she was to look like that. And there was something else, too, something *laid* about her. How lucky somebody was. She gave him the coffee, then went away. He drank it and stared down at the long, slow Middle of the country. Miles, states later, she was back.

"More champagne?" She placed the glass down and took his empty cup away.

"Great. You're married, aren't you."

"I am." She poured. Pinpoints of champagne jumped up over the rim of the glass into the sun. She sat down opposite him. He couldn't help himself. "What big eyes you have," she said finally.

He grinned and shrugged. "Can't say I'm sorry if I'm not."

"Satisfied?"

"I am. I was afraid you were wearing those damn white rubber *pantaloons* down to the knees."

She smiled. "No, I hate them."

"I'm sorry," he said, "that was very rude."

"Well. You do what you can."

That seemed to answer it.

"How did you know I was married?"

He almost said *laid*. "I don't know, just trying to say something smartaleck, I guess. You don't wear a ring, though."

"Actually I've only been married three and a half months. We just never got rings."

"And what does he do while you're flying around? Is he a student? You seem very young."

"He's in Vietnam. I'm twenty-six, he's twenty-two."

"Wow."

"*Wow?*" All the teeth, just for a second, every one of them.

"Wow, you look younger. And wow, it must be awful for him to be in Vietnam."

"It's not too traumatic. I work a lot, and the time goes pretty quickly with the crazy hours."

"What's the *D* for, Miss D. Woods?"

"Doreen."

"Doreen. The only Doreen I ever heard of was one of the Mousketeers."

"And what is Mister John Fitzpatrick called?"

"Ah, ha! Did you check the roster?"

"No. There's a tag on your seat."

"Oh. Fitzie. My buddy back there calls me Fitz."

"He's cute. Is he British really?"

"Yes, really." *He may be cute but it was me you were looking at, lady!* He wanted to say it. To hear her admit it. He had to know if it was really true.

She understood, and told him—with the teeth, the sudden push of the eyes. Fitzie felt better. "What do you do when you aren't working. Read? Rinse out a few things? Do you go out at all? I mean, do you let yourself have any fun? Oh, Christ!"

"What?"

"Forget all that, all right? I really don't want to sound like the Traveling Man."

"Fitzie. That's a good name for you, I think. What are you going to California for, Fitzie?"

"To do a show with Rita Manning."

"Really?"

"Oh, God, no. No. Rita Manning is doing a special. Which is being sponsored by a big company. She is going to do the commercials herself. I wrote one of them and we're going out to have her do it. That's all."

"You mean you're not going to tell me you can get me into something?"

"No. Not that you aren't great-looking enough or anything, but I don't have anything to do . . ."

"Wait! Look, there they are." She slid over to her window. Fitzie went to his. "Oh, man!" he said. The country had rolled over while they were talking. The earth had turned and there were the Rockies reaching up purple for the plane. White snow on the peaks in the sunlight, white on the top of purple and black, all jagged and high and extending for miles. The Great Wall of China, and he was soaring over it to the other side. He had forgotten that the Rockies would be there. The Mississippi, wide, and now the Rockies, so high and solid. And now they were between him and—everything. He was on the other side of them! He was *gone.*

"Oop, the movie's ending," she said. "Back to work. It's been very nice talking to you, Fitzie. We'll be landing soon."

"Doreen? Listen. Can I see you while I'm out here?" *I don't know what I'm doing or why, so please don't put me down!*

"Yes, you can see me out here," she smiled softly. She opened a matchbook from her pocket and wrote on the inside cover. "This is an apartment house. I share with two other girls. Don't call me until Saturday or Sunday, though. I'm not down until then."

"Okay," he said, "I won't be free until then, either."

She said, "Bye," gently, and left him. He looked at the sun hitting his cheek and half of his mouth, reflected in the window. *I did it. Me. I. Did. It. It must have been that easy all along. All these years. And I just never. But now I did. So easy.*

Just before landing, Doreen handed Fitzie his jacket and with it, a brown paper bag. He smiled up at her, with her green eyes, and took the bag and knew there was a bottle of champagne in it. *God, how good it feels! Christ!*

A rented white Mustang was waiting for each of them at the curb outside the glass walls of the luggage pickup area. Fitzie got into the second one and put the top down. If there was any doubt still breathing in him that he wasn't somebody else now, hadn't *got out,* the very air here smothered it. December; gray and raw in New York only hours before; and now this fog of *warm!* Even throttling off into it, tailing Trevor to Century Boulevard, this new kind of air touched without a chill. Where was he? Who was he? Anything seemed possible. He liked his eyes looking at him from the rearview mirror: someone else's. He switched on the radio. Something after *one?* Of course, the three-hour difference. Three hours of his life had happened, but hadn't. He had them back, to do again. Fantastic. The three hours that weren't; in there was the cave that led to Shangri-La! *Lost Horizon.* No, not lost. They were *magic* three hours. The only way he could lose them was to go back. And he would have to want to go back; nobody could make him go back. By God, there was a Santa Monica Boulevard just as Hope said, and he was on it. On it. Gunning along it in a new white Mustang with the top down, keeping Trevor in sight ahead with a new set of eyes.

Block after block, Los Angeles. It all looked to him like Central Square, Cambridge, Massachusetts. Not Harvard Square, which had color. Not even his own Tower Square, Somerville, which at least had squalor. But Central Square. A place you would look for in Woolworth's or Kresge's; no one else would carry it. Cheap, drab, low, new but a little chipped. The thought soured his mood. He lit a cigarette and turned up the radio. Good radio, real rock music—the kind New York played only on FM. Instead of block after block, it became just light after light for him and his spirits rose again; then he followed

211

Trevor's left turn and it wasn't Woolworth's anymore. Tall palm trees along the curbs, a quiet street moving slowly uphill, and houses set in grass that had water shooting up from it. Spanish villas. Miniature castles. Tudors built of Nabisco Sugar Wafers. *So this is the Kingdom of Heaven*, Beverly Hills, on Sunset Boulevard. They were above the city moving east along the side of a cliff. There was a brief pause of sky, then Sunset became the Strip. He was heading straight for Schwab's Drug Store! They veered right and followed the Strip's roll. The traffic was crazy, and he could shoot only quick looks at the places they were passing, the Whiskey à Go Go, the Body Shop, Alfie's. The yellow Chateau Marmont flaking in the sun. Bangled, bearded hippies hawking some newspaper in the street and from the curbs. Girls everywhere, walking, looking in windows, sitting at restaurant tables. None plain. Heels with toreadors. Gene Autry's Continental. Another Schwab's. Jesus, they could get discovered *twice*. The Strip thinned down to delicatessens and dry cleaners, and Trevor led him in another left along a residential street. They turned onto Hollywood Boulevard, then quickly into the Regency Apartment Hotel, dropping down into the dark underground garage, stopping theirs among the seven or eight other white Mustangs stabled there. "Here we are, baby," Trevor's voice echoed within the slam of his door.

The hotel was an atrium, four white stucco walls around a small, turquoise teardrop of a swimming pool sunk in the center. Fitzie's room was on the second level: a balcony that looked up into the hills straight above; sliding glass doors to the large living room; a dining area, a kitchen, a long hall to the two-bedded dark bedroom. Sixteen a night; you could live there, and some people did. He stepped out into his balcony and scanned the hills. Who were they who lived in all those exotic houses up there? Trevor called up from his pool-level apartment, "I just phoned, they expect us at four."

"Who was it, Kreuger?"

"Yeah."

"He say anything else?"

"Not much. Sounded harried, though. Project Rita's not going so smoothly, it appears."

"Serves the bastard right, for getting a month out here."

"My good man! I'll have you know this is a respectable place, we'll have none of your rowdiness," Trevor cautioned, then added in a whisper louder than his voice, "Besides they're all New York ad biggies here, you know.

Competition! Mad Ave West." He was right. Fitzie could spot eyes opening, sunglasses sliding down, ears pointing up from the sunbathers below.

They hit the pool with much cannonballing and splashing, mostly to irritate the loungers, but also, for Fitzie because it was December and here he was, swimming through warm turquoise, tasting chlorine.

They took Fitzie's car, up through Laurel Canyon and down the other side of the hills, Trevor directing, to the studio out in the valley. Kreuger was from one of the other four agencies servicing the sponsor. His was "the agency of control" and he was in charge; an early forties, late thirties man with a low voice and sleepy manner, looking pale and worn under his new tan when Fitzie met him. "Oh, yeah, I've heard of you," he said.

"You, too," Fitzie said.

"You going to be another spike in my cross?"

"I'm going to come in, shoot my spot, and get out."

"That's what they all said, and half of them are still here. We've been shooting for three weeks and only got two spots in the can."

"Whose fault is that?"

"Everybody's, nobody's. Hers. Ours. Client's." Kreuger seemed to grow thinner and shorter with every word. Fitzie sensed that he also was enjoying his agony. "The Brody-King guys are in there now. They should have been out of here a week ago."

"Well, you're going to love us," Fitzie said. "We're going to rehearse with a stand-in tomorrow, take Saturday and Sunday off and shoot Monday." Fitzie was at work. The adrenalin was running, the saber was being drawn from the scabbard, sharp-edged and free of doubts and qualms. He felt sure and knowing and enjoying it.

"Three to one you're pissing in the wind," Kreuger said.

"You read my script?"

"Yeah, I read your script, I read everybody's scripts. That's how you got here."

"Which means you just passed them along, right? Cleared them with Manning's continuity and with client."

"So?"

"So you missed the forest, buddy. No music. No costuming. No singing. No dancing."

"Is that right? I didn't notice, really. What happens, then? What does she do?"

"Nothing. She gets to wear whatever she feels like wearing, and says my words sweetly. We've got photos of her apartment and by tomorrow the set of her living room is supposed to be ready for us to okay. She'll simply show us her quote, home, unquote. Like the old Edward R. Murrow people."

"And talk about furniture polish," Kreuger nodded briskly.

"And talk about *furniture*. We'll just cut to an insert shot of the pro-duct at the end."

"Oh. Wild. You sure made it easy on yourself. And me, it sounds like."

"I wasn't really thinking about that. I just figured every other schmuck would have her do a big production number like the rest of the show. I thought I'd give everyone a break from all that. And stand out in the process, of course."

"Well. Anything I can do."

"One thing," Fitzie smiled.

"What?"

"Stay off my back. And keep client away from me."

"Fair enough. I'm about to have my breakdown any minute anyway."

"Terrific. Just relax and listen to Bing sing."

"All right. And listen. If it all comes off, and *only* if it all comes off, why don't you give me a call back in New York? Get to know each other. You aren't in love with F and F are you?"

"If I couldn't work for F and F, I don't know what I'd do," Fitzie laughed and left Kreuger to join Trevor in the carpenter's shop. "Hey, looks great," he said. He was flying again now. So it works in Hollywood, too. Build a better fuck-you attitude and the world will beat a path to your door.

"How did it go?" Trevor said.

"Beautiful. It has now been officially reported to Control that our script has been altered and will not mention product except by inference and an end shot. It's his ass, now."

"Lovely."

"We also get points for saving his life. All the others have been muffing it. Hey, that sculpture's not right."

"No, but they've got the right one. It'll be here tomorrow."

"And the director, what's his name?"

"Benson. Tomorrow at ten. Loves the script, loves Rita, loves everything."

"So we can get out of here then, right?"

"Fitzie?"

"Yeah?"

"Let's get out of here."

On the way back to the Regency they dropped down to Sunset and went into Greenblatt's to stock up on liquor, cheeses, coffee, chips, orange juice and Coor's beer. Then, gin and tonic in hand, they went prone on the terrace around the pool and caught the last hour of the day's sun. Showered and dressed, they tooled the Strip to the Beverly Hills Hotel and had drinks, but didn't have themselves paged, in the Polo Lounge. Coming back, Sunset Strip was crowded and all bright lights, from cars, doors, signs advertising Forest Lawn, streetlights. The kids, wandering, gaudy Gypsies, milled along the sidewalk on both sides of the Whiskey. They drove to Highland and down to the Au Petit Cafe, parking behind the Ranch Market. They drank vermouth cassis and ate the pepper tournedos, gawking as coolly as they could at all the young girls there, with dates all older and money-looking. "My God," Fitzie said into his coffee, "they're perfected the female body and face out here."

"The men aren't bad either, darling," Trevor lisped.

They sat with scotch at the bar of The Losers on La Cienega, through the poor comic and five topless go-go dancers. Then they drove down Santa Monica to the Pink Pussycat, featuring strippers called Franky Sinatra, Dina Martin or Joni Carson. Back at P.J.'s on Santa Monica they watched the kids dance to two rock groups. More scotch. They drove back to the Strip. Their noses through the Whiskey's jammed doorway: the same as P.J.'s, except only one group. Zang! Zang! Zang! Across to the Body Shop, with its sign outside advertising amateur contests Sunday! More scotch, more strippers. Then still more of the same at the Classic Cat, only with pool tables. They played snooker. Finally, they wre standing on a corner, watching the traffic. A small gang of kids were passing, cloaked shepherds. One girl, about sixteen, hair to the knees, wore a loose, silky shirt: no bra. Fitzie snickered to himself. Bared breasts all night, and he was straining to see hers, a kid on the street passing in the dark.

"What's that?" Another bright doorway. The Melody Lounge.

"I don't know, never been. Want to try it?"

"It's there, isn't it?" Fitzie said. It had become that for him, do everything. Run, sit, drink, look, run. Don't miss anything. Something might be waiting. Inside, an orange girl in an orange dress under a light, singing. At her feet, silver-faced men in tuxedoes playing piano, bass, drums. A wall around them, a very low U-shaped bar with stools

215

along the outside. Fitzie walked around the U and dropped down onto a stool, Trevor following. He was not five feet away from the girl. She was singing love, in soft jazz, and she was sweating orange sweat in the vague delta in the center of her chest just above the top of her strapless gown. She felt—comforting. He could make out now that the other people in here didn't seem to be groups of salesmen as at the other places. They were couples, dressed, and they were listening to the music. A waitress came up quietly, swishing small square napkins and a clean ashtray down in front of them. She was bent between them and Fitzie could smell her perfume. "A stinger, straight up," he said quietly.

"Have you gone mad?" Trevor whispered.

Fitzie grinned, looking at the orange girl again. "Can't stay like this. Have to get sober or stoned."

"Two stingers then."

"Trevor, you're beautiful," Fitzie laughed softly and lit a cigarette. The singer wasn't orange, she was Negro. She was coffee, in an orange sherbet dress. Now he could see that there were more Negroes in the place and seeing them made him miss them in the other places he had been in. So. If the other places had been California, this was New York, then. And that must be why he felt better now, here. The stingers came. "Jesus God," Trevor gasped, "that's fire water!"

"Ssh," Fitzie said.

"Is she any good?"

"She's wonderful. Listen."

Trevor sat quietly, looking at her.

"You don't love her. How can you not *love* her?"

"Just lucky, I guess," Trevor said.

"You're putting me on. You gotta think she's fantastic. She's a stinger singer."

"Old friend, I love her to death. But my heartburn has a bleeding headache."

"Oh, no. But we hafta have another one of these."

"Jesus, no, Fitzie!"

"But we *have* to. See the little sign? Two drink minimum."

"We can just pay what they want. We don't have to drink it if we don't want it."

"But we *want* it!"

"Fitzie mate, if it'll keep you laughing for a change, I'll have four more stingers and go out right here."

"Whaddaya mean, bud? For a change?"

216

Trevor called for another round. "Well, you've kind oi been off your feed tonight, haven't you?"

"Jeez, I didn't think so. How?"

"Little down, little tight?"

"Is that right? I didn't feel like I was."

"Oh, forget it."

"No. Did I spoil anything for you, Trev? Cause, god-damn, if I did, I . . ."

"Hey! No! Not a bit, not a bit. It was me anyway, most likely. I just thought we'd have ourselves a lot of yuks."

"Me, too. And we didn't, did we. Damn. I've been a pain in the ass."

"Rot. Come on, now, bottoms up, down the hatch."

Trevor drove back to the Regency. Getting out, Fitzie mumbled, "What time's it anyhow."

"Half after one."

"No so bad."

"Except it's after *four,* our time."

"Christ, that's right too." And his three magic hours pushed Fitzie face down across the bed in his clothes, straight into thick sleep.

Their work, the next morning, went well. Trevor moved about the set of Rita Manning's living room with clay face and red eyes, saying little, but Fitzie's saber edge was out and brightly sharp and was pleasantly winning each minute, each sentence, each element of the rehearsal and shot-planning with the director, John Benson. Fitzie liked John Benson; for his *being there*—his immediate underfanding of what was being said, of what was wanted, of what might be fresh to try; also for the quickness and easy authority with which the man could direct people and objects to be moved. From the moment they met, they communicated like old partners, and the job went well and fast. A handsome man, all right, with black hair just a little long, John Benson could have been thirty-six or -seven, but might have been fifty. He was much fancier than his name. He wore tight, checked pants over black, medium-heeled boots; a soft, gray mock-turtleneck sweater under a worn black leather jacket like those worn by Chennault's Flying Tiger pilots. "That's exactly what it *is,*" he smiled when Fitzie remarked on it, and turned to show the faded back emblem, just barely visible within the cracks and wrinkle lines, but he said no more than that, so

217

Fitzie dropped it and went on with business. They had sandwiches and milk brought in and kept going through the lunch, letting the union people take their hour. Trevor stayed, although muttering a few times about "going out for a heart-starter." By two, it seemed solid and trimmed. It had gone so well they feared something must have been overlooked, so they stayed on, going over it again. But it was done tightly after all and they found themselves finally just sitting around with coffee. John Benson chatted with charm and showed interest in them, and in their plan for next week especially, offering encouragement, tips and even some specific contacts. Fitzie suddenly felt guilty. They were keeping him.

"Nonsense," he laughed at this, "I'm enjoying you. You're fresh air from the East!"

"Well, we really don't want to impose," Fitzie said.

"Believe me," Benson said, "you haven't any idea how unusually . . . *professional* this was today. One forgets the New York drive. It's refreshing. You'll light a fire out here with no trouble at all."

"That's great to hear," Tevor said.

"Of course, it's not shot yet," Fitzie said. First things first. The job, then the plan. Old Jesuit saying.

"All she has to do is show up," Benson said. "She's a remarkably fast study."

"Have you worked with her before?" Fitzie said.

"Oh, yes. We're old chums. A minute will be nothing to her. She'll love it."

"Good," Fitzie said.

Then Benson slapped his knee with an idea. "Say. Do you have any plans for this evening? Are you committed at all?"

"No."

"I'm tied up for dinner, but later I'm having a few friends in, do you think you might find it fun to come join me? Here's my card. *If* you feel like it, please come. I'd like it if you did, but promise me now, feel no obligation whatsoever—'kay?"

"That's very nice of you," Trevor said.

"John, look, we don't want to . . ."

"If I didn't want you, I wouldn't ask you. And I look forward to Monday whether we see you tonight or not, all right? Now I really have to get a move on. Ciao!"

"See you," they said. Trevor whammed Fitzie on the shoulder. "*See?* Did I tell you, or what?" He imitated Benson's stage manner: "It's all going to *happen,* my good man. Ha-ha!"

"Trev?"

"Yeah, man?"

Fitzie grinned. "What's *chow* mean?"

Trevor whammed his shoulder again.

At the Regency, they both went unconscious and woke so late they had to skip dinner. At the wheel of the Mustang, Fitzie said, "You don't think it's too late, do you?" And Trevor replied, "No, he said *later,* and it's only just past eleven." They were up into the hills now, climbing the nearly perpendicular road. Only speed, it seemed, kept them from toppling back on their roof. "Can you see numbers?" Fitzie asked, watching the road, clicking to high beams and honking his horn before each blind corner. "Yes, still a way to go."

"Where's he live, in a nest?"

"What must it be to come down?"

"Yeah. Remind me to drink a lot."

"Oop, easy now, coming up. Yes, that's it." Trevor pointed. They got out. "I think my nose is going to bleed," Fitzie said. John Benson opened the door after a short wait. "Oh! You did come, I'm so glad. Welcome!" Benson wore an orange Air Force jumpsuit with some Airman First Class Gold's name stenciled on it. The center zipper was open narrowly down the front, nearly to the navel but not quite. His bare feet were in black leather sandals. Fitzie was glad they had worn turtlenecks and not ties. He wondered whether Benson was wearing underwear under the suit and was sure he wasn't. He felt a little squeamish, but stopped it: he must stay *open!* He had to be his work self. He couldn't come off goofy in any way. "Hey, this is great," he said, looking around. They were standing in a small foyer with bare wooden walls covered with framed pencil sketches, charcoals and some brass and copper reliefs. Looking up, Fitzie saw that all the walls ended at about ten feet; the whole beamed roof was the only ceiling. "Oh yes, I love it," John Benson took their jackets. "The others are down on the lower level. That's why it took me a while to answer the door. We can join them later. I must show you around."

He led them past an oriental-looking room divider to the left. "This must be the kitchen," Trevor said and they all laughed. It was one, long open room with dark tile floor and a long wall unit with copper pots and pans dangling overhead. The room turned at the end, and they suddenly stepped into a vast, open space with eight walls of glass. "Quick, what is it?" Benson said.

"The window of a space ship," Fitzie said.

"The *Nautilus*," Trevor said.

"*Very* good," Benson laughed. "Dull people say ski lodge or observation tower. Come out." They stepped outside onto a wide deck that ran the entire width of the house, turning octagonally with the windows. "Incredible!" Fitzie said. So *this* was Los Angeles, lights, lights, lights for as far as the eye could see! An enormous, horizontal city of millions of lights, spreading to the edges of the sky, trying to mirror the entire universe.

"We're lucky tonight," Benson said. "The smog can cover the whole of it."

"Which must help you not take it for granted," Fitzie said.

"Oh, but you couldn't," Benson said, leaning between them on the railing. "The sunrises, the sunsets from here. I couldn't describe them for you. Even this, now, come here." He walked a few paces, to the center of the house. "See?"

"My God," Trevor said, "it's different."

"Yes. Every angle has its own specialness," Benson smiled. The owner.

"Jesus," Fitzie said, "to have this all of the time, as part of your life."

"Yes, but the smog *frees* you from it often enough."

"Why would you want to be freed from it?" Trevor asked.

"Well, it's why, I think, the suicide rate is highest in San Francisco and Sweden. The people are surrounded all the time by such incredible beauty that if they *fail*, why they must blame it on themselves. You know, if they can't do well *here*, they must be really low, really no good."

"The antithesis being true then of, say, New York," Fitzie said.

"Exactly. There, everything is against you. It's dirty and crowded and expensive and mean. So if you fall on your face, well, it couldn't be your fault. And if you succeed! Then you must be quite the guy."

"I never thought of it that way."

"That's just about enough profundity for one night," Benson laughed, and Fitzie spotted the strange shade in his eyes just before it went away. Sadness? Loneliness? Pain? They turned and reentered the house, closing the glass. Fitzie sat on the long white couch to be facing the view. Trevor took one of the large, leather-slung director's chairs opposite. "'Let's get a drink and then we'll go down and meet my other friends," Benson said, and went to fill the orders.

"Is this the bloody *end,* or what?" Trevor whipsered.

"Unbelievable."

"If these aren't right just say so," John Benson called. He carried three huge, orange glass goblets. "Jesus, there must be a fifth in this!" Fitzie said. "Well, it makes it easier on the host," Benson bowed.

They drank from the glasses.

"Let's go downstairs, shall we? I've really neglected them. We'll go this way so you can see my sleeping area, then you'll have had the full tour." They followed him around the end of the wall and into a space filled by a huge bed, covered with one great fur throw. A cork wall rose between the bed area and the small next room where Benson was now. The cork was covered with photographs —all of startlingly beautiful women in various poses, mostly nude. One girl predominated, a slender Chinese or Japanese. Most of the pictures bore inked notes. At the doorway to where Benson and now Trevor waited, Fitzie's eye fell on a snapshot of a man standing in front of a large flowering bush and wearing a short gabardine jacket with a fur collar—over his naked body. His penis was long and circumsised and hung straight down halfway to his knees. Fitzie looked ahead in time to see Benson watching him. Benson looked away toward the white walls of this new, tiny room between bedroom and foyer. It didn't just have pictures, it was a gallery. A wrought-iron railing circled the top of a spiral staircase to the lower level.

Fitzie went down last, holding his glass tightly. At the bottom, a narrow hallway with a door in each wall, both open: a bedroom here, a bedroom there. At the end of the short hall, a room the size of the one upstairs above it, and with an identical wall of spaceship windows: they would still have their city of lights to look at. Floating in the center of the space squarely beneath a hanging Tiffany lamp with four or five erect shadows around it, a pool table. A game was going, bright balls of color on the new green in the white tent of light. Fitzie followed Benson and Trevor into the stand of shadows, which turned to people, and the first face to be presented to him was the girl of the upstairs pictures, the wispy Oriental. "Fitzie, this is Freddie," Benson introduced them. Up close she was silky, and lovely, but Fitzie still couldn't tell, so he asked her, "What are you, Freddie? You aren't Japanese, are you?"

"Half Chinese, half Irish," she smiled. Her black eyes snapped.

"Wonderful. What a mix. I am too," he said. He loved her.

"Half Irish?" she said.

"Half Chinese." They laughed and Benson introduced the others, resting his orange arm lightly across Freddie's shoulders, under the black waterfall of hair: Mine. There were three women, one guy. He was Philip Rendel, a well-set, tall man with sandy hair. He wore a beige blouse and close-fitting slacks. The hair was combed forward, Roman emperor style, on top, and hung long all around the sides and back, a sixty-year-old Dutch boy. He was a talent agent. Of the three women, two were young. The other was Mrs. Garvey, forty-six or -seven in white lounging pajamas, very slim and straight-backed, with a composed, waiting face. The others were chicks. One, Joanna, was Swiss, dark, curvy, a secretary on the verge of becoming a starlet. The last was Penny, a little older, probably twenty-five, and short, with very large breasts and long hair. When Fitzie asked her what she did she answered, "A housewife," and he said, "Oh."

It was all loose and chummy and easy for the first couple of hours. The pool never stopped. Music came steadily from the Fisher stereo system against the wall. Those who weren't playing danced. Fitzie went up to Mrs. Garvey, who didn't want to dance. She lived farther down the hill. Her husband, a producer, was in Mexico.

"Features?" Fitzie asked.

"Special distribution films," Mrs. Garvey explained.

"Skin flicks?" he smiled.

"Yes."

"Could I ask you something personal, Mrs. Garvey?"

"No. But go ahead."

"Where is the little boy's room?"

Mrs. Garvey smiled like someone who wears braces, and said, "Right through that door," nodding toward the wall.

"Thank you," he chuckled, and went through the door. He felt for the light switch but stopped. There were the walls of glass again. Los Angeles was illuminating the bathroom. His hip struck something. His vision cleared and he saw it was a short, brass bathtub railing to prevent anyone from stepping into the *double* bathtub sunk in the floor facing the windows. Fitzie stood at the rail and applauded softly. Then he turned and stepped to the toilet. Urinating in the half-light, he turned his head and spoke aloud to the windows. "Hey, L.A. How about this? Big enough for ya? No? Piss on ya, then." Still laughing, he returned to the poolroom. Benson was walking with Mrs. Garvey toward the opening to the hallway. He walked past the game and the dancers and came up behind them. "Hey, none of that, now," he said.

They turned, Benson laughing, Mrs. Garvey actually blushing. "Mr. Fitzpatrick!" she said. "I'm going home."

"But I wanted to talk to you," he said.

"Darling, you are so sweet. And I would love to stay. But I like it when just John is here. We have soup and such nice talks, don't we, John."

"Yes, we do," Benson said kindly to her.

"Well, listen, Mrs. G," Fitzie said with a burlesque wink, "you put in a tub like that one in there and I'll come up and have soup every night with you!"

She tittered like a nun. It released them. She shook his hand with her cool, bony little feather of one and said, "Young man, you come up to John's sometime, no party, and I'm sure I'd love to have a nice chat with you."

Fitzie said, "I'll do that. I really will." Benson and Mrs. Garvey continued on to the stairs, Benson saying, "Be back shortly," and Fitzie turned back to the—party. It was supposed to be a party, was it? Joanna handed him a cue stick. "Hey, Fizzie, shoot for Chon, huh?" she said.

"Jawohl." He missed the shot. "Nix gut, huh Fräulein?"

"I am Sweese, not Deutsch!" she flared. Big brown eyes, black hair, white blouse, wide belt, leather skirt to her crotch, knee boots over leotards. "Well, they already made *The Sound of Music*, what are you going to do now?" he said. He could feel his eyes turning cold.

She smiled and said *fuck you* in Donald Duck talk.

Fitzie answered *fuck you, too* in Donald Duck talk.

"Oh! You can do that too!" she laughed.

"Yeah. And your English is improving, *shatz,*" he grinned. "Go ahead, take your shot." She did and missed, her skirt way up when she bent. "You've got a lovely ass," he said when she stepped back. She closed her eyes and kissed the air with a big, loud smack. Benson was back. Fitzie handed him his stick. "Here, buddy, I haven't done you much good."

"I think you did Mrs. Garvey some, though," Benson said.

Fitzie didn't answer. Freddie sunk the eight ball and ended the game. "Who needs freshening?" Benson sang, opening a panel in the wall to reveal an inset bar. Fitzie took his glass over. What the hell, nowhere yet. Then, the smell. The sweet smell of punk. Philip was sitting at a low table, lighting a joint. He sucked in a second time, holding it, then passed the brown cigarette up to Trevor. He had the marijuana in Kodak film canisters, a sheaf of papers and a small roller, and began busily to roll more. He made six tight joints and lined them up on the table, like canapes. Okay kids, booze here, stuff there. A new game of pool started, the music played on, the people danced, shot and talked, sipping, smoking. When Freddie handed him the cigarette it was low, nearly a roach, so she wedged it into the bottom of the peace symbol she was wearing around her neck on a thong. Fitzie held the metal and sucked in the last full drag left. "Where does an Irishman meet a Chinese girl, anyway?" he asked Freddie, pulling two more quick nips from the cigarette.

"In San Francisco."

"I'd better get rid of this," he said and started to the table.

"Light a new one," she said and let him lead her by the thong. He did, pulling deeply to the back of his head, and passed it to her. As she inhaled, he rearranged the symbol between her breasts, which he knew from the pictures had large, dark nipples. Stay with me, Fitzie thought, keep me free from hostility. "Who married them?" he said.

"First a priest in a church, then a temple."

"I'll be damned."

"*They'd* be damned. It went over big on both sides my mother tells me," she laughed.

"Well, it sure works. Look at you. The UN should make it a law."

Freddie giggled, "Thank you."

"Why did you come to L.A.?" he asked and began to feel dumb. What school do you go? Do you like gometry? The armpits pouring. She had passed the joint to Penny the Housewife, and had no drink. She was just standing beside him, moving slightly to the music, watching the game. "Oh," she said, "I went to U.C.L.A. for a while." She sounded bored. Oh no, don't be bored with me!

"And what do you do now?" he asked, the words hurting. Christ! But what else could he say?

Freddie sighed. "I've got a job. A temporary thing that's lasted three years. That seems to happen to everybody."

"Yeah," he agreed, not understanding. God, this was hard. A ding-dong had sounded minutes before, sending Benson upstairs. Now he was coming around the hall

224

corner with Fitzie's orange Negro stinger-singer from last night! No, it was another Negro girl, blacker with Afro-cropped hair, but just as beautiful. "Oh, it's Marcy!" Freddie lit up, dancing over to hug her. Fitzie sipped his drink. Why was it such a strain for him? What did people say to each other anyway, that wasn't boring? What did Benson whisper to Freddie, and to Joanna, that made them laugh and say something back? Philip knew, too. And even Trevor—with Penny the Housewife and now, over with their cue sticks, Joanna. Their lips moved, girls laughed. It looked so easy. But what the hell words did they use, for Christ's sake? Marcy evens it up again, four and four. A phone call from upstairs, or from Mrs. Garvey's house? First it's just friends and don't come if you don't want to; then it's a party; now it's all even. To keep me off of Freddie? The old Airman First Class is more secure than that, with those pictures up there. Oh, Jesus, look at me, the wallflower. Over here by myself holding my goddamn glass in my hand, might as well be in the big tub. *Well, Splish, Splash, Oh, the shark, babe.* That's it, here I come. Mack the mick. The others had moved open to let Benson bring Marcy in to them. Penny was back, taking her shot. She also had the joint. Fitzie moved over to her.

"A little lower or you'll scratch," he said. She obeyed and made the shot.

"That's what I need," she squealed, "a couch!"

"You got one," Fitzie said.

"You want?" she said, taking a drag.

He let her put it in his mouth. "Oh, that's the best I've had," he said, exhaling.

"It's good," Penny said.

He was going to say, "New York seems to get much harsher stuff," but *New York* would make her have to say soething like, "Oh, is that where you're from?" which probably would be too heady—that was the mistake he had been making.

"Fitzie, say hello to Marcy Parrot," Benson said, leading her up.

"Hello to Marcy Parrot," Fitzie said and shook her hand. Warm, a little squeeze back.

"Marcy Parrot, say hello to Fitzie," Benson said then.

"Hello to Fitzie," she laughed, white! and let her fingers drag along his.

"Marcy Parrot," Fitzie said, his hand taking the end of her fingers, "we're going to get you a drink in a glass that belonged to Napoleon," he led her away to the bar, "and

225

then we're going to get you a dance with the nineteen thirty-six marathon winner, and we'll even get you a little puff of the wonderful thing if you so desire. From darling Penny there. You know Penny, do you?"

"I know Penny," Marcy laughed, big, going along.

"Penny was my second wife. What'll it be?"

"Vodka and bitter lemon. And who was your first wife?"

"Josephine. That's how we got the glasses."

Marcy laughed.

"No, none of that," Fitzie said. "You get three gulps of your drink and then we put our glasses down and we dance."

She looked around the room. "But where's the marathon winner?"

"My dear child, you are breathing on him."

"Yeah? Who'd you beat?"

"Beat? It isn't over yet, love! They're still waiting for me to stop. Every step I take is pure dance."

She had a laugh that gushed. "Oh, stop!" she said.

"And lose ten bucks?"

She gushed and put down her glass. They danced. He had it, now, he knew. Act the ass and the world doesn't get bored with you. Moving opposite Marcy, he felt the pot get there, the light ballooning inside, the coldness in his leg bones and feet. The record ended and they hugged. Her arm around his middle, his around hers, they walked back to the table. Passing Penny, he stopped and kissed her neck. "Best damn wife I ever had," he said, still holding Marcy.

Penny looked up and held his eyes.

"Let me know when you need more coaching," he said.

"I will," Penny said. "Come back." But, moving Marcy away, he noticed that when Philip came over to her, Penny put her hand up into the back of his Dutch boy wig.

"And did you meet old Trevor?" he said.

"Yes," Marcy and Trevor said. Trevor held Joanna's hand.

"Trevor was my third wife," Fitzie said. "Too masculine, though, I hate butch girls."

"Hey, you're there, man," Trevor laughed, there too. They looked at each other, then burst out laughing, bending over. They couldn't stop. Each time they looked at each other they broke up. Tears ran from their eyes. It spread. Marcy gushed loudly, then Joanna caught it. Fitzie took Joanna's hand and pulled them all outside to the railing and pumped hysterical laughter out into the air and down over the lights below. Turning to lean his back on the railing, momentarily spent, Fitzie saw Benson coming out of one of the doors off the hallway, heading toward them in bare feet. Fitzie looked at the pool table: no Freddie; only Philip and Penny, shooting. Benson stopped at the open glass, the big smile came on and he said, "Hey, gang. I'm afraid that'll bring the *gendarmerie* down on us, okay?"

Like kids in church, they all put their hands to their mouths to suppress their giggles and scurried inside where their dammed-up laughter came shooting out all the louder and sillier. The four clutched each other for support. Benson slid the glass shut and went back to the hallway door. Fitzie was sure the jumpsuit zipper was lower than before. He couldn't get a footing; the others seemed to have fallen down to sprawl on the ledge of after-laughter weakness, but he was still dropping—to empty sadness. He tried to stop it; he took the joint from Philip, but couldn't drag on it. He passed it to Marcy. He retrieved his drink, but it went down like water. It angered him. Damn, he had come so close, too. He knew he wasn't sober by any means but that made no difference. He had landed, hard. That bastard of a nun in his ear again. He ducked into the bathroom. No good. The tub wasn't funny anymore. It was just a weird bathtub built for two. He leaked in the darkness, then flipped on the fluorescent bulb and confronted himself in the mirror. Jesus, he was green. "You jerk," he said aloud with disgust and went back. Marcy handed him a cue stick and pressed herself affectionately against his chest in a brief, smiling hug. Philip and Penny were dancing. Trevor was racking the balls. He stood and watched, feeling Marcy's body connecting with his through her arm around his waist, her hip against his, and discovered: his sex had shut off, too. He hadn't an ounce of horniness left. And vaguely, he felt relieved, saved; which made him hate himself even more.

He only hoped that it didn't show and that he could fake it. The game helped. He noticed Philip and Penny moving away and going to the hall opening. To ballroom number two, he guessed. Everybody's doin' it, doin' it. He shot a long one over a lot of green, sunk it and left himself a good setup. This made him feel better and he walked around the table for his next shot. "Very pretty, laddie," Trevor said. "Thank you, thank you," Fitzie said. "And now, for my next trick, we shall arrange for Joanna

227

to lean way, way over." He took the shot. "Oops." He had made the ball, so had to keep shooting.

"Zat's what you get," Joanna laughed.

"All right, then," he smiled, "this will make you lie on the table." He studied the table. Oh, wrong: Philip and Penny returning, coming up. He chalked his cue. Penny, in a whisper: "He's beautiful, Marcy."

Marcy: "He still asleep?"

Who? Benson? A peephole in the door? Fitzie shot and missed.

"Tough luck," Philip said, "a lovely try, though."

"Thanks," Fitzie said. "Who's beautiful?" he said to Penny.

"Oh, come see him." He followed her to the hallway. The door was closed on Benson and Freddie. Penny led him into the other room. A small, red plaid blanket on the double bed, with a tiny head popping out of it at the top: a child, a boy of about two with curly black hair and a mocha face, handsome and sound asleep. "Jesus Christ," he whispered. Leaning down, Fitzie's head was close to Penny's and when he turned to look at her he saw she wasn't thinking about the baby. They straightened and their mouths came together. No arms. Her tongue came into his mouth, fully, not playfully, then withdrew and they broke the kiss and went out of the room. Penny went to rejoin Philip at the bar. Fitzie returned to Marcy and said, "He's dead to the world. What's his name?"

"That's Earl."

"What is he, about two?"

"Not quite."

"He's big then."

"Yeah. It was so late, I couldn't get anyone to come sit for me," she said.

Half-fooling, Trevor made an incredible bank shot that worked, running his ball straight to the pocket but for a hair. "Oh!" everyone breathed. Fitzie yelled, "Oh, baby! You were screwed, what a beautiful shot!" to cover his leaving Marcy to go put his arm around Trevor's shoulder. His decision had been made. He didn't make it; it had been made. Marcy was shooting. "Listen, babe, I've got to split," he whispered to Trevor.

"With her?" Trevor grinned.

"No. But I need the car. Are you in with Joanna, you think?"

"Sure, take it. But why, mate? What's the trouble?"

The matchbook cover tucked in his wallet signaled just

in time. Fitzie took it out and showed Trevor. "Doreen Woods? Who's that?" Trevor said.

"The stewardess. I'm supposed to pick her up at the airport, for breakfast," he lied.

"You bugger! Why didn't you tell me?"

Fitzie winked. "It wasn't definite. I wanted to see, maybe something better would turn up."

"Wait now," Trevor said. "When'll I see you? I was thinking maybe we could drive down to Tijuana for the weekend."

"Get blown by a twelve-year-old?"

They laughed.

"I don't know," Fitzie said. He had to get out! Why don't we play it by ear. See how you make out and how I make out, and get together later, at the hotel. Maybe all go down together."

"Whatever you say, ducks. Go get her."

"Good. Tell lies here for me, will you? I want to just fade. And thank Benson if you see him again," Fitzie said and walked straight to the hallway without looking, past the doors, one open, one shut still, up the winding stairs to the gallery, found his jacket in the foyer and stepped out of the house. The air was cool now, like a night in the East. The Mustang started. He went down, faintly sad that he wouldn't get to watch the sunrise from Benson's deck.

When he woke, he lifted the phone and asked the clerk the time. Ten something. Was Mr. Williamson in? I'll try him. He doesn't answer. Thanks. No, no message. He lay there, his arm across his eyes against the brightness, the complete, trash can bum. Head throbbing. Finely shaking knees. Flaming eyes. He lurched himself up to sit on the side of the bed. The pain filled his head and snowed slowly down into his shoulders and chest. He opened his eyes: he was still high! He giggled. It hurt his throat. "God, I'm having a good time," he said aloud and laughed—the hell, it's only pain. He stood up and sat down again immediately. He stood again and made it. He walked down the long hall and into the living room. *It shouldn't be like this,* he thought. *It should be a room and a shower. All gaudy and foam rubber. That's a hotel room. This is a frigging apartment. You can't just stay here, you have to live here. But you can't live here. Because you're all by yourself.* He was naked. He got a can of beer, pulled its pop-tab and guzzled it. That felt good. Hair of the dog. It was too bad he was going to miss Tijuana, he had always wanted to see it. *Why are you going to miss it? You can find Trevor.* Because, that's why. He sat on the bed and cradled the phone in his neck. "Hi. Get me the L.A. airport. I don't know who. Whoever goes to San Francisco. P.S.A. Great, thanks" How about that, a shuttle. Just like New York to Boston. Terrific. The one city in the states he had to see before he died. And now it was so close. He had to go to San Francisco, right now.

He lit a cigarette and thought of the matchbook. He took it out of his wallet and looked at the script that was almost printing, very lovely. *Annette! Bobby! Cubby! Doreen!* Screw it. He dropped the cover into the ashtray and watched it burn. He pulled the flattened AWOL bag out of his B-4 bag and packed it. The bag with the champagne in it stood on the dresser. He pressed it in on top of a shirt and zipped the bag closed. He almost left a note for Trevor at the desk, but didn't. This was better. This way Trevor would see him having the green-eyed blond stewardess, understand and approve. Good old Trevor would prefer it that way. Everybody would.

He had a window seat and didn't want to talk to anybody. He half listened to the three men sitting opposite and beside him in the end, double seat: a burly man of forty, thick, who had to be a warrant officer a man about Fitzie's age, and a kid of eighteen—sailors or merchant mariners on shore leave, all excited but only the kid showing it. He babbled away. The others grinned patiently, but their eyes babbled right along with him. Fitzie wanted to hide his hands; theirs were so used and hard-looking. He also wanted to tell the two older guys to quit sliding him glances of apology for the kid's greenness, to quit thinking he was somebody who knew something. He wanted to tell them how he wished he were one of them, going to get drunk and laid and have a Big Time in Frisco. But he wished that only offhandedly; it felt too good to be really alone, getting even farther away, to where he might be able to make things stand still long enough for him to maybe see where the hell he was. It didn't help much, it turned out, to just go with it.

Where the Atlantic would have been, on the right, choppy, black and white-capped, Fitzie watched the Pacific, on the left, flat and bright blue. He wasn't flying to

Boston, he was flying to San Francisco. He dozed. The elevator-drop of the plane woke him and he watched the city rise at him through the clouds. Not unlike Boston, but on hills. There was the Golden Gate, red—and dull, industrial red at that. Shit. Then hills up between him and the city and down, solid, *rumm!* onto the runway; made it again. In a matter of minutes he was going to be in San Francisco—what the songs were about, what the movies had helped conjure in his head as more than another place; an Atlantis. Bogart in taxicabs down its hills, fighting under the bridge. Aldo Ray in khakis. Hello, goodbye to it from the decks and bridges of how many destroyers, subs, carriers? And now he was about to be there and alone. He stepped up into the bus, only fifty cents; didn't they realize?

Outside the terminal, it was warm differently than in L.A.; it wasn't summer in December, it was a May early afternoon in Boston. He carried his raincoat slung over his AWOL bag and walked along the strange, familiar streets. He knew nobody, he had money in his wallet and didn't have to be anywhere until Monday morning. He had never felt so loose and light and *out*. Blocks ahead of him, a cable car crossed and he hurried. Maybe he would be able to still see it. Maybe another would come. He nearly spoke to the passing people, especially the girls and women, even the old ones. Because they wore stockings and heels and skirts and bright coats and walked *fast*. At the cable car corner, he stopped and looked down to the right and could see only one roof, getting darker and smaller above the thick traffic. But up, left, he could see three of them, two going up, one inching down the steepest city street he had ever seen. He looked across at a green, small park with benches and iron picket fencing. He would go sit there and let the sky and hill and buildings fall down onto him. Then he noticed the light post he was standing beside. It was odd and old, not like the real ones arching high above, and there was a straight row of them along the curb, like the gas lamps in parts of Charlestown only ritzier, like those in Louisburg Square. Cabs were pulling in and out to doorman's whistle. He walked along the lamps. The Saint Francis Hotel! How was that familiar? He had been here in an earlier life. They had a room and he took it, for one night, on the second floor. Chinese girl elevator operators! He brushed the thought of Freddie away quickly. He had to stay alone, with the city, if he was going to make it.

He came to his number, unlocked the heavy door and

stepped in. Now, this was a hotel room. One L-shaped room, it was an extravaganza of wasted space. Fitzie smiled at it and loved it. The bed way over against the far right wall looked lost in the warehouse of a room. The desk, dresser, chair, end tables, even the television looked like doll furniture until he walked up and touched them. The bathroom was old, the tile had heavy cornices jutting out all around. Perhaps from memory, the blackening mirror saw only fine features in soft light. He looked at himself in it from the doorway and held the expression he had caught on his face, it so pleased him: hard-good, not hard-worn, young enough, honest, the touch of a tan. "Hi there, I'm Harvey Farquahar," he said. He frowned, he winked, he snarled his upper lip, he turned and looked back quickly, surprised, he stuck out his tongue. He walked back to the dresser cowering on the far wall, pretending he was walking downhill. That was it, it was an Ernie Kovacs room. The bed would come sliding after him and pin him to the dresser. He emptied his AWOL bag into the two top drawers, standing the champagne bag upright against the mirror. Well, so much for brooding. He couldn't do it. There went the picture he had been relishing of himself sitting, smoking, staring, thinking for hours, alone, *figuring things out*. He stepped back for a look. Good. Clothes he was fond of: the cuffless, close gray worsteds, the low black boots, the soft green blazer, the coarse, blue dress shirt, no tie. A wash of the face to clear the eyes and he'd be off. What was it that Benson had said about suicide and San Francisco? He couldn't bring it back. Something weird, probably.

It did smell like Boston. Water. Salt water, from the other side of that mountain of a street up there, the cable cars like ski tows. He stopped. Listen to that. Those trolleys didn't go clang-clang-clang, the car men *played* them bells, *clingaclingitycling, clangaclangityclang, clunga* . . . He would walk with no purpose or direction. *Gump's*. He'd heard of that, too, like the Saint Francis. He went in. A matronly saleswoman leaned against a case, the corner denting her black flannel behind. She was facing away. He walked up to her shoulder and said, "Just looking," making her whirl, saying, "May I help you?" She had a great cackle of a laugh and punched him in the shoulder with it. He laughed and went on, then out to the street again. He walked, looking at the faces, moving uphill, tasting the expectation that in the next minute he would spot a face that he knew, like Shirt from the ice

232

cream factory, Shaz Rafferty from Craig Street, or some-body. "Hey, Shaz, how's it goin'?"

"Hey, Fitzie. Long time no see."

"Still up Raytheon, Shaz?"

"Oh, yeah."

"Shirt! It's me! How the hell are ya?" Wow, that suit must have been five hundred bucks.

"Fitzie! You're all grown up. *Now,* you gonna come work for us, huh?"

"Any day, now, Shirt, any day."

"I'm way up, now, kid, way up there."

"I'll do it, I'll do it. Give me a gun. Tell me who you want bumped off."

All the faces now were Chinese. He looked up at the sign. There really was one! *Grant Avenue, San Francisco, California, U. S. Aaay!* He could hear Pat Suzuki's voice banging it out. He walked along the shops, climbing uphill, in and out of the shade under the awnings. Reams of glass and delicate wood mobiles hanging and tinkling in the soft breeze. He ran his hand along the wood of the sidewalk bins holding fish, beans, some sort of roots. Old people in long kimonos and saucepan caps mixed with young, dressed modern. Any minute Charlie Chan would come bounding in his white-suited copulence out of one of the dark doorways, followed by one or two sons in their crisp suits, saying "Pop." Near the peak of the hill, he entered a small, bright store. He moved about the shop, feeling large and clumsy. He picked up a harmonica and carried it with him. Then he took down a tiny, bright yellow silk kimono with orange and black flowers on it, held it up for size, and draped it over his arm. There was a V-rack of small prints on crinkly paper. He selected three lake scenes. He placed the load in a pile on the counter near the lady shopkeeper and browsed some more. He took three tiny decks of cards and three adjustable-size finger rings, each with an oriental symbol set in silver on its black face. A hand-carved wooden hair barette. A woman's long, slender, silk throat scarf, smoky pink. A set of six slim silver bracelets. She wrapped each thing separately in black tissue paper, put them all into a small black shopping bag and handed Fitzie the bag. He said, "Thank you," and went outside again.

At the long scarf, he had remembered. But by then it was too late, he couldn't very well have put everything back. He could send them to her in the mail, for one thing. Or leave the bag on a bus. Or give all of it away. No, if he got killed by a car it'd be with him, and Janice would never have to know the truth. He'd hold on to it for a while, anyway. He found it wasn't hard at all to simply drop it and think only about that scrawny old cat there taking the sun in the doorway.

He reached North Beach: old Scollay Square: Forty-second Street. He crossed, walking left, to keep going uphill, the draw of the water stronger all the time. Topless, topless. The neon sleeping in the tubes of all the signs. The come-on sidewalk posters and photos cold and fading in the daylight. Yet all warm, somehow, and friendly to him, all built and put out there for him, alone. He turned the corner at Big Al's. He had heard of that too; it had come to him in a dream. Then up steeply once more into kind of Beacon Hill streets, only brighter and cleaner-looking. Colors of ice cream made the houses happier-looking. Caramel. Pecan. Pistachio. Young people going in and out like Harvard Square, older than hippies but Provincetown-looking. He wasn't waiting to see old friends now, he was waiting to see himself coming up, breathing heavily, carrying a brown paper bag with celery sticking out the top, and french bread, instead of his black little shopping bag. "Hi," he would say when he passed him.

"Can't talk now," he would answer and go on.

He was down now and walking along the waterfront. He came to a small green mall and he could see the bay and headed toward it, running smack into an 1890 post-card come-to-life. Here was the turntable where the cable cars ended and people were right now turning one around, pushing its rear end. He rushed into them and got a hand onto the car just before it stopped moving. They really still did that, and now he had done it. The other pushers hopped on. He walked down across the grass. An old sailing ship was tied up, open to the public like the *Constitution* at Charlestown. Fitzie walked to the small public beach and looked at the bay, almost at eye level. It had no waves and looked dark gray and oily, like Revere Beach at low tide, but he wasn't disappointed; it looked chipper and blue further out and off to the left under the Golden Gate. He followed the concrete walk along the narrow beach. Nobody was in the water, but there were several people on blankets and newspapers taking the sun and further on he passed rows of bleachers facing the bay as if it were a football field; here were many more people, lying flat, sitting back on their elbows with their eyes closed, several with shiny aluminum reflectors like collars around their necks. Past the beach, the walk stepped

234

higher and followed the water wall. A grass slope rose and was covered with college people reading books and listening to transistors and drinking malt liquor from cans on blankets. He boosted himself up the stone retaining wall and walked up through them to the crest of the slope, to an open Cyclone Fence where more people were leaning to look down at the Italian men playing boccie in their shirt-sleeves in the courts below. Fitzie smoked a cigarette and watched, tickled by the gusto and machine-gun talk. He hadn't seen boccie since East Boston—*Eastaboss!*— when he used to pass the courts on the way to the shipyard where his father worked. The sound of drums called him away. He passed back down through the spreads of students and jumped down to the walk. A loose crowd was clapping around a row of five Negro boys along the wall, beating high Cuban bongo drums. In front of the drums an extremely fat Italian-looking girl in a black bikini and long stringy black hair was dancing, with shouts and red-lipped laughs, opposite a tall Negro with gray hairs in his black beard, wearing a black beret, a gold earring in one ear and a garishly beautiful poncho of Mexican colors. Her breasts and belly fat, her navel a little smile in it, heaved and joggled to the drumbeats and she was sweating but she knew what she was doing and it was very good. The crowd, and Fitzie, wished they could get to wherever she was, and egged her to "go!" The man was as cool and graceful as a Gypsy elder. When the drums quit and they finished, the crowd yelled "Olé!" Laughing, Fitzie turned away and started back along the beachwalk. He felt drunk. And, as fat as she was, as he watched her dance, the drums filling his head, the girl had turned him on. He didn't feel lustful but his drive was back, and he felt glad. After it had run out on him last night, he hadn't been sure it would ever return. *Did he ever return? No, he never returned, and his fate is still unknown. He can ride forever 'neath the streets of Boston.* Now he felt all there again, and kept walking, all the way back to Fisherman's Wharf.

It was noisy and crowded with people and creeping cars. He poked along the stalls through the smell of shrimp and fish, looking into the shops and restaurants. He saw Joe DiMaggio's. Ted Williams had had it way over Joe, of course, but they had had their own DiMaggio, Dom, in center wearing eyeglasses; Bobby Doerr, Johnny Pesky, Walt Dropo, oh yeah. Fitzie saw he was at one end of a passageway through a restaurant and he saw water at the other end of it. He walked through and came out to a small pier running around a square little harbor closed in by the buildings, with fishing boats rocking hull to hull, a full fleet of them, it seemed, docked there for the diners to look out at. It was Gloucester. Then he went back and walked out of the Wharf, heading for the tall tower he saw up on top of a hill. He felt like an insatiable camera full of endless film. To be like this all the time! Going, seeing, hearing, not thinking, not *doing* anything. The street ended, swerving abruptly up and back on itself, Fitzie sticking with it.

The street was as steep as the Hollywood Hills road. It slowed his pace and drew out the sweat. Woods rose to his left, the backs and roofs of houses sank on his right. The houses weren't poor, but they looked more like *house* houses than those in Benson's cliff; they had porches and wash lines. People could live in them. He had to stop and rest. His legs hurt. Finally, he made it to the top, to the entrance to Coit Tower. He was on Telegraph Hill!— another old familiar place to him. And the Tower he knew was the Bunker Hill Monument. He rode the elevator to the top and looked out. There they were: the city-on-a-dolphin's-back, the bay, the bridges, the sun, the sky, sails and white wakes, Alcatraz. After the delightful shock of his first look at it all, nothing happened. He wondered if it was the same for the Grand Canyon or the Taj Mahal. He knew it was true for Manhattan from the Empire State Building and for Paris from the Eiffel Tower. *Well, there it is. Yeah. That's it, all right.* And nothing more to be done about it, except to stay looking, or leave. But, hell, what should happen, anyway? It was enough for it just to be all out there and beautiful to see. He went down the inside of the tower and out into a small parking lot. He stepped up into the ledge of the stone wall there: the same view, a little smaller and lower, and better because here he could feel the wind in his face and the heat of the sun. His eyes dropped down into the trees before him, and he saw the steps. Goddamn. But there hadn't been a sign; none that he had seen, anyway. Still, he should have used his head. There *had* to be steps. They couldn't expect everyone to have to climb that blasted hill. As he looked, two young boys ran hopping up the wide, stone, gradual stairs. Christ, *kids* found them without any trouble. He jumped off the ledge and started down the steps, but stopped. He turned and went back up and across the stoned lot, around the Tower and onto the sidewalk of the street he had labored up. Having dragged himself up

236

this way, he'd be damned if he'd give up the earned pleasure of running back the same way.

At the bottom, he stamped to a trot and then to a walk. Long breaths in and out, gasping for air. He had been out for hours. He must have walked a hundred miles. He was pooped, and he was starving. He had eaten nothing since lunch the day before; only the beer this morning. Plodding along, he had just the one, sweet dilemma: should he get something to eat here, some seafood, perhaps, on the Wharf, and then take his cable car ride? Or should he get his ride now, in case they should become extinct—there was one coming down now, up ahead—and eat someplace back downtown? In the Saint Francis, itself, maybe? Or the Top of the Mark! Another place he knew well; they might be expecting him at the Mark. But then the place, one he didn't know, hadn't ever heard of, came up to him and let a roar out through its door. Seeing it, smack on the corner of Powell and Hyde, a step away from the turnaround, the Buena Vista Café, was too much. He would gamble that the cars would be let exist awhile longer despite their beauty.

It was a long, narrow place with windows all along the street front and a bar, liquor here, dinner-counter further down, along the wall. It was packed and noisy with voices. Fitzie stood inside the door behind two guys waiting ahead of him. At first burst, the Buena Vista, inside, hit him wrong. It smelled of Upper East Side New York, one of the singles bars with atmosphere up the ass, where the clevers and the dollies with big shoulder bags met to slay each other. The two guys got signaled by the head waitress and dissolved into the melee. He stepped forward. He had been wrong. It was all right. Nothing seemed placed for any effect other than use. He especially went for the table setup. There were stools at the bar, all taken, with standers behind and between, but the rest, the floor, was filled with a few huge, round tables instead of a lot of little ones. It was like Europe; you had to share. The waitress's name tag said Marie, but Fitzie thought it should have been Bertha. She looked like a hard, tough Kate Smith. She came struggling out of the crowd to stand next to Fitzie, the chief of staff returning from the front to assay the situation with the commander. "You want the bar," she reported, "but all I got's one hole at number two."

"That's okay," Fitzie said, "I'd rather sit. I'm going to eat."

"Ah, you're the darlin'," she said and bulldozed a path

237

for him. She turned and pointed to a space between a girl and a soldier near the window. "In there okay?"

"Terrific."

"You need the menu?"

"What have you got for a hangover?"

"New Orleans gin fizz."

"I'll have that and ham and eggs, two scrambled, and a lot of bread."

"And the Irish coffee," Bertha said.

"You got Irish coffee? Great. Perfect."

"Dearie, this is the home of Irish coffee," she said and squeezed past him to go back. "You go sit down now and we'll fix you up in a jiffy."

He sidled as unroughly as he could into his chair. A framed *Time* article on the wall credited the place with inventing Irish coffee. Fitzie had always thought it had been a bartender at Shannon Airport, but would take their word for it, as long as they'd give him enough. It wasn't Europe: if anyone at the table had look at him, they weren't now. No smiles, no nods. He reached down and tucked his shopping bag on the floor under his chair and rested his arms on the table, to wait. He felt awkward. Anyway, it was good to be sitting. He hoped he didn't smell, after all the sweating. He lit a smoke and sent his eyes around the table counterclockwise. The GI next to him was with a buddy, both SP-4s, in greens, Corps of Engineers, Airborne, Vietnam ribbons. They were being talked at by a girl, scrubbed brunette, clicky teeth. Beyond Teeth's mummified date, an obvious ensign, a blonde was in the middle of telling some elaborate story with her hands to the face of the girl next to Fitzie. Listening, she had her head turned, so he could see only her short black hair. But her faded blue man's shirt was untucked by her leaning, and Fitzie could see above the top of her low dungarees a thin crescent of her bare back and the waistband of her panties. They were black. At least that was something nice to drink a gin fizz by. Which arrived just as he thought of it.

"There ya go, dear," Bertha passed it in, behind heads. "Be back in a while." Fitzie drank a mouthful. It had eggs in it, just what he needed. He felt better already. He wished Teeth there would shut the hell up for a minute, but this was fine. You could probably stay here forever, for all they cared. He smoked and just sat there, then drank more of his drink. Time for a little peek at the black panties and skin—but, as if she had heard, the girl sent one arm back and tucked the shirt back down into the little gully. Ah, well. We'll have none of that, anyway. Besides, she was probably a Saint Bernard. His food came. Bertha passed him the bread and told him, "You want to wait for your coffee." He wanted to go bury his head in those big bosoms for talking to him like that and for bringing him all this wonderful food.

He ate, thinking about the taste of each chew of each mouthful. *That's old Mr. Fitz. Been coming in every day for thirty years, the same time. You could set your watch. Bertha will take care of him. He won't have anyone else.* He tried, but couldn't keep Teeth's jabbering out of his head altogether. She was sparkling, "Being an airline stewardess, I get to meet . . ."

Not like the one I know, Fitzie thought. *Well, now I can tell Trevor I was with a stewardess and not be lying.* He kept eating, trying to listen only to the sound of his own chewing; then he made a pact—she could yak while he was eating, but if she hadn't stopped by the time his Irish coffee arrived, well, he'd cut her throat. But Bertha knew. She knew the second he had swallowed his last bite and was there handing him his glass of black magic. He took it and passed her his plate, utensils and empty fizz glass, and when he looked up, Teeth and date had risen to leave. Bertha was taking away everything he didn't want. A middle-aged couple wearing sunglasses immediately took the vacated chairs, smiling and nodding to everyone at the table. Fitzie smiled and nodded back. The GIs retreated to their beer with audible relief. Fitzie sipped the hot black through the cool, sweet white. Bullseye. He did it again, then lit a cigarette and did it again, small sips, each to be relished, eyes fogged, for as long as possible. Suddenly he knew the girl on his left had turned to him. He could feel her face. She was grinning slightly at him when he looked. Inside he felt a jolt and his face warmed red before he could stop it: Saint Bernard? Bite my tongue, what a face! She was carved from Swan soap, with just a hint of rose beneath the skin. Her lashes, like her brows and her hair, were real and black as a cat's fur. They stretched up and out, very long, over her huge, round eyes. Blue. Blue as snow at night. And he had seen her black panties and the skin of her back! The grin became a small smile when she said, "Excuse me, we want to ask you something," and finished, the smile was a small laugh. There was also a slight accent to her words.

"What?" he said. "Ask."

"Have you really been on a hunger strike?" she said and she and the blonde giggled out loud.

"That's right," Fitzie smiled. "Down with farmers."

"*Farmers!*" the blonde parroted him. "What's the accent?"

"Irish," he said.

"I'm Irish," the black-haired girl said, "and I don't talk like that."

"You are?" Fitzie said, "I thought that was a brogue in there. Where from?"

"Glasgow," she said and stopped her laugh with two fingers to her lips. The blonde didn't stop hers; she was fleshy but very pretty. Her mock leopardskin bra showed through her white, fluffy blouse and she made Fitzie think of Hollywood. "I think you're both tipsy, you know that?" he said.

"Oh, now. A Pioneer, is it? Guzzling the fizzes?" the Glasgow girl said.

"What's that you're drinking?" he said.

"Pimm's cup," the blonde said.

"When we're through," the Glasgow girl whispered, leaning close to him, her vaguely grassy scent reaching him, "we cop the cups. I've got five at home. They expect you to, anyway."

"Is that right," Fitzie said and went back to drinking his Irish coffee. He smoked and looked around the place. It was turning less bright outside. A cable car crept diagonally up across the side window. He heard the Glasgow girl whisper something to the blonde. He turned back and laughed as they did, making fun of them. He stopped before they did. Then the Glasgow girl said, "Cat got your tongue?"

"Nice day. Warm."

"Now here's a nice Mister Funny, it looks, who'll talk to us, I said to Luce, and now here you are a Mister Stuck-up."

"Okay, so talk. Just don't giggle anymore," Fitzie said.

"Good," she said. "What's your name?"

"What's yours?" he said. He needed time to improvise. John Lindsay? Harvey Farquahar? Lester Buttery?

"I'm Chrissie Peterson. And this is Lucille Cole. We call her Luce, because she tends to be when she drinks."

"Oh, Chrissie! That's *terrible.* What's got into you?" Luce protested, flouncing the yellow hair. To Fitzie, she said, "I'll tell you something. This one has never acted like this before in her life. Miss Mouse. It must be you. What's your name?"

"Fitzie," he said, jarred off his alias search. "Is it me?" he asked Chrissie.

"Could be," she said, straight and low, then, quickly, "Fitzpatrick?"

"Right," Fitzie said.

"John? Thomas! Brendan. Brian. Sean. Richard?" Chrissie fired.

"Fitzie," he said.

"Good enough," Chrissie said. "You look like a Fitzie."

"You look like a Chrissie, too. And I guess I'd better not say you look like a Luce, huh?" They laughed. "How you doing on the Pimm's cups?"

"Dry as a bone." Chrissie dropped her cup into her handbag.

"Chrissie!" Luce whispered. "No, we're fine."

"Ah, come on, give you something for your hope chests." He called Bertha and ordered them two more.

"That's very nice of you," Luce said. Fitzie looked at Chrissie, catching her; she had been staring at him. She dropped the lids quickly. Her bravado, it seemed, was fragile; if she lost it, things could be awkward. "Well, let's hear it, big mouth," he said to her, "the gentleman's plying you with liquor. The least you can do is act plied."

"Do you live in San Francisco, Fitzie?" Luce asked.

"No, he's from New York," Chrissie said.

"A mystic, are you?" he said. "It's Boston, though, smartie."

"Come on, Chrissie," Luce said, "how did you know he doesn't live here?"

"The way he took the place in when he came in." She let her eyes openly admit to him that she had been watching him. "You like San Francisco?" Chrissie said.

"Yeah. It's really something else."

"You're among your own, child, that's all."

There was something in Chrissie's inflection that he felt he had to defend himself against, something too *knowing*.

Chrissie said, "You should get around and see it all."

"Well, I have seen some." Fitzie told them of his long day's walk.

"That's terrific," Luce said. "I'm here almost two years and I've never really just walked all around."

"Have you, Chrissie?" he said.

"Oh, yes."

Luce suddenly said, "Hey, we'd better drink up and get going."

Chrissie turned. "Ow, is it late already?"

"A quarter to six," Luce said.

"I've got to move soon, too," Fitzie said, so they wouldn't feel bad about leaving him, after starting it. And so he wouldn't feel that he was being left by them, by anybody.

"Going to do the town, are you?" Chrissie asked.

"Yeah, someone's going to show me the sights," he lied. "Why?"

"Well, I was just going to say that if you feel like it, well, here—" she took a pencil from her purse, jamming the second cup in, tore the tab off an envelope and wrote on it. *At least it's not a match cover,* Fitzie thought. "This is a dancehall, where Luce and I work weekend nights. If you find yourself with nothing to do, or something. Oh, I don't know, just take it!"

Luce stood up. "Chrissie, you're so brazen, wait till I tell. It was nice talking to you, Fitzie."

"You, too," Fitzie smiled up, holding the slip of paper. Luce's body blossomed, a blonde's body. When Chrissie stood, he saw she was taut, but not thin. In her shirt and dungarees she was a body, but not a boy. Her breasts pushed round when the shoulder strap of her bag dragged the shirt tighter. And he saw her bottom was full and solid in the denim pockets when she squeezed past behind him and started through the crowd. She touched his face with her eyes. "If I don't see you, bye, Fitzie," she said.

"See you, Chrissie." He didn't know whether he meant that he would, or goodbye. The tourists were talking. The soldiers looked close to being loaded now, and bored sleepy. Despite his precaution, Fitzie did feel left; not by them, by her. By Chrissie. Hell, what had they said to each other? Nothing. Hello, goodbye. She'd probably go home, get sober, and go to work, forgetting she had even met him. The same with him. If only she hadn't had that *thing* about her, whatever it was, that crazy sense of her knowing him and his knowing her, the way he had known the Saint Francis and Grant Avenue and the whole place. But she was just another stranger, another strange girl, the city was full of them, California was sure as hell full of them! The world was full of them, he supposed, and he just had never realized it, having been so caught up for years in his own intense little life. And besides. Also. Anyhow. Come to think of it. Come to think of it, balls. It was all getting too complicated again. To be sure Chrissie had got away, he drank another Irish coffee, then settled his tab with Bertha. Outside, the air was cool, blue water and Fitzie stood on the corner in it.

"Hey, dearie, wait up!" He swung around. It was Bertha, swinging his black shopping bag. "You forgot your package!"

"Oh, Christ. I did. Thank you very much."

"That's okay, lucky I caught you. Come again, now. Ooo, getting nippy, ain't it."

"Yeah," he said, and she went back in. A cable car was being turned around on the stand below, but Fitzie waited as it creaked out of the park and began its climb up the hill. He stepped out into the street at the corner as it approached and, having done it all his life, waited for it to go by him almost entirely before he left the ground and landed on the narrow step of its rear platform. He didn't step up, but hung there holding on to the worn steel handbar and watched the Buena Vista, the park, the beach, the sailing ship, the Wharf sink away beneath him. The sun had left splashes of purple, gold and red suspended in the sky above where it had dropped into the sea. The car strained higher and higher, letting more and more of the city gather in from the sides for Fitzie to see. He squeezed the cool bar tighter to help himself stay aware that he was really there and looking at just the moment when all this colored grandness was happening. Toward the top, shadows were thrown from the building tops, the air turned cooler and he felt a draft of sadness. It was the time to go inside the city. It was the time to have someplace to go. The hills, the streets and the sidewalks seemed not just *there*, waiting, anymore; they were moving conveyor belts now heading to places. Fitzie had been on the bright side of alone, now he was passing onto the dark side.

The wall switch lighted the small twin dresser lamps. While he was out, the bed had slid back to its place on the far wall. He set the shopping bag beside the champagne bag on the dresser. Now that he was there, he didn't know why he had come back. He stood in the middle of the room. The ceiling, the whole top of the hotel, opened on its hinges like a box and the person way up there in the helicopter spotted him through his binoculars. *There he is. Yeah, that's him. No, he's alone, standing there like an asshole. We found him.* Christ. No matter where he was he always felt that he should be someplace else, was *supposed* to be someplace else. He just wasn't used to being by himself, that's all. Aah! It must be like a guitar, just strum stupidly, and it's loneliness. Know the chords, and it's freedom. Okay, then let's see. He walked straight to the phone and called room service for two Beefeater gibsons, on the rocks. There. Have a drink, listen to some music, make your plans. Goddamn it, Bibles and TVs but never a radio anymore. He clicked the television set on

243

and blacked out the picture with the brightness control. Some sound better than none. Now, what. A shower! Of course. Change the clothes, freshen up. You've had a long day. The drinks came on a tray. Nice. One glass, a pitcher of more stuff, a little bowl of ice. He carried the drink to the bathroom and turned the shower on, full and hot. That's better, get the thumb out. Man, it's Kovacs's room, live it up. Fitzie walked the mile from bathroom door to dresser, downhill all the way, down in the Russian crouch, the Groucho Marx walk. With buddies through Harvard Square, himself in front, pausing at every hydrant, meter and pole to lift their legs without falling. Hey, you in the chopper up there, take your pictures now!

A showerhead for some cattle baron, played by Sidney Greenstreet. He set the glass on the sink, then got in and showered, even his hair. No flowered showercap of Janice's. He got out and took towel and drink with him into the other room, now a refrigerator room—oh, that Ernie! —with ice everywhere, icicles for drapes, everything blocks of ice. He dried himself up and down and around the floor, and dressed to the tune of Ted Mack droning a Geritol commercial in the dark screen. *A little traveling music, Ray!* Yut-tut-tutta-tuttut-tuttut-tatta, *and away we go!*

It was night now, dark and cool. He walked, *The Fly!* halfway up the street-mountain, then trotted out and hopped a cable car. On the flat, he jumped down because a lot of other riders got off there. He followed them up a hill, and there was The Mark Hopkins and the Fairmont, duelers facing each other atop the hill. Fitzie went in and had a drink at the bar of the Fairmont, then crossed and went up to the Top of the Mark. The waitresses wore Ann Sheridan, Golden Nugget Saloon gowns. One got him a table at a window and a gin and tonic. Outside, unlike L.A., like Manhattan from the Top of the Sixes but without the perforated towers. Purple, rolling, creased, twinkling. The city down and out there, big; him here, small and what, down and out inside? No! Well, maybe. A little. He looked around inside the place. Were any of these people from some ad agency up here for booze and supper before going back to jerk themselves off until midnight? Probably not, it was Saturday night, and it was San Francisco. They were just people, having drinks, on their way to eat, to a show, home, somewhere.

Come on, come on, come on, drop yer cocks and pick up yer socks, get a move on, snap out of it, forget your frigging *self* for at second, come alive, wake up and die

244

right, on your feet, on your way, it's a big, wide, wonderful world we live in, be a goddamn *tourist*, then, it won't kill you. You've done the Fairmont and the Mark, you're staying at the Saint Francis, what next? Fitzie paid and went down humming, moving lively, back out of doors and into the high air. His mind dropped the reins for once and his milkhorse body did just fine; he found himself on Grant Avenue, right back on his old route. Hong Kong! Singapore! He walked, happy, then hungry; so up the stairs to the second-floor restaurant, busy, mixed faces but mostly Chinese, and behind the maître d' to a window table only a little above the sidewalk and street. No, no drink, but soup, oh yeah, and this, and some of that, and oh, that's special is it? By all means then, thanks and hurry. Fitzie waited, watching faces bobbing along thickly below, but then caught a tidy lady from Kansas City looking at him, not listening to her three lippy sisters. Oh, lady, I know, I always hate to see anybody eating alone, too. But really, it's okay, see this? The nice private smiling-to-myself? Sure. Thinking of something nice that happened. Chrissie turned in her chair in his mind. It surprised him, but worked with the lady. It was harder getting rid of Chrissie. All through his meal he kept sending her away, but she kept coming back, cocking her head, wagging her tail, blinking the big eyes, waiting. As if she were with him. As if she were his.

Fitzie drank the whole fat pot of tea. It took a while, smoking, digesting, sipping, and he found himself starting to give in and pat her. Yeah, yeah, I like you, too, but get out of here, will you? I have to go now. He could feel her pining at the top of the stairs, watching him go, and he felt torn but kept going. Away, away. He walked to Broadway. It was still early. He found Gold Street. The Roaring Twenties was dark and quiet, bar glasses and waiters polished and waiting. He had a Chivas at the bar. People started coming in and music began, but it stayed peaceful so he had another. Scotch in his mouth, circles of water on the bar made into eyes, wheels, cells, barbells with his swizzle stick, idly—alone was good now, a good way to be. He walked back to Broadway, then, and into a door, and sat and watched the All-Girl Topless Band. All the girls wore pasties and he missed the nipples of Sunset Strip. Then, one girl had Chrissie's face. *Damn, she was looking for him.* Then the drummer had the face, then the lead singer with the guitar. Finally he took the face himself and pasted it onto the huge blonde bass player with the cave-woman dugs and that broke it. Out and up

245

the street. Another watered scotch, more pasties. In and out. In Big Al's and out. La Bodega. The Cobacavano. El Mexico Cantino. He couldn't seem to find a place he could stay. Either he got bored or Chrissie found him. At last he was standing on a street corner out of the main push smoking a cigarette and hearing it for the ten-millionth time in his life: *What the hell am I doing here?* In high school and college they would barrel down from Boston to stay at the Y.M.C.A. (the *Hotel Yimca,* their mothers thought), hit Times Square and Forty-second Street and nowhere else, go home and say they'd been to New York. This was the same. Christ, he wouldn't be caught dead in those dives now, yet here he was hitting them in San Francisco as a grown man and wondering what was wrong. He flipped the cigarette away, Brian Donleavy, and walked away from North Beach, the milkhorse taking over for him again while his mind went on mumbling and fretting. The horse went right, tired. Fitzie went back to the hotel.

He lay on his back on the bed. The bed didn't slide. The floor seemed to have leveled off while he was out. Kovacs must have moved on. Oh, beautiful. Some Mister Funny. Come to San Francisco, to *Alexandria* for Christ's sake, all by yourself, for all intents and purposes a totally free agent—and tie your cringing old cord to a fucking over-sized hotel room. Just beautiful. Have a good time, Big Bopper o' mine, just don't cross the street and be home when the lights come on. Yes, it's me and I'm a kid again, a nun-whipped, self-whipped *sincere* jerk of a kid. Ernie, I don't blame you. I'd leave too. Even as an adult, God forbid but never mind, even as an *adult,* I could have gone to a play, a concert, a movie, a show, a museum, a lecture, even. At least it would have been something and I'd still be *out,* where something would be possible! Instead of here in my cribbie scratching my balls at ten fucking forty-five on a Saturday night. Jesus. Even my hotel could be a parish facility. There's the church, Father, and the school, the usher's club, the rectory, and the hotel; I'm sure you'll be happy here at St. Francis's, now I'll show you to your room. Hey, maybe there's a Nocturnal Adoration Society doing its stuff tonight.

"All right!" Fitzie yelled out loud and it rang around the room, rebounding from every corner, and he was off the bed and on his feet. Kovacs, you bastard, I love you, you didn't leave! A giant spring under the bed. An ejecting mattress—Boing! and you're up and out, ha-hah! I'll go find a crummy bar called Pat's or The Shady Nook where

the bums from the boatyards and the ice cream plants and the sanitation department will be, playing the pinball and the shuffleboard, maybe a bowling machine, and I'll drink boilermakers, a shot of Schenley and a draft here, friend, and I'll get loaded, blind, and get them to sing "Soldier Boy" and "Galway" fucking "Bay!"

The hell you will, laughed Ernie in an echo chamber, moving the eyes in the picture on the wall.

The hell I will, said Fitzie like John Wayne, whirled and socked the base-weighted, roly-poly, life-size nun balloon to the floor in the middle of the room. He was out and gone before the rocks in her feet sprang her back upright.

From the corner where he had the taxi pull up, the place looked like a movie theater: a blast of yellow light in the middle of a dark block. He walked toward the yellow, hearing his heels on the sidewalk and reading the marquee: GALAXY BALLROOM. *Tonight. Danny Dunne and the Tuners. Dancing. Cocktails. All invited!* The ticket booth was not at the sidewalk, it was to the rear of the large lobby, next to the carpeted, grand staircase, and Chrissie was inside it, looking down. To Fitzie, approaching between the encased photographs, she looked like the mechanical Gypsy Fortuneteller waiting within her glass box for a penny to bring her to life. Then, as he was nearly up to the glass window and shelf, she was Snow White, asleep forever, from above, top half only. She hadn't heard him. He stood and looked in through the small open talk-hole in the glass. She was reading a Modern Library book. He said, "Hi," through the hole.

The eyes came up, then the whole head as she came awake. "Coo!" she laughed. "You did come. I didn't think you would." She lifted her hands and let the pages flutter across.

"You'll lose your place," he smiled.

"Well, where did you go?" she asked. "Did you have a good time?"

"Oh. Just around, you know. North Beach."

"Lose your friends?" she grinned.

"No friends," he said. "I came to see you."

She colored slightly. "Too bad you didn't come earlier. It stops at midnight, but that gives you nearly an hour."

"What's up there, anyhow?"

"Dancing, and a bar, and loads of people."

"Can you go up?"

247

"Oh, no. I have to stay here. And then I have to stay until one, to help with the books. Sometimes longer. Luce is up there, though."

"I came to see you, Chrissie," he said.

"Oh," she said, as if she hadn't been the one who had pushed the envelope scrap on him. Of course she could say that she simply gave him the information because he was new and alone in the city and might like to know where he could meet people, hear music, dance and have a drink. Except something had damn well happened between them and she knew it and had been sending those beams out from her booth all night until they found him and wouldn't let go. And here he was, by God! "You know what?" he said.

"What?"

"I think somebody has had her bluff called."

"Half," she said.

"Half what?"

"Only half a bluff."

"All right, what do you want me to do, then?"

"Go up and see what's doing and I'll come find you. I'll have to see if somebody'll spell me here."

"Okay. And you look wonderful, by the way," he said. She wore a navy blue dress, nearly black, that crossed below her bust leaving a long cone open from the neck. Around her neck and fluffing in the cone she had a smoky pink scarf exactly like the one sitting in the shopping bag back on his dresser. He couldn't tell what the dress did below her waist. "Thank you," Chrissie said, "you don't look bad yourself. You've changed your shirt."

"How much to get in, anyway?" he asked.

"Two Pimm's cups. You paid in advance."

"No, really. I don't want you . . ."

"It's all right, really. Go ahead, now, and I'll see you."

Fitzie climbed the stairs and checked his coat, then entered the main room. He couldn't believe it. *He was in an Irish Club, in Boston, and it was nineteen fifty-something!* The band, Danny and all, had ducksasses, from combs dipped in large-mouthed slickum bottles, and wore powder blue, one-button roll zoot jackets over royal blue pegged pants, shoestring ties on white shirts. Danny rolled back and forth over his spread legs—the better to make his saxophone wail. His *saxophone. Wail.* Jaysus *Haitch* Christ! Kovacs, you've gone too far.

The bar was rimmed with men, arm to arm, drinking and laughing. The dancers were doing a polka now, which brought a few of the bar boys out and into the arms of a

Maureen or Coleen. A few. Three out of a thousand. Fitzie gladly stayed with the brighter lads, ordering a drink and keeping his eye on the top of the staircase beyond the far end of the bar. Then, "Fitzie!" He turned on his stool, knowing it had to be Luce. "Hi," he smiled.

"How *are* you?" Luce sparkled. She was a wedding cake, in a white gown tight at the top to barely cup the jiggling boob-tops. And around her, not two but three big-grinned Greek boys in sailor suits. Clearly, America was all they had dreamed it would be.

"Fitzie Fitzpatrick, I'd like you to meet Nicky and uh, Nick and Nick." The Greeks nearly danced together, this brought such a laugh from them.

He laughed too and shook their hands. Luce was the Good Fairy. An Archangel. Our Lady. Virginia Mayo.

"I can't get *over* it!" she laughed. "How long have you been here? Oh! Wait till I tell *Chrissie.*"

"I saw her. She's coming up as soon as she can."

"Oh, she's *never!* Is she?"

"Yeah. Why? It won't get her in any trouble, will it?"

"Oh, no. In fact, they're always trying to get her up but she won't. Oh, I'm so excited!"

"Listen, Luce, what are you here, like a hostess?"

"Yes!" she said, the bonfire back. "It's really a fun job, we usually get a party going and go off someplace, it's terrific. You always get a date, anyway."

"Chrissie go, too?" he asked.

"Oh, no. Well, sometimes, if she feels like it."

The Greek boys were getting restless. "Okay, Luce," he laughed, "your fans are waiting. See you later, maybe, huh?"

"Oh, gee, that'd be swell. Oh, though, Chrissie has to stay until one, you know, and . . ."

"Go ahead, love. We'll worry about that later." And off she went with them, trailing stardust like Tinker Bell. So. Now. Chrissie. Something else. Something else altogether. He nearly missed her. He kept watching the space above the stairs, but had forgotten the dress. He had been watching for the boy in the shirt and dungarees, and now when he looked he saw the woman standing there in the short blue-black dress with the pink at the neck. The over-flap went to three tiny gold buttons close at the waist, then dropped straight down the short distance to end well above the knees. Chriss-ie! Jesus, don't go. Here I am, I'm coming.

"Oh, there you are," she fluttered brightly. Lost child found. "I thought you must be out dancing."

249

"No." He took her arm and walked her back to the bar. When he felt the tightness in her arm, he loosened his already light hold on her; as strong as she seemed, she felt breakable. She sat up with her back to the bar, hands in lap, and smiled at him, standing. "Now, what'll you have?" he said.

"He'll know when he spots me," she said.

Sure enough, in two minutes the bartender came up with a drink. "There you go, Chris girl."

"Vodka gimlet," Fitzie said.

"Vodka gimlet. On the house, too."

"A regular B-girl, aren't you," reaching past her for his own drink. "Must spend a lot of time on these stools."

"You bet." Toughly.

"That ain't the way I hoid it."

"Oh, so you've seen Luce, have you? Might have known she'd spy you quick enough. Or did you go looking for her?"

"Lady, let's get something straight, okay? I didn't come here to dance or to drink or meet nice people or see Luce, for Christ's sake. I came here to see you again, and nothing else."

"Okay," she smiled, "but you don't have to curse."

"So," he smiled.

"So, you're seeing me," Chrissie said.

"So you're something delicious to see, too. I thought so this afternoon, tonight and right now. But am I wrong or am I feeling a chill?"

Chrissie, drinking, frowned, put her glass down and licked her lips. "Fitzie, you're wearing a wedding ring. What am I supposed to think about that?"

"That I'm married. And that I would be just as married if I didn't have the ring on, but would be a liar."

"Points for that, I guess."

"All right, but just tell me something. And tell the truth, because I know the answer already. Did you see the ring before you gave me this place or after?"

"Before. Before I even spoke to you."

"Then what am I supposed to think about that?"

"I don't know," Chrissie said sadly.

Then he said, "Well, are we over that or not? Can we be?"

"Can you?" The eyes smaller.

"Yes," he said.

"Easily, all the time, old habit?"

"No. Not that easily at all, if you have to know. And

never before, really, and I don't care if you believe that or not."

"Well, I'm not sure if I even want to believe it. That may be worse."

"How about you, can you be over it—without my getting into it, which I won't?"

"Yes," Chrissie said, "I guess I can. I did this afternoon, then it came back. But yes. Why not."

"Then while we're at it, what about you? You some kind of a weirdo, lovely Chrissie?"

Chrissie smiled, the great eyes touching him again. "Yes," she whispered then, "I'm a weirdo."

"Come to think of it, let me see that hand of *yours*."

She laughed and laid in onto his. "No ring, but are you married?" he said.

"No," she said.

"Are you a liar?"

"Not about that."

"Have you been married?"

"Yes."

"You don't ask, I don't ask?"

"Right," she laughed and closed her fingers briefly over his.

"Phew!" Fitzie said. "That was hard. Hey, listen, we've had enough of the nitty-gritty, love, let's be funny and laugh a lot now. Do you like to dance?"

"Not to that."

"Well, Danny and the boys seem to be taking five anyhow. Want another drink? I'll buy you all the freebies you want."

"Yes, you can. But I have to go back downstairs for a while, then I'll come back."

"Can I come down with you?"

"No, you mind the spot. I shouldn't be long." Her Scottish rolled thicker when she said, "If you've found somebody you'd rather talk to than me, just ignore me."

"And what will you do?"

"I'll go away."

"Really?"

"Yup. I'll kill her, then go away."

"That's better. Now get out of here."

One last touch of the eyes on his face and Chrissie walked away along the rail of sitting and standing, drinking men. With a slight, sweet twitch of her bottom caught by no eyes but Fitzie's. A small warm wave rose and broke gently within his chest. He took the stool and leaned on the bar over his drink. Ladies' choice. A mass hernia swept man-to-man around the entire perimeter of the bar. The revolving ball above the dance floor began to move again, sprinkling its love flakes over all. Near the last *doo-ah, doo-ah* ... Fitzie felt her behind him, then heard her. "No luck, huh?" she said.

He spun the seat around, another wave breaking in him. "It's about time."

"Why you. I wasn't long at all! Don't have to go back till closing either."

"It's ladies' choice. You have to ask me to dance."

Chrissie rolled her eyes. "All right, may I have this dance, sir?" She laughed and led him by the hand around the bar to the love flakes-on-purple. They stood facing each other, grinning, while Danny and the boys lifted the spoon out of "I Love Paris" and dipped it into the even thicker "Moonglow." They came together and began moving, slowly, to the padded beat. "God, you feel good," Fitzie said. Her grassy air reached him then, too late for him to say he liked that, too.

"I forgot how nice it was to dance like this," Chrissie said.

"Was?"

"Is. Oh, *is*."

They stopped talking. They danced, covering no more than a small oblong. His right hand, the edge of his thumb, could feel, faintly, the back strap of her bra through the soft dress. He wondered if it was black, as her panties had been in the afternoon. And he wondered what color her panties were now—black again? The same ones or fresh? White, maybe. Or pink, like her scarf. But not high and floppy. Low and tight. Bikinis even, maybe. Then he wondered how her breasts looked in the bra. Then out. He could feel them against him; the right one, anyway, his wallet was getting the left, damn wallet he should have put it in his back pocket. She was close, but by no means putting it to him; yet he could feel her hipbones now and again, and the tops of her thighs—and the hollow, the unfeelable hollow nothing in the middle, he could feel most keenly of all. *Oh, no, don't! Stay down. Go back to sleep. Think about something else. Oh, yeah come on, ruin everything*. Fitzie turned his body slightly back and left to open the chaperone's inch between them, but Chrissie's right arm pulled her back in against him. His horn pressed hard right into her hollow and she stiffened abruptly. He could feel it in her arm on his back, in the hand he held, in her back beneath the bra. Yet she didn't pull away. "I'm sorry," he said.

"I know. It's all right," she said and her stiffness went away. And then, then! she let them have it both ways, laughed very lightly and said, "The old Mae West line, right? Do you know it?"

Did he know it. He could even do a fair Mae West. He said, "something like 'Oo-ah, is that a pistol in your pocket or are ya glad to see me?' " They both laughed. The song ended. They walked off the floor and back to the bar. Fitzi's erection, foiled and enjoyed, fainted. They smoked and smiled at each other, now easy together. The purple got put away noisily as the lights roared up for a last polka, then the inevitable "Good-night, ladies." The cover onto the drums, still vibrating. The stampede to jam at the coat check counter. All lights up. Drill over, dismissed. "Well, that's it," Chrissie said.

"What happens now?" he asked.

"Now I have to go help with the receipts. About a half-hour if I'm quick. You can stay, the bar stays open."

"Then what?"

"I don't know, then what?"

"Can't we go someplace? What would you like to do?"

"Go home to sleep, probably. I'm really tired."

"Oh, come on."

"But the night's over, isn't it," she said. "It's morning now."

"But we just met."

"You came late," she said, almost sadly. This could be enough, be all. *That was very nice.* It could end now. It was up to him. Chrissie helped a little. She said, "We'll have a nightcap and talk when I come back, okay? I'd best get started," and left. Fitzie stayed straddling his stool, watching the sons and daughters of Erin, the Oliver Plunkett marching band, filing up in disorder to be issued their coats. "Okay here, bud?" the barkeeper asked. "Do it again," Fitzie said. Luce in a big black shawl bounced out of the throng with the last of the Nicks. "We're leaving now. Are you waiting for Chrissie, would you want us to wait?" She smiled eagerly.

"I don't think so, Luce," he grinned, "she may be a while."

"Okay, then." Just as she suspected. Luce gave him her hand to shake. "If I don't see you, it was great meeting you."

"You, too," Fitzie smiled. "Bye." He waved to Nick.

Employees came out of the walls to look tired and sit at the bar and nearby tables, to drink and watch the last of their patrons go away once more into the outside. Fitzie felt simple and content in the still, weary glare of the place, and when Chrissie at last came gliding up through the air of the staircase and through the glare toward him, he felt happy and excited. She was something, all right, and it was for him. She flew up to her seat, waved her finger to the bartender, and smiled at Fitzie a waiting, asking smile.

The bartender came up with a cup of coffee. "Oh, I'm sorry, Ned. I should have ... let's make it another drink tonight if that's all right."

"Okay, Chris, no sweat."

Fitzie asked her, "Is this your only job?"

"It is. There's not much I can do, if the truth be known."

"Does it pay you enough?"

"No, but I don't need much. Nobody needs as much as they think they do."

"And everybody needs more."

"No. I take some courses at State. I keep busy."

"I thought all Scotch girls were nurses."

"A lot are, the ones that come out."

"But not you."

"No. I came out as a domestic. I was sponsored by a professor at N.Y.U."

"Is that right? So you lived in New York!"

"Right on Washington Square for nearly two years. It was lovely."

"Did you like the Village?"

"Well. Once I got over it, I loved it."

"What brought you out here, then?"

"My husband."

"Sorry, I forgot. We said we wouldn't do that."

"No, it's all right. He was the professor's son, although he didn't live at home. He graduated and came to Berkeley for a master's and I came with him." She paused to drink. Fitzie wanted to ask, but held it back: if he didn't, he wouldn't be obliged to tell or be asked anything in return. He said "Chrissie," to tell her they could get off it now. She smiled. "Please. Unless it bothers you. I've never even told Luce. He was into drugs even in New York. I thought it would go away, he wasn't an acid-head or anything. But we no more than set foot out here than he wigged out completely. So we never really left each other, I mean. He just went and I didn't go with him. He's still in the Haight someplace right now. As far as I know, anyhow. I haven't seen him for eight months or more. The divorce like came in the mail overnight. His father. He's a love, poor thing. Sends me a little check every month. I'll be glad when I can send it back."

"Chris?"

"The great thing is, it didn't hurt me any. I wish it didn't happen, but it did, it could've been worse, and I'm on top of it and out of it." She held her glass up and clinked it against Fitzie's. "Here's to faith in yourself."

"How old are you, Chrissie?"

"Twenty-six coming up. I was older than Lou, maybe that should have helped but it didn't. Maybe that was what was wrong."

"You as hungry as I am?"

"Starving."

"Then what do you say we go get something to eat?"

"We shouldn't, should we Mister Fitz."

"Don't you want to stay with me for a while?"

"You know I do. But it can't be any good. You're not really there, are you."

"I don't know if I'm here or not, okay? But it can be good. I won't do anything to make it not good, if you know what I mean. No your place. No my place. Because if we don't, we'll never know, and probably always wonder."

"One more I-almost-did-but-didn't."

"Got many of those?"

"Bushels."

"Me too. And the older I get the more I realize *something* is better than *nothing.*"

"If you asked me what I'd really like to do, it's be to go see the water. And to hear some music. There's a place called the Trident, in Sausalito, on the bay across the bridge."

"I'll rent a car and we'll go there, then."

"No, it'd be closed anyhow."

"Then we'll just drive until we see water, you must know some place. You know, I've never *touched* the Pacific?"

"No, no. I don't want you to rent a car. But it's starting to be an adventure, isn't it! Oh, what can we do?"

"We can't just go to a restaurant, some place with music?"

"Oh, no. Anybody could to that."

"I know. We can go to a deli, if you've got any here, and we can buy some bread and meat and stuff and go eat it someplace."

"Lovely. There's all-night supermarkets. That's what we'll do."

255

"And where'll we go?"

"We can think of that later." She was all excited now. "Where are you staying?"

"The Saint Francis."

"Perfect, I live not far from there. If we're going to be tinkers on the streets I'll have to change to some warmer duds. You can wait in Union Square park for me. Maybe we'll even have our picnic there!"

Chrissie wanted to keep waiting for a bus, but he hailed a cab. The cabbie waited outside the store while Fitzie bought italian bred, ham, cheese, mustard, a bag of potato chips and two big apples, then dropped them at Union Square. He sat on a bench with the bag of food and watched Chrissie run out of sight across the park walk. Then he abruptly jumped to his feet and hustled across the street, into the Saint Francis's lobby and up to his room. He rinsed out the gibson glass, put it and the one from the bathroom into the bag holding the champagne, fitted that into the larger bag, then ran out and down again. She was standing there when he got back, her afternoon shirt and dungarees overwhelmed now by a great, heavy-looking shaggy sweater as long as a coat. "Hey, mister, have you seen a beautiful girl around?" he yelled, running up.

When he saw the eyes his grin froze.

"Oh, Chrissie," he said, "what did you think?" He put the bag on the bench and wrapped his arms around her. Her arms didn't come up; she just fell heavily in against him. "I thought you'd be much longer," he said into her hair. He held her. Finally he moved her away a little and the face came up. The eyes were wet still, but not welling now—receding back to normal. "Soft-ie."

"Like hell," she said. "Off guard, that's all. Not used to it."

"Well, Christ, what do you do, live in one of these trees?"

"The third from the corner," she said, embarrassed.

"I didn't just go off to the john or anything, you know. Or to take a sweater off some poor old night watchman, either!"

She giggled. "What did you get?"

"You'll see. Now, where'll we have our feast?"

"Oh, I don't know."

"Well, I do."

"Where?"

"We have to have the water, right? And it'd be nice to go where we met, wouldn't it?"

"The city beach. Of course. Good. Good and nutty. But that's a long way."

"Can't we take a cable car?"

"No, they're stopped now."

"We'll get another cab, then."

"Ow, the money."

"Do you want to walk?"

"Lord, no."

"Then shut up and come on," he said, and they crossed to a cab at the hotel. Getting in, he said, "It's not really my money, anyhow. I'm letting Madison Ave. spring for me. For a change."

"So, it's the adverts is it?"

"The *adverts!*" he laughed. "Yeah, it's the adverts, all right." They were sitting at brother and sister distance on the taxi seat.

"I should have known," she said.

"Do I look it? Excuse me, I think I'll kill myself."

"No, not slick."

"What, then?"

"I don't know. Alert? *Finished,* that's a good word."

"I'm finished, all right," he said toward the window.

"Oh, now. Not so melodramatic if you please. It can't be all that corrupt and phony or whatever else it's always called, can it?"

"No, it's not. Especially from three thousand miles away. It looks less significant all the time."

"Are you good at it?"

"I'm terrific."

"What do you do, do you *make* the ads and the telly things?"

"Yeah."

"And do you like doing that? Is it any fun?"

"It is, to tell the truth. I get a tremendous bang out of it. You have to go through a lot of crap in between, and that takes a lot out of you, but when I get a job going, something really good, yeah, I really get my rocks off. I suppose that's enough justification right there for doing something."

"No," Chrissie said after a pause, studying the cabbie's neck, "I should think that's a justification of *you*. Not any business you're in."

"Say that again?"

"Well, I don't know. But it seems that that would be more what *you* give *it*, rather than what it gives you. Couldn't you get your bloody *rocks* off, whatever that means, at something else? At anything you might want to do?"

"Wow," Fitzie said. "That's a thing. I never thought of it that way. Here's to faith in yourself, huh? Wish I was brought up that way. Aah! But enough about you. Let's talk about me!"

Fitzie pulled her hand up from her leg and kissed it loudly. "You're beautiful. Hey, driver, can't we pick it up a little?"

"I can't drive and listen, too," the driver said, stepping on the gas. Fitzie, Chrissie and he, Jerry Corrado, laughed. "Okay, we'll shut up," Fitzie said.

"We're just about there anyhow," Corrado said. "Whereabouts?"

"Down beneath the park," Chrissie said. They were passing the Buena Vista, still going within gold light and smoke. Fitzie paid him through the window.

"Oh, man," Fitzie said. They stood on top of the low concrete wall and faced the bay. The beach was a short gap, its black grayed only dimly by the few streetlamps along the wall and the night-lights of the sleeping sailing ship off to the right. Then the water, solid and moving but with only the weakest flop of waves, its surface glittering with lights it had carried in from moored boats out in the bay. The Gate a long arc of distant light away high to their left. The scene wasn't beautiful, as he had expected: too much black. Yet it was all more powerful than Fitzie had anticipated. Because he was actually there, with this other person, this girl who was so real and who had come here with him, *for* him. They stepped off the wall and dropped to the sand, their fingers locked, Fitzie holding the bag and his raincoat against his chest. The beach in both directions was deserted. "Cold?" he asked her.

"Yes, but the air's good, isn't it. I'll make it make me warm."

"Thatta babe," he said. They stopped walking when they were well within the black, beyond the gray of the lights and before the twilight of the water. Fitzie set the bag down upright in the sand. "Want to put my coat on?" he asked.

"No, spread it out. For the picnic."

He opened the coat out and sat down. He pulled off his boots and socks and yanked the tight worsted slacks up to his calves. "I am about to be baptized. I am going to step

258

off the continental United States into the Pacific. Come with me."

"Okay." She undid her sandals. "It's only the bay, though."

"Not to me."

"Not to me, either, then."

"Let's go." Holding hands again, they walked into the water. Chrissie stopped after three steps. "Any more and I'll get soaked," she laughed.

"This is fine." They stood still, together, facing the bay. The water was warmer than the air. The bottom was mucky. "We are off, aren't we," Chrissie said.

"Yup. Three feet, three miles." Three magic hours. "Want to turn around and look at the country?"

"No. And when we go back we'll walk backwards and pretend we're still out here."

"Okay." They walked backwards out of the water and stopped to let the small surf lick the muck off their feet. "You know what we have to do now?" he said.

"Eat! That's what."

"First we have to run around in a great big circle and get nice and warm. When you're running around, see, you're not really on the ground or in the country. So we'll be in the water and in the air. Half the time, anyway."

They turned and trotted along the water's edge, then ran faster up into the sand, through the black, coming around in the gray, then back into the black, stopping at the coat. Chrissie dropped to the coat and fell back, heaving. Fitzie sat down beside her. "There. Now you're warmer, aren't you?"

"Oh, yes," she said and laughed up in broken gusts.

"Okay, now!" He opened the bag and dropped all the food onto her belly, bringing her up. "Here," he said. "You fix the sandwiches, and I'll prepare the surprise."

He pulled the bottle into the air.

"Bubbly!" she sang. "Oh, what a man! What would I do without you!" Untwisting the wire cork-holder, Fitzie knew she meant that no more than Bubbly! but it lit on his mind like a mosquito. And like a mosquito trapped in a sleeping bag, he couldn't kill it or whisk it away—he had to let it stab and draw its quotient of blood. It did—what *will* she do without me?—then flew off. He grabbed the unbound cork, bottle wedged between knees, and pulled it out with a great yank. Chrissie applauded the *Thop!* like a child. He poured champagne into each glass. They clinked glasses and Chrissie drank one long mouthful, half the glass. "Ohh, that's the stuff!" Fitzie poured all of his into him and it washed him clean: keep it simple, stupid, don't make so much of yourself. "And you even had the bread sliced," she praised him, busily layering meat on cheese.

Fitzie poured more champagne, and they ate like chicken thieves. Too full for the apples, they bunched the leavings into the bag and put it off the coat on the sand. They lay on their sides, close and facing, smoking cigarettes and sipping from the glasses. Smiling at each other's smiles. Chrissie's eyes touching him again, reaching and touching. Fitzie knew there would be no more real talking now. Only "More?" when he finished his champagne, and "No," from her as she passed him her empty glass. Warmth came to him from her, although his body was the wind shield. Of course. As if he hadn't known. It was there. It had been there, from the first contact in the afternoon, else there would have been no contact. And not knowing it, dodging it, skirting it, he of course had known it. And now, of course, they were going to do it.

So this is how it is.

His mouth didn't push her head back onto the coat. It merely covered hers, which opened, and her head eased back by itself. Their tongues rubbed gently. When they stopped, she opened her eyes and said, "Surprise!" very softly. Fitzie said, "Really?" and she said, "No." They kissed again, this time his hand finding the gap he knew would be at the top of her dungarees in back, feeling the skin there and moving, open flat, slowly up her back to beneath the strap and then around the front lifting as it went until the bra was limp above her breasts and his hand covered her left breast, rubbing the hard nipple very gently back and forth. Their mouths broke and Chrissie said, "You're so expert," as her lips moved to his throat; she said it to mean it pleased her, nothing more. But even as he lifted the shirt and sank to replace hand with mouth on her breast, even as calm and as giving as he felt, he cursed God for letting her say it. Because *expert* had flashed *Janice* and forced him to admit that he was committing the worst possible sin against Chrissie that he could: he was going back to Janice and was making love to her, as he always had. He felt Chrissie's hand wedge between their bodies and heard the deep click of the snap unlocking. His going hand brushed hers departing and plunged gently into the heat, moving as slowly as the parting zipper, over the softer low-skin and into the hair. *Easy. Nice. She mustn't know.* He actually wanted to stop; he cared about her too much. But he knew, and now the moist lips of the larger, sweeter mouth in the now-

260

rocking, rising head confirmed it: to stop would be as despair—unforgivable. The sin must be committed to prevent the sin, and perhaps make none of it sin at all. To help, he forced the words *Chrissie, Chrissie, Chrissie, Chrissie* out of his mouth. "Oh, now, please," she said strongly, the opposite of whimpering. "I want it so much, I feel so empty." Clothes down, off, her grassy scent rising lush as mown hay. Fitzie prayed *help me, help me, she's so alone and alone.* Without answer. Or answered, punished: No! He entered, was taken deeply, and came on the third stroke. 'Oh, Christ, I'm sorry." Chrissie had frozen in midair, paralyzed, disbelieving such cruelty. He quickly sent his hand. "No." "Please," he said, "let me. My mouth, anything, I want to give you . . ."

"No," she said wearily. She rose out of his hold and had her clothes back up and closed in one movement. The panties were white.

"We can wait, just a little while," Fitzie said.

"No," Chrissie said flatly, "it's all right."

He felt trapped in the warehouse office, the swirling lights and sirens coming fast, alone with the victim of his crime, desperate to convert victim to sole friendly witness. And in a hurry. He didn't have much time; he had to be good. She sat with her chin between her jackknifed knees, staring out at the water. He sat up and stroked her rounded back. "Chrissie please," he whispered, "I couldn't help it."

"No. I'm glad."

"No, please," he urged, sidling closer to her solidity. "I want it to be great for you. It can. Please."

Chrissie turned her head on her knees, resting on her ear, and looked at him silently, without a smile. The eyes didn't touch; flat, they merely looked at Fitzie's face. "And what if it was?" she said at last. "Would you become my lover?"

"Yes!" Fitzie whispered.

"Ah, see," she said, "our first lie already. Leave it, man. Make it easier for me to get back to where I was." She turned her face back out to face the bay. "It's your bloody old pride talking anyhow." She shut the eyes.

"No. It isn't." His mouth was getting drier.

The eyes opened but not to him, to the water, and she spoke to the water. "Yes it is. I just wish I had some. I did. For such a long time, too. I might have known it'd be for nothing. Let me hurt you a little bit, okay?" She turned her face back to him and said, "For nothing, Fitzie. *Nothing.*"

261

"Okay," Fitzie exhaled. Then he lay down on his back and looked up at the sky.

"What's her name?" Chrissie asked. Her voice sounded far away. He looked. She was standing now, on his coat, above him.

"Janice."

"That's pretty," Chrissie said, moving out of his sight, around his feet to his right side. He stayed looking at where she had been. "I hope she can take care of herself as well as I can. Can she?" he heard.

"I don't know."

"Good man," Chrissie said. "Will you help *me* get started, Mr. Fitz? Will you do something for me?"

"Yes. Anything. What?"

"Promise."

"Yes. What?"

"Just lie there and don't move. Let me do something I think I have to do, then let me go away."

"It's late, Chrissie, and dark. I . . ."

"It'll be late and dark tomorrow night and next week. Where will you be then?"

Fitzie closed his eyes. Some answer.

"All right, then?" she said. Her voice seemed right over his ear now.

"All right," he said. When the champagne first struck his skin, at the temple, it felt cold and he flinched. But as it kept coming and streamed across his forehead and cheeks and down over his closed eyes, he realized it was lukewarm and sticky, where the air dried it. He heard the bottle hit the sand and her move away over the sand, step by step, not hurrying. Then he couldn't hear her at all. Fitzie rolled over onto his stomach, freeing the last drops to run from hiding out of his ear and eye creases. He stood, wiping his eyes. She had made it across the grass and was at the curb in front of the empty, shut-up Buena Vista Café. The last he saw of her was the bottom of her big, bulky sweater. Unbuttoned, it flounced up slightly as she broke into a little run and turned the corner.

It was approaching four o'clock Sunday afternoon before he found a church having late Mass and confessions. As if he were in some earlier century that had no telephones, he had searched by foot since one o'clock, simply spotting steeples and heading for them. This one was large and plain. It was in Chinatown, but the people with whom

262

he had been sliding along the pew nearer to confession seemed to be all Italians. And he was only one person, an ancient, snow-headed crony in black, away from the curtain before his mind caught up with him. He said, "Excuse me," three times and finally had to nudge her on the shoulder to get her to let him by. He knew she thought he was trying to get ahead of her, so he genuflected and walked away quickly to put her at ease. He went down the center aisle and joined the congregation awaiting Mass. In Somerville, they had all gone up to Saint Anthony's whenever they had something really bad to confess, and talked fast because the priests there didn't understand much English. Now here he was, trying the same old thing. And what could they tell him anyway? Tsk-tsk, like Joe Palooka. Four hundred rosaries. Seventy times seven litanies. Two Hail Marys. Shit, he knew what he had to do. He had to do something harder than any of that. A priest came out and began Mass. Fitzie watched it like something on a small-screen TV set. He kept trying to grab the firefly of his Fanny Glass Jesus Prayer but his reflexes were as good as dead so he quit. When the time came he got out on the line for Communion and shuffled up toward the rail as in the Army to get a penicillin shot. He got it, hard and sharp in the mouth, and went back to his seat. The wafer stuck to the roof of his mouth, but finally went down, scraping all the way. He liked the prayer, and tried to say it aloud and mean it, but the way the damn old guinea said it:

> Maya you Body, oh Lorda,
> Whicha I havva eat,
> Anna you Blood whicha I
> havva drink,
> Cleava unto my vera soula.
> Anna granta that no tracea of sin
> befound inna me,
> Whoma dese pure anna holy mystery
> havva renew.

made Fitzie bow his head and cement his teeth together to keep from laughing into the hearing aid of the little man in front of him. To boost the penicillin and get his mind away from the laughter coming, he tried to utter the simple, "Give me strength, O Lord," but that only flashed on his screen as tiny letters in Dagwood's thought-balloon. So he released the laugh within a hand-muffled cough, blessed himself, genuflected and hurried up the aisle and out of the church.

Seven

"... WELL, your ass, buddy. Your goddamn fucking, hateful *ass!* You bastard! God how you must hate me. If you can't stand me, can't stand the sight of me, why the Christ don't you just say so. Admit it. I'll get out. I'll get out so fast you won't know what happened. But, oh, no. *I'll go along, I'll give the dumb shit a thrill, so she won't guess she's nothing!* But you can't do it sober, can you! No, you have to go get blind. Boozed out of your mind. Does that make it easier, Fitz? Then you can look at me without throwing up, huh? Oh, isn't he nice. Isn't he nice to her. Thoughtful! Loving! A real sweetheart! Everybody has to love good old Fitzie, don't they. Well, not everybody, baby. Who the hell needs it? Who *needs* it! Who needs *you*, anyway? Why don't you just start staying in there. Get a room. A *pad*. That'd make you happier, wouldn't it? And you can take somebody from *work* out. Somebody you can stand. Somebody funny and with-it. Not like me. Not that dumb ass of a bore. I'll just stay here. It's where I belong anyway. Isn't it? Make it easier on all of us. That way I won't say anything to embarrass you. And you won't have to quit your fun and drag your long puss out here and put up with us. Jesus, how you must suffer. Boy, you must go out of your mind. Poor you. Well, TS, fella! I feel for you but I can't quite reach you. Think about it, prick. Think what a *real* winner you can be without us in your way. Well, go ahead! Don't let me bother you. Because, boy, is that not where I want to be! You. You son of a bitch. Well, now I know, anyhow. Thanks for that. What a fool. It's about time I found out just what the hell I am. I only wish to God I admitted it a long time before this! That's all. Goddamn it to shit anyway. Fitzie. Big deal! Tough guy. So smart. A real killer. A real, fat-headed shit is what you are. Let me know if I'm boring you, now. Let me know if I'm keeping you *up!* He needs his sleep, you know. Big day tomorrow. Oh no, that's right, too. Tomorrow's Saturday. A big nothing! Need anything done, Janice? Want to go out, Janice? We got anybody coming, Janice? Christ, it must drive you up a wall. Well, you don't have to put up with it anymore, you can get the fuck out of here, and let me *live* for a change. If I can still remember how. Wait! You open that pompous mouth once and I'll jump right out that window. Explain that to the neighbors, buddy. But of course, you could, couldn't you. Poor Janice, she just went screwy, I guess. Oh, poor Fitz. There, there, don't blame yourself, we know you did all you could. You pisspot. You phony bastard shifthead. Oh! Am I being too loud for you? Go ahead, frown your ass off. I'll get a hell of a lot louder than this. I'll get as loud as I feel like! You hear me? I don't give a shit who I wake up, either. I don't care who hears me. Because it's the truth and you know it and don't say you don't. And you give me one cute little word, one, *one* cute little Jesuit horseshit word of yours and I'll make you regret it. I'll make you wish you were dead, because I wish *I* was! I'd be better off. You're not in the *city,* now, you know. I'm no client you can bullshit. But don't worry. You'll have plenty of time for that. You'll have more than you ever had with me hanging around. And I hope to Christ you choke someday and fall dead in a meeting. Or on *location* somewhere! That's what I hope."

She still loved him. They had just got home. It was late Friday night, around one in the morning. He had returned from California Tuesday, the day after shooting his commercial. Screaming, Janice was moving around their bedroom in a bra and half-slip, a little drunk, smoking. Fitzie was sitting over the open toilet in the bathroom off their room, forearms on thighs, watching her. He was trying not to smile, knowing there was no way she could understand why he should be smiling at her. Smile, he wanted to grin, to laugh, to roar. Janice didn't know it, but she was breaking a fever; thinking she was destroying them she was healing them. They had had a date to see *The Prime of Miss Jean Brodie* with another couple. They were to all meet for drinks first at the Algonquin Hotel, Janice going there from the train. Trevor had come back from the Coast with Fitzie, losing the courage, at the last minute, to stay and go job hunting alone. To try to make it up to him, and to kill time between work and the Algonquin, Fitzie had gone to have a few with him in the Madison Avenue Longchamps—and had too many, too fast, on an empty stomach, and for too long. He left Trevor fifteen minutes after he should have met Janice and the others. Far from helping, the freezing night seemed to make him drunker. The faster he ran, the slower he went. On Forty-fourth Street, he stepped off the curb between two parked cars and pissed in the street. Janice and the couple were hurrying out the door as he reached it. He knew he couldn't manage anything more than a grinning gurgle, but the time saved him; they had less than five minutes to make the curtain, and had to run all the way. In the dark, laughing a thin stroke behind the others each time during the play, he came sober, or at least lucid and in control. He remembered it only as a disjointed sequence, but was able, remarkably, to make a few apparently nonabsurd comments about it later over supper in the Allied Chemical Tower, and salvaged, he felt, the evening from being a totally bad scene. He liked the couple. Still, he knew he had wounded Janice. She had been humiliated, and he would have to take a roughing-up of one degree or another later. She had stayed completely silent all the way home in the train, letting him know how hurt she was, and when he got back from driving the sitter home, she had had a straight bourbon in the kitchen and was taking her second one upstairs with her. He had shut up the house and turned down the heat and followed her. He was down to his skivvies and socks when she opened up, and although afraid she would take it as a put-down, he had to go to the toilet anyway. He took it humbly, at first, his head down contritely, nodding *yes, yes, you're right, I'm sorry*. When she would pause at the bureau to pull on her drink he would raise his face to take her slung eye-whacks full on the mouth.

But then it didn't stop! And then, the further she went hurtling into overkill, when she actually got fierce and wilder, swifter and deeper, he began to realize. It wasn't just him. She had been as squelched and made miserable by their life as he had. He began to feel the smile take shape way down within him. The louder and sharper Janice slashed at him on the outside, the warmer and wider the smile grew inside, rising slowly up toward his mouth. Thinking of what she was doing and where he was, what he was doing while she was doing it, only pumped more delight into the smile: he was emptying out at one end and being filled up at the other! He knew that if he laughed she would hit him with something, so he waited. She finished her drink and finally came down to sit-crash on the bottom of the wide bed and began to roll her white panty-stocking off in fuming, defeated fury. Fitzie had finished and flushed before but had remained on the seat watching her. She still loved him! He still loved her! Thank God. "Hey," he said from the seat.

The stockings to her knees, she didn't lift her reddened face. "Just shut up, will you? Save it for someone who won't throw up."

"Janice?"

"Stick it."

Fitzie was off the seat, had his shorts up and was heading for her, still in the crouch, before her eyes could raise. He knocked her back on the bed with a hand on each of her bare shoulders and held her down, straddling her to sit on her belly. "You bastard!" she hissed and spit. It hit his throat. She churned and kicked and strained up with the frenzy, of an alligator. "You filthy drunk!" she cursed through her teeth.

"I'm not drunk," he said. The smile was out now, like the sun in the morning. In her wild turnings, one of her hands would reach him now and again and she would pinch the flesh of his sides with the bite of pliers. All Fitzie could do was swallow his "Yow!" and press down harder on her until she lost her hold. Once, her mouth found one of his wrists and she snapped her teeth into it so deeply he let the "Yeah!" scream through the room. It scared her and she pulled her teeth away. Even that merely interrupted his manic grin. At last she quit. The head stopped, the arms dropped, the legs fell still. Her labor over, Janice lay pinned under him with her eyes closed, heaving her breath out through her nose and mouth, her stomach lurching and sinking against his groin.

Fitzie didn't ease his hold on her. "All right," he said, "now you listen. You're right. Okay. Everything you said, you were right. But listen. You weren't talking about just tonight, for Chrissakes, were you. You think I don't know. Well, I'm telling you I know. Now, I know. You meant everything. You meant us being out here in this fucking place. And me going in the city, and getting all hung up on work, and making bread and being good and all that shit, as if it wasn't all shit. Okay. I know. You have to believe me, though, I *didn't* know before. I had my head up. It's all lousy. And it won't stop being lousy, I'm kidding myself." Still leaning heavily, he braced his left arm across beneath the chin of her closed face, freeing his right to pull her stockings the rest of the way off, then his own underwear. She might have been dead or doped. He opened her legs and shoved himself inside her, hands on her shoulders again, and she never moved; only her face tightened for a brief moment. He didn't move himself. He

267

just stayed up within her, still straddling her only now lower, across her hips, closing her legs in around him. "Janice, I'm telling you I'm sorry. I'm telling you I do love you, you're not nothing to me. I don't know what the hell we'll do. But I know what we *won't* do. Fuck them all. You hearing me? I don't *have* to do anything anymore. I'll do what I can do, so we can live, but that's all it'll be. Janice. Christ, Janice." He shut up and began to move in her hard. At first it felt like hurt, like rape. But then she answered him. Her arms came up in answer, her hips rose in answer after answer. It went for a long time with them. All hint of hurt washed away. When it hit it wasn't together it was her first and then him, and when he opened his eyes his face was on hers and he felt the wet beneath and around her eyes and he kissed her tears, then wiped them with his fingers. Then, still silently, they moved up to their pillows, put out the light, and slept, holding each other beneath the covers. He knew she hadn't really known that he had left her, that there had been a Chrissie. He knew he had got through that. Yet he knew, too, that she had *really* known it all, better than he, before it had even happened. So he hadn't had to include that in his confession or in his firm purpose of amendment or in his sorrow. He had only had to tell her what she didn't know. Now he had done that. She had forgiven him. And they slept.

When the phone screamed later that night, cracking its black whip through the air, Fitzie and Janice were not wrenched up out of warm sleep and bed by the hair. They had already come awake after about an hour, had gone down to the kitchen for cocoa and calm. They were smoking and talking. Janice had said, "It's all insane, isn't it."

"Yeah, I guess," Fitzie said, "but no crazier than what we were doing. Pretending everything was wonderful and terrific. Going along unconscious."

"That's what I meant. I don't think facing it is insane. I think *it* was insane. Buying the myth or the lie or whatever it is."

"Listen, lady. We made it, right? Grew up. Reached that *condition* they all said was there. Stable, happy, successful—what? Where you know everything, that's it. Ha."

"We died, that's what we did," Janice said. "But that's

268

what's weird, it's so hard to tell when it started. How the hell did it happen?"

"Well, I guess the thing is to be glad we came out of it now. What do you do if you're forty or fifty and suddenly decide it's all crap?"

"I don't know. I suppose it's no different, no harder or easier. You just go ahead and do what you think's right."

"Which is *what*? I don't know *what* to do."

"I know," she said. "Christ, we've got a house, three kids, twenty-four thousand dollars a year . . ."

"Thirty."

"What do you mean?"

"If I had been in . . . better shape, I meant to tell you before. We're making thirty thousand dollars a year, as of today. One for each year. That's something, huh?"

"So you go get stoned and we go for each other's throats. Wonderful."

"It doesn't make it any harder to get out, though," Fitzie said.

"No. We can't let it, anyway. But I'm not sure getting out is the thing to do. Get out where?"

"How do I know?" Fitzie said. "It's harder here, though, I think. Like you need the money here. We could probably live fine on a hell of a lot less someplace else."

"Oh, come on, you've said it. *League,* right? New York is big league, everything else is the minors."

"That was before."

"You'd still think of it. And I'd rather be unhappy and rich than poor and still unhappy!"

Fitzie laughed. "You're probably right."

"The trouble is, what's happy?"

"Happy for me right now is to tell them all to go fuck themselves. Quit. Don't do anything for anybody. Do something for *me*, for once. Feel like we're running our life. I wonder if anybody does that?"

"A 'peculiar solution,'" she said, "that's what we need."

"Where'd you get that?"

"Remember Beverly Withers?"

"That gave the party. In Brooklyn. Yeah. He was computers."

"Right. Well, I met her in the city last night when I was going to meet you, heh-heh, at the hotel."

"Heh-heh."

"She stopped me on the sidewalk and I didn't have any idea who she was, honest to God. She looks fabulous. Lost all that weight, and remember how gray she looked? All gone. Anyhow, she's got a job and bought a brownstone, right across from where they lived when we were there. And he lives in Jersey."

"What? They split?"

"That's just how I reacted. I was shocked. But yes, except not exactly. The thing is, she lives in the brown-stone with the kids, has a great job someplace, and he comes on weekends, right?"

"Yeah?"

"When he's not staying there! And that's it. They stay together three, four weeks, until it gets rough, then they separate . . "

"Until they can't take *that* anymore."

"Right."

"Jesus Christ."

"They call it their peculiar solution, which I thought was great."

"So find ours, huh?"

"Yes. I mean theirs is a marital thing, between them, but isn't that what we're talking about finding? God, it's two-thirty almost, we . . ."

Ring!

"Mother of God!" she said.

"Jesus Christ!"

Ring!

He grabbed the receiver and pulled it frantically from its cradle. "Hello?" he said, feeling his heart hard and loud, full of the fright he could see in Janice's face. "Yeah, hi, what's the matter? Oh, my God, oh no." It was his father. Fitzie's mother had died an hour before. His father didn't say *dead* or *died*. He said *gone* and kept saying it until it was the only word Fitzie could get clearly through the breaths and sniffings and fluid, formless words pouring down through the wires from Somerville through the cold earpiece and into his head and body standing in the cold kitchen in New York.

"What is it?"

"My mother."

"Oh, dear God, what?"

"She's dead," Fitzie said. "Dad. Dad, listen. Pop. Hey, come on. I know. Daddy, come on, cut it out." Inside, he felt nothing. No sorrow. No shock, now that the first bullet had pierced and gone through. But then he did feel something. Not now, oh, please not now. Tomorrow, next week, later, sometime, when I can handle it, when I've got *us* straightened out. And for Christ's sake, stop it and talk to me! Pull yourself together! His voice was kinder and softer than his thoughts and kept saying, "Come on, Dad,

270

please. Stop, all right? I know, I know, come on, now."
Fitzie could see him at the other phone in the other
kitchen, his face purple-red; he knew who else would be
there, his grandmother—Ma, his mother's mother—and his
Aunt Honey from upstairs, and his sister Katherine, sixteen now. And no better, Fitzie knew, than the father,
even if he could get him to give the phone to one of them,
which he couldn't. "Daddy? Pop? Listen. I'm going to
hang up. Get some sleep. Take a pill or something. I'll be
up first thing in the morning. Okay? Did you hear me? I
have to hang up. No, you hang up, now. And I'll see you
first thing in the morning. I know, man, I know. I'll be
there. Hang up, now, huh?" Fitzie sat back down at the
kitchen table and lit a cigarette. Janice laid her hand over
his. "Oh, Fitzie, my darling, I'm so sorry," she said.

"Comes right out of the blue, doesn't it."

"How did it happen?"

"Christ, I don't know. He broke down right away. It
was only an hour or so ago. It must have been her heart."

"So it was real, all along."

"I guess. I always thought it was just menopause or
something."

"But you saw how she looked last summer. So gaunt."

"I never really thought about it, I guess," Fitzie said.
"You know. Nobody ever dies, for God's sake. Other
people had deaths, not me. Just my two grandfathers."

"My God, I can't believe it," Janice said. "She was so
young. How old was she?"

"Not very old. I don't know. I'm thirty. She was forty-
eight, then, or forty-nine. My father's fifty now."

"My father was almost that when I was born," Janice
said.

"Yeah. They were always young. I always had the
young mother and father. Now she's dead and I don't feel
anything. Jesus, that feels weird. He's a wreck and I don't
feel a thing. Man, everything at once, huh?"

"It hasn't hit you yet, that's all. God wanted her with
him, as my mother would say."

"I'll have to remember that. I'll tell them that, all the
people. Oh, Christ, I have to go up there, don't I."

"Fitzie!"

"Yeah, but it'll be that whole wake thing, won't it. Oh,
Jesus, I dread the thought. I hope somebody knew enough
to call an undertaker and get the body the hell out of
there."

"Of course they did!"

"You never know. I'd better get up there fast. What's

the first shuttle, eight? How's our money? How's the blasted wake work anyhow? Bury her Monday, you think? The Jews have the right idea, bury them right away, *then* mourn."

"Listen, go to bed now so you can get up in the morning."

"It'll be all of them there, won't it."

Ma came down from upstairs and let him in. She was the only one there and she looked as placid as ever, except for the watery eyes. Ma looked, Fitzie had discovered early, like Jimmy Durante. She had always lived upstairs over them, at first with Pa, the truckdriver whose last words to Fitzie had been to get on the P.O., then with Honey and Evelyn, his mother's sisters. For years now, after Evelyn married, it had been just Ma and Honey upstairs. Honey and his sister Katherine were in town, Ma told him, buying black. His father had dropped them at Lechmere to get the train in, but hadn't come back. He walked down the long, narrow hall, past the tiny bathroom, to the kitchen, got the number from the book still hanging from the pantry door by its chain, and called Doctor McGuire. A quack, Fitzie had always thought, an old Middlesex Medical doctor who perhaps hadn't been one of those who had bought his diploma, but who should have been dropped years ago. McGuire sounded as if he were chewing tobacco. The other, over a year ago, had been a stroke. This wasn't that. This, as far as they could tell, had been a "coronary." "Why?" the old man added. "Do you want an autopsy?"

"No, I don't want a fucking autopsy!" Fitzie slammed the receiver down. It could have been the first time his grandmother had ever heard the word in her sixty-odd years, from the look on her ever-sad face. She ran away from it down the hall and up the front stairs to her own flat, saying she'd better be up there in case anybody called. From the kitchen, Fitzie watched her blue housedress take on color briefly from the small square window of the outside front door, then turn out of sight. He wondered who she was. Who had *she*, his mother, been? He was sorry now he had frightened her away: if he could find out who Ma was, maybe it would help him learn who *she* had been, so he would know what he had lost, what had gone out of this house of theirs, of his, hours before. Ghosts. Shadows. On school days, he only

272

knew that she would wake him and give him breakfast. His father had always been up and gone before Fitzie woke. Saturday mornings were the only clue, and only those when he woke and stayed in the house. But they were so few and far away now. He turned the gas on and spooned instant coffee into a cup. He hated instant coffee but he knew it was the only kind they, *she,* ever had in the house.

Goddamn it. Everyone you ran into on the street, everyone he knew, Jew, Italian, Irish, German, WASP, could do nineteen hours on their mothers and families at the drop of a word. What she always said, always did, always cooked; how she always looked, always smelled; where she always went or never went. And here he was, not exactly sure of when he last saw her. Grinding his mind to bring one day, one morning, one minute, anything out of the fog for just even a single quick glimpse. He sipped the foamy coffee and lit a cigarette. She'd wash the dishes, he guessed but couldn't see her doing it. Then go for the mail, make the beds, dust, clean, put out the garbage? No, he or his father emptied the trash at night. Ma would come down, though. Yes. The two of them in the parlor looking out at the street. But for how long? All day? And with what words to each other? Come on, come on, one sentence, one phrase! Nothing. The radio! Aunt Jenny, Dan Seymour, Kate Smith, Bob and Ray. Yeah, the radio was on. But that was noons, when he was there for lunch. What did she *do,* goddamn it, all those years. She didn't shop. She'd send him. His father went to the First National on his way home Friday nights, payday. Christ, what was he saying? Could she have stayed in this house, in these rooms, in the parlor with Ma all day all those years, in her twenties, her *thirties?* If anybody ever came he couldn't remember them.

He put down the cup of instant and walked through the house. He hadn't seen it during his twenty years there, either. He first saw it only after he had left it. On his first trip up from their apartment in Baltimore he had walked into it, in his uniform, and first saw where he had lived for twenty years. No, less than that. There had been those four or five years before the war when they had lived down in Rock Harbor where his father was from. But still, all his school years had been in this place. And yet the day he walked in from Baltimore, not gone a month, it was as if he had never lived here. The place looked the same now as it had then, only ten years fuller. He opened the windowed kitchen door and stepped down into the large, unheated room they called the "porch," although it was totally closed off from the back yard by a rear wall of windows and a door. Like every other room in the place, it was full of things. Perhaps that was why he had seen nothing: there was too much to see. The high closet cabinet built into the wall was crammed, he knew, with mops and brooms, the carpet sweeper, the vacuum cleaner, shopping bags full of old pajamas and sheets, Noxon and Johnson's Glo-Coat. The cabinet's top was piled beyond reach with empty Jordan Marsh and Filene's boxes. Next to the cabinet, the huge refrigerator hummed and shuddered in place, it's dust-darkened top a shelf for more things. An old school briefcase of Katherine's, or maybe his. Something with sharp edges in a Sears bag. The opposite wall was hidden nearly to Fitzie's height with more stuff, on the floor, on the two wooden shelves and dangling from nails. In cardboard cartons and shopping bags. A stack of crippled games in their boxes. A toy sewing machine next to what might have been a fuel pump. The ironing board open and up, the iron's cord dangling, a pile of clothes humped damp and ready, plastic sprinkling bottle half-full of water beside it at the edge of the board.

Now he looked out through the windows of the door at the back yard. It was wide, to serve the four flats of the house. Over there, the rectangle of earth near the trash barrel shed. Now bare, it had once bloomed thick and green with Fitzie's Victory garden. Back toward the B&M tracks he could see the stalks of the tiger lilies. Among them, Japanese lanterns would appear in the summer. The lilac bushes still sprawled the width of the yard, hiding the tracks from view. Five whip trees. A train rattled through behind the bushes, but it was all wrong. It was a silver Buddliner. It was supposed to rattle and chug and piss steam and be carrying, first, pigs and cattle to be slaughtered at Squire's, then carrying soldiers, mostly ours, but sometimes Germans, with guards with guns up on top and between the cars; and carrying, once that he could recall, the circus, the colors and cages and animals, in to Boston Garden. This side of the lilac bushes, the clotheslines: half for the other side, half for us. Ma had her own line above, from porch to tree. *She* putting on his red and black lumberjack shirt one winter night in eighth grade to go take in the stiff, funny long johns before he remembered the four Luckies in the right pocket, the pocket she'd been dropping the pins in. The cigarettes had been broken, smashed by the pins, but nothing had been said. That had

274

been before the laundryman. She hadn't used the lines much for years. Fitzie turned away from the window at the thought, and there they were, the two big laundry bags, full of clothes from the bathroom hamper. This was Saturday morning! Fitzie pulled them, damp and heavy, through the door. He hoped they weren't too late.

He walked back into the kitchen and stood against the sink: the cellar door; *their* bedroom; the metal cabinet over the enamel table; Katherine's room; the phone over the low, spilling floor cupboard; then the pantry. He wouldn't go into the bedrooms. Where the hell was his father anyway! The kitchen, like the porch, held so many things. He couldn't place in time the appearance of the large metal Sears wall cabinet. The pantry, with all its height and shelf space, must have simply filled to clogging. The cabinet was closed but still didn't escape the clutter: things were Scotch-taped and pinned with magnets to its face. On the table, the same cream-enamel with green border where he had sat to eat and to study, he now saw a Sony radio, a folded pillowcase, salt, pepper, sugar, one leather glove, Bell's Seasoning, a Phillips head screwdriver, three brown boxes tied with green string—Mitchell's! So that still happened. Tuesday, Thursday and Saturday. There was the loaf of white, the loaf of honey wheat right next to the boxes. And in the boxes: the mocha cakes, thick frosting on jelly rolls with the cherries in the center? The fig squares, maybe. Or a half dozen of those pastry tubes filled with white cream that his father liked so much? Jesus, about a hundred dollars a week ever since he could remember, not to mention the laundryman; they could have bought ten washing machines for Christ's sake! God, how unlike the way he and Janice lived. And the heat, the heat, the nearly solid hotness steadily rising up from the fat coal furnace through the floor registers. He thought of his own sixty-eight, always down to sixty-two just before bed. Ah, well. That's what makes horse races. *Except I come from this, I must be this, too, in some way.* Well, live and let live. *Except she's dead.* Come off it, anyway, sweetheart. Like you know something they didn't? Like you're okay and they weren't? You've had that, baby. Ten years of thinking that. But no more. Not after last night, buddy. Not after last week, last month, last year. They didn't know how to live but you do, huh?"

He wouldn't go into their bedroom, because he knew the picture would be there. Of *her* when she was eighteen or twenty. A beautiful face. Even as a child Fitzie had known it was a beautiful face whether it was his mother's

275

or not. She never lost it, she disguised it with wrong powders and Maybelline and lipsticks and with wrong hairdos. And she grew fat; she never became a Fat Woman, the great Mother Earth largeness, but she had always been overweight enough to make it easy to forget that that face was there. But it had been. It never left until just the two or so years ago, when she had the stroke and went to that gaunt boniness she had awkwardly called her "girlish figure" —only Janice had seen it as cause for worry. He didn't want to see the picture now. He felt for a cigarette. He was out. He would have to go to the pantry to see if his father's Camels were still kept there in the wall carton-dispenser.

Across the room, the phone rang. It was his father, and he broke again briefly at Fitzie's voice. He had been in Droppie's in the Square having coffee. Everything had been arranged. There was nothing for Fitzie to do. It was all taken care of. He was going to go now to get some phenobarbitol, did Fitzie want to wait there or come with him? "No," Fitzie said, "come pick me up, I'll go with you. And listen, if you're in Droppie's, get me some Pall Malls, huh? Yeah, I know, I was just going to take a pack, but get me some anyhow, okay?" Phenobarb! Jesus Christ, who told him that? Who knew enough to tell him that? He pulled the pack of Camels from the slot and the next pack dropped down. He lit one and stayed in the narrow, self-lined pantry. It had always been the coolest room in the place, except for the porch. Canned goods, peas, corn, B&M Baked Beans, four dozen of everything, rising high up the wall. He stood on tiptoe and stretched his arm up to the fourth shelf and eased aside the dust-greasy preserving jars. His hand entered the space blindly, just as it had practically every night for his four years of college at about two in the morning after he had come home from Lamont Library or Janice and had to study more; and once more, ten years later, brought the bottle down. Ostensibly on account of his grandfather, really because of his mother, his father was a teetotaler. Each Christmas he would get two bottles or so, from Mr. Waldo, the owner of the shipyard, along with the bonus check and the turkey, and usually one or more from some jobber or supply house. Up they would go unopened into the pantry shelf. And down they started to come once Fitzie got into college. He cracked the Four Roses, took three big swigs, then returned it to its hiding place.

He walked straight through the dining room to the living room—the parlor—to see if the dented, salt-chipped blue Plymouth had pulled up yet. He didn't look around the dining room because he knew the studio couch was still there under the wall windows and he didn't want to see it. The couch, the goddamned, fucking couch. Covered by day with a nice bright slipcover, the pillow tucked under it on the floor. By night, since he was fourteen, since Katherine was born, it had been his bed. The table his desk, the dining room his bedroom, the only bedroom in the Western world with a built-in china cabinet jammed with dishes and plates used only on Thanksgiving, Christmas and Easter. Fitzie never had anyone come to his house. Even Janice was in it no more than three or four times in the years he went with her. He was always afraid someone would want to know where his room was, and he would have to lie and say *upstairs* and hold his breath and say something else quickly. He was still ashamed of the couch, but was now also ashamed of being ashamed of it—who the fuck was anybody to make him care and squirm that much?

He stood in the middle of the parlor's red, oriental-like rug and looked through the white curtains at the front curb. His father wasn't there yet. The Hood's truck pulled up and Fitzie watched the milkman load his mental case and jump down to jingle along the walk under the side window to the back to leave his order on the landing beside the laundry bags. Another fifty thousand dollars a week. His father had forgotten and gone to the doctor's without him. He had fallen into one of his sleeps across Droppie's counter. Or at the wheel and been killed. Even after TV came, Fitzie's father fell asleep in the parlor every night until it was time, midnight, to go to bed. When he wasn't working overtime, of course. For years he had put in from sixty to eighty hours a week in the yard. Whether he fell asleep up on a mast or down in an engine room, they didn't know; but he did at home. He always managed to have a cigarette going before dozing off and the house was measled with burn spots, especially the parlor. The parlor was the front window of a local furniture store. The divan covered the wall. The Sears television console, with built-in phonograph, the size of a Volkswagen, blocked the wide center window. After those two, the other pieces had to crowd around on their own, often having to turn nearly sideways to fit. When he was newly married and a gardener in Rock Harbor, his father had worked with wood and had made the solid mahogany table with meticulously inlaid top that hid now behind the easy chair and held the tall artificial plant up to the side window for the sun it didn't need. The bookcase holding the set of encyclopedias had come with them and stood unnoticed near the door to the hall, holding the framed picture of Fitzie and Janice's children, a year old, and also Fitzie and Janice's wedding picture. Above them hung Fitzie's college graduation picture, one of his mother with her two sisters as young girls in East Cambridge, a Christ Is The Head of This House prayer. The fish tank on its stand kept to itself in a corner near the divan. Looking at it, dark and empty, Fitzie couldn't remember whether he had known the last of the fish had gone, or was just discovering it now. Ma had won it in a raffle for the Little Sisters of the Poor and it had come complete with fish, light, pump, snails, wavering plants and miniature Japanese garden, with bridge. He had often sprawled on the divan in the dark, chin on arm doily, Four Roses fresh in the blood, and stared forever at the glittering, darting fish. The Plymouth squeaked and honked just in time; the old claustrophobic feeling had begun to move in on him.

Seeing each other across the front seat, they didn't know whether to shake hands, just speak or what. Finally Fitzie said, "Hi, Pop," and broke the man's whiskered, thick face from the inside. His father burst a sob out. His right arm shot up to Fitzie's neck and pulled his head across the seat. His face went into his father's neck. He could feel the internal bleeding through his father's bulk. It didn't go *guiltguiltguiltguilt*. It went something else, something Fitzie had never heard before and couldn't identify. He couldn't do it. He tried. He closed his eyes, listened, felt the pressure of the arm and the edges of the whiskers, thought of the face in the picture, finally remembered something, the way she would add sums and write words in the air with her right index finger, but he still couldn't give it to him. *For Christ's sake, cry, you bastard, cry! Tears, a little water in the eyes. Anything. Let go you son of a bitch, and cry!* But he couldn't. Nothing would come. He thought of trying to say something into his father's shoulder, maybe that would *sound* or *feel* like sorrow, but he couldn't do that either. Then the loud bleeding slowed and stopped, the arm unlocked and Fitzie floated back up to the surface and looked at the grieving man. "Oh, Jackie," his father said.

"I know, Dad, me too," he lied.

"She's gone, bud. We don't have her anymore," his father sighed to the steering wheel, started to dissolve again, held it, lifted his head back up again, and was all right.

"Daddy, tell me," Fitzie said softly. Then, "Want me to drive?"

"Naw," his father said. He sounded like a man with sinus trouble. He looked in the side mirror, let off the brake, and the car pushed into the street. He told him. It must have been one of his first times to tell it; Fitzie figured he had called his mother in Rock Harbor, and had told the undertaker, maybe, but otherwise it must have been no more than the third telling—perhaps even the first complete telling. The way he told it then became the only version. In the next three days, it never varied more than a word from the way he told Fitzie in the car that Saturday morning. He would tell less, but never more. Fitzie interrupted him once, at the beginning, but no one else did. He had picked her up at the house on his way home from work, to take her with him to do the shopping.

"She went with you?" Fitzie said.

"Yuh," his father said. "We were doing that, Fridays."

"Since when?"

"Oh, I dunno, a year I guess." He had a way of tightening his mouth so his lips disappeared inside and he did this now. "She . . . oh, I dunno. It got to be nice, her coming with me. That ain't why she started. Oh, Jack, I'll tell you sometime what it's been like. She got kinda funny a while back. Before the stroke, even. Change of life or whatever they call it. I don't know what the hell it was, but she started thinkin' funny things. You go down cellar?"

"No."

"I finally boarded up the windows in the coal bin with tarpaper. She got the idea in her head I was down there *signalin'* somebody across the street. There's a kid over there now, her husband's up at Harvard. Anyhow, Mum . . ."

"You shitting me?"

"Naw! I'll tell ya sometime. She got real funny. And when it got to the Friday nights I said why don't you come with me then. Christ, you know, bud. I'd get to chewin' the rag with Ernie on the meats and forget the time."

"Yeah." His father was a sleeper and a gabber.

"So she did! And after a while she started to like to come. We'd go into Rexall sometimes and have a Coke after, or drive up to Buttrick's in Arlington."

"Nice," Fitzie said gently outside; inside he was full of fear and screaming *Never mind! Don't tell me! I don't want to know! I haven't got the right! I'll never remember who she was if you tell me this. Later. Tell me later, Pop!*

279

"Well, we just went the First National last night, I was late gettin' out of the yard. We got a DE in that's being a real bitch, I'm puttin' a sonar in her, so we come right home after. She was really in high spirits. Kiddin' me about the way I do the shopping. You know. As if I haven't been doin' the same thing every Friday night all these years." He let out a slight laugh.

Fitzie grinned. His mother would give his father the list in the morning; at night, in the store, he'd pull it out of his pocket when he hauled the cart from its nest near the window and box pile, carry it in his hand all around the store, and never look at it once. He would take two kinds of things: what he knew they needed and what happened to look good to him, which could mean anything from Philadelphia Scrapple to smoked oysters, candied yams or "six or seven slices of that chicken loaf there, too, or whatever it is." Their weekly order never failed to run to six bags, two thousand dollars.

"Anyhow, she went straight to bed and I was unpacking the groceries. She didn't want to miss her Gomer, ya know, and I got her one of them little Sonys for the bedroom. I wasn't hungry but she asked me if I wanted somethin' to eat on account of skipping supper, being so late, and I said naw, I'd have some coffee or something. But she got up and got me some Campbell's mushroom I like and hopped back into bed. Next thing I knew I had my nose in the soup."

Fitzie had to laugh.

"Ha! She told me she'd been waitin' for it, watchin' me droppin' the head up and down over the bowl, you know. Well, didn't she bust when I finally fell in the drink. Get to bed! she said, so I go down and fix the furnace and get a layer or so off the hands in the sink and I've just got the tops of my pajamas on when she sits up off the pillow. I think I'm gonna be sick, she says, and goes over. I just caught her before she hit the floor . . ." It was coming.

"Pull over," Fitzie said. His father did. Fitzie got out and went around and got in behind the wheel, his father sliding over, his hands up under his glasses.

"That's all she said, Jack." He was crying, but not with the convulsions of before. He could talk. "I got her up on the pillow. Her eyes were shut and Jesus, she looked green and I couldn't get her to breathe more than a couple long, like wheezes, they were. I yelled to Kathy in the parlor for a cold facecloth and tried to breathe into her mouth, ya know? But it was too late. She'd gone. She's dead, Jackie-boy, she's *dead!*" His father wept hard into his sun-worn heavy hands. Fitzie drove the car. He had gone through Magoon Square and was passing Trum Field, approaching the bridge before Ball Square. He didn't know where he was supposed to be going. His father came out of it leaving Ball. It was all right, the doctor's was ahead, near Powderhouse Park. Fitzie stopped at the house his father pointed out. His father put his hand on the door handle, but began to talk again. "Ma and Honey come down and got Kath to call the fire department and the priest house. Father Flynn was over in a jiffy they said but I don't remember him. That's when I called you, bud. I guess I got kinda nuts or somethin', I know I scared the bejeezus out of Ma and Honey."

"How's Kathy?" Fitzie asked to keep him talking. "She taking it bad?"

"She's a pistol, that one. Been cryin' when you look at her cross-eyed all her life, then this happens and she's just swell. What a trouper. Did everything with the undertaker and everything. Christ, she *kicked* Ma and Honey out to hear them tell it, and I don't know what she did with me."

"That's great."

"Well, let me get in and get the knockout drops."

"What made you think of this anyhow?"

"Your grandmother on the phone this morning. She said she'd bring it up with her but I said we'd get it."

He might have known it had been her. "When'll she be up?" It would be good to have her around: food would be cooked, dishes washed, empty wise words said to fill the gaps. Even though his mother had hated her, Fitzie didn't and neither did his father, her son. Gram. Close to seventy if not past it, still working some days out on the Point, still going to the beach and to church—Fitzie called her Old Mary and she was the down-Maine, non-Catholic, leather-skinned, rusting but high-bobbing bell in their family harbor.

"She'll be up on the train this after sometime," his father said, then sat staring at the glove compartment.

"Go get the stuff." His father sighed and went out the door. On the sidewalk and then up the doctor's front walk, the bounce still there. Watching, Fitzie saw his father sailor-walking through the shipyard between the lakes of grease, past the generators standing near the docks like grazing horses, past the piles of steel beams, pipes and wooden blocks, to get parts or cut a thread in the machine shop. *Spider*—for the way he walked, the way he scrambled up masts and down straight ladders into engine rooms and holds and galleys. *Spider*, for the way

281

he knew how to do anything and everything, from hauling the drydock cradle, to getting the power back on on Christmas Eve or at four in the morning. After a few minutes Spider bounced back down the doctor's walk and into the car. While they waited for the prescription to be filled, they went into the tavern next to the drugstore. They both had a shot and a beer. "When did you start doing that?" Fitzie asked.

"Just now," his father said.

"Well, take it easy."

"Don't worry about me."

"Do you need anything?" Fitzie asked.

"What do you mean?"

"Like shirts? Do you have enough to get you through? You got a black tie?"

"Christ, no."

"You could use a haircut, too."

"Mother of God, look who's talkin'! The beatnik. Oh, you know what I said I'd do—get flowers."

"Look. How about if I drop you at Angelo's and let you walk home? If I go get the flowers and a couple shirts, will you be able to sack out for a while, you think? Go up to Ma's, maybe."

"Might be a good idea. Suppose it'll be a long haul. Here, get some from me and Katie, and Ma and Honey and you know."

"That's okay, I've got some dough."

"No, here."

"Give it to me later."

"Here, goddamn it!"

"Okay, okay!"

"Go up to Linehan's."

"All right, they'll deliver them to O'Meara's won't they?"

"No, Shanahan's."

"Down East Cambridge? What the hell we going down there for? The Mass'll be at St. Paul's, won't it?"

"Yeah, but Mum didn't like O'Meara and Pa was buried from Shanahan's."

"But Christ, O'Meara's is right across from the church! You been going the Holy Name with Frank O'Meara for years."

"Mum didn't like him," his father said. Mother of Good God, he tried but he couldn't put those words or any like them in his mother's mouth. *I don't like O'Meara. Bury me not from Frank O'Meara's.* Who on earth at forty-eight or -nine votes for their undertaker? What was not to like or like? East Cambridge! Oh, God. The asshole of the universe. She hadn't lived there since high school; he doubted that she'd even been down there more than twice in all these years. Oh, the hell with it, let it go, what the hell difference does it make anyhow.

Fitzie drove his father back to Tower Square and let him out in front of his barbershop, then drove up Jefferson Street to Linehan-the-Florist. The son who waited on him was a few years younger but Fitzie remembered he was Bobby. Bobby recognized him, too. "Hey, aren't you Jack Fitzpatrick?"

"Yeah, how are you, Bobby?"

"Fine, how are you?" Oh, God. So. A pansy in the sixth grade does turn out to be a fag. Oh, Bobby, I'm sorry I split your eye that time. I really am. Because where am I? and what do I know. Fitzie gave him the order and spelled the *From* names to be embossed on the ribbons. "Gee, I'm awful sorry to hear that, Jack. When did it happen?"

"Just last night, early this morning."

"Oh. I'll have to tell my mother. That'll be first wake tomorrow afternoon then and funeral Tuesday. O'Meara's."

"Shanahan's. And don't ask me why."

"St. Paul's or Immaculate Conception?"

"No, St. Paul's."

"Okay. And we'll make them all really nice."

"Thanks, Bobby. Good seeing you."

"Yeah. And anytime you're up this way, Jack."

"Right."

"Kenny'll probably come when he hears. He talks about you every now and then."

"How's Kenny? He in the shop still with you?"

"Oh, yes. We're all in it. Except Tommy, he stayed in the Navy."

"Yeah. I heard that. Well, I'll see you, Bobby. Hello to your mother."

"Oh, she'll be down. I'm awfully sorry, Jack."

Fitzie drove back down Jefferson Street to the Gorin's in Tower Square, felt ashamed and drove up to Harvard Square. He went into J. Press and bought his father two white oxfords and a black silk tie. He came out and started the car but didn't shift it into drive. He didn't know where he wanted to go. Maybe Kathy and Aunt Honey would be back from in town. Maybe Old Mary would be up from Rock Harbor, or calling from North Station for a ride. He should go to Craig Street. But he didn't want to right now. He drove toward Central Square, stopped and had the car washed. Then he went

283

into a Shell, had it filled, and put a quart of oil in it. Now he did know where he wanted to go. He was close to East Cambridge, passing along the flat-gray gullies between the two- and three-decker houses. He turned and drove to Charlestown and came to the parking lot beside the low brick factory near the railroad yards. A few cars. Somebody was working. The same, the same. The same sign, J. L. POWELL AND SONS, up on the flat roof of the ice cream plant. The same spotless red floor tiles and yellow wall tiles up the staircase, the same clean, sweet smell of cream and steam. He opened the heavy upstairs door, but there was no loud pounding noise to engulf him. He walked, his leather heels clicking softly, along the glass walls of the small, empty plant office. The floor opened and he saw that only the bulk machines were working. The man in white turned and left his three women packers. "What can I do for you?" the man said. White paper cap, denim shirt and trousers.

"Hi," Fitzie said, straining past the man at the women. He didn't know them either. "I wondered if it'd be okay if I just looked around. I used to work here years ago and was just passing by and thought I'd come up and see the old place."

"Oh, yeah? When was that?"

"Oh, jeez, ten years ago pretty near."

The man hesitated, then believed him. "Lemme just check my machines and I'll take you around the floor."

"Oh, that's okay, I can just walk around."

"Uh, I'd just as soon," the man said.

"Fine," Fitzie said and started to walk straight toward the back of the plant. The floorman caught up with him as he reached the pint-packing area. It was quiet and clean. "Know what everything is?" the man asked. "Oh, yeah," Fitzie smiled, but the little gnaw had begun inside: he was looking at the corner of the building. The sun passed through the windows to the floor, here, too, but it shouldn't have been able to. It should have been blocked by high stacks of empty copper molds. They were not there. And the end of the Tank was not there either. He and the man reached the corner and turned it, walking across floor space that shouldn't have been there, that should have been covered by tons of Tank. "Where's the Tank?" Fitzie said.

"The what?"

The high, gleaming metal silo further down, where the stick machines and pit should have been, answered the questions all at once, made all the words unnecessary. But he said them anyway, like prayers at a grave. "What the hell is that?"

"That's your Popsicle machine. Automatic."

"Not my Popsicle machine. Mine used to fill this whole end of the place."

"That so. Before my time, I guess."

"Down for the winter?"

"Yup."

"How many's it take to run it?"

"Man, three girls."

"Used to have four and seventeen. I was super on it."

"That wasn't the Pig Alley, was it?"

"Yeah, that was the Pig Alley."

"Heard about that." They were past the neat, quiet silo now and Fitzie didn't look back at it. They were coming back down the other side passing the freezer walls, approaching the sandwich machine. "Used to work upstairs, too," Fitzie said.

"Mix room?"

"Night cleanup. The vats."

"Uh, no thanks. They have a hard time fillin' *that* job."

Well I did it, and I did it great, too! Bet your sweet ass. That doesn't count for anything, huh? Well ask Shirt! Aah, Shirt's probably gone too. The Tank and Shirt on the same afternoon, and himself, too, really. He was no place and had no idea what to do. He was right back where he had been at the end of college—only older, smarter, dumber, scarred. Because it wasn't good enough just to do it, get your pay and go home. If that was all, hell, he could keep doing it for New York forever. But, no, they insisted that you *believe*, when there was nothing to believe in. Which he couldn't do. And if he couldn't believe it, he couldn't do it anymore, either. "Wanta go upstairs?" the man was saying, one eye back on his machines and his chattering, finger-flying women. "No," Fitzie smiled, "this was fine. Thanks a lot."

He drove back to Tower Square, ran into Droopie's and bought a *Globe*. In front of their house on Craig Street he opened the paper. It wasn't in yet; it would be in the Sunday papers tomorrow morning, then. Inside, Aunt Honey turned to water when she saw him. His sister Kathy only returned his hug, the two of them wooden-faced. Old Mary was there tanned and in black, and squeezed him tightly when he bent to her. *"Poor Sonny*

285

Boy." She gave a nice little cry, then told him she had heard doves coo two nights running, which made him laugh. There was one thing to be done. Somebody had to go down in the early evening and tell the hairdresser how they wanted it. Only Old Mary and Kathy were willing, all in whispers so *he* wouldn't hear. Fitzie said it should be Kathy and drove her to the funeral parlor in East Cambridge, vaguely hoping the *sight* of her would reach him. It didn't. All he could see was the head of a body in a casket. No flowers yet. It certainly wasn't *her*, so how could he feel anything? It must have been the same for Kathy, because she talked calmly right over the head, even touched the hair a few times to show the loud Italian woman with the set of curling irons what she meant. Back in the car, Kathy said only, "Honest to God, if she said how lovely she'll look once more I was going to smash her fat face for her." Driving under the streetlights, Fitzie didn't say anything but "Yeah, I know it." *Now who are you, pretty teen-age girl? Hip enough, with the long straight hair and the fantastic grades and the art prizes. Any relations? And what will you do, who will you be, growing up in the same place, the very same place only without her and alone with him? Let me know if there's anything I can do, anything I can tell you or give you, because I'll be damned if I can think of anything. And by the way, how come you aren't broken up in tears, either? Did you know her?*

He had thought it was rotten coffee so didn't drink much, but it turned out Old Mary had slipped the phenobarb into everybody except herself. "For Christ's sake, Gram, *I'm* all right!" he said to her. They were alone in the kitchen, near to midnight.

"You just think so, you're still beside yourself. You'll thank me in the morning. And I'll thank you to mind your tongue in my presence!"

She had asked for it. He brought the fifth out of the pantry threw off three shots across from her at the table, sending her up and around the room clucking her false teeth and wringing her hands in the apron she had brought with her. "You are the most wicked child on God's earth!" she whispered at him.

"That's what you get for slipping me a Mickey."

"It wasn't so long ago I could have whipped you proper, don't forget."

"Oh, you really beat me up, Old Mary. Mean as hell, that's you. That what they teach you in the Baptist Church?"

"All wasted. You didn't turn out no different! Well, the sweet Lord knows full well how hard I tried. Ever since your poor Grandfather died."

"Now you're going to ask me if I remember the time when I was three days old and it was raining and Aunt Phyl and Uncle Rick came down from Kennebunkport and you were wearing . . ."

"Oh! You sass me! Now either git your oh so grown-up self to bed or I'll be sweeping you off the floor."

He started to laugh and answer her but then his eyes opened and her knitting bag of a face was above his on the divan and she was telling him to get up and take his sister to church. "Good God," he said through the fog, "if you aren't the most wicked woman on God's earth."

"That's my pretty boy," she grinned, "now get a move on and I'll have a nice breakfast for you when you get back. We'll let your father sleep, I'm sure dear Jesus knows that'll be better for him."

They walked, cold and half-awake, along the cracking concrete through their end of Jefferson Park. It wasn't a grass and bushes and trees park. It was dirt. One gigantic square of dirt, with a green cement-block park house where Fitzie, his father, and Pa used to go for their showers for a quarter. It was good to live so close to Jefferson because you could put your skates on at home and just toe-run over, squeak-slicing into traffic-packed street snow. Tiny Mamie's, now called Federico's, still behind the old wooden bleachers, at third base. Devil Dogs, chips, Coke and cream soda—he had to check for the *tonic* caps sunk into Craig Street. Now they left the park, climbing up the concrete stairs to the street. He looked down at the fence-enclosed swings and slides area. The same. So what. They walked across the gray wooden railroad bridge and the strip of metal where bridge met street went *kaklop* when a car hit it—just as it always had. It was all the same. Shitty. And here it was. St. Paul's boys school, grades one to nine; nuns to the fifth, brothers from then on. Seven stories of ancient, dirty brick, an ocean liner at dock. The schoolyard behind a green wooden fence, blacktopped, no longer a rolling desert of brick. Stickball. Tubba Warren, a three-inch metal dart up his behind, off to the hospital. The basement called the *Dungeons*. Candy Room, Band Room, Scout Room all filled with the stink of urine from the toilets. Seventy-five to a class. Old brothers from Newfie who dozed while you smoked and read *The Vixens* in 7-A. Tough, young guys from the Bronx and Brooklyn in black robes, one going after Bobo Cochran in the top hall, taking the buckle of Bobo's garrison belt across the face three times, then breaking his nose with a punch. Old weirds like Brother Septimus, who had stayed on so long beyond the line that he could wig out and smash Kevin Burke over the head with the window pole, calling him and the rest of 8-A "scurvy ass fuckers!"

He was glad to be past the school and going by the Rectory, then turning down the side to go into the eight o'clock Mass—Down. There were Upstairs people and Downstairs people. Fitzie and his family had always been Downs. Most of the parishioners who went to the Eight went downstairs. The Nine was about even, up and down. The Ten was mostly up. Inside, it was dark with a forest of standing people. Fitzie dropped two quarters on the desk in front of the usher. The people sat, catching him and Kathy walking up the side aisle. Looking for pew space, he could feel the eyes of the nuns and high school girls filling the center aisle benches on both sides: pitying Kathy, sizing him up, tasting the sweetness of somebody else's time of sorrow. An MTA driver pushed in for them, they genuflected and knelt on the foam-padded kneelers. Fitzie was eight, twelve, twenty, eighty. Nothing surprised him. Of course that was Father "Sweathead" Gaffney up there; just because Fitzie himself had served him for years meant he shouldn't still be there? And of course he was facing *away,* at the same old altar, turning his IHS to the people: this was St. Paul's, this was Somerville, this was Boston, this was nineteen fifty, not nineteen sixty-seven, nearly sixty-eight. Okay, push it, then; it's something to do. The kid on the right, the Bells, that's me, watching for the signals, listening for the cues: *Dominus Vobiscum,* ET CUM SPIRITU TUO! loud and clear, let 'em hear it down the back. And there they are, the bunch of plaster grapes there in the altar's right front panel. The wine? The Blood? The *tits,* boy! A whole bunch and all for me. Those are Peggy Brady's, those are Susan McKenzie's, those are Sister Mary Francis's, and those are Maureen Sheehan's. Squeeze them, kiss them, lap them, pull them. *Stop! Stop! Get behind me, Satan. I'm sorry, Jesus, in there in the tabernacle, I'm sorry!* The paten's off, up to the middle, genuflect, run for the wine cruet. Back quick for the towel, hand the other kid the finger dish, then up again to bow the head and smell the holy smell of Sweathead Gaffney mumbling off the altar card. *La-va-bo, mmm, mmm, mmm . . .*

Jingle-Jangle? Jingle-Jangle? What's that other me doing, that's no way to do the Sanctus; you can't push all those people to their knees, you have to make them *want* to. Move a little, jerk. Are the chime keys still there, imbedded white and cool in the rug? Yes! Still there. Now that was the way. Some had it, some didn't. I did. I could've really been a good piano player. The Sanctus? One-two-three. But just right. Then the hands-over-chalice: one—pause, make them *die* for it!—three-two. The elevation of the Host—the high point, this is it—five, four-three-one . . . two! Then again—can you do it?—for the chalice: five, four-three-one . . . two! Beautiful. The last, the *Domine non sum dignus,* easy, with the left hand, throw it away: three, two . . . one. No, no, that's all today folks, that's all and there ain't no more. Eat your hearts out. The ushers stormtrooped down the aisle with their baskets for the first collection and jarred Fitzie back. Gaffney was still only warming up and Fitzie had already finished. He couldn't make it. He waited until the Faithful Assembled started to slide their behinds forward to stand for the Gospel and leaned to Kathy: "Let's go."

"What's the matter?"

"Stomach," he lied. In a crouch, he led her into the aisle, the moment of the big *Stand!* and hurried up to the front side door and out. Sorry, Father, Sisters, but mourning and all that, you understand; the Lord will, even if you don't.

"You all right?" Kathy asked, sliding off her new black mantilla.

"Yeah. Yeah. The air feels good." He brought both a *Globe* and an *American* from the kid with the wagon at the curb. Walking, he had Kathy hold the rest of the papers as he found the obituary page. Man, was it in there. He couldn't believe it. SUDDENLY IN SOMERVILLE it began in boldface. A headline! Some idiot had had to write a headline for it! If it had been for an ad he would have rejected it; yet here it was in print to announce his mother's death. Oh, find the one who did that! Promote him to ship arrivals, I think the kid's really got it.

"Is it in?" Kathy asked.

"Yeah, it's there."

"They get it all right?"

"Yeah. It's all right," he said and took the papers back from her. To outdo Old Mary, he got into the car instead of going into the house. Without questioning, Kathy got in with him. He drove down to the S. S. Pierce's in Inman Square and bought food: doughnuts and pastries for the morning, a baked ham, cold cuts, macaroni salad and cheese for later, whenever they would have to eat. Old Mary pretended to be delighted and thankful for the supplies and packed it all away, including the doughnuts and pastries. Fitzie's father was up and the three sat down to Old Mary's eggs and bacon and toast. Although a total abstainer up until yesterday afternoon, his father, having slept, washed and shaved, had the look an alcoholic has when sober and off the liquor: cleaner than a child; startlingly, shining clean. After eating, Fitzie and his father went into the sunny, tight parlor to smoke and read the papers until it was time to drive to East Cambridge for the first wake. Fitzie would peek over the top of the *Globe* magazine section to perhaps catch a clue, take a reading. There must be something missing, *her*, for his father: how would it show? If it did, Fitzie couldn't see it. His father sat there on the divan behind the *American*, quiet except for his breathing. The only unusual part of it was something Fitzie didn't notice while he was there but realized later, driving the Plymouth. His father had not dozed off; he had stayed awake. Oh, Pop, oh, Spider, what were you thinking and what are you feeling now, going to see her?

Even scrubbed by a Sunday afternoon sun in December, East Cambridge looked scabby and sickly to Fitzie. There had been a time when a few Irish winners thought they could stay in East Cambirdge and turned some of their money into large, grand houses with porches and gables and wide center halls. When they realized they were building on the ash heap of a city dump they quickly moved out to West Roxbury, Belmont and the Newtons, where their lace curtains could be aired without letting in the smell of swill and the screams of sour tongues. Most of the homes they left behind were quickly taught humility by being cut up into flats. A few were allowed to hold on to their grandeur by being converted into funeral parlors. J. P. Shanahan's was one of these. A silked squire visiting with dirt-caked serfs, the house stood at a brace on a corner, a clean, fine mustard yellow with olive green shutters all around, up and down. A careful, polite sign, like those in front of country Episcopal churches, spoke respectfully from the lawn behind the unchipped black, wrought-iron fence. Inside the heavy maple door, its brass a mirror, J. P. Shanahan's had achieved the right smell, the subtle but crucial line dividing royalty from pretender: it smelled like its higher-up-the-line brother. It smelled like a priest's house. A unique, telling smell. The oiled, carved woodwork of doors, floors and moldings;

the richness and thickness of the muted oriental rugs; the stillness, the somehow unstuffy stillness of the air; the Popes Pius, John and Paul in oil; the assorted prints of Jesus and His Mother; the tone of the voice of the man, the pastor or curate, or in this case the Funeral Director. The original J. P. Shanahan was long dead. This was the son, about the same age as Fitzie, and he walked up to Spider at the head of the entering group, and took his hand and said, "Mr. Fitzpatrick," in such a protective way that his father's stiffened shoulders immediately collapsed, the arms coming up and the awful, loud blubbering wailing out through the still air and onto the immaculate chest of J. P. Shanahan Junior's blue wool suit. He dissolved so utterly that Fitzie couldn't punch in the undertaker's putty face, he had to put his arm around his father's bowed back and whisper to him to "Take it easy, Pop. Thatta way. Let it go. Okay. Okay, now." Old Mary and Kathy helped. Ma let out one long moan, then held it. Aunt Honey echoed Spider, but weakly.

That was the beginning of the first wake and there were three more. Sunday evening, Monday afternoon, Monday evening. The first was the worst because not so many people came in the afternoon, and they had to stay without enough to take their attention away from the body; but especially because the first involved confronting *her* for the first time. The women stayed back in the foyer by the small stand reading FITZPATRICK, with an arrow, in white plastic letters pushed into furrowed black felt, like the show times of movies. The men entered the first room, walled with folding chairs, and crossed it to the opening of the rear room. Here Fitzie halted Shanahan, at his father's other side, with a light tap on the arm. He grinned thinly and whispered, "Hey, Buzz off, huh, Charlie?" He guided his father to the coffin, then just let him go, looking but not watching. It wasn't loud. His father paused, staring, at the kneeler then stepped up on it and went in to her. He kissed the face and the neck and clutched at the hands, crying into her, talking into her. When movement stopped, with a sudden, defeated slump, and only crying, not words, came back, Fitzie stepped up and put his hands on his father's upper arms and eased him up, off and back. Then they knelt down beside each other, blessed themselves, and stayed there long enough to say three or four Hail Marys although Fitzie didn't say a word of prayer. What was there to say? *Don't send her to Hell or Purgatory?* If He could do that to somebody like her, then He wasn't anything to pray to. *Spare him, help him?* Too late for that now. He wished he knew what his father was saying or thinking or praying. That was it: a nerve had been cut, a wire was down somewhere. It wasn't that he wasn't there, that he was still in New York in *his* life and dreaming all this. No, he was here, all right; and this was a part of his life, not anything apart from it. It was simply that the connection he had always thought was there wasn't. It either had never been there. Or it had, and had been broken off. Slowly, strand by strand? Abruptly, with a snap and a spark?—it didn't matter. There was a short circuit between him and them, the people, the place and the past; a gap across which no message could pass, either way.

Maybe that was a shame, a sin. Even so, to suddenly realize it, kneeling there beside *him* before *her* among *them* and *it all*, made Fitzie suddenly untie inside and feel better. It freed him. It sent a feeling of relief, of being let go, through him so intense that he felt physically faint and put his face down into his hands. He didn't have to hate them anymore. He was free to love them at last, without the hate and the guilt for having the hate. For he had hated them and had known it. Hate-in-love: the worst kind. Not in his heart or in his mind, Fitzie had hated them in his nerve ends, in his hungers and pushings. He had hated them generally for being who they were and for being what they had been forced to be, having been born when and where they had been born. Specifically, he had hated them for having to leave Rock Harbor for Craig Street (to get work). And for sending him back summers to Rock Harbor from when he was seven until he was sixteen (to get him away from Craig Street). And for not owning the house on Craig Street (the rent was still less than fifty dollars a month), and for sending him to St. Paul's in clean shirts and socks (so they'll see we are a good family) when nobody else had them, and for telling him to *don't think you're a big shot* (he who profits anything in the world suffers the loss of his soul), and for making him do his homework (so you won't have to depend on your hands like me), and for sending him on to college (it's up to you; we, of course, would love you to) and at the same time not sending him (this insurance will take care of your first year; you'll have to work; you'll have to live at home but we'll buy your clothes and you'll never have to pay for bed or board and try not to be late for supper) while all along they really could have (he was back from Europe in New York before he uncovered the fact that Spider had been making and spending, on nothing, over ten thousand a year for years) but never knew it. Never knew it. They had never known it, any of it. And he had never known that they never knew. Now, unexpectedly, suddenly, he did know, and the need to hate went away. Hate died the day after his mother. Now he could love them and love her. Perhaps, then, it wasn't a coincidence. Perhaps she died for him, perhaps that's who she was. Because now he knew what to love them for. For never hurting him. For never stopping him. For letting him go. And now for telling him that they still weren't stopping him. That was love and what else do you want.

He lifted his head. He wanted it all to be over so he could tell Janice. But it was far from over, it had just begun. He and his father went and sat on the first two family chairs. Kathy and Old Mary knelt now, Ma and Aunt Honey waiting for their turn to perform the rite of the eyes: to her hands on the beads, to her face, up to the sashes on the flowers, down to the coffin, finally to their own hands. Every visitor, Fitzie was to notice, did the same; the rite of the eyes was involuntary and invariable. Monday afternoon's wake was nearly as grim as the first, longer than the hours it took. The night wakes were seemingly quicker because of the hordes of people who came. Not that this was an Irish wake; outside of South Boston, there were few of those anymore. Still, these night wakes for Fitzie's mother weren't that unlike a wedding reception. They would sit there, his father, then him, then Kathy, Ma, Honey, his other aunt, Evelyn, and Old Mary— all eyes red and puffed except his and Kathy's. The people would come, in the outside door, to the right through the outer parlor lined with earlier arrivals now chatting or waiting stony-faced for the decent time to leave or for the Rosary to start, then in to the kneeler for the rite of the eyes, then up, an endless stream of them, and over to start with the husband, the father. They were relatives from both sides, from the North Shore and the South, in from Ayer and Worcester. They were neighbors. They were friends: of *theirs*, of Ma's, Honey's, Kathy's, even Fitzie's. Janice's family came. The guys from the yard came, appearing like the off-shift from the mines after an accident: grimy, short, and all together. Sons and daughters never seen before, or friends and relatives, came, to represent or accompany whoever it was who *knew* her or him or them. Up they would come with: *Lord I'm so sorry what can I*

293

say so young just my Edna's age she's with God now rest her soul why haven't we seen you all these years better fast than suffering like Theresa Sawyer six years with C I've written to my Tommy in the missions and he'll this isn't little Jackie you poor boy and you her first your mother was so proud used to see her at the nine always so nice Helen Moody saw it in the Record *and called us Ernie's at the Guard for the weekend but he'll be up tomorrow God looks after them He's borrowed from my Artie and my mother in the same month can you imagine Doctor Kelly had to put me on sedatives but I have my Little Flower we went to O'Meara's never dreaming and Paula's Joe said we must have the wrong night but they sent us down we had to call a cab one of those niggers he charged us two dollars the nerve of them they're so fresh my God but doesn't she look wonderful a sign she's happy in Heaven tonight watching over you have my deepest sympathy Spider anything I can do we never know do we sorry sorry what can I say.*

There was little to say in reply. Fitzie's father would tell his story to some, but it was usually only *thank you, I know you are, thank you for coming, oh yes, of course I remember, I went to school with your Eddie, thank you.* Knowing so few of the forms and faces made it harder for Fitzie, especially the having to sit still and look up into each wave as it broke. Finally, about half-way through the Sunday night wake, as it neared its full tide, he could take it no longer and left his chair between his father and sister. He went and stood at the end of the family row and manned the visitors' register book on its stand with its tiny light and ballpoint pen from somebody's desk set. This was better. Now as they left Old Mary and faced him standing there he could take the initiative and say, "Hello, I'm John, the son. Would you mind signing here?" and get only their diluted, second-wind of sympathy and homilies. It made him feel useful and from this point he could gauge the whole flow from door to family and manage to get his father out and down to the smoking lounge more and more often. No, it wasn't unlike a wedding reception after a while. It was possible to forget why he and everybody were there. Bubbles of laughter, even, would soar up from this group and then that in the front room and downstairs. Stranger yet, he discovered how many girls and younger women were willing to ping-ping their eyes at his—even after they knew who he was; and that he could ping receipt of the message and enjoy the game without guilt. It never became *flirting at your own moth-*

er's wake! to him, it just happened. He was relieved to see that his father had crossed over to some other-state of numbness, some chamber of control that encapsuled him almost visibly and let him get through each session of waiting in a room beside the dead body of his bride, mate, lover, wife of over thirty years. His protective spell would lift only at the end of each wake, after the people had cleared out and the women were getting their coats and he would be left alone with *her* for a little while before having to leave for the house and the bed where she had been. Fitzie would watch, virtually stand guard, as his father would go to her, to speak to her, to touch her and to weep. He would signal the end to it by going over to kneel on the kneeler and look as if he were praying. Then he would drive them back to Craig Street. Old Mary would pass them their drug in cocoa, tea or milk. Fitzie would wait, no matter how long it took to outlast her, until Old Mary herself retired, then he would bring down the whiskey out of the pantry and throw down four or five shots at long intervals, sitting at the kitchen table.

Janice arrived at the beginning of the last hour of the last wake, Monday night. From his central control station at the book, Fitzie saw her down the hallway as she stepped swiftly through the front doors dressed darkly but not in black and looking young and very New York, her face glowing from the winter air and the frenetic scurrying he knew she had done to get out of their house and to Boston. He couldn't see her pass through the front parlor but knew the look of the eyes that would be on her from the gallery. The maverick, she broke the rite of the eyes, looking only once and quickly at the face and not at all at the flowers or coffin. She knelt briefly in prayer-pose then stepped over, bending, to his father, taking his hands and smiling slightly as she spoke to him. Then down the line quickly, past his empty chair, kissing Kathy and letting serious concern briefly flash into her face. When she reached Old Mary, it was more a grin than a smile—on both their woman faces: they know something or other together. Following her, waiting for her, Fitzie now knew how to conjure up tears; he could imagine her, *his,* there in the coffin instead of her, his father's. That would make him feel very sorry for himself, sorry enough certainly to cry. But then, he knew now there wouldn't be any need to do any of that, there would be no need for him to cry. "How are you?" she said and kissed his cheek.

"Fine. You made it okay. I told you you didn't have to."

"Well, Joey turned out to be all right. I thought sure he was coming down with something."

"Who'd you get?"

"I finally called The Service in White Plains. A nice big mammy in a uniform."

"Five hundred a day?"

"A thousand. Listen, what should I do now?"

"Stand here with me."

"No, I don't want to do that."

As if she had been listening, and she probably had, Old Mary came up and said, "Janice, you come, I want you to meet our Sonny-boy's great aunt and uncle up all the way from Newburyport," and whisked her off down the hall to show her off again to the front parlor. Later, he left them in Craig Street and picked her up at her mother's and they went to Fantasia's by Fresh Pond and he drank three martinis with her. "Feels like visiting day at Sing Sing," he said. Before falling to sleep in the dark on the parlor divan, it felt peculiar to know she was in a bed only two miles away and he was here.

The beginning of the end: he drove them to East Cambridge, to J. P. Shanahan's for the last time Tuesday morning. All black, all Cadillacs and gleaming, the flower car, the hearse and the two family limousines slunk at the curb in front of the funeral home. Private cars to be in the procession had purple flags tied to their antennas. Shanahan's men wore morning clothes. One stood inside the door near the clock and called off the names of the people waiting and directed them to their assigned cars. Fitzie passed the keys of the Plymouth to his Aunt Evelyn's husband Don and followed his father and the women inside to pay their last respects, to see his mother's face for the last time. When her turn came, after Ma and Honey had passed Fitzie's empty bookstand, Kathy knelt and finally cried. When she had gone, Fitzie's father went in hesitantly. Fitzie waited. He didn't watch. He stood in the empty, sunny front parlor looking out a side window at hedges through curtains and listened. His father's word-sounds grew longer and louder, moans, and Fitzie didn't go in. Let him go, get it all out now once and for all before the church. The soft sound of shoes on carpet turned him around. It was Shanahan creeping toward his father and holding something small and square in his hand. "Hey," Fitzie said low.

The man stopped and smiled pityingly at him.

"What's the matter?" Fitzie said.

"Why, nothing," Shanahan said, holding the smile. He spoke like a suit salesman in Saks. "I have something to give to your father."

"Oh. I'm letting him get it all out of his system."

"Yes. That's always best. And we still have time. All the cars are filled now."

"Good. What have you got there, anyway?"

"Oh, these," Shanahan smiled, pleased, glad to be asked. He passed them up to Fitzie, a deck of four Polaroid Land Camera color snapshots of his dead mother laid out in the casket among the flowers, from different angles.

"Jesus Christ!" Fitzie hissed through clenched teeth.

"It's another little service we like to provide. To remember, or sometimes to send to those who live in California or somewhere and couldn't make it," Shanahan explained, holding his palm up.

Fitzie held on to the pictures. Looking again at them, he said, "You're crazy, right?"

Shanahan answered with a look: shocked and hurt, yet the *understanding* coming over him immediately.

Fitzie shoved the pictures into his pocket. "Just get the fuck out of here," he told Shanahan and walked in, got his father and led him away, outside and into the first Cadillac. He never looked at the casket. He sat with his father in the car and tried to talk enough to keep him from watching the flowers being run out of the house by the men and then the casket awkwardly bounced down the stairs and into the hearse. But his father saw it anyway and burst out again. They drove slowly through and out of East Cambridge, Fitzie watching the shabby houses and tawdry stores and junkyards pass by. The needless stupidity of it, was all he could think of. This long, unnecessary ride, only to be outdone by the one to follow the funeral. His mother was to be buried in Rock Harbor, some forty miles up the North Shore. Well, at least that should give a lot of people a good excuse to go home or back to work and keep it small. How his mother could have wanted to be waked in East Cambridge and then buried to rest in Old Mary's Protestant town was totally beyond his comprehension. But he let it go, let it go. The lines are cut, the wires are down, let it go. He climbed the high stone steps to St. Paul's between his father and sister, holding each by the arm. Shanahan's men helped Ma and Old Mary, behind. Inside the cathedral-size front door they stopped behind the casket wagon and waited for the priest to swish up the center aisle ahead of the altar boys bearing cross, candles and holy water bucket. He whispered to Kathy, "*Low* Mass?"

She nodded yes.

"Why?"

"He said she wouldn't want a High."

Jesus Christ Almighty! That did it, that was the end. Now he'd never known anything again. Oh, she wouldn't, huh? Oh, I see. What'll you have? Oh, a Low Mass, please. The priest mumbled the prayers and splashed water all over everything and everybody. Where it hit the waxed casket it puddled, small and shiny. They walked up the aisle to the front and slid into the first pew. There was a good crowd. They watched as the priest pulled on his black vestments over the white, lacy cassock, then began Mass at the foot of the five-stepped altar. Fitzie couldn't let it go. Here, in St. Paul's *Upstairs,* he was on the congregation end of a *Low* funeral Mass and it was his mother's, his own *mother's!* Here, right here in the same, unchanged, magnificent upstairs church, where there was more of him than in any of the rooms of the school or in the dirt of the park, where every saint worth paint floated in full color up on the ceiling, each as big as a balloon in Macy's Thanksgiving Day parade, where the Transfiguration itself had six whole stained-glass windows high above the Tank-sized altar, where he had made a fairly good living on undertakers' tips from sixth to eighth grade on *High* funeral Masses, eventually attaining a taste of stardom as *the* master of ceremonies. Who's got *master?* Fitzie, who else. Master! Most parishes had *priests* as masters at high funerals. St. Paul's had Fitzie. Master, the coveted climax to a career of service from server to censer or incense bearer to acolyte, the *kid* who moved around up there with the celebrant, the deacon and the sub-deacon, turning parchment pages, moving bodies with the bow of the head, holding the book for the gospel singer—the playmaker of the Mass. At least three funerals a week for three years when the others were having religion or history or English, with a wedding or two on the weekends in the spring: six, ten bucks anyway, on the average. Not bad for a twelve-year-old, and on school time, at that! This was the hardest of all for Fitzie to let go. *Toreador* for scores of other people's funerals, to now have to sit in the bleachers at this skinny, pauper's Low funeral Mass for his own mother! The priest was younger than himself and looked pale and hung over and in a hurry. Just then, though, the polished, blond wood sacristy door creaked open a foot and two handsome young priests walked out and went to the posh throne-kneelers at the side of the altar. It was Janice's brother Tommy and his friend Father Mike Rafferty, friends of Fitzie, the only two priests in the world Fitzie liked because they goddamned things honestly, without faking it to appear regular, and came to New York two or three times a year in civvies to hit the shows and the Monkey Bar with Fitzie and Janice. They had been at the wake last night but hadn't mentioned this. Perhaps they had been in the congregation, saw what was being pulled and ran up to try to make a save? Whatever, they were up there now and made it all look better, gave it some class and Fitzie wanted to yell up to them. This is worth a couple of biggies, guys. A couple steaks at Downey's, a couple quarts of the good stuff; I won't forget you for this, baby.

The power of the Mass was such that it accomplished what Fitzie had been unable to. It overshadowed his father's abject grief at his loss, his crushing awareness of the reality of each of these irrevocable moments. He started to doze. Gently, secretly, Fitzie nudged him awake. But the poor Mass was quick about it, at least, and soon the priest was down walking around the casket with the incense and water and saying the last prayers over the dead. St. Paul's hadn't let the priest face the people yet, but they had replaced the Latin with English for these prayers—just in case there were any eyes in the ranks who thought they could get away without bawling. He talked to God out loud about Fitzie's mother by name, begging Him to give her a break. Had Fitzie let himself listen he too might have relented and given the priest the applause-substitute he wrung from the others. But he didn't.

Fitzie had dreaded the long convoy ride to Rock Harbor. He felt he had stayed too long already, felt impatient to get out and away and back to his own life. But once they were all out of the church and into the cars, a sort of cease-fire of grief was called. By their hearts, he supposed, which like anything else can go so long and take so much and then no more. They smoked. People on sidewalks stopped and removed their hats, standing on the curbs. In Everett there was an old city worker who didn't notice them and blew his nose through his fingers into the street.

"There's the mayor," Fitzie said and the car laughed, even his father. The cars moved faster once they reached Route 1, then turned onto 128. The wind whistled into the heated car through the windows cracked a little at the top to let the smoke out and reminded them how cold it was, and how clear and sweet the air turned the farther away from Boston and nearer to the sea they drove. In Rock Harbor the air was the winter ocean itself. They got out at the town cemetery, as clean and quaint and groomed as the nearby country club, where Fitzie had caddied for so many summers, where he had tasted his first beer, filched from the trunk of a member's Continental, and where he had touched his first bare breast, at night, on the seventh green. He looked over hedge and gulley at the clubhouse in the sun, while they waited, then read the name of his grandfather on the stone near the green canopy where Shanahan's men were setting up. Nineteen forty-eight. Flags had flown at half-mast in the town that day because he had been a selectman. Only the Salem paper intimated how it had really happened. Fitzie had cried that time, all right. When it was time, they huddled around under the canopy and listened to the town priest's words fly up and off in the windlicks from the close-by sea. Dirt *was* thrown. There *was* a hole in the ground, green-sheeted or not. And the woman in the casket *was* lowered down into it, through the sheet. One sound out of his father, a foghorn, a ship's bleat in the night. Fitzie held his father's shattered bulk and at last felt the spurt behind his own eyes and then the hot, wet tears came down over his cheeks and to his lips. Like the wind, like the sea, like the town, they were salty. They came because they saw, they knew now that all a man can really have is another to love and to love him, and for that other to be boxed and lowered into a hole in the earth forever is a terrible thing to happen. So Fitzie cried, and crying walked his father away and to the car, feeling very sorry, for the first and last time, that their line was cut, that there was no way for him to pass even a word in through to the man.

Old Mary had food in her kitchen for the mourners and for Shanahan's men. She had no liquor, but plenty of coffee, tea and soft drinks and plenty of sandwiches and salads and desserts. His father and Kathy would stay in Rock Harbor for a couple of days. Ma, Honey and the rest had rides home.

He and Janice didn't talk much until they were at Logan that evening, waiting for their plane. He had only one, weak scotch sour and it made him feel a little high. "You must be beat," Janice said. "But I suppose you'll go to work tomorrow," she said, too, with a smile that had vinegar in it.

"No, I won't be going to work tomorrow," he mimicked her.

"Wow. The world's coming to an end."

"Christ, I hope not."

"Christmas'll be pretty grim for them, won't it."

"Yeah. Maybe we can have them down. Old Mary too."

"Sure. You think they'll come?"

"How the hell do I know? Mary will. We'll ask, that's all we can do."

They ran to their plane. It was a Whisperjet and it took off on time, making its lovely boomerang sweep up and out over Winthrop, then around climbing, to head south. From the window, Fitzie could see the lights of the prison at Point Shirley and Revere Beach on the other side; then he could make out Charlestown, East Boston, downtown, Somerville, Cambridge and the Newtons before lights were swept beneath trees and it all became dark. He turned to Janice and said, "Excuse me, miss?"

"Leave me alone or I'll call the stewardess."

"Well, I don't mean to be rude, but I was wondering if you'd like to come spend the night at my place? You do have nice thighs. I can see them."

"Hmm. I'll have to think about it. What's the catch?"

"Just one."

"What?"

"You'll have to have your loop removed."

"Oh yeah? Why?"

"Because I don't have enough kids. I want more."

"Oh. I see. You're going to stop making money *and* have more kids."

"Yeah. See, I've decided everybody is rotten except you and me, and I want to get a lot of *us* running around to piss them all off."

"Okay. But can we do it tonight anyhow?"

"Oh, I suppose so. It won't count, though."

They laughed. The plane made good time all the way but when it reached La Guardia there was a stack-up and they had to circle for more than a half-hour. It was a little scary, but at least between them they had enough cigarettes

301

to smoke. The only aggravating thing was, the longer they circled the hornier and more impatient Fitzie grew to get down and on his way.

More Bestsellers Now in SIGNET Editions

Recent Bestsellers Now in SIGNET Editions

☐ **LISTEN TO THE SILENCE by David W. Elliott.** A total and unique experience—gripping, poignant, most often, shattering. A fourteen-year-old boy narrates the chronicle of events that lead him into, through, and out of an insane asylum. "Each page has the ring of unmistakable truth . . . a well-written tour de force, another **Snake Pit** . . ."—**The New York Times Book Review**
(#Q4513—95¢)

☐ **THE SUMMIT by Stephen Marlowe.** Intrigue, blackmail, treachery and romance, THE SUMMIT is a wire-taut novel as devious as LeCarre, as fast moving as Ambler or Greene—chosen by **The New York Times Book Review** as one of The Year's Best Criminals at Large, 1970 . . . "A shining example of the political extrapolation that pumped new lifeblood into the espionage novel in 1970." (#Y4632—$1.25)

☐ **SANCTUARY V by Budd Schulberg.** A gripping study of men and women under the most extreme kinds of pressure in a Cuban political haven. Writing with power, compassion, and with a rare gift for characterization, Budd Schulberg reconfirms with SANCTUARY V his position as one of America's master storytellers.
(#Y4511—$1.25)

☐ **THE STUD by Jackie Collins.** A novel about the ambitious, fast living—and loving—people among the swinging "in-crowd" of London's discotheque scene . . . and Tony Burg, ex-waiter, ex-nothing—now elevated to the rank of superstud. (#Q4609—95¢)

THE NEW AMERICAN LIBRARY, INC.,
P.O. Box 999, Bergenfield, New Jersey 07621

Please send me the SIGNET BOOKS I have checked above. I am enclosing $_____(check or money order—no currency or C.O.D.'s). Please include the list price plus 15¢ a copy to cover mailing costs.

Name_____

Address_____

City_____State_____Zip Code_____
Allow at least 3 weeks for delivery